1. This book may be kept three weeks. It is to be
   returned on / before the last date stamped below.
2. A fine of 25c will be charged for every week or
   part of week a book is overdue.

HARD REVOLUTION

HARD REVOLUTION

A NOVEL

GEORGE PELECANOS

ORION

First published in Great Britain in 2004
by Orion Books,
an imprint of The Orion Publishing Group
Orion House, 5 Upper St Martin's Lane,
London WC2H 9EA

All characters in this publication are fictitious
and any resemblance to real persons, living
or dead, is purely coincidental.

A CIP catalogue record for this book
is available from the British Library

ISBN (hardback) 0 75285 630 8
ISBN (trade paperback) 0 75285 631 6

Printed and bound in Great Britain by
Clays Ltd, St Ives plc

To Sloan

'You inherit the sins, you inherit the flames.'

Bruce Springsteen, 'Adam Raised a Cain'

PART 1

Spring 1959

ONE

DEREK STRANGE GOT down in a three-point stance. He breathed evenly, as his father had instructed him to do, and took in the pleasant smell of April. Magnolias, dogwoods, and cherry trees were in bloom around the city. The scent of their flowers, and the heavy fragrance of a nearby lilac bush growing against a residential fence, filled the air.

"You keep your back straight," said Derek, "like you're gonna set a dinner up on it. You ain't want your butt up in the air, either. That way you're ready. You just blow right out, like, and hit the holes. Bust on through."

Derek and his Saturday companion, Billy Georgelakos, were in an alley that ran behind the Three-Star Diner on a single-number block of Kennedy Street, at the eastern edge of Northwest D.C. Both were twelve years old.

"Like your man," said Billy, sitting on a milk crate, an *Our Army at War* comic book rolled tightly in his meaty hand.

"Yeah," said Derek. "Here go Jim Brown right here."

Derek came up out of his stance and exploded forward, one palm hovering above the other, both close to his chest. He took an imaginary handoff as he ran a few steps, then cut, slowed down, turned, and walked back toward Billy.

Derek had a way of moving. It was confident but not cocky, shoulders squared, with a slight looseness to the hips. He had copied the walk from his older brother, Dennis. Derek was the right height for his age, but like all boys and most men, he wished to be taller. Lately, at night when he was in bed, he thought he could feel himself growing. The mirror over his mother's dresser told him he was filling out in the upper body, too.

Billy, despite his wide shoulders and unusually broad chest, was not an athlete. He kept up on the local sports teams, but he had other passions. Billy liked pinball machines, cap pistols, and comic books.

"That how Brown got his twelve yards in eleven carries against the 'Skins?" said Billy.

"Uh-uh, Billy, don't be talkin' about that."

"Don Bosseler gained more in that game than Brown did."

"*In that game.* Most of the time, Bosseler ain't fit to carry my man's cleats. Two weeks before that, at Griffith? Jim Brown ran for one hundred and fifty-two. The man set the all-time rushing record in that one, Billy. Don Bosseler? Shoot."

"Awright," said Billy, a smile forming on his wide face. "Your man can play."

Derek knew Billy was messing with him, but he couldn't help getting agitated just the same. Not that Derek wasn't a Redskins fan. He listened to every game on the radio. He read the Shirley Povich and Bob Addie columns in the *Post* whenever they saw print. He followed the stats of quarterback Eddie LeBaron, middle linebacker Chuck Drazenovich, halfback

Eddie Sutton, and others. He even tracked Bosseler's yards-per-carry. In fact, he only rooted against the 'Skins twice a year, and then with a pang of guilt, when they played Cleveland.

Derek had a newspaper photo of Brown taped to the wall of the bedroom he shared with his brother. With the exception of his father, there was no one who was more of a hero to him than Brown. This was a strong individual who commanded respect, not just from his own but from people of all colors. The man could play.

"Don Bosseler," said Derek, chuckling. He put one big, long-fingered hand to the top of his head, shaved nearly to the scalp, and rubbed it. It was something his brother, Dennis, did in conversation when he was cracking on his friends. Derek had picked up the gesture, like his walk, from Dennis.

"I'm kiddin' you, Derek." Billy got up off the milk crate and put his comic book down on the diner's back stoop. "C'mon, let's go."

"Where?"

"My neighborhood. Maybe there's a game up at Fort Stevens."

"Okay," said Derek. Billy's streets were a couple of miles from the diner and several miles from Derek's home. Most of the kids up there were white. But Derek didn't object. Truth was, it excited him some to be off his turf.

On most Saturdays, Derek and Billy spent their time out in the city while their fathers worked at the diner. They were boys and were expected to go out and find adventure and even mild forms of trouble. There was violence in certain sections of the District, but it was committed by adults and usually among criminals and mostly at night. Generally, the young went untouched.

Out on the main drag, Derek noticed that the local movie house, the Kennedy, was still running *Buchanan Rides Alone,* with Randolph Scott. Derek had already seen it with his dad. His father had promised to take him down to U Street for the new John Wayne, *Rio Bravo,* which had people talking around town. The picture was playing down at the Republic. Like the other District theaters on U, the Lincoln and the Booker T, the Republic was mostly for colored, and Derek felt comfortable there. His father, Darius Strange, loved westerns, and Derek Strange had come to love them, too.

Derek and Billy walked east on the commercial strip. They passed two boys Derek knew from church, and one of them said, "What you hangin' with that white boy for?" and Derek said, "What business is that of yours?" He made just enough eye contact for the boy to know he was serious, and all of them went on their way.

Billy was Derek's first and only white playmate. The working relationship between their fathers had caused their hookup. Otherwise they never would have been put together, since most of the time, outside of sporting events and first jobs, colored boys and white boys didn't mix. Wasn't anything wrong with mixing, exactly, but it just seemed more natural to be with your own kind. Hanging with Billy sometimes put Derek in a bad position; you'd get challenged out here when your own saw you walking with a white. But Derek figured you had to stand by someone unless he gave you cause not to, and he felt he had to say something when conflict arrived. It wouldn't have been right to let it pass. Sure, Billy often said the wrong things, and sometimes those things hurt, but it was because he didn't know any better. He was ignorant, but his ignorance was never deliberate.

They walked northwest through Manor Park, across the green of Fort Slocum, and soon were up on Georgia Avenue, which many thought of as Main Street, D.C. It was the longest road in the District and had always been the primary northern thoroughfare into Washington, going back to when it was called the 7th Street Pike. All types of businesses lined the strip, and folks moved about the sidewalks day and night. The Avenue was always alive.

The road was white concrete and etched with streetcar tracks. Wood platforms, where riders had once waited to board streetcars, were still up in spots, but the D.C. Transit buses were now the main form of public transportation. A few steel troughs, used to water the horses that had pulled the carts of the junkmen and fruit and vegetable vendors, remained on the Avenue, but in short order all of it would be going the way of those mobile merchants. It was said that the street would soon be paved in asphalt and the tracks, platforms, and troughs would disappear.

Billy's neighborhood, Brightwood, was mostly white, working- and middle-class, and heavily ethnic: Greeks, Italians, Irish Catholics, and all varieties of Jew. The families had moved from Petworth, 7th Street, Columbia Heights, the H Street corridor in Northeast, and Chinatown, working their way north as they began to make more money in the prosperous years following World War II. They were seeking nicer housing, yards for their children, and driveways for their cars. Also, they were moving away from the colored, whose numbers and visibility had rapidly increased citywide in the wake of reurbanization and forced desegregation.

But even this would be a temporary move. Blockbuster real estate agents in Brightwood had begun moving colored families into white streets with the intention of scaring residents into selling their houses on the cheap. The next stop for upper-Northwest, east-of-the-park whites would be the suburbs of Maryland. No one knew that the events of the next nine years would hasten that final move, though there was a feeling that some sort of change was coming and that it would have to come, an unspoken sense of the inevitable. Still, some denied it as strongly as they denied death.

Derek lived in Park View, south of Petworth, now mostly colored and some working-class whites. He attended Backus Junior High and would go on to Roosevelt High School. Billy went to Paul Junior High and was destined for Coolidge High, which had some coloreds, most of whom were athletes. Many Coolidge kids would go on to college; far fewer from Roosevelt would. Roosevelt had gangs; Coolidge had fraternities. Derek and Billy lived a few short miles apart, but the differences in their lives and prospects were striking.

They walked the east side of Georgia's 6200 block, passing the open door of the Arrow cleaners, a business that had been in place since 1929, owned and operated by Bill Caludis. They stopped in to say hey to Caludis's son, Billy, whom Billy Georgelakos knew from church. On the corner sat Clark's Men's Shop, near Marinoff-Pritt and Katz, the Jewish market, where several of the butchers had camp numbers tattooed on their forearms. Nearby was the Sheridan Theater, which was running *Decision at Sundown*, another Randolph Scott. Derek had seen it with his dad.

They crossed to the other side of Georgia. They walked by Vince's Agnes Flower Shop, where Billy paused to say a few words with a cute young clerk named Margie, and the Sheridan Waffle Shop, also known as John's Lunch, a diner owned by John Deoudes. Then it was a watering hole called Sue's 6210, a Chinese laundry, a barbershop, and on the corner another beer garden, the 6200. "Stagger Lee" was playing on the house juke, its rhythms coming through the 6200's open door.

On the sidewalk outside the bar, three young white teenagers were alternately talking, smoking cigarettes, and running combs through their hair. One of them was ribbing another, asking if his girlfriend had given him his shiner and swollen face. "Nah," said the kid with the black eye, "I got jumped by a buncha niggers down at Griffith Stadium," adding that he was going to be looking for them and "some get-back." The group quieted as Derek and Billy passed. There were no words spoken, no hard stares, and no trouble. Derek looking at the weak, all-mouth boy and thinking, Prob'ly wasn't no "buncha niggers" about it, only had to be one.

At the corner of Georgia and Rittenhouse, Billy pointed excitedly at a man wearing a brimmed hat, crossing the street and heading east. With him was a young woman whose face they couldn't see but whose backside moved in a pleasing way.

"That's Bo Diddley," said Billy.

"Thought he lived over on Rhode Island Avenue."

"That's what everyone says. But we all been seein' him around here lately. They say he's got a spot down there on Rittenhouse."

"Bo Diddley's a gunslinger," said Derek, a warmth rising in his thighs as he checked out the fill of the woman's skirt.

They walked south to Quackenbos and cut across the lot of the Nativity School, a Catholic convent that housed a nice gymnasium. The nuns there were forever chasing Billy and his friends from the gym. Beyond the lot was Fort Stevens, where Confederate forces had been repelled by the guns and musketry of Union soldiers in July of 1864. The fort had been re-created and preserved, but few tourists now visited the site. The grounds mainly served as a playing field for the neighborhood boys.

"Ain't nobody up here," said Derek, looking across the weedy field, the American flag flying on a white mast throwing a wavy shadow on the lawn.

"I'm gonna pick some *porichia* for my mom," said Billy.

"Say what?"

Derek and Billy went up a steep grade to its crest, where several cannons sat spaced in a row. The grade dropped to a deep gully that ran along the northern line of the fort. Beside one of the cannons grew patches of spindly plants with hard stems. Billy pulled a few of the plants and shook the dirt off the roots.

"Thought your mama liked them dandelion weeds."

"That's *rodichia.* These here are good, too. You gotta get 'em before they flower, though, 'cause then they're too bitter. Let's go give 'em to her and get something to drink."

Billy lived in a slate-roofed, copper-guttered brick colonial on the 1300 block of Somerset, a few blocks west of the park. In contrast with the row houses of Park View and Petworth, the houses here were detached, with flat, well-tended front lawns. The streets were heavy with Italians and Greeks. The Deoudes family lived on Somerset, as did the Vondas family, and up on Underwood lived a wiry kid named Bobby Boukas, whose parents owned a flower shop. All were members of Billy's church, St. Sophia. On Tuckerman stood the house where midget actor Johnny Puleo, who had played in the Lancaster-Curtis circus picture, *Trapeze,* stayed for much of the year. Puleo drove a customized Dodge with wood blocks fitted to the gas and brake pedals.

On the way to the Georgelakos house, Derek stopped to pet a muscular tan boxer who was usually chained outside the front of the Deoudes residence. The dog's name was Greco. Greco sometimes walked with the police at night on their foot patrols and was known to be quick, loyal, and tough.

Derek got down on his haunches and let Greco smell his hand. The dog pushed his muzzle into Derek's fingers, and Derek patted his belly and rubbed behind his ears.

"Crazy," said Billy.

"What you mean?"

"Usually he rises up and shows his teeth."

"To colored boys, right?"

"Well, yeah."

"He likes *me.*" Derek's eyes softened as he admired the dog. "One day, I'ma get me one just like him, too."

TWO

AFTER DELIVERING THE *porichia* to Billy's mother, the boys returned to Fort Stevens. There they saw two brothers, Dominic and Angelo Martini, standing in the middle of the field.

"You wanna move on?" said Billy. The last time they'd met, Dominic Martini had ridden Derek hard.

"Nah," said Derek. "It's all right."

They approached the boys. Dominic, sixteen, stood a couple inches shy of six feet and had the build of a man in his twenties. His skin was dark, as was his perfectly pompadoured hair. His black eyes were flat. He had dropped out of Coolidge on his last birthday and was a pump jockey at the Esso station south of Georgia and Piney Branch. His brother, Angelo, fourteen, was similarly complected but lacked the size, good looks, and confidence of Dominic. His slumped posture said that he was aware of the difference.

"Billy," said Dominic. "See you got your shadow with you today."

"His name's Derek," said Billy, a forced strength to his voice.

"Relax, Billy boy." Dominic smiled, dragged on his cigarette, and gave Derek the once-over. "Wanna fight?"

Derek had expected the challenge. The first time they'd met, he had seen Martini do this to another kid who was minding his own and crossing the park. Dominic, he supposed, liked to lead with the question, let everyone know from the start that he was in control. It knocked the other guy off balance and was a way for Dominic to gain the immediate upper hand.

"Not today," said Derek.

"Maybe you wanna run to yo' mama instead."

Dominic's mention of his mother and his idea of a colored accent caused Derek to involuntarily ball his fists. He took a breath and relaxed his hands.

"Now, look here, I don't mean you gotta mix with *me*," said Dominic. "Wouldn't be fair. I don't pick on no one littler, see?"

You ain't all that much bigger than me, thought Derek.

"I was thinkin' of you and Angie," said Dominic, and as the words left his mouth, Angelo's eyes dropped.

"I got no quarrel with your brother," said Derek.

"Knock it off, Dom," said Angelo.

"I'm talkin' to *Derek*," said Dominic.

Derek knew he could take Angelo. Shoot, the boy's chin was down on his chest; he was al*ready* beat. Derek figured that Angelo feared colored boys the same way many other white boys did. And that fear would be the difference. But there wasn't anything in kicking Angelo's ass for Derek. Wasn't any way he could win.

"You got your mitts?" said Derek.

"Yeah, we got 'em," said Dominic. "So?"

"Me and Billy," said Derek, "we'll take y'all on in a ball game instead. How about that?"

"Fine," said Dominic. "But first say you won't fight."

"Dominic," said Angelo in a pleading way.

"I got no need to fight," said Derek.

"That ain't the same thing. Say what I told you to say or step to my brother and put up your hands."

"Okay, then," said Derek. "I won't fight." He didn't mind saying it. He had not backed up a step, folded his arms, or looked away. His body said that he was not afraid. Dominic could see it. He *knew*.

"All right," said Dominic. For a moment, Derek saw something human in Martini's eyes. "Let's play ball."

The Martini boys had a bat, a hardball, and two mitts stashed in the ammo bunker built into the base of the fort's hill. Basically, the game was stickball, but without the wall. Base hits were calculated by landmarks — the flagpole, the fort's commemorative plaque, et cetera — with the crest of the hill the ultimate goal. A ball hit over "the wall" of the fortification line was a home run.

Derek had the superior swing, and even Billy was a better athlete than the Martinis. Soon it was apparent that the contest was done. When Derek knocked out his third homer, Dominic said he was bored and stopped the game. After putting the playing equipment back in the bunker, Dominic turned to Derek.

"Say, you ever had any, man?"

"Sure have," said Derek, which was a lie. He had rubbed a little over-the-shirt tit off this older girl in his neighborhood, had a reputation for starting the young boys off, but that was all.

"Sure you have," said Dominic, laughing a little and lighting a cigarette. "Me, I get it all the time."

He told Derek about the Fort Club, which he and his friends had recently formed, and how they drank beer and pulled trains on girls inside the bunker on Friday nights. Derek issued a small shrug, enough to stave off another conflict, not enough to let Dominic think that he cared. It wasn't the reaction Dominic wanted. He pulled something from his pocket and held it in front of Derek.

"You know what this is?"

"That's a cherry bomb."

"How about I set it off?"

"Go ahead."

Martini lit the fuse off his smoke and calmly dropped the bomb into the muzzle of one of the cannons. The cherry bomb exploded, and its report was surprisingly loud. A janitor came out of the church, yelled something at the boys, and walked toward them. Angelo and Billy jogged in the direction of 13th Street. Derek and Dominic followed the other two out of the park, walking at a leisurely pace.

"You and me," said Dominic, "we ain't gonna run from nothin', right?"

Derek had the feeling that this afternoon would come to some kind of bad, the way a boy always knows that the direction of the day has turned. It was as if he were walking, willingly, from the sunny side of the street to the side covered in shadow. He had been raised to understand the clear difference between right and wrong, and he knew that, right about now, he should head back to the diner with Billy. But he was attracted to that shadowed side just the same. So when Dominic suggested they go over to "the Sixth," just to "fuck around some," Derek did not object.

THE SIXTH PRECINCT station was on Nicholson, set to the left of Brightwood Elementary. The station structure, all brick fronted with columns, looked like a small schoolhouse itself. A goldfish pond was set beside the concrete drive that horseshoed the rear of the station. The boys approached it from the right side, grouped themselves beside a tall oak, and studied the building through a chain-link fence.

"There's the cell block right there," said Dominic, pointing to the right side of the building. "They ain't got nothin' but old spring cots for you to sleep on."

"How do *you* know?" said Billy, challenging Martini but secretly impressed.

"Our old man told us," said Angelo. Their father had slept off public drunks in the station a couple of times in the past year.

"Not just that," said Dominic, annoyed. "I been in there myself." He had never actually spent the night in the jail, though he had aspirations. Dominic had been written up for a field investigation, which was less dramatic than "a record," for throwing a rock through a window of the elementary school.

Back behind the main structure was a garage housing several Harleys for the motorcycle cops. One of the precinct's three squad cars, a high-horse Ford, was parked in the lot, beside a black unmarked, also a Ford. The boys of Brightwood recognized the squad car numbers, 61 to 63, printed on the sides of the vehicles. They knew the names of the desk sergeant and homicide cops and the beat police as well. Among them was an Irish cop whose status had been elevated to legend after he had taken a .45 slug in the gut. The Sixth also had one uniformed colored cop, William Davis, and the hated Officer Pappas, a Greek who was especially tough on kids. He had made it his mission to bust the fathers and sons, some of whom were fellow Greeks, who ran numbers and occasionally fenced out of their businesses up on the Avenue. Pappas had a pencil-thin mustache, which the boys thought of as a French look that bordered on feminine. They had nicknamed him Jacques. When he was on foot patrol, they taunted him from rooftops and alleys, calling out to him with high-pitched voices, "Jaaacques, oh, Jaaacques."

Officer Davis came from the front of the building and walked to squad car number 62. Davis was tall and lean, his uniform perfectly pressed, his service revolver snapped into its holster. Derek wondered what you had to do to become a police. Must be something to it to make Davis walk the way he was walking. Chin up, close to a swagger. It seemed like the man had pride.

Dominic Martini picked up a rock. Derek grabbed his wrist.

"Don't," said Derek.

Derek's action surprised both of them, so much so that Dominic didn't resist. He dropped the rock, shook his hand free, and stared at Davis.

"Look at him," said Martini with contempt. "He really thinks he's somethin'."

He *is*, thought Derek Strange, studying the police officer as he got into the Ford. That's a *man* right there.

BUZZ STEWART FED gas into the tank of a '57 DeSoto Fireflite, a two-tone red-and-white sedan fitted out with whitewalls and skirts. A cigarette dangled from his lips as he worked the pump. He wasn't supposed to smoke anywhere near the tanks, but there wasn't anyone at the station, including his boss, big enough to tell him not to. As he replaced the pump handle and took the money from the square behind the wheel, he thumb-flicked ash off his Marlboro and put the smoke back in his thin-lipped mouth.

"Hey, Buzz," said Dominic Martini, walking by with a bottle of Coca-Cola in his hand.

"Hey," mumbled Stewart.

Stewart watched Martini, an Italian kid who worked weekend nights, join a group of younger boys at the edge of the Esso station lot. One of the boys was Martini's no-balls brother. The other was some fattish kid, looked like another spaghetti-bender to him. The third kid was a nigger. Now, why would Martini want to run with a colored boy? He'd have to give Dom some shit about it the next time they talked.

Stewart walked across the lot, patting his Brylcreemed blond hair. He admired his veins, like root tendrils, standing up on the inside of his forearms and popping out on his biceps. He felt strong. He went six-three and one ninety, none of it waste. Some guys thought they could challenge him, all that harder-you-fall bullshit they had to tell themselves 'cause they were small. Stewart could back up his size and didn't need to be pushed to prove it.

He went inside the station. The manager, built-guy once, fat-guy now, was sitting behind his desk, doing his usual heap of nothing. "Party Doll" was coming from the radio, Buddy Knox with his stutter-step vocals, then that nice guitar break with the walkin' rhythm behind it coming in right after. Stewart liked that one. It wasn't no Link, but it was nice.

"We talk?" said Stewart.

"Go 'head," said the manager, not meeting Stewart's eyes.

"When am I gonna get a chance in them bays?"

"When you take the course."

"I could take apart an engine and put it back together with my eyes closed."

"Maybe they could use you at the circus," said the manager. "But the sign out front says 'Certified Mechanics.' You wanna be one, parent company requires you to take the course."

Fuck a course, thought Stewart. Last course I took was at Montgomery Blair, and that was when I was sixteen. I didn't need no courses then and I sure as hell didn't need no high school degree. You didn't have to sit in no classroom to know how to work on cars.

"Maybe later," said Stewart, jerking a thumb toward the clock on the wall. "I'm out." He took the bill roll he kept in his pocket, undid the change belt he wore around his waist, and put both on the manager's desk.

"Wait for me to count it out," said the manager.

"If it's wrong, you'll let me know."

"You in a hurry?"

"Yeah," said Stewart. "I got places to go and people to meet, and none of 'em are here."

Stewart walked out.

"Big maaan," said the manager, but only after Stewart had left the office.

Buzz Stewart got into his bored-out '50 Ford, outfitted with headers and dropped near to the ground. The paint job, a purple body over a blue interior, had been customized. He and his crowd named their cars and scripted the names on their right front fenders. His read "Lavender Blue," because of the color scheme, and also for that Sammy Turner song. He was proud of the name. He had thought of it all by himself.

Stewart cranked the ignition and drove north out of D.C., toward his parents' house in Silver Spring.

A little ways over the District line he drove under the B&O bridge and passed the Canada Dry plant on the left. He and his boys used to hit the plant on Saturdays, when there wasn't but one security guard on duty, and steal as many cases of ginger ale as they could carry. In a nearby wooded area they dumped out the soda, then turned in the bottles to local merchants for pocket change. You could make a few bucks like that, but it had ended one day a few years back when a gray-haired guard happened upon him and his group. Luckily, Stewart's best bud, Shorty Hess, was behind the guard and knocked him out with a crack to the skull from a length of pipe he kept slipped down his jeans. They were afraid at first he'd killed him, but it didn't make the newspapers or nothin,' so they guessed the old guy lived. Since then, he and his buddies had gone on to bigger things, like break-ins. For fun they liked to race cars, drink beer and hard liquor, run coloreds off the sidewalks, and fuck girls. They also liked to fight.

Stewart drove to his house. He lived with his folks in a detached place on Mississippi Avenue, between Sligo and Piney Branch. The house, a square of bricks fronted by a wooden porch, sat on nearly a half acre of land. In the back was a freestanding garage where Stewart worked on vehicles. Beside the garage ran a large garden plot where his mother would plant vegetables — corn, tomatoes, bell peppers, and the like. Stewart had recently turned the soil for her, as she would begin planting her summer crop soon.

Inside he found his father, Albert, sitting in his upholstered chair in the living room, drinking Old German beer and smoking a straight Camel. Al bought his beer for $2.50 a case and went through a case every two days. He was watching a *Cisco Kid* rerun on TV. Albert was as big as his son and nearly bald. Like his son, he was neither handsome nor ugly, with no features of prominence or note, a bland, perpetually scowling man, thin lipped, small eyed, quick to anger and judge.

"What *you* doin'?" said Al, not turning his head.

"Nuthin'," said Buzz, staring openmouthed at the TV.

"You get paid?"

"Yesterday."

"You eighteen now, boy. Time you started paying rent."

"I know it."

"Then pay it up."

"I will."

"When?"

Stewart went past the kitchen, where his mother, Pat, was

sitting at a Formica-top table, smoking a cigarette. She wore a housedress with a floral print, one of two she had bought years ago at Montgomery Ward's and wore on alternate days. Her gray hair was pinned back in a bun. She still had lines around her mouth from when she used to laugh. Her eyes were a washed-out blue. Relatives on her side claimed she had been pretty once.

"Carlton," she said, using her son's given name.

"Yeah, Ma."

"You staying for dinner?"

"Nah, I'm going out. I'll take a sandwich or somethin', though."

"You think this is a restaurant?" called Al from the living room.

"Yeah," said Stewart, raising his voice. "Can I get a steak? Make it medium. And I'll take one of them fine brews you drinkin', too."

"Stupid sumbitch," said Al.

Buzz Stewart went down to his room.

THREE

FROM THE SIXTH Precinct station house, the boys walked back up to the Avenue. Dominic Martini bought a bottle of Coke from a red cooler up at the Esso station and assured his boss he'd be there on time for the late shift. On his way back to the group, he said, "Hey, Buzz," to a big guy, his sleeves rolled up to show off his biceps, who was pumping gas.

Dominic passed the bottle to his brother, who then passed it without thinking to Derek. Derek took a pull from the bottle and handed it back to Dominic. Dominic wiped the neck off before putting it to his mouth. As he did this, he locked eyes with Derek.

Eventually, they made their way to Ida's, the department store up on the east-side corner of Georgia and Quackenbos. In addition to selling household goods, the store clothed most of the kids in the area, colored and white alike. The PF Flyers on Derek's feet were from Ida's, as was the old Boy Scout uniform in Billy Georgelakos's closet. Ida's was the uptown equivalent of the downtown Morton's.

The boys entered the store, hit one of the aisles, and went toward the back. The employees were busy with customers and no one had taken note of them yet. There was no good reason for them to be here, as none of them had any money to spend, but Derek had a good idea of their intent. Still, he went along. Almost immediately he saw Dominic take an Ace comb out of a bin and slip it into his back pocket in one smooth motion. Angelo, sweat on his upper lip, did the same.

"Let's get outta here, Derek," said Billy.

"Yeah, you pussies take off," said Dominic.

"Who you callin' pussy?" said Derek, regretting his words as they left his tongue.

"*Do* somethin', then," said Dominic. "Prove you got some balls on you, *Derek.*"

"I will," said Derek Strange.

Dominic smiled. "See you out on the street."

Derek went farther into the store and cut down another aisle as the Martini brothers vanished. Billy stayed with Derek. Derek came upon the tool and hardware section, saw a padlock, thought his father could use it for something. He must have stood there for a full minute, staring at the lock. He looked around, saw no one in the aisle, and slipped the padlock into the right front pocket of his blue jeans. He started walking for the front of the store, Billy at his heels.

As they reached the entrance doors, he felt a hand grip one of his biceps. He tried to shake it off and run, but the person who held him held fast.

"Hold on there," said a man's voice. "You're not going anywhere, son."

Derek gave up his struggle. He was nailed, and down somewhere deep he knew that he deserved it. He cursed himself silently and then cursed himself out loud.

"Stupid," said Derek.

"That's right," said the man. He was a stocky white man with broad shoulders. He wore a cardigan vest, an open-necked shirt, and had a pair of eyeglasses perched atop his head of black hair. Strange read the name tag on his chest: "Harold Fein."

"You have anything in your pockets, son?" said Fein, turning to Billy.

"No," said Billy.

"Then get out of here, *now.*"

"Can't I wait for my friend?"

Derek felt some affection for Billy then, the way he'd called him "friend." Until now, Billy was just a kid he'd been put together with, almost by accident.

"If you're gonna wait," said Fein, still holding Derek's arm, "you're gonna wait outside. Now, I *know* you, and your mother, too. Don't ever let me see you involved in anything like this again."

Billy said, "You won't," but it was to their backs, as Fein was already leading Derek to the back of the store. They went through a narrow opening into a low-ceilinged stockroom.

Fein instructed Derek to take a seat. There was a padded chair behind a desk cluttered with paperwork and a hard chair beside the desk. Derek figured the padded chair was Mr. Fein's. He sat in the hard one. On the desk was a triangular block of wood with a brass plate. It read "Receiving Manager." Also on the desk were framed photographs of a little girl and what looked to be a two-year-old boy.

"What's your name?" said Fein, still standing.

"Derek Strange."

"Where do you live?"

Derek told him he lived down on Princeton Place, in Park View.

"I've got to go check the manifest on a truck," said Fein.

"You just sit right there. Put the padlock on the desk before I forget about it. And don't think about runnin' out, 'cause I know where to find you, hear?"

"Yessir."

It took a while for Fein to come back. Maybe thirty minutes or so, but it seemed like hours to Derek. He was miserable, thinking on what his mother and father would say when they got the phone call. Angry, too, for allowing himself to get baited by Dominic Martini, a boy he didn't even respect. Why he felt he had to prove himself to Martini, he couldn't say. Derek had done some bad things, and he'd do more bad things in the future, he knew, but he vowed that he would never do a *stupid* bad thing for no reason again. He hadn't been raised that way.

Fein returned and took his seat. He shuffled the papers on his desk and put them in some kind of order. Then he folded his hands, rested them in his lap, and turned his attention to Derek.

"You did wrong today," said Fein.

"I know."

"Do you?"

"Yes, sir."

Fein exhaled slowly. "I saw those other boys steal those combs. There's no trick to it; we have mirrors up in the corners of the store. Do you know why I didn't grab them first?"

"No, sir."

"Because it wouldn't have done them any good. I've seen them around. The older one, especially, is already . . . Well, he's on a path. I'm not going to speed things up for him, if you know what I mean."

Derek didn't, exactly. Later he would think on this day and understand.

"So now you're wondering, why me?" said Fein. "It's because you're not like that other boy. I watched you and your

friend in that aisle. You hesitated, because you know the difference between right and wrong. Then you made the wrong
decision. But listen, it's not the end of the world, if you *know*
you made the wrong decision."

Derek nodded, looking into the man's eyes. They had
softened somewhat since their first encounter.

"Derek, right?"

"Yes."

"You know what you wanna be when you grow up?"

"A police," said Derek, without even turning it over in
his mind.

"Well, there you go. You need to start thinking on how
you're going to live your life, even now. Everything you do as
a young man can affect what you become or don't become
later on."

Derek nodded. It was unclear to him where the man was
going with this. But it sounded like good sense.

"You can go," said Fein.

"What?"

"Go home. I'm not going to call your parents or the police.
Think about what I've told you today." Fein tapped his temple
with a thick finger. *"Think."*

"Thank you, sir," said Derek, rising up out of his chair as
if shocked.

Harold Fein moved his eyeglasses down from the top his
head and fitted them on the bridge of his nose. He returned his
attention to the work waiting on his desk.

Billy was sitting on the curb outside the store. He stood as
Derek came to meet him.

"You in trouble?" said Billy.

"Nah," said Derek, "I'm all right. Where the Martini
boys at?"

"They left."

"Figured they would."

"We better be gettin' back to the diner, Derek, it's late."

Derek put a hand on Billy's shoulder. "Thanks, man."

"For what?"

"For waitin' on me," said Derek. Billy ducked his head and grinned.

They walked southeast on Missouri Avenue, toward Kennedy Street. The shadows of late afternoon had begun to lengthen, and they quickened their steps. Down in Manor Park a car went by, its radio playing "You're So Fine" by that group the Falcons, had that singer Derek's father liked. The sound of it, and the sight of the colored men in the car, made Derek smile. He felt clean, like he'd just walked out of church. The way you do when you confess.

BY MOST FOLKS' estimation, Frank Vaughn had it pretty good. He had survived a tour of Okinawa, married a girl with a nice set of legs, fathered a son, bought a house in a white neighborhood, and was making a fair living with a pension waiting for him down the road. Men gave him wide berth, and women still looked him over when he walked down the street. Coming up on forty, he was where most men claimed they wanted to be.

Vaughn had a sip of coffee, dragged on his cigarette, and fitted it in a crenellated plastic ashtray his son, Ricky, had bought for him at Kresge's for Father's Day. Imagine a kid buying his old man an ashtray. Might as well have given him a card to go with it, said, "Here you go, Dad, hope you croak." But the kid wasn't clever enough for that. The ashtray must have been Olga's idea, her idea of a joke. Like she'd last a week if he wasn't around. What would she do for a living? No one pays you to shop, watch television, or talk on the phone with your girlfriends. Least not that he was aware.

Vaughn snatched the sports page from the newspaper

sections piled at his feet. Redskins president George Marshall, in the process of renegotiating a lease with Calvin Griffith, was threatening to build a new stadium down at the Armory grounds if he didn't get his terms. Former welterweight champ Johnny Saxton had tried to hang himself in a jail cell after he was caught robbing a five-and-dime. Saxton, who had beaten Kid Gavilan, Carmen Basilio, and Tony DeMarco before he hit the skids, had previously been arrested for trying to steal a fur cape and a pack of smokes. Former Washington Senator Jim Piersall, another candidate for the laughing house, said he was "unhappy" about being traded from Boston to Cleveland. When, exactly, thought Vaughn, had Piersall ever been happy? Audacious and Negro Minstrel were the long-shot daily double picks at Laurel. And the Nats had taken the Orioles two to one when Killebrew doubled in the eighth.

Vaughn dropped the newspaper on the floor and yawned. There was nothing about the straight life that excited him. These days, he could only get jazzed when he walked out that front door, to his other life on the street.

He sat back in his chair and took in Olga, who was building sandwiches on the counter beside the sink. She was wearing black pedal pushers she had picked up at Kann's, a top from Lansburgh's over in Langley Park, and a new pair of shoes on her feet. All of it courtesy of his Central Charge card. It kept her happy and it kept her out of his hair, so what the hell.

Olga walked toward him, carrying his sandwich. She had a plain face that had hardened over the years. The heavy eye shadow she wore, the hair-sprayed helmet of hair, the pancake makeup, and the red-red lipstick did not enliven her, but rather reminded Vaughn of a corpse. She had kept her figure, at least, though it had flattened out somewhat in the back. She still had nice legs.

"Here you go, honey," she said, putting the plate down in front of him.

"Thanks, baby doll," he said.

Olga picked up one foot and wiggled it around. "Capezios. You like 'em? I got 'em over at Hahn's."

"They're all right," he said with a scowl. He wasn't angry that she'd bought them. He couldn't have cared less. But he was expected to react this way. And now she'd justify the purchase.

"I needed a new pair," she said. "And I've been saving every place else. Honey, I've got a full book of S&H Green Stamps. . . ."

He blocked out the rest of it. Her voice reminded him of flies buzzing around his head. Annoying but harmless. He grunted almost inaudibly, thinking of how he must have looked. Sitting there, acting like he was listening but not really listening at all, giving her his canine grin, his eyes heavy lidded and amused, slowly nodding his head.

Finally, when she was done running her mouth, he said, "C'mon, Olga, let's eat."

He finished his cigarette while she went to the stairs by the foyer and called up for their son. He heard her add, "And go down and get Alethea, tell her to come up, too."

As Olga placed the other setups and drinks around the table, Ricky came in, twelve years old and flouncy-bouncy in that way of his that made Vaughn fear his son was gonna be a swish, and took a chair. He had been up in his bedroom, standing in front of the mirror, most likely, doing the twist or some other crazy dance he had learned from watching that guy, Dick Clark. It hadn't been long since Ricky was nuts over Pick Temple, that TV cowboy, and now his interests had gone to girls in sweaters. Vaughn hoped. He loved his kid but had never understood him. He should have tried to get closer to him, especially when he was younger, but he didn't know how. No one gave out road maps on how to be a father. Vaughn tapped ash, thinking, All you can do is the best you can.

Alethea entered the kitchen wearing one of those old uniforms of hers, a shapeless white dress that could not hide her shape. Vaughn watched her walk to the table, hoping to get a look at her legs as the sunlight from the kitchen window went through her dress. She held her head erect and her shoulders square as she crossed the room and took a seat. She wore no makeup, and her hair was hidden under some kind of patterned scarf she always donned when working at their house.

Vaughn put her at about forty. She wasn't young, but she was all woman. He wondered what she did to her husband when the lights went out. He thought about it often. Sometimes he thought about it when he made love to his wife.

You couldn't call Alethea beautiful or anything close to it. Her skin was dark and she had those prominent colored features that Vaughn didn't go for. No one was gonna mistake her for Lena Horne. Her eyes, though, they did it for him. Deep brown, liquid, and knowing. If there was something, one thing about her, it had to be her eyes.

Olga had a seat at the kitchen table. Alethea closed her eyes, put her hands together, and soundlessly moved her lips. The Vaughns were not themselves religious, but they sat quietly while Alethea said her grace. When she was done, they began to eat.

"How's it going today, Alethea?" said Olga.

"I'm on my schedule. Gonna get to that laundry next."

"You feeling okay?"

"Fine."

"How's your family?"

"They're fine. Everyone's fine."

Same old conversation, thought Vaughn. Olga, influenced by her girlfriends in the neighborhood who sat around talking about segregation and civil rights when they weren't talking about their nails or pushing around mah-jongg tiles. Olga, with her guilt about paying Alethea "only" ten dollars a day, when that was the fee Alethea herself had quoted from day one. Olga, still trying to make Alethea feel like she was one of the family; Alethea polite but not giving up anything of herself. And why should she? For Chrissakes, she was their maid. Get in, do your work, earn your money, and get back downtown to your people. Vaughn understood this, but Olga, who wasn't out there, could not. Okay, so some folks were pushing for equality, and Vaughn had no problem with that. But nobody wanted to mix, not when you got down to it. People wanted to be around their own kind.

"Olga," said Vaughn, "give me some potato chips, pickles, or somethin', will ya, honey? This is . . . this sandwich would leave a bird hungry, right here."

Anything to shut up Olga's yap. But when she returned to the table with a jar of sweet pickles, she tried again.

"Alethea, isn't it awful about that boy down in Mississippi?"

"Yes," said Alethea, "it sure is."

"They lynched that boy!"

"That's what the newspapers say." Alethea's voice was void of emotion. She kept her eyes averted from Olga as she replied.

"The way they treat those Negroes down South," said Olga, shaking her head. "When do you think this will stop?"

"I don't know," said Alethea.

"Do you think it will get better for your people soon?"

Alethea shrugged and said, "I just don't know."

When they were done, Olga cleared the table. Vaughn watched as she separated Alethea's plate and glass from the others she had put in the sink. Later, Olga would wash Alethea's things more thoroughly than she did the rest. Vaughn noticed that Alethea was watching Olga arrange the dishes.

Alethea turned back to the table and, for a moment, looked into Vaughn's eyes.

FOUR

Down in his room, Buzz Stewart turned on the fourteen-inch Philco that sat on his dresser and switched the dial to channel 5. The Saturday edition of *The Milt Grant Show* was still in progress. Local band Terry and the Pirates were on-stage, and the kids were dancing up a storm.

Milt Grant's show was on Monday through Saturday on WTTG. On Saturday, Milt went up against the nationally tele-cast *American Bandstand*. Everyone knew that Milt Grant had come up with the concept first, but the preppy kids and those whose parents had desk jobs had gone over to Dick Clark. To Stewart, the kids on *Bandstand* looked like pussies and fakes. The kids with rougher edges and rough tastes, greasers and the like, and those who liked their rock and roll on the raw side, had stayed with Milt Grant. Hell, Link Wray headed Grant's house band. That was enough to make Stewart go for him right there.

Many of the famed Milt Grant's Record Hops were held in the Silver Spring Armory, not too far from Stewart's house. At these events, packed to the walls with kids from local high schools, Stewart saw acts like the Everly Brothers, Fats Domino, and that wild boy, Little Richard. Stewart wasn't much of a dancer. At the hops, he leaned his back against a wall, his sleeves rolled up to show off his arms, and watched the girls. But sometimes, especially when the colored acts got up there and cut loose, he wished he'd learned a few steps.

After the Grant show was done, Stewart took a shower. Then he returned to his bedroom, where his mother had placed a turkey sandwich and a bottle of RC Cola on his nightstand. He played some singles on his Cavalier phonograph while he ate and dressed. First was "Bip Bop Bip," by Don Covay, on the local Colt 45 record label. Then a Flamingos tune, and "Annie Had a Baby," by Hank Ballard and the Midnighters, and finally, as was his pre–Saturday night ritual, Link's "Rumble" before he went out the door. Anything by the Raymen got him fired up.

He said good-bye to his mother, sitting at the table, smoking another cigarette. She told him to have fun and he said that he would. Out in the living room, his father, half lit now, looked him over. Stewart wore black Levi peg-legs, thick-soled loafers called "bombers," and a bright orange button-down shirt under black leather. His hair was thick with Brylcreem and it rode high and stiff on his head.

"Where'd you get that shirt?" said Albert.

"What's wrong with it?"

"You look like a nigger."

Buzz Stewart left the house.

DOWN IN THE basement of the Vaughns' split-level, Alethea folded the family's clothing, warm from the dryer, on an ironing board set under a naked bulb. She timed her day so that she could have this relatively light chore after lunch, when she tended to grow tired. All that food sitting in your stomach, especially that bland, tasteless food Olga Vaughn made, just made you want to lie down and close your eyes.

It was quiet down here, pleasant and cool. All the toys sitting around the basement, things Ricky didn't use anymore and probably never had used much, gathering dust. In Alethea's opinion, they had spoiled that boy, not an uncommon thing to do with an only child. When really all any child needed was love, food, shelter, and a good example of how grown men and women should conduct their lives.

Olga had become barren after the birth of Ricky, Alethea guessed, which was a shame for the boy. A child needed a sibling to play with and also to confide in when things got tough. Frank Vaughn was not the kind of man who could find a way to be both a father and a friend to his son. For Frank, it took too much effort and thought. He should have spent more time with Ricky, though, even if it was not in his nature, as the child had become something of a mama's boy. Boys like that grew up to be lovers and layabouts, the kind of men who leaned on their women far too much. But Ricky was smart and kind. Most likely, despite what he hadn't gotten in his home, he would find his way.

Alethea stopped for a moment to stretch her hurting back. The pain could have been a mind thing, thinking too much on the fact that she'd turned forty a couple of years ago. But she was getting out of bed slower most mornings, no question about it. Wasn't her imagination or the date on her birth certificate giving her those pains. You worked this kind of labor six days a week all these years, what did you expect? She wasn't going to think on it all that much, because none of that worrying ever did anyone any kind of good.

The Lord would show her the way.

She could see a doctor about her back, she supposed, but money was tight, like it had always been. Another ten, twelve dollars a week would help, and she felt certain she could get it, spread out among the six households she worked on her regular schedule. Wasn't one of those families could argue that she didn't deserve a two-dollar raise. But seventy-two would put her over the salary of her husband, who was making sixty-five a week on his job, and that would be a problem right there. You never wanted to be making more money than your husband. A situation like that, it could kill the lion in your man.

Alethea folded a pair of Olga Vaughn's white panties.

"Oh, Lord," said Alethea, chuckling at the thought of Olga, trying to make conversation at lunch.

Lunch should have been Alethea's time of rest, but truly, at the Vaughns' it was the most challenging portion of her day. Olga insisted she eat with the family when all Alethea wanted was one half hour of peace. She accepted it, the way you had to accept most anything your boss asked of you, but it was a chore, more work, like being forced to take a role in a play. When Olga was talking to you, she was so *aware* that she was talking to you: Look at me, world, I'm talking to a "Negro." The whole lunch thing was her way of telling herself, and her friends, most likely, that she was pure of heart, better than those people "down South." But she wasn't any better. Matter of fact, she was worse, 'cause with a race hater from *anywhere,* least you knew where you stood. If Olga was so pure, then why was she separating Alethea's dishes in the sink?

Don't want to get any of that colored on you, do you, girl?

"Forget it," she said aloud, not liking her resentment, knowing it to be a trait that went against her Christian teachings. To herself she said a small prayer of forgiveness.

She began to fold Frank Vaughn's underwear, extra-large-size boxers. Big man, Frank. She wondered . . . never mind. Wasn't a sin to think about it. It was just natural curiosity about a physical thing, is all it was. She knew, though, that he studied her in that way. She felt his eyes on her all the time. But she never did think of him like that, not even for a moment. In any kind of world he was not her type.

Frank Vaughn would be upstairs in their bedroom now, taking his afternoon nap, like he always did before going off to work. Probably he went off to sleep quickly, like uncomplicated people tended to do. That was Frank Vaughn in a word: uncomplicated. If you asked, she'd bet he would tell you the same. Unlike his wife, this was a person who knew who he was. Not good, exactly, but clear. He must have done bad things on his job, had to have done bad things, she supposed, 'cause that's the kind of job it was. In the end he was just a man. *All man*, if you had to say it short.

Anyway, this family here was no business of hers. She would always be polite to them, but she was uninterested in being their friend. This was something Olga and most "good" white folks would never understand. The thing of it was, she had her own friends, took pleasure in her *own* world. Her own family, too. A good man and a good provider who she loved fierce, and two strong, fine-hearted sons.

AFTER FRANK VAUGHN woke from his nap, he showered and shaved in his master bathroom. He left both the door to his bedroom and the bathroom door closed, as it blocked out the rock-and-roll music coming from Ricky's room.

Vaughn could blame himself for that, as he had bought most of Ricky's records. Occasionally he paid retail down at the Music Box on 10th and at the Jay Perri Record Shop, next to the Highland Theater on Pennsylvania Avenue in Southeast. But most of the time he got them hot from this colored fence he knew down near 14th and U. This fence owed him a favor for something Vaughn didn't do to his kid brother, so often these records came free.

The records made Ricky happy, and that made Vaughn

feel good. Still, Vaughn couldn't stand the sound of the shit. Sinatra, Perry Como, and them, they were real singers, and some of the broads like Peggy Lee, June Christy, and, God, Julie London were pretty good, too. Elvis? He sang like a hopped-up spade, and the way he wiggled his hips was just, well, it was suspicious. These days, at least you didn't hear him every time you turned on the radio. Presley was in Germany now, wearing a uniform. Kids had short memories, so maybe he would just fade away. In Vaughn's opinion, that was good.

Vaughn found his can of shaving cream between Olga's private things, a box of Modess and a bottle of Lysol douche. He lathered his face and used a straight razor to shave himself. He had large features, jowly cheeks, and a squarish head. His teeth were crooked and widely spaced. His eyes were blue and lazy. He liked to think of himself as a less pretty Mitchum. Some of the younger guys at work called him Hound Dog. He figured it had something to with his determination on the job and something to do with his looks. And there was that god-damn Elvis song. The name didn't bother him, though. Long as they respected him, he didn't mind.

He dressed in a white shirt, black tie, and gray Robert Hall suit. He opened the drawer of the nightstand beside his bed and extracted his .38. He checked the load, then slipped the service revolver into the clip-on holster he wore on his belt.

Olga came into the room. She smiled crookedly and ran her hands down the thighs of her pedal pushers. He walked over to her, pulled her to him, and kissed her roughly on the mouth. She grabbed him tightly around the waist.

"You're gonna make my gun go off."

"And you'll mess up my lipstick."

"I already did," he said, showing her his smile. He pushed himself against her to let her know he had it. Tired of her as he got sometimes, she was still his lover as well as his wife. Olga did like to buck. She had always been a wildcat in the sack, once you tuned her up.

36

"Let's go out this weekend," she said. "See some music and have a few cocktails. We haven't done that for a while."

"Where to?"

"Xavier Cugat's playing down at Casino Royal."

"The hell with him."

"Abbe Lane's on the bill."

"Okay, baby doll. We'll see."

He kissed her again, slipping her his tongue before breaking the embrace. He liked to give her something to remember him by while he was down at work.

Vaughn left her there. He didn't bother to knock on Ricky's door to say good-bye.

Down in the foyer, he took his raincoat and hat from the closet. The April evenings were cool and damp, so he would need the warmth. Also, he liked the way the getup looked. The coat-and-hat rig reminded him of the cover of *No One Cares*, with Sinatra sitting at the bar, staring into his whiskey glass, looking as though he'd just been punched in the heart. A night wolf, wounded and alone. Vaughn liked to think of himself just like that. The image pleased him.

Alethea came up the stairs as he was about to go out the door. She was wearing a clean raincoat over her street clothes and had removed her scarf and combed out her hair.

"You wanna ride somewhere?" said Vaughn. "I'm heading into town."

"I'm just gonna walk up to Georgia and catch the bus. It takes me straight home."

"You sure?"

"Thank you, but I'm fine."

He was usually going to work as she was getting off. He always offered her a lift, and her answer was almost always the same.

"I ask you somethin'?" said Vaughn.

"Long as it's not too personal," she said, letting him know in her tone that she would take no offense either way.

"Are you happy?" said Vaughn.

Alethea Strange hesitated. It was an odd and unexpected question, but Frank Vaughn's eyes said that he truly wanted to know.

"Most of the time," she said. "I'd say nearly all the time I am. Yes."

"You look it," said Vaughn.

Outside, Frank Vaughn got into his '57 Dodge Royal, a two-tone, two-door rose metallic V-8 with a push-button transmission parked in the driveway of his house, on a suburban block between Wheaton and Silver Spring. Alethea Strange walked toward Georgia Avenue and stood at the bus stop with two other domestics who were waiting for a D.C. Transit bus to take them south over the District line, to the familiar faces, smells, and musical cadences of the voices that told them they were home.

HIS FATHER HAD got his blood up, but that feeling soon passed when Buzz Stewart cruised up the street in his car. He got WDON, Don Dillard's R&R record show that was broadcast out of a bunker on University Boulevard up in Wheaton, on the radio and turned it up. Dillard was spinning the Chantels' "Maybe," one of Stewart's all-time favorite songs, and this made his spirits rise. When it was done, Dillard signed off, as sunset had come, and WDON held only a daylight license. He thumbed the dial up to WINX on 1600, which aired till midnight. Then he pulled a Marlboro from his breast pocket and lit himself a smoke.

Walter Hess's car, a dropped-down 283 Chevy painted candy apple red, was parked outside the doughnut shop on Pershing. In script on the front right fender it read "Shorty's Dream." Stewart cut in behind the Chevy, let his car idle, and honked the horn. Hess was inside the doughnut shop, most likely working the pinball machine they'd rigged for multiple plays. Once they'd pried the glass off the top with Hess's knife and gotten to that button, it was easy. The owner never knew what was going on.

Walter came out of the shop a few minutes later. He wore an outfit similar to Stewart's, only in much smaller sizes. Walter's friends called him Shorty. It was not said with derision but rather with respect. He was tightly muscled and a fighter who would do damn near anything to win. One of his front teeth was chipped and his eyes were comically, some would say pathetically, close set. Some people claimed he didn't know how to read, and others went further and said he was retarded, but never to his face. Guys were afraid of him and girls prayed he wouldn't ask them to dance. He was funny looking, but in a scary way.

"Me or you," said Hess, approaching the open window of the Ford.

"You," said Stewart, killing the ignition. "We'll switch up later on."

Stewart took off his bombers before getting into Hess's Chevy. It was a ritual practiced by many of the car freaks in their crowd, who took pride in their flawless interiors. Stewart only removed his shoes for Hess. They had been best buds since their grade school days at St. Michael's, the Catholic elementary in the neighborhood. Both had been labeled as troublemakers early on. No teacher, not even a nun with a hot ruler, could tell them what to do.

No one could tell them anything now.

FIVE

DEREK STRANGE AND Billy Georgelakos neared the Three-Star Diner a little past closing time. Inside the area's apartments and row houses, men and women were having their first beers and highballs, listening to the radio, arguing, making love, and changing into stylish threads. Freshly washed cars cruised the strip, rhythm and blues coming from their open windows. It was coming up on Saturday night, and the pulse on Kennedy Street and behind its walls had begun to pick up.

The boys entered the diner. Mike Georgelakos sat by the register counting out the day's folding money and change. Darius Strange ran a cleaning brick over the grill, stripping it of any excess grease. Ella Lockheart, the Three-Star's counter-and-booth waitress, poured watery A&P brand ketchup into bottles marked Heinz. As was her custom this time of day, Ella had found the gospel hour on the house radio. A tune called "Peace in the Valley" was playing.

The diner had been set up in the forties. A Formica-top counter held fourteen armless red-vinyl swivel-top stools. Three four-seat booths, upholstered in red, ran along the plate glass that fronted the store. All food and drink was prepared and served from behind the counter: prep, colds, and hots. At the far right of the diner the counter elbowed off. This area was hidden behind a ceiling-hung plastic curtain. Behind the curtain were a stainless-steel automatic dishwasher and a double-tubbed sink with an industrial-sized tube-and-spray nozzle. Three walls of the diner were white plaster. The fourth wall, the one that ran behind the counter, was covered in white tile.

"*Vasili,*" said Mike to his son. "Derek."

"*Ba-ba,*" said Billy.

"Mr. Mike," said Derek, unable to correctly pronounce the family's last name.

Darius Strange glanced over at his son without breaking the rhythm of his chore, looked him over, and nodded. Derek Strange lifted his chin in return.

"C'mon, boy," said Mike, "help me count the money. Derek, the mop's waitin' for you in the back."

Derek found the bucket, strainer, and mop back by the dishwasher. The place had a utility man, addressed only by his nickname, Halftime, but he left early on Saturdays to allow Darius's son the chance to earn a little money. This suited Halftime fine.

Derek took up the webbed rubber mats behind the counter and rinsed them out in the sink. He carried the mats back through the small storage room, one by one, and laid them out in the alley to dry in the sun. He then waited for Ella Lockheart to fill the salt and pepper shakers, change into her street clothes in the back room, and leave the store. Lockheart, in her early thirties, was light-skinned, rail thin, pretty, quiet, unmarried, and deeply religious. She said to Derek, "Have a blessed day, young man," before going out the door.

Derek mopped the floor while his father sat on a stool and

read the sports page of the *Post*. His chef's hat, which he wore at all times while working over the grill, was on the counter by his side. Mike was showing Billy how to enter numbers in a green-covered book. Derek had seen the pages of the book once, a grid of lines with small figures penciled into the squares.

Derek strained water from the mop to the point that it was damp, and put it to work on the floor. He made sure to get the area at the base of the stools, where grease tended to collect.

"Elgin Baylor had thirty-four last night for Minneapolis," said Darius Strange, raising his voice some so his son could hear him while he worked. "Thirty-four in a *championship* game. That's the Lakers playin' against Russell, Cousy, Sam Jones, and them. That is some kind of accomplishment, wouldn't you say?"

"Sure is."

"Boy's got that quick first step."

"Yep."

"Came out of Spingarn, too," said Darius, naming Baylor's high school alma mater, off Benning Road in Northeast D.C. "The Green Wave graduates some superior athletes."

Derek smiled to himself as he worked. Partly it was because of the way his dad always liked to make his point with those local-boy-makes-good stories. But mostly he was smiling 'cause he liked the deep sound of his father's voice.

Darius Strange looked over at his son, bent over, pushing the mop. It was good for the boy to have this chore. After inspecting the finished floor, Mike would give Derek a dollar, which was walking-around money and also a simple work-and-reward lesson. The boy had a twice-a-week paper route, too. Darius wasn't worried about Derek the way he was worried about his older son, Dennis. Basically, Derek was good.

It was nice that Derek could see him working this steady job here as well. Plenty of boys never did get to see that kind of example. Someday Derek would know that this had all meant something with regard to what he himself would become.

But beyond that, Darius Strange did enjoy, and take pride in, his work. After the war he had taken several jobs involving hard, mindless physical labor, finally landing in the kitchen of the house restaurant of a downtown hotel. He was a dishwasher there, but he closely watched the activities of the line cooks and chefs. One of the cooks, a white steam-table man, was nice enough to school him in the details of the job. It wasn't long before Darius felt he was due for a promotion. But the manager wouldn't bring him along, so he left and got his first cooking job as a grill man in a greasy spoon in Far Northeast. The owner was a hard, bitter white who looked upon him as an animal and paid him pennies, but he got what he needed there, and when he had learned his trade he started looking around for something else. He signed up with Conway's Employment Service, down on 6th Street, which listed him as "Cook, Colored," and soon they had hooked him up with Mike Georgelakos, who had just let go of a good man who was bad behind drink. Georgelakos offered Darius forty dollars a week to start. Five years later, he was pulling in sixty-five.

"I'm finished," said Derek Strange.

"Go talk to Mr. Mike," said Darius.

Mike Georgelakos got off his stool behind the register. He was not much taller standing than he was sitting. He was bald on top, with patches of graying black hair on the sides. His nose was large and it hooked down over his mustache. Mike's shoulders were broad, his chest barrel shaped. Both of these traits had been passed down to Billy.

Mike walked the house ceremoniously and inspected the floor. When he returned he gave Derek a clean dollar bill.

"Here you go, boy. Good job."

"Thanks, Mr. Mike. Catch you around, Billy."

"You, too, Derek," said Billy, standing beside his father, smiling a little at his friend, sharing the secret of their day.

At the door, Darius Strange turned to give a short wave to Mike Georgelakos, as he always did.

"*Yasou*, Mike," said Darius.

"*Yasou*, Darius," said Mike. "*Adio.*"

Out on the sidewalk, Derek said to his father, "What's that Greek talk mean, anyway?"

"*Adio* means, like, adios. And *Yasou?* It's just a greeting, a, what do you call that, a salutation. All-purpose, kinda like aloha. You know, how they do in Hawaii?"

Derek Strange looked up at his father. Strong and handsome, with a neat mustache and closely cut, pomaded hair. He had to go six-two or six-three.

"Speaking of Hawaii," said Darius Strange, "Globetrotters gonna be comin' to Uline. They're playin' the Hawaiian team, the Fiftieth Staters? I just read the announcement in the paper. You feel like goin', I can get us tickets."

"Yeah!"

"Trotters got this young giant, Wilt Chamberlain, played for Kansas. They're payin' him sixty-five thousand dollars a year. I'd like to see what that boy can do to earn it."

"He come out of Spingarn, too?"

"Stop playin'," said Darius Strange in a stern way, but Derek could see a smirk breaking on the edge of his lips.

They got into Darius Strange's car, a '57 Mercury he had picked up at a lot on 10th and New York. It was a repossession deal, nineteen dollars a month on an eight-hundred-dollar balance. There had been a "special" interest rate put on it, a kind of penalty imposed on colored buyers. Darius was aware of it, and he knew it was wrong, but he accepted it just the same. Any way he looked at it, he would be paying on that car for the next four years.

DARIUS STRANGE DROVE up Georgia Avenue, his son at his side. They passed Ida's department store, where Derek had found trouble earlier in the day. It now seemed to him to have happened a long time ago. He was safe with his father now, and all of that mess he'd gotten into was tucked far away.

Just up above Piney Branch Road, near Van Buren, Darius Strange pulled into the lot of the soft–ice cream place, had mirror chips embedded in the stucco of its walls. The name of the place was Beck's, but everyone called it the Polar Bears because of the animal statues out front.

Darius killed the engine, gave Derek some change, and told him he'd meet him back at the car. Derek went to the service window, bought a tall swirl of chocolate on a cone, and had a seat on the curb. His father had walked to the Hubbard House to buy one of their layered chocolate pies. Derek Strange looked forward to this Saturday ritual all week long.

As he ate his ice cream, he watched his father cross the street with the pie box in his hand. A group of white boys drove by in a dropped-down Chevy and yelled something at his father from the open windows of their car. His father returned, expressionless, and made no mention of the incident. But Derek had heard their laughter, and the sound had cut him deep.

The last stop on their route home was Tempchin's Kosher Meat Market, a butcher shop between Shepherd and Randolph, down on 14th. In the store, Darius Strange said hello to Abe Tempchin, the proprietor, a thick, balding man who always seemed to have a smile on his face. To Derek, the place smelled funny, and the customers in here, white folks but not exactly, talked funny, too. Kinda like Billy's father, Mike.

"The holy man come in today?" said Darius Strange.

"Yes, he was here," said Tempchin.

"Let me get one of those chickens he got to, then."

Derek knew that Tempchin kept a shack full of live chickens behind the store. His father had told him that the rabbi, "the Jew version of a minister," would come to the store and kill the chickens, an odd thing, Derek thought, for a man of God to do. His father had explained, "That's what makes 'em kosher," and Derek had asked, "What's *kosher* mean?" "I got no clue," admitted his father. "But your mother thinks the chickens here are better than the ones at the A&P."

They drove southeast into Petworth and Park View. Darius Strange parked the Mercury on Princeton Place, a street that graded up off Georgia. Row houses holding single and multiple families, mostly colored now, lined the block.

"Go on and get your mother some milk," said Darius as he set the brake.

"Okay," said Derek.

Derek went down the block to the east side of the Avenue. On one corner was the neighborhood movie house, the York, and on the other was a small grocery, one of many neighborhood markets scattered around the city. He picked up a bottle of milk and took it to the counter, where the owner, a Jew the kids called Mr. Meyer and the adults called just Meyer, sat on a high-backed stool. Mr. Meyer knew Derek and the other members of his family by name. He marked the purchase down on a yellow pad and thanked Derek for his business. Darius Strange settled his debt with Meyer on payday, or the first of the month, or sometimes whenever he could.

Derek came out of the market. A girl he knew was standing on the corner, wearing a store-bought dress. She was his age and his height, and she had breasts. She had dimples when she smiled. She was smiling now.

"Hi, Derek," she said musically.

"Hey," said Derek, stopping in his tracks. He had the milk bottle in one hand, but the other was free. That hand felt awkward hanging there, so he put it in the pocket of his blue jeans.

"Don't you know my name?" the girl said. Lord, thought Derek, she has got some pretty brown eyes.

"Sure, I know it."

"Why you don't call me by it, then?"

"It's Carmen."

"*I* know what it is. You don't have to *tell* me it! You should be polite, though, and call me by my name when you see me."

Derek felt his face grow hot. "Why you got a Puerto Rican name, girl?"

"It's not Puerto Rican. My mama thought it sounded pretty, is all."

"It's all right," said Derek.

Carmen Hill giggled and began to tap one foot on the sidewalk. She was wearing patent leather church shoes, must have had something on the tips of those soles for dancing, 'cause they made a sound.

"Why you laughin'?" said Derek. "I ain't tell no joke."

"That how you give a girl a compliment? My name is *all right?*"

"It's pretty," said Derek quickly, and before he lost his nerve added, "Just like you."

He turned and went up the street. He passed a German man, one of the last whites on the block, who had once thrown hot water at him and his brother for playing too close to his house, and a boy he recognized who was cradling a Daisy lever-action BB rifle he had gotten for his birthday. Ordinarily Derek Strange would have stopped and checked out the gun. But he kept going, looking over his shoulder at Carmen Hill, still standing there tapping her foot, smiling that smile, her eyes alive, those deep dimples of hers . . .

That girl bothered him nearly every time he saw her. Least he had had the nerve to tell her she was pretty. He wondered what her smart self thought of *that.*

At 760 Princeton, he took the steps up to his home.

SIX

THE FAMILY LIVED in a row house that Darius Strange had di-
vided into two apartments. A single mother who worked
at the cafeteria down at Howard University, not much more
than a mile away, lived in the bottom unit with her three wild
sons. Darius had bought the house after answering an ad in
the *Washington Post* that read, "Colored, NW, Brick Home."
After putting three hundred and fifty down, he had secured a
GI Bill loan at 4 percent. His nut was eighty-six dollars a
month, and so far he had not missed a payment. The tenant
downstairs was often late with her rent, but she was trying her
best, and often he let her slide.

The Strange unit consisted of two bedrooms, a living
room/dining area, and a galley-style kitchen. The furniture
and appliances were old but clean. A screened-in porch, where
Derek Strange often slept on summer nights, gave onto a view
of a small dirt-and-weed backyard and then an alley. The alley,
and the grounds of Park View Elementary up the block, were

the primary playgrounds for the boys and girls of Princeton
Place and those on Otis Place, the next street to the south.

Derek Strange entered the apartment. His father had settled in his regular big old chair, the one facing the television
set, a new twenty-one-inch Zenith with Space Command remote control. He had the latest *Afro-American* spread out in his
lap. On the TV screen, James Stewart and Stephen McNally
were firing rifles at one each other, both of them having found
protection in an outcrop of rocks.

"Young D," said Dennis Strange, eighteen, tall and lean
like his father, dark skinned like the entire family. Dennis was
seated at the table where the Stranges took their meals. He,
too, had a copy of the *Afro-American* before him. There were always extras around the house.

"Dennis," said Derek.

"What you been doin', man?"

"Playin'."

Dennis rubbed his fingers along the top of his shaven
head. "With your white-boy friend?"

"So?" Derek stared at the gunplay on the TV screen. The
sound of ricochet was loud in the room. "Why they tryin' to
kill each other, Pop?"

"One man took the other man's Winchester in the begin-
ning of the movie," said Darius Strange. "They just gettin'
around to settlin' it now."

Derek looked at the tabloid-sized newspaper in his father's lap. Derek and his best friend, Lydell Blue, delivered the
Washington edition of the newspaper to neighborhood sub-
scribers on Tuesdays and Fridays, earning roughly two dollars
a week each. This was real money to them. Derek always tried
to read the paper, too. Unlike the stuff he read in the *Post* and
the *Star*, the stories in the *Afro* described his world.

Often, though, the stories scared him some. The front
page of the latest issue talked about this boy Mack Parker, only
twenty-one years old, who got beat half to death and dragged

out of his cell by a lynch mob down in Mississippi. His mother was sayin', "Oh, Lord, why?" 'cause no one had seen Parker since the mob threw him in a car outside the jail. Reminded Derek of the story of that boy Emmett Till, which Dennis was always goin' on about, who got murdered down there for nothing more than whistling at a white girl.

But in this apartment, with his mother, father, and big brother, Derek felt safe.

"Where Mom at?" said Derek.

"Kitchen," said Dennis.

Derek walked by the *Life* magazines stacked on a table by the sofa. The cover story of the issue on top was one in a continuing seven-part series called "How the West Was Won." Darius Strange had collected every one. Dennis called it "How the West Got Stole" just to annoy their father. The same way he made fun of those programs his father loved to watch at night during the week: *Wagon Train, Bat Masterson, Trackdown,* and the like. These days, seemed like Dennis and his father were at each other all the time.

Next to the eating table sat a Sylvania hi-fi console combination with records stacked on top. His father listened to some jazz, but mostly the rhythm and blues singers who had started out in gospel. Derek liked to look at the album covers, photos of people like Ray Charles and that Soul Stirrers singer, and a big boy on the Apollo label named Solomon Burke. He wondered what it was like to sing for all those people up onstage, have that kind of money, have the finest women and the Cadillac cars. He wondered if his father, who smelled like grease, sweat, and burned meat when he came home from work, was envious of these men's lives. Derek didn't like to think on it too much, because it made him feel bad to imagine that his father would ever leave their home.

As Derek tried to walk by him, Dennis grabbed hold of his shirt and pinned his arms at his side. Derek managed to place the bottle of milk he was holding atop the stack of records. Once he had done this, he tried to break free, but Dennis was too strong. Derek did the only thing he could, dropping to his knees, taking Dennis down with him. They hit the floor and rolled.

"You can't get away from me," said Dennis.

"Punk," said Derek.

"Call me that again and you'll be lookin' like one of them polio kids. They'll be havin' to fit you for some of them braces and stuff."

"That's enough," said their father, his eyes on the TV.

Derek rolled Dennis so that one of Dennis's hands was pinned beneath him. Derek felt around and tried to get purchase on Dennis's other hand. Instead he grabbed Dennis's crotch.

"You like that, boy?"

"Like what?"

"You got your hand on my rod!"

They rolled into the hi-fi and laughed.

"I said that's enough," said Darius. "I ain't even finished payin' on that console yet."

Darius Strange had bought the hi-fi and the television on time. He had first gone downtown to George's, on 8th and F, but the salesman there, a chubby white man, had treated him with disrespect. When he walked in, Darius had heard Chubby laughing with one of his coworkers off to the side, talking about he was gonna sell that guy a "Zenick" and saying, with his idea of a colored voice, "Can I put it on laysaways?" Chubby hadn't thought he'd heard him, but he had. Darius hadn't raised a stink about it, but he'd left right away and driven over to Slattery's on Naylor Road, where the man himself, Frank Slattery, had written him up for the Zenith and the Sylvania, gotten him credit, and delivered it all the next day. The colored money got put together with the white money in the register, and once you counted it out come closing time, you couldn't even tell the difference. That's what Chubby didn't understand.

Like the car, he'd be paying on these things for a long while. Darius didn't worry on it, though. He expected he was going to be working for the rest of his life.

"You gettin' strong," said Dennis, looking his younger brother over with admiration as they both got to their feet.

"Bet I can take you soon, too."

"You can try," said Dennis. He made a head motion in the direction of the kitchen. "Go ahead, man."

"I'm gone."

Dennis chuckled as he pushed Derek's forehead with the flat of his palm. He tried it again and Derek ducked away, snatching the milk bottle off the record stack and walking through a short hall back to the kitchen.

"Boy wrinkled my shirt," said Dennis. "I was gonna wear it tonight, too."

Darius Strange looked over at his older son. "You goin' out?"

"I'm fixin' to. Why?"

"Who you goin' out *with?* That no-account I seen you with down on the Avenue?"

"Kenneth?" said Dennis. "He all right."

"He ain't look all right to me."

"Well, you don't have to worry. We just gonna drive around a little with his cousin, is all. Maybe check out that All-Star Jamboree they got down at the Howard. They got Baby Cortez and the Clovers on the bill. Anyway, I won't be late."

"Don't be. You comin' to church tomorrow morning with us, right?"

"I'm going to temple. There's a service in the afternoon."

"Temple," said Darius with a grunt. "You mean that place on Vermont Avenue?"

"Minister Lucius presiding," said Dennis.

"He gonna be *presidin'* now, huh?"

"The man is a disciple of Elijah Muhammad."

"I know who that is." Darius tapped the newspaper in his

lap. "There's an advertisement your man paid for right in here. Calls himself the Anointed Leader. Asking for donations, says he wants to build a hospital. Ain't they got hospitals already in Chicago?"

"This one's for our people."

"Oh. If you so taken with him, why don't you send him some of your money?"

"If I had any I would."

"The man is just another hustler. He ain't no better than any old pimp you see out here on the street. And he ain't even Christian."

"That's the point. Jesus is the white man's god."

"Don't let your mother hear you say that, boy."

"Look, to me the Christian church is like that paper you readin'. Supposed to be for us, but it's not. You see the ads they run in there?" Dennis picked up the newspaper in front of him, opened it, and read off the page. "'Black and White Blanching Cream — a brighter, *lighter*, softer, smoother look.' Here's another one: 'Dr. Fred Palmer's Skin Whitener.' And the pictures of the women write these social columns they got? Those women all got light skin, and the way they got their hair fixed, I mean, they look like they're trying to be white. So who is hustling who? What you think this newspaper is trying to sell us here, huh?"

"I got eyes. You might think I'm blind, but I am not. Things are changing slow, but they're changin'. It ain't all good in this world, but for right now, it's what we got."

"You just gonna settle for *what we got*, then."

"You're young," said Darius. "Sooner or later you're gonna see, you got to go with some things to get along."

"You mean like last summer, when we went down to the shore? Remember when you got Jim Crowed, how you just *went along?* How'd you feel that day? How you think it made us feel?"

Darius had driven the family down to the Annapolis area,

looking for Highland, the beach that allowed colored. But he drove to the wrong place, and before he could back up and turn around, he got told by some man in a booth that they didn't allow his kind. Got told this in front of his wife and sons. Anger was what he felt. Anger and shame. But he didn't answer his son.

"Things ain't changin' quick enough for me," said Dennis. "I don't want to just get along. And just so you know, I'm gonna be goin' to that march next week, too."

"What march is that?"

"Youth March for Integrated Schools. They say twenty-five thousand strong gonna meet down at the Sylvan theater."

"Mind what you get yourself into."

"I know what I'm doin'."

"You think you do," said Darius Strange. "But y'all start rising up too hard, they gonna start doing you like they did that boy in that Mississippi jail."

"I ain't worried."

"Course not. Like I said, you're young."

In the kitchen, Derek Strange put the bottle of milk in the Frigidaire and went to the sink, where his mother stood washing dishes. There was a window over the sink, but at present it did not let in much light, as Alethea Strange had taped cardboard to the bottom panes. She did this so the humans in the kitchen would not scare the birds that had built a nest in the window frame outside.

"Hey, Mama," said Derek, touching his mother on her hip.

"Derek," she said, looking him in the eye. Sometime in the past year, her youngest had reached her height. "Anything special happen today?"

"Nothing special," he said, thinking of the incident at Ida's, wondering if he had just told his mother a lie. "How about you?"

"Oh, you know, just work." Alethea moved a bottle of

Kretol roach killer that sat on the sill and peeled back a corner of the cardboard on the window before her. "Look here, son."

Derek leaned forward on the counter. A mother robin was feeding her babies in her nest. Three featherless heads were going after one half of a worm.

"Where the father at?" said Derek.

"He's still around, I expect. He built the nest and now the mother is taking care of the kids. How we do around here."

Derek nodded. His mother had told him this many times before. He watched her tape the cardboard back in place and leaned his back to the counter.

"Lydell came by," said Alethea.

"Yeah?"

"Was looking to see if you wanted to go fishing up at the Home. Said he'd come back to pick you up in a little while."

"Can I go?"

"Yes, but not for long. Sun's gonna be going down soon anyway, and your father and me were thinking we'd go to a movie tonight. Want you back in the house before we go."

"What movie?"

"I wanted to see that one, *Imitation of Life,* 'cause everyone's been talkin' about it. But you know your father; he said he wasn't gonna pay to see no 'weepie.' He was pushing for some western, but I am not getting dressed to go out and see some show with men got dust on their clothes. So we made a compromise. We're gonna go see that new picture *I Want to Live!* down at the Lincoln."

"The one where they put that woman in the gas chamber, right?"

"Well, yes."

"Dag, I'd like to see that, too."

"You're not ready to see it. Now listen, your brother will be going out. You can stay here a couple of hours by yourself, can't you?"

"Sure."

"We won't be late. We've got church tomorrow."

"Yes, ma'am," said Derek Strange.

ALVIN JONES AND Kenneth Willis sat in a car in the alley behind Jones's grandmother's place, sharing a ninety-seven-cent bottle of imported sherry. Willis, in the passenger seat, was thumbing the wheel of the radio dial, trying to find a song that Jones could get behind. He stopped searching as a DJ introduced a record. The tuned kicked in, followed by a woman's vocals.

"Who is that bitch?" said Jones.

"Man said Connie Francis," said Willis.

"She can't sing a note. But I would fuck her to death if I ever got close to it."

"She's too old. Anyway, I seen her picture in a magazine, and she ain't all that great."

"I don't care *what* she looks like. I would fuck the life out of that white girl anyway."

"She's Spanish."

"So?"

"I'm just sayin'."

"What's the name of that song she's singin'? 'My Hot Penis'?"

"'My *Hap*piness.'"

"What I said."

They were in Jones's Cadillac, a '53 sedan, a basic radio-and-heater model that was no Coupe DeVille or Eldorado. It had the Caddy symbol on it, though, and that is what Jones cared about most. It was a start. He had bought it on time from Royal Chrysler on Rhode Island Avenue for eight hundred and ninety-five. He had lied about his job status to get the credit. He'd owned it for three months and had made one payment so far. They could go ahead and repossess it, they wanted to. He wasn't gonna pay on it anymore.

"Where we goin' when we done with this bottle?" said Jones.

"Told my boy Dennis we'd swing by and pick him up, ride around some. Boy's a grasshopper, man. Figure he might have somethin' we can burn."

"That tall boy lives over on Princeton?"

"Yeah."

"He ain't no more than a kid."

"He's my age."

"That's what I'm sayin'."

Alvin Jones was twenty-two. His cousin Kenneth Willis had just turned eighteen. Jones was feral, thin, light-skinned, and small of stature. Willis was dark, medium height, buck-toothed, and skinny, with thick wrists that said his frame would fill out soon.

"How you know this Dennis from?" said Jones.

"We both in the navy reserve."

"Huh," said Jones, and then laughed.

"What's so funny?"

"Picturin' you in one of the sailor suits. You know, that uniform looks like a dress to some of them navy boys. Heard them ships be crawlin' with faggots."

"I ain't no punk."

"You better not be one. If you was, it would be my blood duty to put a size ten up your motherfuckin' ass."

Willis grabbed the crotch of his slacks. "This here is for bitches only, Alvin."

"So is this," said Jones, raising his fist. "You got a point?"

"Don't be callin' me no punk," said Willis.

"Shit, just find some got-damn music on that box."

Kenneth Willis turned the radio dial and got a Fats Domino tune, "I Want to Walk You Home," on WUST. Now, that was how a song should be sung. Willis looked across the bench at his older cousin, who knew so much.

"Alvin?"

"Huh."

"What it felt like when you killed that boy?"

Jones hit the bottle of sherry and used his sleeve to wipe his mouth. "I ain't planned to kill him."

"*Planned to* got nothin' to do with it. He dead whether you meant him to be or not."

Two nights earlier, Jones had called a liquor store he knew delivered and asked for a messenger boy to bring out a bottle of Cuban rum, a fifth of French cognac, and a bottle of Spanish sherry. He had taken the selection right out of an ad the shop had run in the *Evening Star*. When the boy, young buck wearing a hat, had arrived at the address, a deserted row house in east Shaw, Jones had come out of the shadows and put the muzzle of a hot .22 to his temple. The boy gave up the money he had on him without any kind of fight. Jones shot him anyway, and watched the boy's last moments with fascination as he shivered and bled out on the street. He had always known he would kill a man someday and had decided just then that it was time to get it done.

"It felt like nothin'," said Jones. "Boy was breathin' and then he wasn't."

"You cold, man."

Jones shrugged. "We all headed to a bed of maggots. I was just helpin' the boy along."

The response chilled Willis. In some way it excited him, too. He reached for the bottle and took a long pull.

"You ain't said nothin' to no one, right?" said Jones.

"No one," said Willis.

"Don't *even* be talkin' about it with your friend."

"You *know* I won't."

Jones took the bottle, put it to his lips, and drank off the base. "That's the end of the evidence right there. I already done drank the rum and the cognac up."

Willis wiped at his forehead. "I am high."

"I am, too," said Jones.

They drove out of the alley and stopped on the adjoining street, where Willis got out and rolled the empty bottle down a sewer. He and Jones then headed for Princeton Place to pick up Dennis Strange.

SEVEN

"Dennis?"

"What?"

"I was looking at this police officer today, studyin' on him, like."

"So?"

"I was thinkin' I'd like to be one my own self someday."

"A police?"

"Yeah."

"You gonna keep all us Negroes in line down here, huh?"

"What you talkin' about?"

"Never mind."

Dennis and Derek Strange sat on the front steps of their row house in the last hour of daylight. On the sidewalk, three girls were playing jump rope, and on the north side of Princeton a woman pushed a baby carriage down toward Georgia. The light from the dying sun was like honey dripping on the street. Derek thought of it as "golden time."

"What about you?" said Derek. "What you gonna do?"

Dennis fingered the marijuana cigarette he had slipped into his pocket before leaving the house as he thought about the question. He didn't mind answering, as long as it was Derek and not his parents who were asking. Not that he was thinking on his future all that much. Lately, all he looked forward to was getting high. This older cat on the next street over had introduced him to reefer a few months back, and Dennis had taken to it from the start.

"I don't know. Continue on with the navy, I expect, when I get out of Roosevelt. Learn some kinda trade. Let the government put me through college, maybe. Knowledge is power, little brother, that's what they say."

"The navy. That means you got to go away?"

"What you think, man?"

"I don't want you to," said Derek, trying to keep the desperation that he felt out of his voice.

"It's just natural that things gonna change around here, D. You'll be missin' me at first, but soon you'll be lookin' to get out yourself. Like them baby birds Mama's always goin' on about. They ain't gonna be stayin' in that nest forever, right?"

"I guess."

"Go on, young man," said Dennis, pushing on his kid brother's head, hoping to lighten the sadness that had come into his eyes. "It's gonna be all right."

A Cadillac came up Princeton and pulled up behind Darius Strange's Mercury. Though there was space behind him, the driver of the Caddy touched his bumper to the rear bumper of Darius's car.

A man and a young man got out of the car and walked up the sidewalk. Derek had met the younger one, Kenneth, a friend of his brother's from the reserves, and didn't like him. He bragged on himself too much and talked all the time about what he had done or was going to do to girls. Kenneth Willis didn't look like he was headed anyplace good.

The other man, the older, smaller one with the light skin, didn't seem like someone Derek would care to hang with, either. He was dressed in black slacks and a thin purple shirt, looked like silk. He was what Derek's father called a no-account, or a hustler, or sometimes just a pimp. You could tell by the way his father's lip curled when he said it that he had no use for this kind of man.

Dennis rose from the steps as the two from the Cadillac came up the walk. Derek got up and stood beside his brother.

"Damn, Alvin," said Dennis, "ya'll ain't had to hit my father's car." He said it with a smile, to let them know that he was not angry. It made Derek ashamed.

"That your old man's Merc?" said the one called Alvin, who was the driver of the Cadillac. "Thought he *had* a job."

"He does."

"Car look like a repop to me."

So what if it is? thought Derek. Don't mean you had to bump it.

Alvin Jones lit a cigarette from a pack he produced from a pocket in his slacks. He carelessly tossed the spent match on the weedy front yard as smoke dribbled from his mouth and nose.

These men, with their bloodshot, heavy eyes, looked like they were on something. Derek had heard about things some people used to make themselves crazy in the head. But as they stepped closer, he could smell the alcohol coming off them. He recognized that stench from a wino he often came in contact with in the neighborhood. These two were drunk.

"That your brother?" said Alvin, looking Derek over.

"His name's Derek," said Dennis.

"Where you hidin' Dumbo at?" said Alvin Jones.

"What, all a y'all got names start with *D*?" said Kenneth Willis.

"My father's idea," said Dennis, looking at his feet.

Don't apologize to them for our father, thought Derek. Don't you ever do that.

"Musta got little man all angry, talkin' about his family," said Willis. "Lookit, Alvin, he got his fists balled up."

Derek relaxed his hands. He hadn't realized he had formed them into fists.

"Damn," said Jones, "we ain't mean to *upset* you, little man. What, you want to steal me, somethin' like that? Come over here, then, you got a mind to. I'll let you have a free swing."

Derek felt Dennis's arm come around his shoulder. He felt Dennis pull him in.

"He's all right," said Dennis, making a head motion toward the Cadillac. "C'mon, let's go."

"You bring that gage with you, man?" said Willis.

"Shut up, Kenneth," said Dennis, losing the pleasant tone he had been trying to maintain. "Ain't you got no sense?"

Jones and Willis laughed.

Dennis turned to Derek. "Go on, Young D."

"Why you got to go with them?" said Derek, not caring if Willis and Jones could hear.

"I won't be late. There go Lydell, lookin' for you."

Derek glanced up the block, where Lydell Blue was coming down the sidewalk from the direction of Park View Elementary, two cane poles resting on his shoulder. Derek walked north and met his friend. They shook hands, then tapped fists to their own chests.

"Us," said Derek.

"Us," said Lydell.

Lydell, stocky and muscled, with the beginnings of a mustache, handed Derek one of the poles. They were headed up to the Old Soldiers' Home, where they would jump the fence that surrounded the property and fish the pond on the wooded grounds. They hardly ever got a bite, but no one bothered them there, and it was a nice place to sit and talk. Lydell was Derek's boy going back to kindergarten. He had always been his tightest friend.

"You all right?" said Lydell, studying Derek's troubled face as they walked up the street.

"What is gage, Ly?"

"That's marijuana, man. Don't you know nothin'?"

"I knew," said Derek, feeling a drop in his chest. "I was just wonderin' if *you* knew, is all."

Derek turned his head, watched as his brother and the other two went toward the old Cadillac, watched Dennis put his hand to the handle of the back door.

Don't get in that car.

Derek Strange heard doors open and slam shut, and then the ignition of an engine. He and Lydell Blue walked east through the last of golden time as dusk settled on the street.

STEWART AND HESS went over to Mighty Mo's, a drive-in with car-side service at the intersection of New Hampshire Avenue and 410. It had been built in '58 and was the hangout for their crew and others. This was where they went to plot out the action for the rest of the night. Hot rods and lowriders with names like "Little Dipper," "Little Sleeper," and "Also Ran" were scattered about the lot. Rock and roll came from the open windows of the rides, their freshly waxed bodies gleaming under the lights.

Stewart and Hess hooked up with their friends. They ordered the signature burgers and onion rings through speakers, and were served by waitresses who ran the food from the kitchens out to the cars. The young men and women washed it down with beer. The night went on like that, engine talk and boasts and eye contact with the girlfriends of others, and soon enough the buzz of alcohol and deep night had come. It was time to go out and run the cars.

64

Hess and several others began to drive out of Mo's. In a corner of the lot, apart from the younger ones, stood Billy Griffith, Mike Anastasi, and Tommy Hancock, all leaning on their cars. These were the most feared, badass white boys in the area. For sport they frequently went into D.C. and picked fights with groups of coloreds. The most famous fight had started at the Hot Shoppes down at Georgia and Hamilton and continued on to the Little Tavern across the street. It was said that Griffith, Anastasi, and Hancock took on ten coloreds and beat the living shit out of them. As the story got around, the coloreds numbered twenty.

Stewart nodded at Billy Griffith, the most demented of the three, as he and Hess drove by. Griffith had a legendary rep. Men of all ages talked about him in bars and quieted when he walked into a room. Buzz Stewart could only hope that people would someday see him that way, too.

STEWART AND HESS drove out Route 29 to the area around Fairland Road. It was not far from downtown Silver Spring, maybe five miles on the odometer, but it was country. By ten o'clock there was little traffic, and those who were parked along the shoulders were there for fun.

A quarter mile had been marked off. Small bets had been made back at Mo's and at other area hangouts. Hess pulled over near a group of their friends and watched a race between a Chevy and a Dodge. Then a guy arrived towing a trailer holding a '31 Ford sedan without tags.

"Man claims it's got a five-twelve rear, dad," said Hess.

"What he claims," said Stewart.

The driver of the Ford dragged a hopped-up '50 Studebaker and blew its doors off.

"Whew," said Hess. "He wasn't braggin'."

They watched more races and drank more beer. Stewart saw a peroxide blonde named Suzie who he had dry-fucked one time in the back of his car when both of them were falling down on gin and Coke. He couldn't remember nothin' about her except the smell she'd left in his car. He started toward her but changed his mind. He could have that any old day, he wanted it. What he wanted tonight was a different kind of action. Three beers had been whispering to him, and now four talked in his ear, telling him to kick somebody's ass.

But Hess wanted to take a run at some snatch, so they went over and talked to a couple of tough girls they recognized, one who was okay, one who looked like a pimply duck. Both of them were wearing tight jeans. They got the girls into the car and after they'd switched to boy-girl and he'd gotten everyone to take off their shoes, Hess drove them through some farmer's cornfield for laughs. The girls were as drunk as they were, and soon they found a place to park. Stewart took a walk with the okay girl while Hess stayed in the car with the pimply duck. Later, after they had dropped the girls at a field party off Peach Orchard Road, Stewart admitted that he hadn't gotten anything off his girl, not even tit. Hess claimed he got his fingers wet and with an outstretched hand offered Stewart a smell.

"Get that shit outta my face, Shorty," said Stewart.

Hess cackled like a witch. "You ready to go sportin', Buzz?"

"Yeah. Let's pick up my ride."

They switched cars at the doughnut shop, bought more beer down below the line, and drove into the District, looking for something or someone to fuck up.

Their next stop was the Rendezvous, down on 10th Street in Northwest. The bar was jammed with rough old boys, bikers, and women who liked their type. The place smelled like alcohol and sweat. Link Wray and his Raymen were up on the bandstand. Link was wearing leather and rocking the house.

Stewart and Hess stepped up to the bar and ordered a couple of drafts. Stewart got a man's size and Hess ordered a fifteen-center. It looked like a girl's glass, but Hess didn't care. The fifteen-cent glass was tall, fragile, and skinny. You could break the head off it easy, if you had to, and use the jagged edge to open up some joker's face. Hess had a sip and put his back to the bar.

The band did a number with sometime vocalist Bobby Howard, then another. The Raymen were at their most raucous on their instrumentals, but Howard had a good voice for this kind of rock. It was known that Link couldn't sing. He had caught TB overseas when he was in the service, and the doctors had removed one of his lungs.

"Here he goes," said Stewart happily, and they watched Link use a pen to punch a couple of holes in the bands' speakers. It was how he got that fuzz tone out of his ax, and it was a signal that the band was about to lift off.

Which is how it went as the band kicked into "The Swag" and then an extended version of "Rawhide." It was a sound that no one else could seem to get, a primal, blood-kicking kind of rock and roll, and it energized the room. People were dancing into one another, and soon punches were thrown, and many of the people who were fighting still had smiles on their faces. Link himself was said to be a peaceable man, but sometimes his music incited righteous violence.

"You in?" said Hess, his eyes on a fight that was building in numbers on the edge of the room.

"Nah," said Stewart, who just wanted to enjoy the music for now. "I'm good."

Hess put his glass down on the bar, made his way into the crowd, and started swinging. His first punch met the temple of some guy who turned his head right into it, knocking him clean off his feet. Hess thinking, Some nights you just get luckier than shit, right before some other guy, looked like Richard Boone, up and split his lip with a straight right.

AN HOUR LATER they were parked up on 14th Street, way north of Columbia Road, drinking beers and huffing cigarettes. "The Girl Can't Help It" was playing on the radio, and Stewart was tapping his finger in time on the steering wheel.

Both of them were drunk stupid but still adrenalized from the fight. Stewart had waded in after Hess had caught that right and they had cleaned house from there on in. The most prideful thing about it was they weren't even tossed. In fact, they had walked out on their own two feet as the band played "Rumble" to their backs. Stewart would always remember the way that felt, like Link was playing that song for him. They should have been satisfied, but they still had energy to burn and felt that the night was not yet done.

"What you figure he's doin'?" said Hess, looking down the street to where a young colored guy stood by himself.

"Pretty obvious he's waitin' on a bus," said Stewart, thinking, as he did sometimes, that someone had taken a scalpel to Shorty's brain. Hell, the boy was right there at the D.C. Transit stop.

Hess touched at his lip. The blood had congealed some, but it still seeped out occasionally, as the split was deep. He put his cigarette in the other side of his mouth and had a drag.

"What you gonna do?" said Hess.

"What you mean?"

"Like, with your life?"

"I don't know." Stewart hadn't weighed it much.

"I'm thinking of enlisting in the Corps."

"Think they'll take you, huh?"

"Why wouldn't they?"

"Ain't you never heard of a Section Eight?"

Hess rubbed at his crotch, thinking of the duck-looking girl he'd had. She'd fought him some when he jammed his fingers down those panties of hers. Maybe he had been a little rough with her, but shit, they said don't, you *knew* they meant do.

"You know that girl I had tonight?" said Hess.

"I seen her on *You Bet Your Life*. She dropped down from the ceiling and almost hit Groucho."

"Stop it. That girl was the most, man."

"The most ugly. Had to be to get with you."

The two friends laughed. And then Hess's eyes narrowed as he tried to focus on the colored boy down the street.

"Let's try and peg that coon, Stubie. You wanna?"

"Sure," said Stewart. "Why not?"

Stewart hit the ignition and cruised slowly down the street. He kept the headlights off.

"He's watchin' us," said Hess. "He's trying not to, but he is."

Hess reached over to the radio and turned it way up, Little Richard's wail of release hitting the night. The colored boy turned his head in the direction of the Ford.

"Now we got his attention," said Hess.

Buzz Stewart drove his car up on the sidewalk and punched the gas. The colored boy took off.

"Run, nigger, run," said Hess.

"How many points if I hit him?"

"Say five."

Stewart laughed as they closed in on him. The boy leaped off the sidewalk and hit the street. Hess cackled as Stewart cut left, jumped the curb, and felt his four wheels find asphalt. At the last moment, when they got dangerously close, Stewart braked to a stop.

They watched the boy hotfoot it down the street. They laughed about it on the ride home.

DETECTIVE FRANK VAUGHN checked in with his lieutenant down at the Sixth Precinct house and changed over to a black Ford. He drove around town, talked with his informants, and interviewed potential witnesses on a recent homicide involving a liquor store messenger who was lured to an address by a phone call, then robbed and shot dead. He had a few bourbons at a bar near Colorado Avenue and didn't pay for one. While there, he phoned a divorcée he knew who lived in an apartment on 16th, near the bridge with the lions. He and the divorcée, a tall, curvy brunette named Linda, had a couple of cocktails at her place and some loose conversation before he fucked her on her queen-size bed. An hour after he had entered her apartment, he was back on the job.

Late that night he was called to the scene of a murder on Crittenden Street, down near Sherman Circle. The colored kid who'd bought it, eighteen years old, had been stabbed in the neck and chest. Uniforms had begun to canvass the neighbors but had turned up nothing yet.

Vaughn would do his job in a methodical, unhurried way. There wouldn't be much pressure from the white shirts to make a quick arrest. A dead colored boy was not a high priority. Hell, it would barely make the papers.

The mother of the victim had arrived on the scene and was crying hysterically. The sound of her grief turned Vaughn's thoughts to his maid, Alethea Strange. She had two sons, one the same age as Ricky, the other about the same age as the dead kid lying on the street. He'd met them once, and her husband, when he'd driven her home in a hard summer rain.

He shook off the thought. Every murder was a tragedy to someone, after all.

DEREK STRANGE LAY in his bed, listening to a scratching sound. The wind was moving the branches and leaves of the tree outside his window. A dog was making noise out there, too. Had to be the Broadnaxes' shepherd, barking in the alley that ran behind the house. That's all it was. A tree he climbed regular and a dog who always licked his outstretched hand.

Dennis was still out with his friends. Their parents had re-turned from the movie and gone to bed.

Derek felt his blood pulsing hard inside him. He wanted Dennis to come back home. He wanted him under the same roof as his mother and father. It was safe here when they were all together in this house.

He got up, went to Dennis's bed, and slipped underneath the sheets and blanket. His brother wouldn't mind that he'd switched. Derek smiled, smelling Dennis in the bed, knowing then that he could rest. He closed his eyes and fell asleep.

As he slept, shadows crept across the wall.

PART 2

Spring 1968

EIGHT

Coming out of Sunday school at St. Sophia Greek Ortho-
dox Cathedral, a boy heard a slow, carefully enunciated
voice echoing from outdoor speakers. The voice was com-
manding and somehow welcoming. The boy walked down
the front steps of his church and headed in the direction of the
voice.

Around him, fathers were gathering their wives and children. Men were laughing with one another and smoking after-
service cigarettes. The day was pleasantly cool. The smell of
tobacco smoke and the scent of dogwood and magnolia blos-
soms were in the air.

The boy neared a big man with a friendly, wide-open face,
scarred on one cheek, who was on the sidewalk talking to another aging Greek. The big man smiled at the eleven-year-old
boy, who had curly brown hair and wore a blue blazer with an
attendance pin fixed to its lapel.

"You ready, *Niko?*"

"Not yet, *Papou*. Soon."

"Where you goin'?"

"Gonna see what's goin' on over there. I'll be right back."

"Okay, boy. Meet me at the *karo*."

The big man watched his grandson cross Garfield, go down a set of concrete steps, and disappear into the grounds of the National Cathedral.

The boy followed the voice and walked through a lawn landscaped with azaleas and other shrubs, finally reaching the edge of a huge crowd. He made his way into the middle of the crowd, which was mostly white, but a different kind of white than he and his grandfather and friends. His grandfather called these people *Amerikani*, or sometimes simply *aspri*. They were facing the loudspeakers that had been placed outside the cathedral and they were listening to that voice, sounded like a black man, which was coming from somewhere inside the stone walls. From the look of concentration on their faces, the boy could tell that what was being said was important.

"*. . . we are not coming to Washington to engage in any histrionic action, nor are we coming to tear up Washington. . . .*"

The boy turned to the man beside him and tugged on his suit jacket.

"Excuse me," said the boy. "Who is that?"

"Dr. King," said the man, who did not take his eyes from the loudspeakers as he answered.

"*. . . I don't like to predict violence, but if nothing is done between now and June to raise ghetto hope, I feel this summer will not only be as bad, but worse than last year.*"

Some of the men in the crowd looked at their wives as this was said. These same men and women then glanced at their children.

Soon the boy grew bored, as he did not understand the meaning of Dr. King's words. He walked from the cathedral grounds back toward the property where his own church and people stood. His grandfather was leaning against his gold '63 Buick Wildcat, parked on Garfield. He flicked the last of his cigarette onto the street and opened the passenger door for the boy. Then he got under the wheel of his car and turned the ignition.

"You went to hear the *mavros,* eh?" said the grandfather, pulling away from the curb.

"I heard a little," said the boy. "Is he good?"

"Good?" The grandfather shrugged. "What the hell do I know? I think he believes what he's sayin'. Anyway, he's stirring things up, that's for sure."

The boy reached for the radio switch. "Where we goin'?"

"To see *Kirio* Georgelakos, over on Kennedy Street. He ran out of tomatoes. I told him we'd drop some by."

The boy, whose name was Nick Stefanos, fiddled with the dial of the radio, stopping it at 1390. He found a rock-and-roll song he liked on WEAM and upped the volume. He began to sing along.

"What the hell?" said the grandfather, also named Nick Stefanos, with a gruff voice. But he was not annoyed. In fact, he was amused. He looked across the bench and gave the boy a crooked smile.

BIG NICK STEFANOS parked his Wildcat in the alley behind a fastback Mustang, got a crate of tomatoes out of his trunk, and called through the screen door of the Three-Star before he and his grandson walked inside. He dropped the crate in the small storage room before going through a doorway leading to the dishwashing area behind the counter.

"*Niko,*" said Mike Georgelakos, holding a spatula, leaning over the grill, his bald dome framed by patches of gray.

"I put the tomatoes in the back."

"Thanks, boss."

"*Tipota.*"

Nick and his grandson went around the counter, nodding at Billy, Mike's son, who was working colds. Billy, a younger, taller, hairier version of his father, wore an apron and kept a ballpoint pen lodged behind his ear. Over by the urns, a thin waitress pulled down on a black handle and drew a stream of coffee into a cup. The two Nicks found seats on empty stools.

All the booths and half the counter seats were taken. Mike Georgelakos opened for a few hours on Sundays to catch an after-church flurry that occurred between noon and one o'clock. Many of the customers wore dresses and suits. Gospel music came from the radio set on the AM station that normally played rhythm and blues.

A black cop and a white cop, both in uniform, sat at the counter having breakfast. Before them were cups of coffee and plates of eggs, potatoes, grilled onions, and half smokes. Occasionally they said a few quiet words to each other, but mostly they worked on their food. A couple of teenage boys sitting in a booth with their mother stared boldly at the backs of the police officers, studying their size and the service revolvers holstered on their hips.

"That your new car out back, Billy?" said the older Nick.

"It's a two-plus-two," said Billy Georgelakos, his eyes on the club sandwich he was making on the board in front of him.

"*Orayo eine.*"

"Yeah, it's nice."

"*Tha fas simera?*" called Mike from behind the grill.

"No food today," said Nick Stefanos. "Just a quick *caffe* for me and a cherry Co-Cola for my boy."

The frail, pretty waitress drew a coffee for the older man, poured a shot of cherry syrup into a glass of Coke she had pulled from the soda dispenser, and served them both.

"Ella, you do good work."

"Thank you, Mr. Nick."

They drank up their coffee and soda. The boy was not uncomfortable here, as his grandfather also owned a lunch counter, Nick's Grill, on 14th and S, that catered to blacks. Still, in both establishments he was always aware that he was in a different world than his own.

Big Nick left a dollar under his saucer for Ella. He and the boy went to the register, where Mike had just finished ringing up a sale. It was understood that Mike would not give Nick money for the tomatoes and that sometime in the future the debt would be repaid in kind. Also understood was that the drinks were on the house.

"How you doin,' young man?" said Mike to the boy. "You all right?"

"Yes."

"Good boy." Mike turned to the older man, whom he'd known for twenty-some-odd years. "You went to church, eh? I heard the *mavros* was supposed to talk down there."

"King?" said Nick Stefanos. "He talked. Got a big crowd, too."

"He's gonna make trouble," said Mike, lowering his voice. "He's gonna get 'em all stirred up."

"Whatever's gonna happen's gonna happen," said Nick with a shrug. He looked across the counter at Mike, carrying twenty pounds he didn't need, sweating, breathing hard from walking down twenty feet of rubber mats. "You can't stop it, *patrioti*, so don't waste your time worryin' about it. You're gonna make yourself sick."

Mike waved his hand. "God*damn*, you know me, I don't worry about nothin'."

"Looks like you can use some help. Where's your grill man today?"

"He don't work Sundays. Between me and my boy and Ella, we can handle it all right."

"Take it easy, *Michali*," said Nick, reaching over the counter to shake Mike's hand.

"You, too."

As Nick Stefanos and his grandson left the store, the two cops dropped some change on the counter, got up off their stools, and walked to the register. The boys who had been staring at them so boldly looked down at their plates as the tall men crossed the room.

"How you like it, boys?"

"I'm gonna be dreamin' about those half smokes tonight," said the white cop, who had the South in his voice.

"That's my signature," said Mike, catching the black cop's eye. "I learned it from a pro."

"How much, Mr. Mike?" said the black cop.

"Two dollars for both," said Mike, charging them two dollars less than he would have charged civilians.

"Have a blessed day, young man," said the waitress, Ella Lockheart, as she passed behind the black cop, who was in the process of returning his wallet to the back pocket of his slacks.

"You do the same."

At the door, the young black cop, broad shouldered, dark skinned, and handsome, turned and called to Billy Georgelakos, standing at the colds station.

"*Yasou, Vasili.*"

"*Yasou*, Derek."

The black cop, Derek Strange, and the white cop, who was named Troy Peters, walked out of the Three-Star and headed toward their squad car, parked out on the street.

STRANGE KEYED THE mic and radioed in to tell the station operator that he and his partner were back on duty. They cruised west down the strip, Peters under the wheel. A few kids were lining up for the matinee at the Kennedy; its marquee read

"Joan Crawford goes *Berserk!*" Bars, cleaners, and other shops were shuttered. A couple of young men dipping down the sidewalk cold-eyed Strange as the squad car passed.

"Go on, fellas," said Peters. "Wave to Officer Friendly."

"Don't you know the po-lice is your buddy?" said Strange. Peters chuckled, but Strange could not bring himself to smile.

This was the part of the job, the open contempt, that got under Strange's skin. Wouldn't have been so bad if he only got it while he was in uniform. But he was reminded of it even when he was not on duty. Once, at a party near Florida and 7th, a woman told him in front of Darla Harris, his date, that what he was doing was a form of betrayal, that, in essence, he was a traitor. But he felt that he was not. He was *protecting* his people. He was doing a job that few were willing to do and that needed to get done. He had convinced himself of this early on so he could get through his day-to-day.

It was true that he had been warned by the experienced black officers to expect this kind of attitude. But he didn't know it would continue to bother him as deeply as it did. He talked about it with his friend Lydell Blue whenever he could, because he could not talk about it with Troy Peters. Lydell had also become an MPD cop, straight out of the army. He knew.

Wasn't everybody. Plenty of people showed him respect. Older folks, mostly, and little kids. Still, as he got into the poorer neighborhoods, he was looked upon as the enemy by everyone, especially by the young. Sometimes he caught it from his own blood. On the afternoon of Strange's graduation from the academy, his brother, Dennis, high on something, had congratulated him, then said, "You a full-fledged member of the occupying army now." Strange was tempted to tell his brother that he had no call to be cuttin' on anyone who had a job, but he held his tongue. Dennis didn't mean anything by it, for real. He had always been against anything that smelled like the system. His parents, at least, had looked at him with pride.

"You hear those two old birds in there, talkin' about Dr. King?" said Peters.

"I heard 'em," said Strange.

"They're afraid, is what it is."

Strange looked across the bench at his blond-haired partner. "Now you're gonna tell me you're not."

"Not in that way. Look, if these people out here don't get some kind of relief, it's all gonna boil over. I don't look forward to that kind of violence. I'm *afraid* of it, okay? But those old guys, what they're afraid of is the change itself. I'm talkin' about how their world is gonna change forever when all of this gets settled once and for all. Me, I welcome that kind of change."

"You welcome it, huh?"

"You know what I mean."

"Okay. But here's something for you to remember while you're bein' so broad-minded. Come revolution time? You go out there and greet *these people* with open arms? Yours is gonna be the first throat they cut."

"Something's coming, is all I'm saying. You can't deny it. It's like trying to stop the sunrise."

Strange nodded tightly. Living conditions had deteriorated as poverty had grown throughout the decade. At present, only one out of three students in the city graduated from public high schools, resulting in a huge unskilled workforce released into a white-collar, government-industry town that yielded few jobs and little in the way of prospects. For many, the promise of the civil rights movement seemed broken. And if the ghetto was thought of by its residents as a kind of prison, then its police force was seen as the prison guard. This perception was exacerbated by the fact that, in D.C., roughly three out of four citizens were black, while four out of five police officers were white. No wonder that crime, civil disobedience, and unmasked hatred were on the rise.

The government, meanwhile, was making eleventh-hour efforts to ease the tension. President Johnson had appointed Walter Washington, longtime head of the National Capital Housing Authority, to be D.C.'s first black mayor. Mayor Washington then brought in Patrick V. Murphy, former chief of the Syracuse police, and put him in the newly created position of director of public safety. Murphy, who was perceived to be more sympathetic to the race problem than Police Chief John Layton, was charged with overseeing both the MPD and the fire department. Immediately, Murphy promoted blacks to higher ranks and stepped up efforts to recruit rookie black police officers. This did not make Murphy popular with senators and congressmen of a certain stripe, who feared that blacks were getting too much power in the federally controlled nation's capital. Nevertheless, a new opportunity had presented itself, and black men and women began to sign on in numbers for the uniform, badge, and gun. Derek Strange and Lydell Blue were two of many who had heard the call.

Disenfranchised Washingtonians, however, considered these efforts to be too little, too late. The race divide remained the nation's powder keg, and its ultimate explosion seemed destined to occur in D.C. In August of '67, arson and minor riots had broken out along 7th and 14th Streets, with rocks and bottles thrown at firemen attempting to extinguish the flames. Since then, unrest and disorder had become almost weekly occurrences. Stokely Carmichael, the high-profile former spokesman for the Student Nonviolent Coordinating Committee, had moved to town. H. Rap Brown was being extradited from New Orleans to Richmond and ultimately to Maryland's Eastern Shore, where he faced charges of arson and inciting a riot in the town of Cambridge. Black Panthers and other Black Nationalist factions had become active and entrenched around the city.

And Dr. Martin Luther King Jr. was promising, some said threatening, to bring his Poor People's Campaign, a massive rally, to Washington on April 22. But first he had to deal with Memphis.

Days earlier, King had led a six-thousand-strong march down Beale Street in support of an ongoing garbage workers' strike in Memphis, where almost all the refuse men were black. Rioting and violence had ensued, ending in serious injuries, scores of arrests, and the death of a sixteen-year-old boy. Witnesses claimed the boy, Larry Payne, had been shot by a white policeman after putting his hands up in surrender. Subsequently, a prominent group of radicals had called for the annexation of five southern states with the intention of forming a separate black nation, warning that the country would have "no chance of surviving" if their demands were not met. A visibly worn down President Johnson stated that rioting could only serve to divide the people, while presidential candidate Richard Nixon declared that "the nation must be prepared to meet force with force if necessary." King had pledged that the Memphis incident would not deter his plans to march in D.C. in April.

"Troy?"

"What?"

"Think we could get through one afternoon without talkin' about all this bullshit for a change?"

"It's not important to you?"

"I hear enough about it in *my* world every day. I just don't need to be discussin' it all day at work."

Discussing it with a white man, Strange might have added. But there wasn't any need to say it aloud. Peters was smart enough to read between the lines.

Strange had been riding with Peters for a while now, but it had only taken one day to know his history. Peters was twenty-nine years old, a devout Christian married to his college sweetheart, Patty, who worked for an American Indian–rights group on Jefferson Place in Northwest and drove a VW Bug with a flower-shaped McCarthy sticker affixed to its hood. Peters had strong feelings on civil rights, women's rights, organized labor, and the war in Vietnam. On all of these issues, Peters believed he was on the side of the angels.

Right or not, his opinions often came off as speeches, like he was up in front of one of those poli-sci classes he had taken back in school. Strange sometimes felt it was his duty to bring Peters back down to reality. Let him know in his own way that while all black people were looking for equality, few were looking to be accepted, or loved, by whites. It was, in fact, just about the furthest thing from black folks' minds. This was something that many of these well-meaning types could not seem to understand.

One thing about Peters, he was different for sure from most of the cops Strange had come to know. A Carolina boy who'd graduated from Princeton, joined the Peace Corps, then signed up for the MPD, he was one of several high-profile recruits with similar backgrounds who'd come to the force with Ivy League degrees in hand, hoping to change the system from the inside. There had even been a *New York Times* article written on these men in which Peters had been quoted, and a *Look* magazine spread that featured a photograph of his freckly, blue-eyed face. He claimed to be embarrassed by all the attention, and Strange had no doubt that he was. Certainly his notoriety and well-heeled upbringing did not endear him to many of his fellow officers, black or white. To them he was just playing dress-up until he got bored and moved on to something else.

Not that Peters was soft. Boys tended to be built bigger and tougher in the South, and Peters was a southern boy all the way. From what Strange had seen so far, he was unafraid to enter into a conflict and had no physical problem subduing suspects on the street. More important, Strange was secure in the belief that Peters would have his back in the event of a situation.

So Peters was all right. He wasn't Strange's boy or anything like that, but he was fine. Strange just wished he didn't try so hard to endear himself to his "black" partner all the time. It got tiring sometimes, listening to the beat of his pure heart.

"I wish I could have been there," said Peters.

"Where?"

"The cathedral. I would've liked to have heard him speak."

"Thought we were done with that," said Strange.

"The radio said four thousand showed up to hear him," said Peters, unable to give it up.

"Gonna be four *hundred* thousand," said Strange, "he comes back in April."

"First he's gotta go back to Tennessee to try and put a Band-Aid on that situation they got down there."

"Fine by me," said Strange. "Let the Memphis police deal with it for a while. Leave us with some peace."

He looked out the window of the squad car, saw a man washing his Cadillac curbside. A snatch of "Cold Sweat" came from its radio. Two kids were dancing on the sidewalk, one of them trying to do a JB split beside the man's ride.

"Maceo," said Strange under his breath.

Farther along, a woman in a gone-to-church outfit walked alone, swinging a handbag, her backside moving beautifully beneath her short skirt.

"What'd you say?" said Peters.

"I love this city," said Strange.

NINE

BUZZ STEWART WALKED through an open bay door, stepped into the cool spring air, and lit himself a smoke. He had just finished changing the oil on a '66 Dart, needed a break, and felt he was due. Behind him, from the garage radio, came that new one from the Temptations, "I Wish It Would Rain." Now, that was a nice song.

"Day in, day out, my tear-stained face is pressed against the windowpane," sang Stewart, soft and off-key, his eyes closed, the sun warming his face. David Ruffin on vocals, you couldn't go wrong there. Course, Stewart couldn't stand the sight of most niggers. But, boy, they could sing.

After Stewart's discharge from the army, the manager of the Esso station at Georgia and Piney Branch had rehired him straightaway. Manager said he hoped the service had made a man out of him, and Stewart assured him that it had. Soon Stewart had been promoted to junior mechanic, a title that allowed him to do simple work: water pumps, belts, hoses, battery replacements, thermostats, and the like. No valve jobs, though, or even tune-ups, because the fat man still insisted he pass the certification course before he could take on those kinds of procedures. Stewart wouldn't do it. He had long ago decided that he was never gonna sit in any kind of classroom again, have anyone laugh at him the way kids used to laugh at him back at St. Michael's just because he couldn't read the long words in those stupid books.

Manager said, "You take the class, you make full mechanic, it's as simple as that."

Stewart said, "Fuck a lot of class," ending the discussion right there.

Stewart liked to work on cars, but he was no longer looking to make a career of it. There were easier ways to make money.

"Hey, Dom," said Stewart, watching Dominic Martini scrape a rubber squeegee across the windshield of a '64 Impala over by the pumps. "You missed a spot. How you gonna get employee of the month like that?"

"I dunno, Buzz," said Martini without looking away from the chore at hand. He had to have known Stewart was cracking on him, but if it bothered him, he didn't let it show.

"Just don't want to see you get off that management track you're on."

"Thanks for lookin' out for me, man."

Stewart grunted. Martini was in his midtwenties, dark and pretty like Broadway Joe. He could have been a movie star, maybe, or one of them gigolos got paid to go on dates with old ladies, he wanted to. And here he was, a pump jockey, still cleaning windshields in the neighborhood he grew up in, a neighborhood gone half spade.

"Dumb ass," said Stewart.

Dumb, maybe, but tough. Unlike Buzz Stewart, who had been stationed in the Philippines for the duration of his enlistment, Dominic Martini had seen Vietnam. Talk was his out-fit had been involved in some real action, too. But Martini, who had been a cocky sonofabitch when he was a teenager, had lost something overseas. Funny how being in the middle of that shit storm had took the fire out of him. Or maybe it had something to do with his kid brother. The boy, Angelo, a weak tit if you asked Stewart, had always been his shadow when the two of them were growing up.

Whatever it was that had turned his lights off, and despite his lack of enthusiasm, Stewart had made Martini a part of his plans. He figured that if something went down, Martini would act without thought and also act with authority. After you've been programmed to kill, thought Stewart, the instinct never left you.

Martini had said that whatever Stewart had in mind was okay. He had said it without enthusiasm, like he said every-thing else, but agreed to come along. Stewart had brought Shorty in, too, soon as he'd done his straight time. Prison had made the little guy crazier than shit, and that could be useful, too. Not that he'd ever been normal or anything close to it. Walter Hess didn't need no Marine Corps to teach him how to kill.

Stewart hit his smoke, hit it again, hot-boxed it so the pa-per collapsed under the draw. He crushed the cigarette under his boot. There was an Olds 88 in the garage beside the Dart, waitin' on its tires to get rotated. It was time to get back to work.

He stopped by his car, a '64 Plymouth Belvedere, double red with a white top, parked along the cinder-block wall of the garage. Stewart babied his ride, a customized 440 with a Max Wedge head scoop, Hooker headers, three-inch pipes, a 727 automatic trans, and chrome reverse mags. On the left front quarter panel, in white script, was written the word "Berna-dette." He'd named the car after one of his favorite songs.

Stewart noticed a smudge on the hood. He grabbed at the

hip area of his belt line, where a clean shop rag always hung, and pulled the cloth free. He rubbed the smudge and removed it. Now she looked right.

———

WASN'T LONG BEFORE Stewart had the Olds up on the lift and was using an air gun to loosen the lugs on the wheels. The old lady who owned the car would be by soon to pick it up.

He had his sleeves rolled up high on his biceps, and as he worked he periodically checked his arms to regard their size. He had always been a big boy. The army had made him big like Kong.

Barry Richards, that fast-talking DJ on WHMC, introduced the brand-new Miracles record, "If You Can Want," saying, "Go ahead, Smokey," before the tune kicked in. It wasn't no "I Second That Emotion," but it was okay.

Walter Hess gave Stewart much shit about his newfound love of R&B. It was true that Stewart had been a rocker way back when, but something had changed in him early in the decade, when he started going to the Howard, down off 7th Street below Florida Avenue, to see the live acts with his friends. Most of the time they were the only whites in the place, but the colored kids were so into the show that there never had been any kind of trouble. None to speak of, that is, outside of the occasional hard look. Stewart always sat in the balcony, where he was less visible, just in case. Because of his size, he stood out too much as it was.

Early on, he caught the big-name acts. For fifty cents, in the early years, you got live performances and a movie, too. Comedians, sometimes, like Moms Mabley and Pigmeat Markham. But mostly musicians, and it was them he would remember most: James Brown and the Famous Flames, Little Stevie Wonder, Martha and the Vandellas, the Impressions, Joe Tex, and Aretha when she wasn't much more than a little girl.

Hell, she was so young then, her father had to be onstage with her, like a chaperone. Stewart had gotten tired of the hits he'd been hearing on the radio, especially that British shit, but what he saw at the Howard put a hot wire up inside him and got him buying music again.

He liked all kinds of R&B. But when he was looking to spend money in the record stores, he kept his eye out for the labels Tamla, Gordy, and Motown. There wasn't nothin' better than the Motown sound. Those blue-gum singers they had down south, Otis Redding and Wilson Pickett and them, some of their stuff was okay, but when they got to grunting and sweating they were way too niggerish for Stewart's tastes. The Motowners, they dressed high-class, in tuxes and gowns, and wore their hair like whites. What they were singing about, you could tell it wasn't just meant for colored. Hell, they could have been singing about things that happened in white people's lives. Sometimes, you closed your eyes, you could even pretend that they were white.

Not that Stewart had given up on rock completely. He and Shorty, sometimes with Martini in tow, still went out to the clubs. And Link Wray remained his man.

Stewart had missed Link's long run at Vinnie's, a rough old bar down around the Greyhound station on H, because those were the years he had been in the service. When he returned, Wray and the Raymen were the house act at the 1023 Club in Far Southeast. It was a bikers' bar, with members of Satan's Few, the Phantoms, the Pagans, and others in the mix. By then that part of Anacostia was going from working-class white to colored, and tensions between the neighborhood residents and the club patrons had begun to boil. In the summer of '66, coloreds attacked the club, cutting power lines, knocking over bikes, and tossing bricks through the 1023's windows. The following week the Pagans retaliated with some righteous ass kicking of their own. Buzz Stewart and

Walter Hess had joined the melee. This was before Shorty went to jail for something else he'd done. But on the bloody night of that retaliation, Stewart had seen him take a gravity knife to some coon's face during the free-for-all. Last Stewart had seen that man, he was running down the street screaming like a girl. Shorty musta cut him good.

Eventually that club had to close. Link moved to the Famous, on New York Avenue, across from the Rocket Room, another rough-and-tumble joint. Stewart followed him and continued to drink there and in other bucket-of-bloods just like it. There was the Anchor Inn, in Southeast, which was known to employ a whore waitress or two; and Strick's, on Branch Avenue, which still had country music; the Alpine, on Kennedy; the Lion's Den, on Georgia; and Cousin Nick's, another Pagan dive, near the bus depot, high on 14th. Coloreds were not welcome in most of these places, though many of these bars were in colored neighborhoods. If one came in and leered at one of the white girls, well, that was his misfortune. You just had to go ahead and stomp his ass.

Inside these establishments, Stewart felt safe with his own. It was like he was with his car-club boys in the parking lot of Mo's, the Chantels were singing from the dash radio, and the calendar still read 1959. But outside the club walls, the attitude had changed. Coloreds weren't looking away when you stared them down. They walked real slow across the street, almost daring you to hit 'em. Young ones especially had that laughing, fuck-you look in their eyes. Clearly they weren't going to take any shit from white boys anymore.

There were other changes as well. Greasers were no longer cool. Hot rods were out, muscle cars and pony cars were in, and Elvis was for squares. Stewart lost the Brylcreem in his hair and let it grow, just a little, over his ears. Some of Stewart's friends got into pot. A few got into worse. Walter Hess still drank beer and sometimes Jack, but somewhere along the line, probably in prison, he'd started in on amphetamines, too. As for Stewart, he stayed with beer and hard liquor. He liked Ten High bourbon and ginger ale. On certain nights, when he wanted to get way outside his head, he went with gin and Coke.

In their day, Stewart and Hess had relied mainly on their fists. Now they never went into the colored sections of town without some kind of weapon. Buzz kept a derringer in his boot; Shorty always carried some kind of knife. They wore the same accessories in the after-hours bars they frequented on 13th and 14th Streets, down in Shaw. Of course, the races in those joints mixed, as a certain tension release came with the late-hour buzz. The patrons were a drunken blur of black and white. The whores were mostly black.

"You got that Olds ready?" It was the fat manager, standing in the open bay door.

"Just about," said Stewart, who had balanced and rotated the tires and was now tightening the lugs.

"The blue-hair's waiting."

"Said I was near done."

Stewart looked out the door. The manager was already waddling back to his office. Out by the pumps, Martini was talking to a big guy wearing a suit and hat, the gas line going into his old-man's Dodge. The big guy had a sleepy set of eyes, and his hair was cut real short. You'd think he was military from the first glance. But Stewart had been around enough to know different. This guy was a cop.

Stewart wasn't surprised. Dominic Martini knew most of the cops in the neighborhood. It was like a game he played, knowing their names. He'd been hanging around precinct houses, watching them, since he was a kid.

Dumb shit, thought Stewart. It was like he looked up to them. Imagine, looking up to a cop.

Soon after, a squad car drove into the lot with two uniforms, colored and a white guy, in the front seat. The driver, the white guy, pulled up near the plainclothesman's Dodge.

Stewart said, "What the fuck."

FRANK VAUGHN LIKED to get out of his car and stretch while the young man at the Esso station gassed up his car. This one had been working here on and off for many years.

On his shirt, the name Dom was stitched onto a patch. There was a long period there when this Dom had been gone. Vaughn guessed he had done an active tour. He had the look of someone the government would snatch. He sure wasn't college-deferment material, and he was no rich man's son. Probably a high school dropout to boot. But plenty big enough to be a soldier. When Vaughn used to come here years earlier, the kid was full of piss and vinegar. Knew Vaughn was a cop and was a smart-ass about it, too. Now it looked like all that attitude had drained right out of his eyes.

"Don't fill it all the way," said Vaughn, who was admiring a shiny, tricked-out Plymouth Belvedere parked alongside the garage. "Leave some room for the tiger."

"Huh?"

"Your sign says 'Put a tiger in your tank.'"

"Oh, yeah," said Dom, like he didn't get the joke. More likely, he heard the same crack ten times a day.

A squad car pulled into the lot. Vaughn knew the occupants. Peters, the Ivy Leaguer, and the colored rookie, Derek Strange. The white knight and his black partner, crisp as a newly minted bill, part of the new look of the MPD. To Vaughn, it seemed like more of a publicity stunt than anything practical. Peters was a high-profile uniform who sometimes got his picture in the papers. Put him next to a colored guy, a good-looking one who could speak in full sentences, to make some sort of point. This is the face of your future po-lice officer.

Vaughn felt that the MPD was hiring black cops too quickly, with little regard for their qualifications. In theory, it was a good idea to have coloreds policing colored citizens. But Vaughn was not sure that he or the department was ready for the change. Like everything else rushing by him these past few years, it seemed to be happening too fast.

This young man was all right, though. Hell, he was Alethea's son, so that wasn't any kind of surprise.

The Ford stopped on the other side of the pump and idled. Derek Strange was on the passenger side, his arm resting on the lip of the open window.

"Detective Vaughn," said Strange.

"How you fellas doin' today?" said Vaughn.

"We're about off shift."

"And here I am, just gettin' on. You need somethin'?"

"Just sayin' hello. You looked kinda lonely, standing out here."

"Thanks for your concern."

The pump jockey turned and had a glance at Strange. Their eyes locked for a moment, and then the jockey looked away.

Strange recognized him. Martini, the teenager from Billy's neighborhood who he'd hung with a couple of times back when they were boys. A JD-lookin' kid, on the mean side, had a little brother who was kind, which this one probably mistook for weak. They were all together that day when Strange had been popped at Ida's for trying to boost a padlock, nine years back.

Strange didn't acknowledge Martini. He didn't look like he wanted him to. Looked like he'd fallen some off that high horse of his. Strange let him be. Strange's father had always told him, Don't be kickin' a man when he's down. Ain't no good reason for it, he'd said. Wrong as it was, though, Strange had to admit it felt good, wearing his clean uniform, looking at Martini, grease all over his.

"Your mother all right?" said Vaughn.

"She's fine," said Strange with a tone of finality. It was plain to Vaughn that Strange was asking him to say no more.

"All right, then," said Vaughn. "You fellas keep your eyes open out there."

"Have a good one, Detective," said Peters, who then put the Ford in gear and drove out of the lot.

Martini replaced the pump handle in its holster. "That'll be five."

"Here," said Vaughn, handing over the bill.

Vaughn walked over to the beautiful red Plymouth parked beside the garage. He studied the car. The owner had named it Bernadette, most likely for his girl. Well, thought Vaughn, young men do stupid things when it comes to young women. Vaughn himself had a tattoo on his shoulder that read "Olga," the word on a banner flowing across a heart. She had been his girlfriend when he'd had the tattoo done one drunken night in a parlor overseas, twenty-four years earlier. After he gotten it, he'd gone into a whorehouse next door and spent the rest of his leave money on a skinny little girl who called him Fwank, had a shaved snatch, and liked to laugh.

Vaughn walked to the open bay door of the garage. A mechanic, farm-boy big, was lowering an Olds to the cement floor.

"That your Belvedere out here?" said Vaughn.

"Yeah," said Stewart, not even bothering to look at Vaughn. He was breathing through his mouth as he worked. Vaughn put him in his late twenties. A greaser, not too bright, whose time had already passed him by.

"Nice sled," said Vaughn.

"Somethin' wrong?"

"It just caught my eye. I'm a Mopar man myself."

"Huh," said Stewart. It was more of a grunt than a response.

Friendly type, thought Vaughn. Okay, then, fuck you, too.

He walked back to his own car, a '67 Polara with cat-eye taillights. It only held a 318 under the hood, not much horse for the weight. Everything on it was stock, straight off the lot at Laurel Dodge. Nothing like the young man's Plymouth, a head-turner and a genuine rocket. But the Polara was plenty sporty for a man who was watching fifty coming up in the rearview mirror. It was a pretty car.

Vaughn lit a cigarette as he drove out of the Esso lot and headed for the station. Sunday was a good shift. Not too much happening, usually. Maybe he'd have a free hour. Enough time to visit his girl.

COMING OUT OF the Esso, Strange and Peters responded to a call, a domestic dispute down on Ogelthorpe. Peters told the dispatcher that they'd take it and got them on their way.

"We parked here?" said Strange.

"There ain't no hurry, rook."

"You're drivin' the limit."

Peters checked the speedometer. "So I am."

Peters knew that domestics usually worked themselves out before the police arrived. Cops who had been around for a while weren't in any hurry to jump into a conflict between a man and a woman, not if they didn't have to.

"Detective Hound Dog," said Peters, giving the Ford a little extra gas as he hit the hill on 14th. "He knows your mother?"

"From work," said Strange.

"I guess Vaughn gets those choppers of his cleaned real regular."

"I guess he does," said Strange.

Strange had told Peters early on that his mother worked reception in a dental office. He was instantly ashamed of himself for doing so and wondered why he had. Now he had to keep up the lie.

"You got plans tonight?" said Peters.

"Gonna catch an early show down at the Tivoli. *The Good, the Bad and the Ugly.*"

"You've seen it twice already."

"Guess I'll make it three times. Anyway, my girl hasn't seen it yet."

"Woman's gonna be a girlfriend to you, I guess she has to like westerns, too."

"She likes that good thing, she gonna have to learn."

"Quit braggin'."

"No brag, just fact."

Peters cut right on Ogelthorpe and slowed the cruiser. "They been playing the theme song from that movie all over the radio, you know?"

"Hugo Montenegro?" said Strange. "That's the bullshit version right there."

They pulled up along the curb, near the house number that had been radioed in to them. A man and a woman, both dressed in church clothes, were embracing on the front porch. The man kissed the woman on her cheek and then kissed her mouth.

"Now he gonna patch things up," said Peters.

"He's working on it," said Strange.

"Why I wasn't rushing," said Peters. "Let's just sit here for a minute, okay?"

"Give him a chance to tell her he learned."

———

BUZZ STEWART WALKED out to the pumps. Dominic Martini had just finished pouring eight gallons into a gold Riviera. He keyed the reset meter as the Buick left the lot.

"What was up with that?" said Stewart.

"Nothin'."

"Nothin', hell. Who were the uniforms?"

"Just cops."

"I mean, do you know 'em?"

"I seen 'em around."

"Shit, you don't get it, do you?" Stewart rubbed at his jaw. "You in or no?"

"In," said Martini.

"Then act like it. You can't be runnin' your mouth to the police and be with me, too. Understand?"

"I wasn't . . . I didn't say shit."

"Good. Shorty and me are gonna meet up tonight. You comin'?"

"Said I was in."

"Be over at my place 'round eight."

Martini watched Stewart cross the lot and disappear into the dark of the garage.

TEN

ALVIN JONES SAT in his favorite chair, a Kool burning between the fingers of his right hand, a bourbon over ice in his left. He had the sports page open in his lap and was squinting as he labored to read the type. His vision was fine, but the whiskey had got to his eyes.

Paper said the Senators had beat the Pirates, five to three, in an exhibition, which made ten straight wins over National League teams. But he wasn't interested in who beat who. Jones was looking at the game's box score so that he could choose the number he was going to play come Monday.

The way Jones had been doing it lately, he'd find his favorite player from the opposing team and make note of his position, then his stats from that particular game. Today he was studying on Willie Stargell. Stargell played first base, that was a 1. He had gone two for four, that was 2 and 4. Put it all together and you got 124. That was the number Jones would play.

But hadn't he played that number last week? He had, and it had been cold. Shit, he wasn't gonna make that mistake again. He went to the Nats box and tried the same thing. He didn't really have any favorites from Washington, though. Del Unser, he was all right but nothing special. Epstein on bag one, okay, sounded like a Jewboy name, so he wasn't gonna go with him, and then you had Ken McMullen at third. Nah, uh-uh, he didn't like the way slim looked with that Adam's apple bobbin' around in his neck. Casanova, Valentine . . . Frank Howard. Might as well go with farm boy; motherfucker could blow the cover right off the ball while he was sending it into the D.C. Stadium bleachers. But Howard played left. How could you make a number out of left field?

Jones dragged down some menthol and had a sip of his bourbon whiskey. Cheap shit, 86 proof, had the Clark's label on it, the store's own brand. He bought the five-year-old stuff instead of the six, unless he was drinking with a woman. Not Lula, a fresh woman. Cheap or no, it did the job and fucked with his head. Said it came from Kentucky, so how bad could it be? He drained the glass, sucked on some ice, and spit the cubes back.

"Lula!" he shouted over a Sam and Dave coming from the component stereo across the room. Unit had everything, even FM. But Jones kept the receiver on AM, where the soul stations were at. He had the dial set on WOOK.

She probably couldn't hear him, back in her bedroom, fuckin' with that kid. Between the music playing and that baby boy of hers, she was out of earshot for sure. Sometimes he wondered how he got himself into this situation right here. Thirty-one years old and he still hadn't learned. He didn't even like kids, and here he was, listening to one bawling day and night. Recently, he'd left another woman because of her child. Once she'd had it, she'd focused her attention on the boy and begun to ignore him. He couldn't have that, but now he was stuck in the same kind of setup. At least this bitch here was getting a steady check. That alone was enough to make him stay.

Jones got up and turned the volume down on the box. He'd had Lula buy it, after a little convincing. Took her down to the Dalmo store on 12th and F, asked the salesman to write it up. The salesman chuckled when Jones called it an "Admirable." How was he supposed to know the brand was Admiral? Way it was printed in the newspaper ad, it looked like Admirable to him.

"Lula!" he shouted.

"What?"

"Bring me a drink!"

That wasn't all they bought that day. Picked out an RCA Victor twenty-inch diagonal color TV with Wireless Wizard remote control, too. Jones told Lula to fill out the credit forms for both items and sign her name to the whole thing.

Before she did, she took him aside. "Alvin, you know I don't have that kind of money."

"All you got to do," said Jones, "is put down the deposit. You ain't have to make any more payments, you don't want to."

"They just gonna repossess it."

"If they want it that bad, they will. Meantime, we got sounds and a color TV."

"What about my credit?"

"You never can fuck up your credit all the way. Always gonna be somebody lookin' to give you credit."

"You sure, Alvin?"

"How I buy everything."

The way he figured it, if he was gonna move into the bitch's apartment and listen to her baby cry, then he deserved to have nice things.

This place wasn't bad, not for what Lula paid. Two bedrooms, if you counted that little one in the back, had no closet, where the baby slept. Wasn't his money paying for it, anyway, so he didn't care how much it was. He didn't work, not a sucker's job, anyway. Neither did Lula, for that matter. Her government checks paid for everything. Which meant he had to hide or be out when the welfare man came around. Inconvenient is what it was, but the price was right, and it was better than being out on the street.

Jones sat back down, took the last drag off his smoke, and crushed it into the ashtray that rested on the cushioned arm of his chair.

He *was* gonna need some money soon, though. You couldn't live off a woman all the time. Man had to look like something when was walking down the street. Have a roll in his pocket if he was gonna talk to a woman in a club and offer to buy her a drink. Cash for things like cigarettes, liquor, and gage. He had his eye on an El D he'd seen at this dealer's lot, too.

So he was gonna have to get up off his ass and do some work. He'd done a bus robbery recently, one late night over on Kenilworth Avenue in Northeast. Stepped onto a D.C. Transit with one of Lula's stockings over his face, showed the driver his .38, and took him for everything he had. Not much cash and too many tokens, but enough money to last him a few weeks. Those were the kinds of games he ran. One hustle, robbery, break-in, or purse snatch at a time. Once in a while something big to make the ride last. He'd been studying on some small hotels on the white side of town, over on 16th. All those places had cash on hand, and safes. That's what this boy of his said, anyway, and this boy knew a lot. Punk motherfuckers worked those front desks, too, so it wasn't like there was much risk. And there was this corner market near Lula's crib, settled their debts with the neighborhood regulars the first of every month. He and his cousin Kenneth had been thinkin' on that place for some time.

He'd made mistakes. Done some jail time for small things, strong-arm robberies and the like. No prison time, though. And he hadn't been caught for any of the homicides he'd done, grudge-type, passion-type, murder-for-hire shit, which could set you up for half a year. A couple of times he'd killed 'cause his blood had got up.

He thought about that last one. How he'd followed some cat out of a bar who'd said something smart to a woman Jones was with. How he'd taken a blade to this cat's cheek in the alley behind a low-rise apartment building, one of those reurbanization projects, the fancy name the government gave to ghettos. Jones had cut him, and the man was bleeding through his fingers and had begun to beg: I ain't mean nothin', brother, and Please not today, Lord, all that. But Jones had already begun to feel that *tick tick tick* coursing through his veins, that *thing* that told him to kill. Jones stuck him right in his chest and twisted the blade before he withdrew it. Must have been the heart he hit, 'cause the blood was bright red and pumping out fast. There was a witness, a young dude, but Jones had fish-eyed the motherfucker as he walked away from the scene. He knew this dude would not come forward. Few in that neighborhood, especially if they were young, would talk to the police. Jones didn't lose any sleep over it either way. He was thinking, Man shouldn't have talked to my woman the way he did.

And then he started thinking, Where is that bitch with my drink?

Lula Bacon came into the living-room area with a glass in her hand, like God had answered his question. He took the glass from her and drank bourbon deep.

"Where you been?" said Jones, wiping the back of his hand across his mouth.

"Puttin' him to sleep."

She stood over him in a sleeveless shift, tapping her foot. She was wearing a pair of pumps with a little cloth bow on top of each one. He guessed he was supposed to notice her shoes.

"New kicks?" he said, giving her a little something, thanking her, in his way, for bringing him a drink.

"For Easter. But I wouldn't mind wearing them out tonight."

"Who's gonna look after the kid?"

"My mother would."

"Well, I ain't goin' *no* goddamn where but this chair. My cousin and his boy are comin' over with some smoke, and I am going to get my head up right here."

"We could go to Ed Murphy's."

"What, I hit the number and no one told me?"

"You just cheap."

Jones liked Ed Murphy's Supper Club, over on Georgia. The kitchen made a mean shrimp creole, and the bartenders poured with a heavy hand. He went there once in a while when he was looking for something fresh. But what was the use of taking a woman out and spending good money on her when he already had her ass for free, right here, twenty feet from the bedroom?

"You ain't never want to go out," said Lula.

"What, you still runnin' your mouth?"

"Lazy motherfucker."

"Shut up, girl."

"Look —"

"I am warning you, either you shut that mouth of yours or, or . . ."

Lula put her hand on her hip. "Or what?"

"You keep talkin', I'm gonna put a size ten and a half up in your ass."

"Ten and a half?" she said, her eyes gone playful. "Now, you *know* you a ten. Why you men always tellin' lies behind your shoe size?"

"If I'm lyin', I'm lyin' on the low side. *You* know that."

Lula smiled.

Jones looked her over in that shift, cut up way above her knees. Nice legs, and they went up to an ass so good, made your friends jealous you'd gotten your hands around it first.

Young girl, just past twenty. She hadn't lost a goddamn bit of shape birthing that kid, either. Big brown eyes, too. Girl looked like Diana Ross, with titties.

Jones put his drink on the floor and opened his arms. "C'mere, girl."

"You're gonna wake the baby," said Lula.

"You the one be makin' all that noise."

She chuckled, and he knew he was there.

"Alvin?"

"What?"

"Can we go out?"

"We gonna have to see."

"I got somethin' you can see right here."

"When?"

Lula lifted her shift up to her waist. She sauntered toward him. The front of her panties was dark where her sex had dampened. The sight of her black mound behind those white panties made him grow. He was a small man, so there was room for them both on the chair. She straddled him there and unzipped his slacks.

"Can we go out?" she said.

"Okay," said Jones.

Jones thinking, After I get my nut, I'll just tell her I had a change of mind.

KENNETH WILLIS HAD bought his Mercury, a green Monterey, because of its flat rear window. With this feature, the Monterey was like no other model on the street. Women, he believed, would like to sit beside a man who drove a car like that.

Lately, though, Willis was having a little trouble making the payments. He had a custodial position over at this elementary school off Kansas Avenue, but it was a low-pay job. Also, he and Alvin had not pulled off any side thing for a while. He needed money. He was counting on having some soon.

Kenneth Willis and Dennis Strange were driving south on 7th Street in the Monterey. Both were high from the marijuana they'd smoked, fifteen minutes earlier, in Willis's shit-hole apartment on H. Dennis was dressed in clothes that were fashionable in '66. His hair was ratty. He held a paperback copy of *Dominated Man* in his hand.

Willis was under the wheel, filling out the window frame with his big body, nodding along to the brand-new Percy Sledge, "Take Time to Know Her," coming thin and crackly from the speaker mounted under the dash shelf.

"Percy be singin' good right here," said Willis. He had big shoulders and lean, muscular arms. He would have been handsome if not for his buckteeth.

"Any motherfucker sound good when you're high," said Dennis Strange.

Dennis preferred the new-sound thing coming up, Sly and the Family Stone, the Chambers Brothers, and them. He dug the way those cats looked, like they were gonna step out any way they wanted to and just didn't give a fuck about what society thought. Percy Sledge? To Dennis he was one of those old-time, lantern-on-the-lawn Negroes, a prisoner to the record company. He dressed in tuxedos. He still wore pomade in his hair. But he wouldn't mention that to his friend Kenneth. Willis wore pomade in his hair, too.

The street was crowded and alive. Families were out alongside hustlers and children playing ball. Women were gliding on the sidewalks, still in their Sunday dresses.

"Damn, baby," said Willis, slowing the car and leaning his head out the window to talk to a girl who was making her way down the strip. "Why you gonna walk like that while I'm behind the wheel? You gonna make a man have an *accident*."

"Don't blame me if you can't drive." She was smiling some but kept up her pace and would not look his way.

"Wanna go for a ride?"

"Uh-uh."

"What's wrong, you got a George?"

"Ain't none of your concern if I do."

"Why you wanna be like that, girl?"

"Go ahead, slick," she said, before turning down the cross street.

"One of them jaspers," said Willis.

"If they don't like you, they must be lesbians, huh?"

"Some bitches just don't like men," said Willis, shrugging.

"You gonna talk to them all, though. Find out which ones don't and which ones do."

"Somethin' wrong with that?"

It wouldn't help any for Dennis to tell Kenneth that there was. Kenneth, who he'd known since they were both in the reserves, was as pussy hungry as a man could be. He'd done some time on a statutory rape conviction, but even that lesson hadn't thrown water on his fire. Dennis didn't know how a man like him could get a job, not even a janitor's job, around little kids. He wouldn't let Kenneth around his own daughter, if he had one. He didn't even want him near his mother, and she was over fifty years old.

"Sure is some nice scenery out here, though," said Willis, his sights already set on another girl.

"Sure is," said Dennis, smiling at the familiar feeling he had, looking at his people, his world.

They rolled slowly past T Street, where the Howard Theater was set just east of 7th. Lately, the Howard had been replacing its stage shows with what they called adult films. Today the marquee read, *Miniskirt Love,* and underneath the title smaller letters had been put up, saying, "Warped Morals of the Mod World." Dennis wondered, Why would anyone care about some rich-ass white kids, doing shit 'cause they bored?

"Where the music gone to, man?" said Willis.

"Acts be goin' places where white folks got money to spend," said Dennis. "Ray Charles just played Constitution

Hall. James Brown, Gladys Knight, shit, they're out there at Shady Grove next week."

"Where the fuck is that?"

"In some cornfield out in Maryland. All I know is, I ain't interested."

He couldn't have afforded to go to those kinds of shows if he wanted to. Dennis Strange had no job. He lived with his mother and father. He sold marijuana in small quantities so that he could afford his own stash. He had a pill habit. He drank too much, and what he drank was cheap. In fact, he could smell last night's fortified wine coming out his pores now. When his head was up, he thought of these things and his shame grew. But that didn't stop him from getting high.

Being up on reefer, it chilled some of his anger, too. That was good, as it felt to him that he'd been angry for a long time. He'd been fired up on the injustices done to his people way before these Johnny-come-lately motherfuckers came out with their black gloves, naturals, and slogans. He was no longer interested in wearing signs.

Early on, during his stint in the navy, he'd gotten involved with a couple of Muslim boys who were into the same kind of ideology as him. Quietly, they'd hung together and talked about Elijah Muhammad and the new world they knew would have to come. They exchanged books like *The Colonizer and the Colonized* and *The Wretched of the Earth*. They talked about institutional oppression, the disease of capitalism, and revolution deep into the night. But Dennis never could get with the personal politics of the Muslim religion. For one, he liked to drink and get high, and he liked his women smart and free. Wasn't any god worth giving those things up for. Then, when Malcolm was assassinated by his own, Dennis got disillusioned all the way. He stopped hanging with his Muslim friends and retreated inside himself.

One night, drunk on Night Train, out there in Chicago

where he was stationed, he tumbled down a flight of stairs and broke his tailbone. He had been coming down out of a tenement where he had gone to cop some weed when he tripped and fell. He blacked out from the pain and the drink. No one got to him until the next morning. When they did he was sober and lying in his pee. His time in the navy was done. He received an honorable discharge and full disability. He walked with a slight limp and always had pain. He was prescribed barbiturates and fell in love with them. He began to receive a monthly check.

Dennis Strange came back to D.C. as a cripple living off the government tit, more bitter and insecure than he had ever been before. He moved in with his parents and did not try to get a job. He got high every day. He went to seminars at Africa House, a couple of SNCC and Black Nationalist rallies, and attended a few meetings organized by the local chapter of the Black Panthers in Shaw. He thought he would be into the Panthers, but he was put off by them, too. True, many in attendance were genuinely committed. But a few of the young brothers were there because they liked the fit of the beret and the cut of the uniform. Others were there for the pussy to be had. Some of them liked to shout; all of them liked to talk. To Dennis, they were dark-skinned versions of those kids with the long hair who hung out at Dupont Circle, on the other side of town. They were playing soldier, but they didn't really want to go to war. As usual, he did not fit in.

He tried to follow Dr. King but felt the reverend was, too forgiving. Time was gone for joining hands. King's followers believed freedom could be got with pacifism and words of love. Dennis knew that America would only respond, really respond, to the sound of gunfire, the sight of blood, and the smell of ashes.

"Goddamn right," said Dennis, the reefer, along with the pill he had taken, hitting him all at once.

"Say what?" said Kenneth Willis.

"Nothin'."

"You talkin' to yourself again."

"Yeah, I know," said Dennis. "Must be 'cause I'm high."

Willis parked the Monterey on a residential block of LeDroit Park, southeast of Howard University, in front of a row house converted into three units.

"This your cousin's new crib?" said Dennis.

"His woman's," said Willis. "She got a baby in there, too."

"From his blood?"

"He's made a couple his own self. But this one's not his."

Dennis Strange looked at the steps going up a hill to the house. There'd probably be at least another flight he'd have to take once inside. All those stairs were hell on his back.

"You can run the shit in to him," said Dennis. "I'll stay in the car."

"You need to come with me," said Willis.

"Why?"

"Alvin says he's got a proposition for us. Wants you in on it, too."

ELEVEN

DOMINIC MARTINI CAME up off Longfellow and turned left, taking Georgia Avenue north toward Silver Spring. His wrist rested on the wheel of his Nova, and a freshly lit Marlboro hung between his lips. Jack Alix, the DJ on WPGC, sprang boisterous from the radio as he introduced a song.

"Here's Gary Puckett and the Union Gap, with 'Woman, Woman,' comin' in at number one!"

The singer started out sincerely, then went dramatic on the chorus, demanding to know if his girl was thinking of stepping out on him. The music swelled around Martini in the car, but it barely registered. His attention was focused on the street.

When he'd gotten back from the service, the first thing he noticed about Georgia Avenue was that it had been repaved. The white concrete and streetcar tracks were gone, replaced by black asphalt. The platforms and watering troughs had disappeared. Everything looked less bright.

The second thing he'd noticed was that there were many more blacks in the neighborhood, up on the commercial strip and in the residential areas as well. Soul music came from radios of cars cruising the Avenue and sometimes it came from the open doors of the bars. Realtors had brought in black buyers and turned white blocks gray, causing many white homeowners to sell their houses on the cheap and move into the Maryland suburbs. Martini's house on Longfellow looked the same as when he left it, but most of the neighbors he'd known in his youth were gone. He felt like a stranger in his hometown.

There were changes inside his house, too. His father had died of liver failure. Angelo was gone. His mother was in a state of perpetual mourning and always wore black. The smell of the pasta sauce simmering in the kitchen reminded Martini he was home. But it was a lifeless place now. Windows were kept closed. The air was still, and the furniture held a thin coat of dust. He often heard his mother sobbing at night in her room.

He had few friends. He had not finished high school and felt cut off from those who did. Some of the kids he'd come up with were away at college, and he seemed dead to those who remained. He had not expected to return to D.C. with a hero's welcome. But he had hoped for respect.

He got it from the old-timers, especially the veterans, but it was different with the young. To many of them, he was a freak. In bars, he no longer talked about Vietnam. It didn't help him with women and sometimes it spurred unwelcome comments from men. When he mentioned his tour of duty, it seemed to lead to no good.

Now he was twenty-five years old, back at the gas station, working the pumps and washing windshields, doing the same thing he'd been doing when he was sixteen. His service benefits would pay for college, but he'd have to tackle high school first. He supposed that he could get that degree if he worked at it, but he knew he wasn't smart enough or ambitious enough to take the next step.

He hung with Buzz Stewart. Stewart rode him sometimes, but he was the closest thing to a friend Martini had. And there was something else about Buzz, something that was difficult for him to admit. Martini had gotten used to taking orders. He had grown comfortable getting up in the morning and having someone tell him what to do. When Dominic Martini looked at Stewart's sleeves, he saw stripes.

Stewart had asked if he was in. To Martini, it had sounded like a command.

Martini went under the railroad bridge in downtown Silver Spring. He passed Fay and Andy's, a beer garden at Selim where he sometimes drank with Buzz and Walter Hess, and hung a right at the Gifford's ice cream parlor on the next corner. He drove down Sligo Avenue, toward Stewart's place on Mississippi. He took a final drag off his cigarette and pitched the butt out the window.

Stewart was okay as long as he was sober. Hess was wrong most all the time. Both of them were ugly when they tied it on. Martini listened to their hate talk but didn't join in. They were all together on some things but not on that. Martini had been that way himself most of his life, but now he was not. While growing up, he had listened to his father talk constantly about niggers, mostly while drunk, and it had infected him. It took a tour of Vietnam to clean the poison from his blood.

It was clear from the start that the men of his platoon were more alike than they ever would have imagined. None of them came from money. None fully understood the circumstances that had brought them to Southeast Asia and put them in the line of fire. All watched one another's backs. In those ways, and in many other ways, they were brothers.

He had forged deep friendships with blacks and whites. He had thought the bonds would last. But after his discharge he lost contact with them. He was embarrassed to write them letters, as he couldn't spell for shit. And anyway, what would he say? My life is fucked. I'm pumping gas and getting ready to do a robbery. What's up with you?

Back in D.C., he was disappointed to find that the old mistrust remained. If anything, the canyon between blacks and whites was wider than it had been before. He tried to make friendly with some black guys who were new to the neighborhood but got limp handshakes and ice-cool eyes in return. Stewart and Hess laughed about this, called him Martini Luther King, Lady Bird, shit like that. They told him that a guy needed to choose which side of the line he was gonna stand on. That even the niggers didn't respect a man who switched sides. But he had lost the heart for that sort of conflict. He didn't hate blacks. He didn't want to hate anyone anymore.

Martini parked his Nova on Mississippi, near Stewart's Belvedere and Hess's ride. He walked beside a small brick house to a freestanding garage beside a large plot of plow-lined dirt, recently turned. Buzz did this every spring for his mother; he had done it even when the old man was alive. Albert Stewart had kicked from throat cancer while Buzz was overseas.

Stewart and Hess were in the garage, standing around Stewart's bike, an old Triumph Bonneville with twenty-four-inch risers. Both were smoking 'Boros and drinking Schlitz out of cans. Both wore Levi's jeans and motorcycle boots. A radio sat on a shelf under an old Esso sign, taken from the station. "7 Rooms of Gloom" came from its speaker.

A droplight had been looped through the rafters and hung over the two men. It cast yellow light upon their pale faces.

Hess threw his head back to kill his beer. He crushed the can in his fist and tossed it into a trash can, half filled with empties, in the corner of the garage. Martini stepped inside.

He said, "Buzz," then nodded at Hess.

"Pretty boy," said Hess.

"Shorty," said Martini.

"Drop that door," said Stewart.

Martini pulled the garage door down to the cement floor. Hess found another can of beer and pulled its ring. He dropped the ring into the opening at the top of the can.

Stewart head-motioned Martini toward a workbench set against one of the cinder-block walls. "Check this out."

Martini followed Stewart to a corner of the bench. Stewart pulled back a tarp covering a lumpen shape. A double-barreled, double-triggered, Italian-made shotgun was set tight in a vise. The barrel and stock had been cut down. A hacksaw lay nearby in a thick film of metal shavings.

Martini hadn't held a gun since he'd turned in his rifle. He had no desire to touch one again.

"Whaddaya think?"

"It's gotta be fifty years old. A bird shooter." Martini could think of nothing else to say.

"It makes its point. A man stares down two barrels of anything, he's gonna give up whatever it is you askin' for." Stewart dragged on his smoke. "Go on, take it out the vise and get a feel for it."

"I don't want to," said Martini.

"I don't want to," said Hess in a girlish way.

"Shut up, Shorty," said Stewart.

"What," said Hess, "you gonna let him pussy out on us now?"

Martini shook his head. "That's not what I'm sayin'."

"What, then?" said Stewart.

"Told you once before. I don't want to see nobody hurt."

"Shit," said Hess, "you didn't have no problem with greasin' them pieheads over there, did ya?"

Martini kept his eyes on Stewart. "All I'm tryin' to say is, I ain't up for no blood."

"You don't have nothin' against getting rich, though, do you?" said Stewart.

"Course not."

"Well, you don't have to worry, then," said Stewart. "The cut-down's for me. All you gotta do is drive. Three equal shares, like I promised. Course, you *will* have to carry a gun, just in case. All for one. But there won't be no need to use it."

"When?" said Martini.

"Soon."

Stewart studied Martini. Martini lowered his eyes.

Hess hit his smoke down to the filter and crushed it under his boot. He looked at the radio on the shelf with something like hate. "Buzz?"

"What?"

"What the *fuck* is this rughead singin' about, anyway?"

Stewart turned to Hess. "That's Levi Stubbs, you dumb shit."

"So?"

"So it shows what you *don't* know."

"Thought we was gonna do some sportin' tonight. I ain't come here to listen to no songs."

Stewart said, "Let's go."

Martini grabbed a can of Schlitz and popped it. Hess casually took a pill from his pocket, popped it in his mouth, and washed it down with beer. Stewart found a small black case in a footlocker, set the case on the workbench, and opened its lid. He extracted his derringer, an American single-shot stainless .38 with rosewood grips, from its place in the red velvet lining. He put one foot up on a stool and slipped the derringer into his boot.

"I'll meet you guys out front," said Stewart. "I gotta say good-bye to my mom."

"WHERE YOUR GIRL at, Alvin?" said Kenneth Willis.

"Back there fuckin' with that kid."

"Must not have been back there all day, though."

"Why you say that?"

"It smells like Charlie the Tuna been swimmin' through here, cuz."

"Yeah, well, *you* know."

Alvin Jones and Kenneth Willis laughed and touched hands.

Jones sat on a big cushioned chair. He had the smell of whiskey on him but had not offered any kind of refreshment to Willis or Dennis Strange. Both were standing in the cramped living room of Lula Bacon's apartment.

Dennis looked down at Jones, compact, freckled, with a yellow color to his skin. Wearing a gold Ban-Lon shirt with wide vertical black stripes, black slacks, and hard shoes of imitation-reptile tooled leather. Dennis could see his socks, sheer, almost, except for the solid parallel lines running through them. The slick brothers called these Thick 'n Thins. This was one slick man right here.

"What you lookin' at, boy?" said Jones. His eyes were golden, the same color as his shirt.

"Nothin'," said Dennis.

"Oh, you *lookin'*, all right. Always lookin'. You into the details of everything, I can tell. Got this outfit at Cavalier, on Seventh, case you wonderin'." Jones wiggled one foot. "I can see you diggin' on my gators, too. Saw 'em in the window of Flagg Brothers. Wouldn't buy my shoes anyplace else."

Those aren't real gators, thought Dennis. And you ain't shit.

"I'll take you down to F Street with me next time; we can hook you up with a pair, too," said Jones, going on despite the fact that Dennis had not replied. "Get you out of them Kinneys you wearin'."

"I don't need you to pick out my shoes."

Jones laughed. "Well, you damn sure look like you could use *some*one's help."

"Why we listenin' to the news?" said Willis, who had gone to the stereo and was reaching for the tuner dial.

"Don't touch that," said Jones.

"I was gonna move it over to OL," said Willis. "All's they doin' is talkin'."

"Uh-uh, man, leave it on OOK. That's me right there."

"They both the same."

"K comes before L," said Jones. "Don't you know that?"

Willis looked at him, openmouthed, and stepped back from the unit. "Say, man, what you fixin' to play tomorrow?"

"Well, I got a problem with that," said Jones. "I was picking Frank Howard for the first number, but Howard plays left. Ain't no base you can draw it from. . . ."

"Seven," said Dennis Strange.

"Say what?"

"Left is the seventh position on the field. It's what the stats man uses when he's making a mark in his book."

Jones winked. "Damn, boy, you smart. All them books you be readin' must be sinkin' in."

"Just tryin' to help."

"Nah, you a smart one, I can tell." Jones showed Dennis Strange his teeth. "A *de*tail man."

Dennis knew Alvin Jones from nine years back, through Kenneth, but it seemed he had always known his kind. Jones had that crocodile smile and those cut-you-for-nothin' eyes that Dennis had seen on certain neighborhood crawlers his whole life. Dennis had returned from the navy determined not to hang with these types, who perpetrated violent shit against their own people and treated their women like dogs. It was Willis, stupid and not as slick, but just as willing to do low things, who had put them all back together. And here was

Dennis, selling reefer for a Park View dealer, taking government disability, high during the daytime, having no job. Just like them. Dennis's father called them no-accounts. Now he was one, too.

"You want your gage?" said Dennis, cutting his eyes away from Jones's.

"You bring it?"

Dennis patted the pocket of his slacks. "Right here."

"Lemme see."

Dennis found a bag in his pocket and handed Jones the ounce he had asked for. Jones opened it and smelled the contents. He hefted the bag to feel its weight.

"It's right," said Dennis.

"How much?"

"Thirty."

"For this here?"

"Didn't grow in no alley."

"Okay. But I'm a little light this evening. I don't have the full amount on me, see?"

"You don't have it *on* you, huh. You gonna get it, though, right?"

"What, you don't trust a brother? You, who's always goin' on about unity, now you gonna act like that?"

"I trust you," said Dennis, hating his weakness and the lie.

"Look here." Jones made a show of glancing around, making sure Lula was not anywhere nearby. "This woman I know, she gonna front me for it."

"When?"

"We'll go over there right now. She's gonna have to write you out a check, though."

"My man don't take checks."

"He gonna have to take one tonight. It's Sunday, man. What you think, they gonna open up the banks just for this girl?"

"Check better be good."

"This girl is square," said Jones. "You can believe that."

Dennis stared at Jones, then looked away.

"Somethin' you wanted to talk to Dennis about?" said Willis.

"We gonna do that on the way."

Jones got up out of his chair and took a hat, a black sporty number with a bright gold band, off a coat tree by the door. He put the hat on his head and cocked it right.

"Thought you was stayin' in with Lula tonight," said Willis.

"I already fucked the bitch," said Jones. "Ain't no need to stay in now."

TWELVE

S O WHICH ONE was the Bad?"
"Van Cleef. The guy they called Angel Eyes."

"See, I thought the little Mexican dude could have been the Bad, too. What was his name?"

"Tuco." Strange smiled. "Otherwise known as the Rat."

"Yeah," said Darla Harris. "Him."

"Tuco was the Ugly."

"But he was bad, too."

"Not exactly," said Strange. "He was more like the dark side of Blondie. Someplace in between the Bad and the Good."

"I like it better when you can tell who the good guy is and who the bad guy is."

"Like, white hat, black hat, you mean. John Wayne and all that."

"Well, yeah."

"That's over, baby. The movies finally be gettin' around to how the world is. Complex."

"I don't get it."

I know you don't, thought Strange. Which is one reason why you and me are never gonna connect all the way.

They were headed east on Irving, coming from the Tivoli Theater on 14th and Park. Strange was under the wheel of his '65 Impala, a blue clean-line V-8 he'd purchased used at Curtis Chevrolet. He liked the car, but it was no Cadillac. Like his father, he'd always wanted a Caddy. Like his father, he didn't know if he'd ever have the means.

"We always go to the movies," said the woman.

"Gives me peace. Sit in a dark theater, forget about what I see out here every day."

"We always go to the movies and the movies are always westerns."

"Tell you what," said Strange. "You like that guy Coburn, right?"

"You mean Flint?"

"Him."

"That's a sexy man right there."

"He's in this new movie, playin' at the Atlas, thought we'd check it out later this week."

The woman raised an eyebrow, looked at Strange with skepticism. "What's the name of it?"

"*Waterhole #3.*"

Darla, who was a dark, cute, Northeast girl, slapped Strange on the arm and laughed. "You are pushin' it now."

"C'mere," said Strange, patting the bench seat. Darla slid over so that her thigh, exposed from her short skirt, was touching his. It was a nice thigh, tight and compact like the rest of her. Strange put his hand on the inside of it and gave it a little rub.

They had been together for a few months. Strange didn't love her, but they were compatible and fit together in bed. He had never pledged fidelity to her, and she hadn't asked him to. If she had, he would have run. Strange often had other women on his mind; there was one in particular who'd been haunting his thoughts for a long time. Anyway, he and Darla got along fine. She didn't make him want to pick flowers for her or write a song in her name or anything like that. What they had was just all right.

"My mother's out with her man," said Darla.

"She gonna be out all night?"

"I expect."

"I'll drop you, then come back over later, if that's all right."

"You got plans right now?"

"You know I always have Sunday supper with my parents."

"Okay." She kissed him behind his ear. "You get some food in you, then come on by."

"Go ahead and find something on the box," said Strange, putting his right arm around Darla's shoulder, settling into his seat.

She turned on the dash radio. At WWDC, she came upon a symphonic instrumental and recognized the theme.

"That's from the movie."

"The bullshit version," said Strange.

Darla got off of 1260. At all-news WAVA the announcer said that President Johnson would address the nation that night. She spun the dial, went right by a rock-and-roll tune, then stopped for a moment on WOOK. Strange caught a couple lines of an Otis Redding, which he recognized as "Chained and Bound," before Darla went past it. She found WOL at 1450, took her fingers off the dial, and sat back.

"Girl, you got a quick hand."

"Tired of listening to that 'Bama."

"He was from Georgia."

"Same thing to me. Anyway, you play him all the time at your crib." Darla smiled as "Love Is Here and Now You're Gone" came up through the shelf speaker. "This is more like it right here."

Just another thing gonna drive me away from her eventually, thought Strange. Woman runs by Otis to get to the Supremes.

"Aw, don't be like that," said Darla, looking at the frown on Strange's face.

"Motown," said Strange dismissively.

"So?"

"Ain't nothin' but soul music for white people, you ask me."

⸻

ALVIN JONES, Kenneth Willis, and Dennis Strange sat in the green Monterey across from a corner store, parked under a street lamp. Dusk had come and gone. The children of the neighborhood and most of its adults had gone indoors. The men had been there, and had been in strong discussion, for some time.

"Go on in, boy," said Jones to Dennis.

"Told you I don't need nothin'."

"Go on."

"And do what?"

"You the detail man. Use your eyes. Come on back and tell us what you see."

"Why would I?"

"'Cause me and Kenneth here are fixin' to rob this motherfucker," said Jones. "What you think?"

They were on a single-digit street off Rhode Island Avenue, in LeDroit Park. The market was just like many others serving the residential areas of the city. It catered to the needs of the immediate neighborhood in the absence of a large grocery store. A green-and-gold sign hung over the door. The door was tied open with a piece of rope. The lights were on inside.

"Go on in your own self, then," said Dennis.

"Can't do that," said Jones. "It would ruin the surprise we got planned for later on."

"Well, you gonna have to find someone else to do it," said Dennis Strange. "'Cause this kind of thing, it ain't me."

"You could use the money, right?" Jones, on the passenger side, looked in the rearview at Dennis, alone in the backseat, his book in his hand. Jones's eyes smiled. "You damn sure *look* like you could."

Dennis ignored the cut. He flashed on his father and mother, his brother in his uniform. He said, "It ain't me."

Jones adjusted himself in his seat, looked at Willis behind the wheel, looked back in the mirror at Dennis. "So you all talk, then."

"What'd you say?"

"All the time I been knowin' you, been hearin' you talk. How the white man be exploitatin' the black man, all that. How these crackers come into where we live and open their businesses. Suck all the money out of our people and never put anything back into the community."

"You got a point?"

"I bet you walk in there, you gonna see some Jew motherfucker behind that counter, doin' just what you claim. All I'm tellin' you is, me and Kenneth, we just gonna go and take back what motherfuckers like that been takin' from all of *us* all our lives. But you go on ahead and keep talkin' about it. Meanwhile, me and Kenneth here? We gonna *do* somethin'."

"Yeah," said Dennis, shaking his head, "y'all are a couple of real revolutionaries."

"More than *you*."

"And what you gonna do with all those pennies you get, huh? Put 'em toward the cause?"

"Gonna be a whole lot more than pennies," said Jones.

"I heard *that*," said Willis.

"Let me ask you somethin', man," said Jones, still eyeing Dennis. "What's the date today?"

"Last day of March," said Dennis.

"And what happens on the first of the month in these places, all over town? I bet you have a market just like this one over in Park View, so you must know."

"The owner collects," said Dennis, answering without having to think on it, knowing then what this was about.

"What I'm sayin'. People in the neighborhood got to pay their debt on that day, otherwise they gonna lose their credit. So we ain't talkin' about no pennies. We get it done before the man goes to the bank, late in the afternoon, we could walk away with, shit, I don't know, a thousand dollars. You do this thing for us, you gonna get yourself a cut."

"And you ain't have to do nothin' but look around," said Willis.

"Be a different kind of thing for you," said Jones. "A little bit somethin' more than talk."

Dennis shook his head. "I ain't robbin' *no*-motherfuckin'-body."

"Ain't nobody asked you to," said Jones. "What I been tryin' to tell you this whole time."

"Go on, bro," said Willis. "We keep lippin' out here, they gonna close the place up."

Dennis laid his book down on the seat beside him. He put his hand on the door release and pulled up on it. He was tired of hearing their voices. His high was gone and so was the low, steady feeling from the down he'd taken earlier in the day. He wanted to get away from these two and clear his head.

"Get me a pack of double-Os while you in there, too," said Jones.

"You got money?" said Dennis.

Jones waved him away. "I'll get you at my girl's."

Dennis got out of the car and crossed the street, a slight limp in his walk. Jones and Willis watched him pass through the market's open door.

"Damn," said Willis, "you are good. All that shit about exploitatin' our people, him bein' nothin' but talk . . . you lit a fire in his ass."

"I can talk some shit, can't I?"

"What if he has a change of mind?"

"He walked in there, didn't he?" said Jones. "Ain't no way he can change up now."

Upon entering the market, Dennis Strange found that it was as he had imagined it would be. Several rows of canned and dry goods, a cooler for sodas and dairy products, a limited selection of fresh vegetables and fruits, a freezer for ice cream tubs and bars, penny-candy bins, a whole mess of nickel candy, and paperbacks on a stand-up carousel rack. A white man, who would be the owner, and a black man, who would be the employee, sat behind the long counter that ran in front of one wall of the store. The white man sat on a stool in front of the register. The black man, also on a stool, sat tight against the counter, a newspaper open before him.

A twelve-inch Philco black-and-white TV, its rabbit ears wrapped in foil, sat on the far end of the counter, the tuxedoed image on its screen flickering amid the snow. Even through the poor reception, Dennis recognized the hunched shoulders, fish-like face, and the old-time-radio sound of the host's voice.

"We have a big show for you tonight. . . . Charleton Heston, Peter Genarro, popular singing group the Young Americans, Frankie Laine, Lana Cantrell, funnyman Myron Cohen, Smokey Robinson and the Miracles, and a young comedian I think you're going to like, Richard Pryor!"

The white man nodded to Dennis. "How you doing this evening, friend?"

"I'm doin' all right," said Dennis.

The black man, who Dennis guessed was the stock shelver, hand trucker, general physical laborer, and muscle for the place if it was needed, looked him over but did not nod or greet him in any way. He was not being unfriendly, but simply doing his job. This was the kind of place where the employees recognized damn near every person who came through the door. Dennis reasoned that he would check a young man like him out, too, if that were what he was being paid to do.

Dennis went to the paperbacks and casually spun the carousel, inspecting the imprints, titles, and authors of the books racked on it. There were several Coffin Ed–Gravedigger Jones novels by Chester Himes, a couple of Harold Robbinses, *The Autobiography of Malcolm X*, and a copy of *Nigger*, by Dick Gregory. Also, books by John D. MacDonald, all with colors in their titles, Avon-edition Ian Flemings, a few Matt Helms, *Valley of the Dolls*, and a ninety-five-cent Dell version of *Rosemary's Baby*. The cover of this one claimed that it was "America's #1 Bestseller." Dennis's mother said that all her friends had read it, but she was going to pass, as she had already raised two devil children of her own. Her eyes had sparkled some when she said it, though. She had been in the kitchen, washing dishes and looking at her baby birds, while she was talking. Dennis smiled a little, thinking of her there.

"We help you?" said the black man from behind the counter. "Gettin' about ready to close up."

"Just checking out these books," said Dennis, moving away from the rack and walking toward the register, where the white man sat. He saw the black man casually slip his hand beneath the counter. "I *will* take a pack of menthols, though."

"What flavor?" said the white man, getting up off his stool and putting his hand up to a slotted display over the register that held the cigarettes.

"Kools," said Dennis.

He noticed that the white man had them in his hand before the brand name had even come out of Dennis's mouth. Course this man would know what brand to pull. Every menthol-smoking brother walking in here was either going for Kool, Newport, or Salem. But if you had to bet on it, Kool was the cigarette of choice, especially for a young cat like him.

"You must have, what do you call that, intuition," said Dennis.

"You hear that, John?" said the white man to the black man, and the black man's eyes smiled. "I'm the Uri Geller of the grocery world."

"You in the wrong business, Mr. Ludvig."

"Here you go," said Dennis, pushing a one-dollar bill across the counter.

This Mr. Ludvig reminded Dennis of old man Meyer, from the corner DGS market where he lived. Same easy manner, same sense of humor, always making fun at his own expense. Prob'ly knew every kid's name who came into his shop. Prob'ly spotted them for penny candy, too, the way Mr. Meyer had spotted him for fireballs, Bazookas, and such when he was a kid.

And the black man, John, wearing a button-down sweater even though it wasn't all that cold, could've been Dennis's father. Same age, about, same kind of physical strength, same kind of resignation in his face as to what he was. A straight man, in a way, to his boss. The way Darius was to Mike Georgelakos, the Greek over on Kennedy. Chuckling at jokes that weren't all that funny, nodding at the same old cornball sayings he heard coming from the man's mouth ten times a day. Doing it because he was of that time. A time that was bound to pass, but still. What choice had they had, really, in the face of feeding their families? Take care of your people, hope that they made a better life for themselves and their own kids when the time came. Or be some shifty, low-ass bum, a nothing that no one, not even heirs, would remember. This man John and Dennis's father, Darius, they had chosen right. Two men who had chosen to *be* men, and in the process had given up some of their pride long ago. Because that is what they had to work with *in their time.*

"You okay?" said Mr. Ludvig.

"Fine," said Dennis, who had been staring off to the side.

"Here you go, friend," said Ludvig, handing him his change.

"All right, then," said Dennis, looking from one man to the other. "Ya'll have a good evening, hear?"

"You do the same, young man," said John.

Dennis walked out the door. The black man, whose full name was John Thomas, came around the counter and went to the plate-glass window that fronted the market. He watched Dennis cross the street.

Dennis went to the Monterey and dropped into the backseat. He handed the Kools over the seat to Jones, who packed them against the back of his hand, removed all the cellophane, and tore a hole in the bottom of the pack. He shook one out, tobacco end first, turned it, and slipped it into his mouth.

"Well?" said Jones.

"You gonna have some problems," said Dennis.

"How so?"

"Place is mined, for one. They got snipers up in the trees, too."

Jones put fire to his cigarette. He blew the match out on the exhale and turned his head to look at Dennis. "You finished?"

"No, there's more. Let me lay it out for you, like you asked me to, so you know."

Jones's eyes were flat. "Go ahead."

"You know where the register always at in these places? It's in the same place here. Except they done went and dug a moat around it. Dropped some cobra snakes in the moat and put a few crocodiles in there to keep 'em company."

"That a fact."

"Uh-huh. And you were right on about the money. There's tons of it, man. Matter of fact, they got a big old safe in that market, exactly like the one they got down in Fort Knox, just so they can hold it all. Odd Job be guardin' it, too."

"Smart nigger," said Jones.

"I think of any details I forgot," said Dennis, "I'll let you know."

Jones's lip twitched. "This a game to you?"

"Told you from the start I wasn't gonna do it."

"You need to understand somethin', then. I hear you been talkin' about this to anybody, especially that po-lice brother of yours, I'm gonna be lookin' for you. And another thing: If I go down for this, for *any* reason, your name's gonna be the first one I mention. 'Cause you was in there, boy; can't nobody dispute that. And whoever you spoke to, they gonna remember your face."

"You scarin' me, brother," said Dennis. "I mean, I am tremblin'."

"You think I'm playin'," said Jones, "you try me out."

"We done?"

Jones breathed out slowly. "Drop this motherfucker off somewhere, Kenneth, before I lose my composure."

"You need to go by your woman's before you drop me anywhere," said Dennis.

"Say what?" said Jones.

"You still owe me thirty. For the gage."

Willis ignitioned the Mercury and pulled it off the curb. Full night had come to the streets.

THIRTEEN

Y OU OKAY, LOVER?"

"I'm fine," said Frank Vaughn.

"Your eyes look kinda funny."

"Yours did, too. A minute ago, it looked like they were gonna pop right out your head."

"Stop it."

"Don't worry about me. I'm just a little dizzy. But it's a good dizzy, babe."

Frank Vaughn pulled out of the woman who was underneath him in her bed. Her name was Linda Allen. She caught her breath as he left her and rolled onto his back. He rested a beefy hand between the pillow and his head. The smell of Linda's sex, the smell of their perspiration, and the smell of the liquor they had drunk and the cigarettes they'd smoked were strong in the room.

"I'm gonna go wash up," said Linda. "You want something?"

Vaughn checked his Hamilton wristwatch. Gray and brown hairs sprouted through the links of the stainless band. "I got time for a short one, I guess."

Linda Allen got off the bed naked and proud, her posture straight. She shook her long hair off her shoulders as she moved. That was for him. Vaughn watched her with admiration. She was a tall, leggy brunette, now in her forties, a divorcée who had never had children and so had kept her shape. Her breasts were pink tipped, heavy, and stood up nice. Vaughn took in the cut of her muscular thighs, her ample round ass, and that warm box that always held him tight. God, this was a woman right here. Reminded him of Julie London in her prime. He had been with Linda for almost ten years.

He thought of this apartment, a one-bedroom in the Woodner, down by the lion bridge on 16th, as his oasis. He visited Linda on his night shifts, one or two times a week. Sometimes he came for what he'd come for tonight. Sometimes he came to rest.

He heard the toilet flush in the bathroom and then the sound of water flowing from the faucet. He reached over to the nightstand, shook an L&M from the deck, and lit it with his Zippo, which was customized with a hand-painted map of Okinawa. He took a deep drag, coughed a little, and lay his head back on the pillow.

His wife, Olga, was the same age as Linda, but the similarities ended there. Olga no longer had any shape to speak of. Her ass had flattened out, as had her breasts. Linda talked very little; Olga talked all the time. Vaughn's ejaculations with Olga were typically no more sensational than urination. With Linda, he came like a stallion. The funny thing was, though, when Vaughn made love to his wife, he experienced emotions he never felt while he was fucking Linda. And he knew the difference was just that simple: One was love and one was just a fuck. A lucky man could get both from his wife, but Vaughn hadn't had that kind of luck. It wasn't anything to cry over. This arrangement worked just fine.

Vaughn heard Linda's heavy footsteps out in the living room. He heard her opening the lid on her console hi-fi. He heard a Chris Connor tune coming from the speakers. That was another thing about Linda; she shared his taste in music. Entertainers who dressed right, musicians who had been trained to play their instruments, singers who sang rather than screamed. None of that rock-and-roll shit that his son, Ricky, now a twenty-one-year-old student at the University of Maryland, listened to in his room.

Linda came into the bedroom, a clean, damp washcloth in one hand, a tumbler of Beam and water over ice in the other. Vaughn rested his smoke in the dip of the nightstand ashtray. She put the washcloth in his hand and sat on the edge of the bed. Vaughn ran the cloth over his uncut member, pushed out the last of his seed, and cleaned Linda's smell from his pubic hair. He sat up, leaned his back against the headboard, and dropped the washcloth to the floor. Linda had a pull of the drink and handed the glass to Vaughn. He rattled the cubes a little and tipped some cool hot bourbon into his mouth.

Vaughn swallowed slowly. "What you starin' at, doll?"

"Big old dog. I'm staring at you." She rubbed her hand over his flattop. "For luck," she said.

"I can use it."

Linda ran her fingers down Vaughn's shoulder, unconsciously touching the tattoo of his wife's name floating in a heart. "Think we can go see some music one night? We haven't gone out in a while."

"Where you wanna go?"

"I like that girl, sings upstairs at Mr. Henry's in Southeast. Remember her?"

"The colored singer, with the trio."

"Roberta Flack," said Linda, recalling the singer's name.

"Yeah, okay."

"Can we go?"

"Sometime," said Vaughn.

Vaughn touched her left breast, squeezed the tip of her pink nipple, and felt it swell.

"You keep that up, you're gonna have to stay."

"I can't," he said. "I gotta get back on the street."

BUZZ STEWART, DOMINIC Martini, and Walter Hess drove downtown in Walter's '63½ Galaxie, a red-over-black beauty, drinking beer all the way. Hess had heard about the Ford from a cell mate of his and bought it from a mechanic up in King of Prussia, Pennsylvania, when he was released. It had a 427 under the hood, a four-speed on the console, small hubcaps, rear skirts, and the chrome dress-up option from the factory. It was the cleanest vehicle of its kind on the street.

Hess worked in a machine shop on Brookeville Road and put every extra dime he earned into the car. He had few expenses outside of beer and cigarettes, the amphetamines he bought with regularity, and the Ford. He lived with his mother and father in a bungalow on the 700 block of Silver Spring Avenue. He bought his speed from bikers who rented a group house on the same block. His pills of choice were Black Beauties. When the bikers were out of Beauties, he bought White Crosses and ate twice as many. Whatever it took to get that tingle going in his skull.

Hess felt he had grown up some since his stay in prison. Certainly he had not hurt anyone as badly as he had in that final incident, the last of several similar but less serious attacks, that got him sent away. He had been standing on Cameron Street off Georgia, smoking a butt outside Eddie Leonard's sandwich shop, when a group of young men drove by in a new Chevelle, yelling out the window at him and laughing, calling him "little greaser" and shit like that. It had got his back up and made him yell back, screaming "college faggots" at them 'cause he'd seen the Maryland U decal on the rear window of their car. Right away, they stopped the Chevy in the middle of Cameron. A big guy wearing a leather jacket with a football sewed over the M got out of the car. Hess pulled his hunting knife, a six-inch serrated stainless job he was carrying at the time, from the sheath in his boot and held it tight against his thigh. When the football player reached him, Hess brought the knife up and stabbed him in the face, just below his left eye. He then opened him up from his cheek clean down to the collarbone. All that blood. One of the college boys puked his lunch it was so bad. Walter Hess knew right away he was going to get sent up for that one. Too many witnesses, and there were his assault priors, too.

He had expected to get offered a deal like some of his friends had gotten back then. Join the Corps and we'll drop the charges, like that. He brought it up to the lawyer the court gave him, but the fancy guy just shook his head. "They don't want people like you," the lawyer said. In his cell at night, Walter would sometimes think about that and get confused. The army trained guys to kill, didn't they? He didn't even need training; it came natural to him. And if they took pretty-boy pussy boys like Dominic Martini, why wouldn't they take a man like him?

"Pull over," said Stewart. "Anywhere around here's good."

"Not yet," said Hess.

Hess drove by the bus station, where people stood out front on the sidewalk, killing time and catching cigarettes. Martini watched the eyes of the young blacks tracking them as they passed. He and his companions looked like trouble, he guessed. Trouble and hate.

"Park it," said Stewart, seeing an empty spot. They were on the 1200 block of New York Avenue, headed for the Famous.

"I need to find a spot closer to the club," said Hess. "I don't want none of these boofers down here fuckin' with my ride."

"Right there," said Stewart. "Shit, Shorty, what you want to do, park it in the bar?"

Hess cackled like a witch. "Think they'll let me?"

They parked and went inside. Immediately they found folks they knew among the white blue-collar crowd. Bikers from various gangs mixed with hard cases, construction workers, electricians' apprentices, pipe fitters, waitresses, secretaries, and young men from good homes who had no business being there but aspired to grit. Some of the women had tattoos, both store-bought and home inflicted. One girl, who called herself Danny and had the tat to prove it, had lost a tooth in a fight with her old man but had not replaced it because, she said, the hole made a good place to fit her cigar. Stewart bought her a CC and Seven as soon as he came in. He had done her one night a year back, before her boyfriend had ruined her face, and felt he owed her a drink. The girl was sloppy, but she was all right. Stewart was feeling generous. He was happy to be with his people.

Martini stayed with beer. Stewart and Hess went over to the hard stuff as Link Wray and his latest version of the Raymen took the stand. Between the British Invasion, the white blues revival, Dylan, psychedelia, and the soul revolution, Wray's music had not gotten much radio time these past few years, but he was still bringing in the local crowds. His set now consisted of his early smashes with some Elvis covers thrown into the mix. He opened with "Jack the Ripper," his last big hit, from '63. The place got moving straightaway. Stewart rested his back against the bar. He saw Dominic smiling, tapping his foot to the music. Hell, when Wray turned up his amp and let it rip, even that dumb shit could find a way to have a good time.

Stewart wondered why the world couldn't be the way it was in here, right now, all the time.

"Buzz," said Hess, standing beside him, a shot of Jack Daniel's in one hand, a draft beer in the other.

"Yeah."

"You see that fuckin' *girl* over there in the corner?"

Stewart looked in that direction. He saw a guy, drinking a beer, grinning, listening to the music, not bothering a soul. Stewart looked at Shorty, his eyes somewhat crossed, nodding his head rapidly for no reason except that the speed was telling him to.

"So?"

Hess threw his head back to drain his mash, placed the empty glass on the bar. "I don't like the way he's smiling."

"Shit, he ain't smilin' at you."

Hess stepped forward. Stewart grabbed the sleeve of his leather and pulled him back.

"Let him be, Shorty. He's just havin' a good time."

Stewart felt the bunched muscles of Hess's arm loosen under his grip.

"Buy me another shot, will ya, Buzz? I can stand another brew, too. Man, I'm thirsty as shit."

Course you are, thought Stewart. All that speed you got in you.

They had two more rounds. After the set, Stewart got a go order from the bartender and motioned Hess and Martini toward the door. They killed a six on the drive uptown.

DEREK STRANGE HAD parked his Impala on Princeton Place under a street lamp and was locking it down when he saw Kenneth Willis's green Monterey coming up the block. Willis slowed and pulled up to the curb, stopping behind the Impala. Strange saw that Alvin Jones, a crawler who never had been no good or brought any good along with him, sat beside his younger cousin. Dennis was in the backseat.

Strange waited for his brother to get out of the car. Jones

leaned on the window lip, crossed his left hand over his right forearm to ash his smoke. As was Strange's habit, he scanned the physical details: Jones wore a gold Ban-Lon shirt and a black hat with a bright gold band. He smiled as his eyes sized up Strange.

Strange straightened and gave Jones his full height and build. It was childish, he knew. Still, there were some things a man never could stop himself from doing, no matter how mature he was supposed to be. One was letting another man know that he had the goods to kick his ass if that's what he had a mind to do.

"Lawman," said Jones. "Must feel all naked and shit, out of your uniform. Where your sidearm at?"

Right under my shirttail, thought Strange. In my clip-on.

"Brother, you gonna hurt my feelings, you don't say somethin' soon."

Strange said nothing. Through the windshield, he could see Willis's big old row of buckteeth as he smiled. Willis, who had done time on a statutory charge, worked as a janitor, lived above a liquor store on H, and thought he was a stud. He saw Jones and Willis touch hands.

"My man," said Jones, his smile gone, looking directly at Strange with his cold light eyes. "Makin' the world safe for Mr. Charlie." Jones took a drag of his Kool and let the smoke dribble from his mouth.

Dennis shut the door and slowly made his way from the Mercury toward Derek, clutching a paperback in his hand, wincing a little as he took an errant step. Sitting in a car, and getting out of it, were hard on his back.

"Remember what I told you, boy," said Jones. "Hear?" But Dennis didn't look his way.

Dennis met Derek by the Impala. Together they walked toward the steps up to the row house where they'd both been raised. They heard more comments coming from behind them. Jones said something about the police and then mentioned

Darius Strange's car, "another repop," which made Willis laugh. The brothers did not turn or acknowledge them. Soon there was the sound of the Mercury turning in the street as Willis drove back toward Georgia.

"What you been doin', man?" said Dennis.

"Worked today. Took this girl to the movies. You?"

"Just drove around some."

"With those two?"

"Yeah."

"Where'd you go?"

Dennis fingered the check in his pocket. "Jones knows this woman. We was just over at her place for a little bit, you know."

I do know, thought Derek. Whatever you were doing, it had something to do with bad. Always would, with Jones and Willis around. Buying or selling something that was wrong. Maybe running for that dealer, Hayes, stayed over on Otis.

"What were y'all doing over at this *woman's* place?"

"Damn, boy, you gonna run me in?"

"Just curious."

"We were gettin' our heads up. You happy?"

Derek looked at his older brother with disappointment. It was a familiar look to Dennis, and he cut his eyes away.

"You gotta get high before family dinner now, too," said Derek.

"Ain't like you never burn it."

"Yeah, but I don't make it my everything."

"Father Derek," said Dennis, shaking his head.

"That woman y'all were visiting," said Derek, not able to back off. "Is she that Bacon girl Jones stays with in LeDroit Park?"

"How you know about her?"

"You told me. Hard to forget a name like that."

"This was another girl, had his baby. Lives over your way."

"Just what we need down here, more children bein' made by no-account brothers like Jones."

"So now you put on that uniform, you lose your color?"

"Bullshit."

"Now you gonna get up on your high horse and look down on the black man, too."

"That is bullshit, Dennis. I'm just pointin' out that this particular cat is wrong."

"I got eyes. You don't need to be lecturin' me on things I can see my own self."

They had reached the door of the house. Derek put a hand on Dennis's arm. "Listen, all I'm tellin' you is, you don't need to be runnin' in place out here. I can hook you up with some kind of job, you let me. I'm always meeting people, got small businesses and such, on my shifts. They'd be glad to do a police officer a solid, help out someone in his family, you know what I'm sayin'? That's the way it works."

"The system, you mean."

"Yeah. Nothing wrong with it, either."

"I ain't interested."

"What you plan to do, then, be some kind of professional victim? Give up 'cause of all this white oppression you always going on about? So, what, all these race-hatin' motherfuckers out here can point to a shiftless nigger like you and say they were right?"

"Shut up, man."

"Or maybe you just gonna keep hangin' with trash like Jones, till something happens you can't fix."

"Told you to shut your mouth."

"You and me, we weren't brought up that way."

Dennis pulled his arm free. "Dinner's ready, I expect."

"You're better than you know."

"I'm tired, man." Dennis lowered his eyes. "Do me a favor, Derek. Let me be."

FOURTEEN

"THERE GOES JULIA," said Dennis Strange, pointing to the screen of the family's color TV.

"Diahann Carroll," said Derek Strange. "That's a fine-looking woman right there."

"Reminds me of your mother," said Darius Strange.

"Talks like a white girl, though," said Dennis.

"Ain't no crime in it," said Darius.

"She be datin' white men, too," said Dennis. "I seen her in this magazine, on the arm of some British cat, one who does those interviews on channel five."

"She's *still* fine," said Derek.

"Got your mother's eyes," said Darius Strange.

Darius sat in his green lounger, the sports page of the *Washington Post* open in his lap. His facial features had begun to sag, and his weight had shifted down toward his middle.

His sons sat on hard chairs beside him. Alethea Strange

had cleared the dinner table and was back in the kitchen putting the dishes in a sink full of warm water.

The apartment was as it had always been. The furniture was the same furniture Dennis and Derek had roughhoused on all their lives. Their father's hi-fi was used infrequently these days and now served mainly as a stand for Alethea's herbs and African violets. Darius had not bought a record for many years. First Ray Charles went country, and then Sam Cooke had been shot dead by that woman back in '64. He had just lost interest after that. And anyway, he was well into his fifties now. The new soul sound was for the young. He had given his records to Derek, who had become a deep rhythm and blues fan, the same way Darius had been years ago.

The men were watching *The Hollywood Palace* variety show on ABC. *Bonanza* had come and gone, and there was little else of interest on the other channels. They were waiting to hear the president, scheduled to speak at any moment. It was rumored that he would be making some sort of major announcement concerning the war in Vietnam.

Diahann Carroll finished her number, a tune from *Camelot*. The show's host, Don Adams, came back onstage and began to introduce the next guest.

"Sorry about that, Chief," said Dennis in a nasal voice. "Yeah, you sorry all right. You and your tired-ass shit."

"Man used to have a comedy act in D.C.," said Darius.

"Was he funny then? 'Cause he ain't never made me laugh once. They want me to watch this show, they *better* bring out Agent Ninety-nine."

"And now, please welcome Diana Quarry and her brother, boxer Jerry Quarry, who are going to perform a very special song tonight."

"He's gonna sing now?" said Derek.

"Gotta do somethin'," said Dennis. "'Cause you *know* he can't fight."

"He decisioned Floyd Patterson," said Darius.

"An old Floyd," said Dennis.

"Government gives Ali his gloves back," said Derek, "he gonna take that man apart."

As the heavyweight and his sibling attempted a rock-and-roll duet, Darius Strange read from the newspaper. "Elgin Baylor had thirty-seven for the Lakers, can you believe it? Now L.A. gonna go on in the west. Man eliminated the Bulls all by hisself."

"Baylor?" said Derek, grinning at his brother. "Who's that?"

"Local boy, right?" said Dennis, winking at Derek.

"Came out of Spingarn," said Derek.

"You lyin'?" said Dennis. "Thought it was Dunbar."

Dennis and Derek reached behind their father, chuckled, and touched hands.

"Quit playin'," said Darius, stifling a grin, not looking up from his newspaper.

Alethea came into the room rubbing her hands dry on a dish towel. She wore a flower-patterned housedress with a cloth rose, similar to those that were printed on the dress, pinned in her graying hair. Except for the gray, the bursts of lines around her eyes, and her wrinkled hands, which had been damaged by the cleaning fluid she'd used through the years, she was a fit fifty-one. Her legs and back gave her problems from time to time, the cost of her domestic work, which she had recently cut to five days a week. But aside from those minor pains, she felt fine.

"Satisfaction?" she said, looking with affection at her men grouped around the Sylvania in the living room.

"Yes, ma'am," said Derek. "That chicken was right. Greens weren't too shabby, either."

"Glad you enjoyed it."

"Could've used a nice bottle of wine with it, somethin',"

said Dennis, smiling at his mother, not meaning anything by the remark.

"You want us to buy that for you, too?" said Darius.

"Darius," said Alethea.

"We pay his way for everything else around here, don't we?"

"He's just havin' a little fun with me," said Alethea.

"I can move out, Pop," said Dennis, "you want me to."

"What I want is for you to work," said Darius. "That's what a man does. Your brother's out there breaking a sweat. He's got a car, his own apartment. That's what you need to be moving toward, too."

Derek couldn't look at Dennis. He had ridden him hard outside the house because he believed in him and thought he could improve his life. But he never came down on Dennis in front of their parents. He wished he wasn't here to witness this now.

The silence that had fallen on the room ended as an announcer broke into the show to inform viewers that the president was about to speak. Derek got up and let his mother take his seat. He found another chair and dragged it close to the set.

"Man looks like one of his beagles," said Dennis.

"Hush," said Darius.

President Johnson began by talking about the war in Southeast Asia. He said that he would immediately order a cessation of air and naval attacks on North Vietnam, except in the area north of the twentieth parallel. He went into an explanation of what this meant in terms of the conflict's history and its progression. Then he indicated that he wanted to speak on something else. His face was somber but somewhat more relaxed than most Americans had seen it for some time.

"*I will not seek, and I will not accept, the nomination of my party. . . .*"

"Damn," said Dennis.

"Can't believe it," said Alethea.

"Man's giving up," said Derek. "You can see it on his face, though. He's had enough."

"So what fool we gonna get next?" said Dennis. "Nixon?"

"That won't happen," said Darius. "I got to believe, you get down to it, the people in this country are better than that. They get in the voting booth, they're not gonna pull the lever for that man."

"Unless they're scared," said Dennis.

"Scared of what?" said Darius.

"Everything," said Dennis. "Us."

Derek rubbed at his face. "Bobby Kennedy gonna step in now. You watch."

"That would work," said Darius. "He's a politician like the rest of them. But his heart seems right."

Alethea nodded. "Least there'd be hope."

They sat there in the glow of the television screen, listening to their president. But soon their thoughts returned to the smaller, more manageable conflicts in their own lives. Derek thinking of his job. Dennis concentrating on his wrong companions and their plans, and, at the same time, his next high. Alethea worrying about her elder son's future. Darius wincing at the sudden, sharp pain low in his spine.

He'd been getting these jolts lately, sometimes on his feet, sometimes while simply relaxing in his chair. A few days earlier, he'd noticed blood in his morning movement as well. There was something wrong with him, for sure. But what could he do? He still had to provide. His wife, God love her, couldn't work any harder than she already did. They were in debt, as they had always been. He couldn't afford to be sick, so there wasn't any use in worrying about it either way.

"I'm going out," said Dennis, getting up out of his seat.

"Where you off to?" said Darius.

"Out," said Dennis, walking toward the bedroom he and

Derek had once shared. "Twenty-seven years old, and you still quizzin' me."

"You stop acting like seven instead of twenty-seven," said Darius, "I'll stop quizzin'."

"Darius," said Alethea.

"Boy ain't gone no further than a child."

Dennis entered his bedroom and found a vial he kept underneath his socks in the top drawer of his dresser, beside a scarred-up baseball he'd had since he was eight. He and his father had played catch with that ball on summer evenings in the alley behind the house, as far back as '48. He stared at the ball for a moment, then closed the drawer.

Dennis shook a red out of the vial, raised spit, and swallowed the pill. He left the apartment without a word to any of them, slipping out quietly, looking to pay his man for the reefer he'd sold, looking for the comfort he found on the street.

In the kitchen, Alethea washed the dinner dishes and passed them to Derek, who dried them off with a towel. Alethea hummed a gospel tune he recognized as she handed him a wet plate. He wiped it hastily and slipped it, still damp, into a sun-faded rubber rack.

"You in a hurry?" said Alethea.

"I'm meeting someone," said Derek.

"That little girl from Northeast, works in the beauty shop?"

"Uh-huh."

"Whatever happened to Carmen?"

"She's around. Finishin' up over at Howard."

"You ever see her?"

"Not lately."

"Shame. Always liked Carmen. Good family, and a neighborhood girl, too."

"Yeah, she's good."

"Nice girl like that, growing up right beside you. Sometimes you can't see the good things 'cause they're too close to your face. Like the story about that man, went all over the world looking for treasure, only to come back home and find —"

"Diamonds in his backyard," said Derek. "I know."

"Guess I've told you that one before."

"You might have," said Derek, smiling at his mother as his hip brushed against hers.

"Well, I hope you've been hearing me all these years."

"It's that brother of his who's deaf," said Darius, coming into the kitchen. He went to the old Frigidaire and grabbed a bottle of beer from the bottom shelf.

"He'll find his way," said Derek.

"He better start. 'Cause he sure ain't found it yet."

Darius got an opener out of a drawer and uncapped his beer. He had a pull from the bottle and drank off its neck. Derek put the last plate in the rack as Alethea dried her hands. The three of them stood in the closeness of the galley kitchen, a space that was tight and badly lit but was as comfortable to them as a warm glove.

"You doin' all right?" said Darius.

"Fine," said Derek in an unconvincing way.

"Rough, isn't it?"

"It can be."

"I suppose you're not gettin' the love you thought you would."

"I'm not winnin' any popularity contests."

"Remember, the good folks, they got no problem with seein' you coming down the street. It's the criminals and the no-accounts gonna look at you and hate. This city is finally getting a police force that looks like its people, so you're doin' something that's necessary and right. You ought to be proud of that."

"It's just hard."

"If it's important," said Darius, "it usually is. You'll be fine, long as you don't get off the path. Get caught up in that power thing, the way some of these police do. Forget why they took the job to begin with."

"I'm straight," said Derek.

"I know you are, son," said Darius.

"You just watch yourself, hear?" said Alethea.

"Yes, ma'am."

Darius looked his son over with admiration. He didn't have to say what he was feeling. Derek knew. He was getting, in a silent way, what every son craved from his father and what few ever got: validation and respect. It was all in his eyes.

"We get your big brother straightened around, too," said Darius, "we gonna be all right."

"BUY ME ANOTHER beer," said Walter Hess.

"They already turned the lights on," said Buzz Stewart.

"That's good," said Hess. "Now I can see what I'm drinkin'."

"He means it's closing time," said Dominic Martini.

"I know what he means, you dumb fuckin' guinea," said Hess. He turned to Stewart with unfocused eyes. "Buy me another beer, dad."

They were in a white bar in a black neighborhood on 14th. The men wore leathers, Macs, and motorcycle boots. The women wore Peters jackets and Ban-Lon shirts. Mitch Ryder was playing on the radio. The crowd was sweaty and drunk-ugly in the bright lights of last call. A fog of cigarette smoke hung in the air.

"C'mon, Shorty," said Stewart, grabbing a sleeve of Hess's jacket and pulling him toward the door.

Hess pulled his arm free as they walked. He stopped at a

woman he did not know who was standing beside a guy who was drinking a Schlitz. The woman had a pocked face and a peroxide streak in her hair. Hess gave her a kiss. Her back was to a wall and she dropped her arms helplessly to her sides. Hess jammed his tongue in her mouth and licked her lips for good measure as he pulled away.

"Hey," said the guy she was with, stepping forward.

"Hay is for horses, *faggot*," said Hess, cross-eyed and grinning.

The man did nothing and said nothing else. A bouncer named Dale, a friend to Stewart and Hess, came quickly from around the stick. He went straight to the guy who had defended the girl and put him up against the wall. Dale's left hand held his shirt collar and pinned him there. He smashed his right fist into the guy's nose. The nose caved, and blood ran down the guy's upper lip and into his mouth. He dropped his bottle and his eyes rolled to white. Dale hit him again. The people in the bar tipped their heads back to finish their beers.

Hess left the place cackling, followed by Stewart and Martini. All lit smokes on the way to Hess's car.

They drove up 14th, all three drunker than shit. Stewart fucked with the radio dial and found a Marvin and Tammi single he liked. He turned it up. Hess double-clutched coming up a rise and the surge pushed Martini back against his seat.

"Slow down," said Martini.

"Slow down," said Hess in a girlish way. He gave the Ford more gas.

"I'm not kiddin' around," said Martini.

"Shut your cocksucker," said Hess.

Over the rise, on a residential strip of 14th somewhere between Park and Arkansas, they saw a young black man walking the sidewalk a block or so south of their car. Hess eased his foot off the gas, looked in the rearview, looked ahead, and saw no one else driving the street. Except for the black man, there was no pedestrian traffic. Hess cut the headlights and slowed to a crawl.

"Buzz," said Martini, "tell him to knock this shit off."

Hess and Stewart kept their eyes down the road. The black man looked over his shoulder and slightly quickened his pace.

"He heard us," said Stewart.

"Course he did," said Hess, "loud as you're playin' that boofer music."

"It's the exhaust system in this piece of shit that's makin' all the noise."

"If you call purrin' noise." Hess squinted. "How come he ain't runnin', though?"

"They don't never run no more, *you* know that. He's daring you, son."

"I should peg that nigger, Stubie."

"Scare him some," said Stewart. "Go ahead."

"Don't," said Martini, the word barely making a sound against the music coming from the radio.

Hess found a break in the line of parked cars, carefully drove over the curb, and got the Ford up on the sidewalk. He cruised slowly down the hill. The black man turned his head again, double-taked, and ran. Hess laughed and hit the gas.

"How many points?" said Hess.

"Make it ten."

They closed in on him quickly. The black man leaped off the sidewalk and hit the street.

"Look at him go," said Hess.

"Like he seen an alligator," said Stewart.

Hess tore up turf as he jumped the curb and got back onto the street. He downshifted, rubber crying as the tires struggled for purchase on the asphalt. He pinned the gas pedal and narrowed the distance between man and car. In the backseat, Martini's fingers dented black vinyl.

The young man suddenly cut right and headed for the space between two parked cars, a purple Chevy and a white Dodge. Hess followed. The Ford fishtailed, then found its feet again.

Stewart looked over at his friend. "Hey, Shorty."

They were on the young man startlingly fast. Hess jammed the middle pedal to the floor, but the speed was too much for the brakes, and the Ford went into a skid. The young man's head turned. Stewart thinking, Damn, his eyes are wider than shit, as the Galaxie lifted the young man and took him into the front quarter of the white Dodge. At the point of impact, all the occupants of the Ford were thrown forward. Stewart and Hess jacked into the dash; Martini's head bounced off the bench. They sat there dazed, the world spinning slightly, the blare of the radio and something else ringing in their ears.

Hess swallowed blood. His mouth had hit the wheel violently and the collision had split his upper lip. Stewart touched a deep gash on his brow, felt wetness there, pulled back a finger smudged with red. With a shaking right hand he cut the radio off.

They cleared the dizziness from their heads. They looked through the windshield. They saw the young man, arms twisted, torso misshapen, lying at an unnatural angle on the hood in a quickly spreading pool of liquid, pinned to the Dodge. Lights came on in row houses that had been dark moments ago.

"We need to get ourselves gone, Shorty," said Stewart, seeing Hess working the shifter through the gears but doing nothing else.

"What?"

"*Haul ass.*"

The young man's body slid off the hood as Hess put the Ford into reverse and flipped on its lights. A single beam shot out from the front of the car. They pulled back, and a fine spray of blood erupted from the young man's mouth as he rolled onto his side in the street. One hand reached up as if to grab at something. The hand dropped. The body moved in spasm and then didn't move at all.

Hess hit it. He drove up 14th as sirens gathered in the distance. Martini closed his eyes. Stewart put a Marlboro between his lips and pushed the lighter into the dash. Hess goosed the gas and shifted for speed, muttering all the while. He was wondering just how bad he'd fucked up his car.

VAUGHN WAS COMING up 16th Street in his unmarked, freshly fucked and relaxed from his last highball, listening to his dash radio, his two-way turned down low, when he heard the news about LBJ's decision. The newsman on WWDC said that local reaction to the announcement had been swift.

"Scores of local college students, some reportedly barefoot, danced in celebration, singing 'We Shall Overcome' across from the White House in Lafayette Park. Many wore McCarthy bumper stickers on their backs. . . ."

"Christ," said Vaughn. He only hoped his son wasn't among the celebrants. Way his hair was hitting his collar, he'd fit right in.

A call came in from the station. Vaughn pulled the mic from its cradle and responded. It was a hit-and-run on a residential block of a two-syllable cross street on 14th. He hit the gas. By the time he got there, uniforms, ME suits, and a meat wagon had already arrived.

In the flashbulb light of an MPD photographer, amid the strobe of the cherry tops, Vaughn saw the twisted body lying in a slick of blood on the street. The young man, Vernon Wilson, age seventeen, had been IDed by the contents of his wallet. Uniforms had begun to canvass the residents, but as of yet no one claimed to have seen a thing, though one man said that, through his screen windows, he had heard the squeal of tires, loud music, and a collision. Headlight glass, bits of a grille, and a Ford insignia were found near the body. The light of a flashlight revealed red paint on the dented portion of the white Dodge where the crime had taken place.

Vaughn walked up and down the block and examined the general area. Tomorrow he'd try to determine the make of the Ford by having his lab man, who was good with cars, study the grillwork, logo, and shards of glass. Vaughn would put the word out at the usual body shops to look out for damage to the fender, headlights, grille, hood, and front quarter panels of a red Ford. He'd visit certain garages that had a history of breaking down or repairing vehicles associated with criminals and crime.

If it was determined that this was something other than a homicide, then his involvement would end. It might have been a garden-variety blind drunk who had hit the kid, panicked, and fled. If so, then the hope would be that the driver would wake up sober, see Jesus, call the police, and turn himself in. But Vaughn was almost certain this would become one of his.

North of the death spot, the grassy strips framing the sidewalk had been tracked and dug up in spots, telling Vaughn that the driver of the Ford had deliberately gone off the road. Also, the car had burned rubber on the street, with skid marks at the scene, indicating recklessness and acceleration. It was as if Vernon Wilson had been hunted. The loud music meant the driver or occupants were young and, to some degree, enjoying the game, too.

It was highly doubtful that Wilson was connected to someone of importance in some political way, so there would be no pressure to solve the case. This was, at bottom, a colored kid with a broken neck, a low priority at best. Still, Vaughn would do his job.

DENNIS STRANGE STOOD in the alley that ran behind Princeton and Otis. He struck a match and cupped his hand around the flame. Masking its flare, he lit the joint he'd rolled, drew on it, and let the sweet smoke lie in his lungs.

A dog was barking at the north T of the alley, up near Park View Elementary. He knew from the deep sound that the dog, a long-haired German shepherd, was the family pet of those people, the Broadnaxes, who'd recently lost a son in the war. They'd had that animal for fifteen years. He could identify most every dog around these blocks by their barks. It was a thing that happened when you stayed in one place so long. In his case, too long. Wasn't natural for a man to be staying with his parents past a certain age, he knew. But then, he hadn't planned it. Problem was, he never had planned a thing.

Dennis let the smoke out and took more in.

Up in the kitchen of his parents' apartment, the circular fluorescent in the ceiling had been shut off. He could see the blue light of the television playing on the walls, bleeding out from the living room, where his father still sat. Watching a western if there was one on; if not, one of those cop things.

Dennis had delivered the check to his man, James Hayes, the longtime dealer who lived over on Otis, and had gotten some smoke in return. Hayes was on the old side, not flashy, dressed clean, quiet. Lived alone and occasionally entertained women friends. Every neighborhood seemed to house dealers like him, one for gage and one for heroin. Sometimes, but not often, the same man sold both. Many of the adults living in the vicinity knew what the man did to make his living, and as they grew, the kids learned, too. Most of the time, people decided to go about their business and let him be.

Dennis drew hard on the reefer and felt it hit him like a kiss.

You didn't talk to the police. That was the rule. Not unless some violent shit got perpetrated on an elderly person or a kid. In the eyes of many, a snitch was worse than a criminal. That's just the way it was. Even his father, about as straight as a man could be, felt that way.

Not that his father didn't admire Derek and his uniform. It was understating it to say that he did. Loving his son the policeman was different, though, than loving the police. To go to a police for something that could work itself out or be worked out by means other than the law, well, that was wrong. Dennis felt that way for sure. Course, it did present problems sometimes. Like that thing that was gonna go down tomorrow with Alvin and Kenneth. If his father knew about something like that in advance and one of those involved was his friend, what would he do?

The reefer had begun to work on Dennis's head. His thoughts grew grandiose and bold.

Okay: He wasn't gonna stand back and let those boys rob that market. Way Alvin was wired, he might just murder that older brother behind the counter if things went wrong. And he, Dennis, would have that on his head. Another thing to add to his list of shame.

He could do something about it. Something that would make his father look at him the way he looked at Derek. The way he himself looked at Derek in his mind.

"Oh, shit," said Dennis, chuckling at the thought, liking the thought, staring at the joint burning between the fingers of his hand.

Maybe I'll let this high come on me full now, he thought. Walk around a little, think up a plan.

That would be a change for me, thought Dennis Strange. A plan.

FIFTEEN

O N MONDAY, DOWN in Memphis, the body of sixteen-year-old Larry Payne, shot and killed by a white policeman, lay in state at Clayborn Temple African Methodist Episcopal Church, the starting point for the previous week's march led by the Reverend Dr. Martin Luther King Jr. Hundreds of blacks came to the church to pay their respects under the gaze of National Guard troops. King would return the following day to Memphis, where he was scheduled to lead another march on Friday.

On Monday, around the country, politicians commented publicly on LBJ's withdrawal from the race and his new, relatively dovish stance on the war in Vietnam. Former Vice President Richard Nixon, the leading Republican candidate, said that "a bombing halt in itself would not be a step toward peace." California governor Ronald Reagan stated that "de-escalation has usually resulted in the death of more Americans" and added that he "would favor a step-up of the war."

Robert Kennedy, Eugene McCarthy, and Vice President Hubert Humphrey publicly expressed support for the president's decisions while scrambling behind the scenes to capitalize on this unexpected opportunity and position themselves more favorably for the upcoming race. Johnson himself, in an unusually candid and relaxed speech to the National Association of Broadcasters, said that there were "some things that a president cannot do to buy popularity" and admitted to his "shortcomings as a communicator."

On Monday, in D.C., working-class people went about their day-to-day. Derek Strange and Troy Peters patrolled their district. Buzz Stewart followed Walter Hess to a garage in Hyattsville, Maryland, where Hess dropped off his Galaxie to be repaired. Then Stewart drove Hess to his job at the machine shop and went on to his own shift at the Esso station, where Dominic Martini was already on the clock, pumping gas. Inside the Three-Star on Kennedy Street, Darius Strange stood over a hot grill, trying not to think of the pain in his back, while Mike Georgelakos patrolled the diner, operating the register and making small talk with the customers. Ella Lockheart served food around him. Kenneth Willis cleaned an elementary school off Kansas Avenue in Northwest. Alethea Strange cleaned a house on Caddington Avenue in Silver Spring. Her older son, Dennis, rode down 7th Street in a D.C. Transit bus.

Dennis Strange, carrying a book he had been reading, got off the bus between Florida and Rhode Island and walked east into the low-number streets of LeDroit Park. He found the market with the green-and-gold sign over the door and went inside.

The old Jew, Mr. Ludvig, sat behind the counter, the *Post* spread out before him. The market's black-and-white set was on channel 5, playing the local interview show, *Panorama*, had that young dude, the son of the sportswriter Shirley Povich, as the host.

Mr. Ludvig raised his head as Dennis entered the shop.

Negative recognition came to his watery eyes. Then he forced himself to smile. "You're my pack of Kools. Am I right?"

"That was me," said Dennis, "but not today. I'm lookin' for that man works here, goes by John."

"Mr. Thomas is in the stockroom."

"I speak to him?"

Ludvig looked Dennis over, then got off his stool slowly, grunted, and walked into the stockroom. Dennis heard muffled voices, and in short order Ludvig returned.

"Walk around to the alley. John's getting ready to have a smoke break. He'll be out back."

The alley bordered two residential blocks, all row houses, with the market the only commercial property on the strip. Street cats and kittens scattered as Dennis walked the cracked concrete. Up ahead, a boy was throwing a tennis ball against a wall of bricks. The boy studied Dennis, then held the ball to let him pass.

"Little brother," said Dennis, and the boy lifted up his chin by way of greeting. "No school today?"

"Told my mother I was sick."

"Can't be too sick, you out here playin'."

"Yeah, well, you know."

"Knowledge is power," said Dennis, holding up the book he carried. "You need to be goin' to class."

"What my moms said," said the boy. "But she at work."

"You take care of yourself, now, hear?"

Dennis went on. John Thomas was beside the market stoop, sitting on an overturned milk crate, having a cigarette. His eyes tracked Dennis as he approached. Though the day was cool, there was a film of sweat on Thomas's face. He was older than he had looked in the artificial light of the market the night before. Natural light brought out the lines, in startling relief, that hard work and time had put on his face.

"Young man," said Thomas.

"How you doin'?"

"Doin' good." Thomas's eyes went to the book under Dennis's arm. "You enjoying that?"

Dennis glanced at the cover of the just-published *Soul on Ice* as if he had forgotten he was carrying it. Young people of different colors and classes were talking about it citywide. It outraged some and energized others. It tended to get a reaction out of all who read it. Dennis was reading it for the second time.

"Eldridge Cleaver speaks the truth."

"On some things he does," said Thomas. "I will give you that. Never had it all explained to me before the way he does, even though I've been livin' it my whole life. My son, young man about your age, passed it on to me. Hard for me to get with all of it, understand. Harder still to get with the man himself."

"What you don't like about him?"

"He's a rapist, for one. That right there, I mean, it goes against my Christian upbringing to follow a man like him."

"He did his time."

"As he should have. But that kind of violence against another human being . . . don't see how anyone can look past that. Now, you take a man like King, well, that's a leader right there. The reverend's coming from a place of peace. Course, you bein' your age and all, you probably too impatient for all that."

"I respect the man. Ain't no question he's good. But some young black men and women feel like that passive resistance thing ain't gonna get it no more."

"What you think works, then? Fire? You seen what happened in Watts. You young black men and women burn this society we got, what you got ready to take its place? This market here goes to ashes, black *people* like me gonna lose our jobs. This market here goes to ashes, black *people* in this neighborhood got no place to buy their groceries to feed their kids. You see what I'm sayin'? You got to have somethin' built before you start tearin' down."

"I hear you. And I know you might not like it. It might not even make sense to you. But it's coming just the same."

"I don't need to be readin' that book to learn about the problem," said Thomas. "What we all need now is some kind of solution that's not gonna hurt our own people."

"People always gonna get hurt in a revolution. Ain't never been no easy one, right?"

Ludvig appeared in the doorway to the stockroom and cleared his throat. "Everything okay out here?"

"Yes, Mr. Ludvig," said Thomas.

Ludvig looked from Thomas to Dennis, then disappeared back into the store.

Thomas set his eyes on Dennis. "Say what you came to say. It's obvious you're here to get somethin' off your chest."

"Does it show?"

"It did last night. Looked like you had something you wanted to tell me then." Thomas hit his cigarette, tapped ash to the concrete. "Might as well do it now."

Dennis nodded slowly. "Couple of dudes I know, they fixin' to knock this place over."

"The ones was sittin' in that green Monterey, waitin' on you to come out."

Dennis cocked his head. "Yeah."

"Don't look so surprised. I knew you was wrong the minute you walked into the market. Y'all should've left out of there right away, 'stead of sittin' on the street debating or whatever it was you was doin'. Parked under a street lamp, too. I watched you people from the plate-glass window. My eyes haven't failed me yet. Got a good look at the driver, dark-skinned dude with funny teeth, and the other fella, with his hat. Even gave me time to take down the license plate number.

Stupid. But then, anybody low enough to try something like that ain't gonna be all that smart."

"I guess not."

"You guess. Hmm." Thomas took a drag off his cigarette, exhaled slowly, keeping his eyes on Dennis. "When?"

"This afternoon."

"I been tellin' Ludvig, everyone grew up in this city knows these markets got cash on hand the day credit comes due. Been tellin' him for years he needs to change that up."

"That was their plan. Hit y'all before you make your deposit."

"And what was your part in it?"

"They had me come in to look the place over. But I didn't tell 'em nothin', man."

"Not a thing, huh?"

"Didn't even tell 'em about that gun you keep under the counter."

"You got good eyes."

"Some say I do. Some say I'm good at details."

"So you smarter than your friends and you got talent. A conscience, too. Question is, why you runnin' around with the likes of them?"

"I don't know," said Dennis. "I been on a wrong road, seems like forever. Hard to change direction, I guess."

"You just did. Least you put your foot the right way." Thomas took a last hit off his smoke and crushed the butt under his shoe. "What's your name, son?"

"Dennis Strange."

Thomas smiled a little. He was missing some teeth. "Uh-huh. Okay. I knew a Strange once, had a *D* name, too. Veteran. Used to see him at those banquets at the Republic Gardens, in the Blue Room, up on U? It's been ten years since the last one I went to, though."

"His American Legion meetings," said Dennis, remembering his father in a jacket and tie, straight of posture, leaving the house.

"Post Number Five," said Thomas. "He's your kin, then."

"My father. Goes by Darius."

"Darius, right. Grill man. He still stayin' up in Park View?"

"Princeton Place," said Dennis. "Right off Georgia."

"Good man," said Thomas.

"Yes," said Dennis. "My whole family's good." He glanced away, embarrassed at his show of pride. "Look here —"

"I know. We didn't have this conversation."

"It's not just that. One of those boys, the driver you saw . . . I been knowin' him from way back."

"You made a choice," said Thomas. "The right choice."

"Just don't want to see him get shot or nothin' like that."

"Whatever happens to that boy is gonna happen eventually, whether he pays today or a year from now. He's just headed that way. But you don't have to worry about him gettin' hurt. What you think you saw me reaching for, under the counter? That wasn't no gun. Wasn't nothin' but a lead-filled club. Shoot, I haven't touched a gun since I was in the Quartermaster Corps, back in the war."

"What you gonna do, then?"

"Gonna do my job," said Thomas. "Don't suppose you'd want to give me the names of those two you been runnin' with."

"Can't do that."

"Didn't think you could. No matter. We'll be all right. Like I said, you did good."

"I ain't been here. No matter what happens, I was not here."

"We're straight." Thomas reached his hand out. Dennis shook it. "You keep on that road, hear?"

"I'm gonna do my best."

Dennis turned and went down the alley the way he'd come. John Thomas watched him pass that boy who threw that ball at all hours against the brick wall. Then he pulled his bulk up off the milk crate and went inside the back door. He moved through the stockroom to the store, where Ira Ludvig had returned to his stool.

"Better make that bank deposit, Mr. L."

"It's too early."

"Think you better do it now," said Thomas in a strong way.

Ludvig looked up. Thomas rarely used that tone with him. When he did, Ludvig listened.

"Okay. You hold it down for a while?"

"I'll be fine," said Thomas.

After Ludvig left the store, a green deposit bag under his arm, John Thomas made a phone call and left a message for William Davis. He'd been knowing Davis all his life, since their days growing up in Foggy Bottom. Sergeant Davis, now a man of late middle age, had been one of the early black hires on the force. Ordinarily, Thomas wouldn't expect much response after making a call like this. After all, police didn't have the time to be deploying men on suspicion of a crime yet to be committed. But if John Thomas asked him to, Bill Davis would do something, for sure.

Ten minutes later, Thomas got a call back. He told William Davis everything he knew and some things that he suspected. Davis asked how he had come upon the information, and Thomas said it was mostly what he'd observed the night before, and part intuition. He didn't mention the young man, Dennis Strange.

"John, are you sure?"

"I ever bother you before with somethin' like this?"

"Well, you ain't in the habit of sellin' wolf tickets."

"There it is."

"But you understand, it's tricky."

"Boy gonna knock us over, he's bound to have a gun, right? Chances are, he's doin' this today, he's done somethin' like it before. Man's got prior convictions, you get him with a gun on his person, you got call to put him in a cell."

"Now you gonna tell me how to do my job?"

"I never would."

"Okay, then," said Davis. "I'll take care of it. And I'll send a couple of uniforms to sit outside the market for the rest of the day, too. How about that?"

When Ludvig returned to the market, a squad car holding two patrolmen was already parked on the corner of the block. Ludvig replaced the empty deposit bag where he kept it, in a drawer under the register. He went over to the plate-glass window that fronted the store and looked out at the street.

"Those cops been out there long?" said Ludvig.

"Not too long."

"I wonder what's going on."

"No idea. Doesn't do any harm to have them out there, though."

Ludvig stared at his longtime employee. They had never once socialized outside of work, but still, he considered Thomas a friend. Ludvig didn't know how he would ever run the business without him. Sometimes he wondered who was truly running things, but he was not a man with a strong ego, so the question was irrelevant in the end.

"John?

"Sir."

"Why'd you have me make that deposit so early in the day?"

"You know how I been tellin' you to change up? Thought today would be a good day to start. I just had this feeling, you know?"

"This feeling wouldn't have something to do with that guy came to see you, would it?"

"Nothing at all," said Thomas. "We were just talking. Turns out I know his father."

"He looked suspicious, is why I asked."

"You know how it is when you get to be our age. Most young men walkin' in here, unless we know 'em, they look like trouble, to us."

"True," said Ludvig.

"That boy's good," said Thomas.

Troubled, thought Thomas. But good.

SIXTEEN

PAT MILLIKIN'S GARAGE, a cinder-block structure on a stretch of gravel running behind a strip of parts and speed shops, was off Agar Road in West Hyattsville, in Maryland's Prince George's County. There was no sign to identify the place, but a certain kind of customer knew where to find it, and Millikin was never at a loss for business. He catered to the chop trade and specialized in rentals. For a hundred bucks, a man could get an inspection certificate for his rag. Services and products aside, what Millikin truly sold, and guaranteed, was silence.

Millikin's brother, Sean, a three-time loser, had been incarcerated on a manslaughter charge with Walter Hess up in the Western Maryland prison. Hess was no particular fan of the Irish, but Sean was white, and in the joint that made them allies. Sean had told Hess about his brother, Pat, and what he could do for him if he ever got jammed up. Hess had given Pat some referrals, and he and Stewart had used him for a couple of minor things in the past. Hess needed Pat now.

Buzz Stewart drove his washed-off Belvedere down Agar Road, listening to "Jimmy Mack" on the radio, enjoying Martha and the Vandellas, one arm out the window, a Marlboro burning between his fingers. He was following Hess, who was behind the wheel of his Galaxie and doing the limit. Hess didn't want to get pulled over for any reason now, especially not here. The PG County cops had a rep for taking no man's shit. Hess figured he'd drive slowly, not blow off any reds, and get the Ford over to Pat's. He accomplished that, he'd be fine.

Shorty, hell, sometimes he just went too far. Wasn't any good reason to run down that colored boy, but it was done. Get the car fixed up and put it behind you, that was the thing to do. Dominic Martini, with all that Catholic guilt he had, was the weak link. Way he was acting after it happened, it was like he wanted to confess. Stewart had to make Martini understand, you could confess all you wanted to, wasn't nobody, priest or God almighty himself, could bring that colored boy back. But Stewart didn't think Martini would be a problem. He just needed to be told. Martini was a follower and always would be.

They found Pat Millikin's garage. Hess drove into the open bay, where Millikin had left a spot for the Ford, and cut the engine. Stewart parked outside, behind a plum-colored Dart GT. He got out and locked down the Belvedere.

A hard-looking, big-limbed colored guy was sitting on a folding chair outside the garage, having a smoke. He studied the Belvedere and as he did a small smile came to his face. Stewart figured he was admiring it, so he nodded at him, expecting something back. But he got nothing in return. Stewart thinking, Every place you go now, it's the same way.

He walked into the garage, where a radio was playing "Cherish." Millikin, pale and freckled, with horseman arms, walked around the Ford, giving it the eyeball, assessing the damage. He wore coveralls with the sleeves cut off. A cigarette dangled from his lips. Where he walked, Hess followed.

"Well," said Millikin, "you didn't lie."

"I did it," said Hess. "I fucked it up royal."

"What'd you hit, a moose?"

"A monkey," said Hess, glancing at Stewart, giving him a grin.

"We just had an accident," said Stewart, warning Hess with his eyes. "Too much drinkin', is all. But you know, we didn't exactly leave a note on the guy's windshield with our, uh, insurance information."

"Say no more," said Millikin.

Right about then, Hess noticed that the colored guy, the one who was sitting outside when they'd rolled up, had followed Stewart into the bay. Hess wondered if he'd heard the monkey comment. And then he wondered why he was sweating over it. He didn't care.

"Lawrence, come here," said Millikin.

Hess and Stewart watched the hard colored guy cross the concrete floor and inspect the Ford. He looked at it carefully. He said "yeah" and "uh-huh" and looked at it some more. He put his hands in his pockets and looked at Millikin.

"Well?" said Millikin.

"Gonna take some work," said Lawrence.

"No shit," said Hess. He turned to Millikin. "The question is, when and how much?"

"Got to check down in Brandywine," said Lawrence, still talking to Millikin like Hess was not there. "See if I can't raise the parts at the junkyard. Otherwise I gotta order them from the factory. 'Nother words, I'm gonna have to let you know."

"You heard him, Shorty," said Millikin. "I can't give you a price just yet. Timewise, we'll just have to see how it goes."

"Yeah, okay."

"Pat," said Stewart. "We get a minute here?"

"He's all right," said Millikin, meaning Lawrence.

"A minute," said Stewart.

Lawrence walked out of the garage without a word.

"I'm gonna be needin' a rental," said Stewart. "With plates. Something fast but no flash."

"When?"

"Soon."

"I'll find you somethin'," said Millikin.

"You used to work alone around here," said Hess.

"I needed more help. I got another place where I work on projects like this one. This here location is too visible, if you know what I mean. So I have to have another man."

"Yeah, well, I don't know *Lawrence* from Kingfish. He don't make me too comfortable."

"Lawrence did time, just like you. He doesn't talk to the law, just like you." Millikin's eyes caught mischief. "Matter of fact, now that I think of it, he ain't all that much different than you."

"That's a laugh," said Hess.

Millikin flicked his butt out the open bay door. "I'll let you know when you can pick up your car."

Hess and Stewart walked from the garage. Lawrence Houston was back in his seat, staring ahead, working on another cigarette.

In the Belvedere, up the road, Hess shook his head.

"Ever notice how they always have these real high-class names?" said Hess. "Couldn't be plain old Larry. Had to be *Lawrence*."

"Your mother named you Walter, didn't she?" said Stewart, looking at Hess out the side of his eyes. "No one ever called you Wally, right?"

"It ain't the same thing."

"I guess it's like Pat said. That coon back there, he ain't all that different from you."

"Aw, *shut* up, Buzz."

Stewart smiled, reaching for the radio on the dash.

KENNETH WILLIS TOOK the last of the garbage cans from the cafeteria to the Dumpsters behind the school. Willis carried the can up on his shoulder, the way some men carried a sport jacket, casual like. He was strong enough to do it, too. Unlike his supervisor, an old man with the name of Samuel, who Willis called Sambo to hisself. Always yessirin' everybody, keeping his eyes downcast, and scratching at his head.

Carrying a full trash can that way, it showed off the muscles in his arms. At work, he rolled the sleeves of his shirt high so that the ladies could see what he had. Wore his pants tight for the same reason. He could feel the eyes of a couple of the female teachers they had at the school studying him as he walked the halls. Some of the little girls who went to the school there, sometimes they'd be noticing him, too. Even if they *were* too young to know what was making them feel warm inside.

Coming out the back door, he dumped the garbage into this big old green container and put the can down on the asphalt. He reached into his breast pocket, withdrew a Kool, and lit himself a smoke. He dragged on his cigarette and watched the kids the way he liked to do. They had finished their lunch and were out there on the edge of the playground, kicking a red rubber ball around on a weedy field.

There was this one girl Willis had been keeping his eye on. Did her hair in braids and always came to school in some kind of skirt. Wore little white socks on her feet. Girl was only ten, but she already had an ass on her like a girl of thirteen. Willis had checked out the mother when she came to pick the girl up around dismissal time. If the mother was any kind of road map to where the girl was headed, well, this girl was going to a real good place.

Not that he was into little girls or nothin' like that. He did have a few things with some young ones now and again, and that last thing with that fourteen-year-old, the one who'd put him in jail. Fourteen? Shit, the way that girl moved her hips?

Only a full-grown woman knew how to gyrate like that. But that was behind him, anyhow. He had to be careful now who he put his eyes on. He'd gotten this job, even with his priors, because someone had been lazy in looking into his past. He didn't want to lose this position, not yet.

Wouldn't be long, though, before he was out. This market thing, and then a couple of hotel jobs that Alvin had been talking about. Willis would throw away this piece he was wearing, had his name stitched across the front. Like they thought he couldn't remember it, had to write it on his shirt. And these dirty pants, always smelled like food the kids had thrown away no matter how hard he scrubbed them in the sink. This was not a job for a man like him. He needed to start living right. These mothers that came to get their kids, and these teachers, and some of these kids, all of them who looked away when he smiled, had to be because he was a janitor. After those jobs with Alvin, he'd come back in his street threads, driving a new car, maybe a Lincoln, and see how they looked at him then.

Willis dropped the cigarette to the asphalt and crushed it. He had one more look at that girl out there. He wondered what color panties she had on underneath that skirt.

He turned and went back into the school, headed for the janitors' room, where Samuel was having his lunch. It was time to go to work. Not to do this bullshit work right here, but to do the work of a man.

Willis stepped into the cramped room, poorly lit by one bulb. Samuel was sitting at a table, eating a sandwich his wife had made him, drinking one of those little cartons of milk he'd gotten from the cafeteria, the way he did every day. Him and those baggy-ass clothes, with those clown patches of gray around a bald-ass head.

"I feel poorly," said Willis, putting a palm to his stomach.

"That right," said Samuel.

"Tellin' you, I'm sick."

"Uh-huh."

"I just came from the bathroom, man. Didn't know so much could drop out of one man."

"Maybe you got yourself a worm."

"Sumshit *like* it, that's for damn sure."

"You better go home, then," said Samuel in a tired way.

"Thanks, boss."

"Don't forget to punch yourself out."

Okay, thought Willis. I'll go ahead and do that now. You just sit there, eating your sad-ass, sorry-ass sandwich, and let me go. Shoot, blind man in a coffin could see he wasn't sick. Strong as he looked? Now Samuel was gonna stick around, making his pennies, while he, Willis, went on that thing with his cousin and scored some real cash. Wasn't no trick to getting free to do it, either. You could fool this fool here every single day.

Samuel Rogers watched Kenneth Willis punch his time card, then watched him walk from the room. He chuckled under his breath. Boy thought he was fooling him. He didn't mind giving Willis the afternoon off, even if it meant more chores for him. Rogers plain didn't care for Willis. Him with his sleeves rolled up to show his muscles, and that hungry-wolf way he looked at the women and even the little girls. Him hiding those soiled magazines in the office, back behind the lockers, like he was getting away with something. Not knowing enough about himself to admit what he was.

Through the years, Samuel Rogers had seen many of these slick young ones who thought they were too smart to work. Them thinking he was some kind of fool for sticking with it. Them who were in such a big hurry to get in the unemployment line. Samuel just did not like to be around that kind.

Man wore his pants too tight, too.

OLGA VAUGHN STOOD beside her husband, Frank, who was seated at the kitchen table, having a coffee and a smoke. They had just finished lunch. Olga had gone up to their bedroom and returned with a new pair of boots, looked like something out of the 1930s, on her feet. She had drawn a cigarette from Frank's pack and was moving it, unlit, to and from her mouth in a cigar smoker's pantomime. She had her free hand cupped alongside her hip, as if she were holding a tommy gun.

"Whaddaya think, Frank?"

"Who you supposed to be?"

"Faye Dunaway!"

"She's a blonde. You got hair like the ace of spades."

"I'm talkin' about the look." Olga glanced down at her feet so that Frank's eyes would go there, too. "I got 'em down at the Bootery on Connecticut. They're called gunboots."

"You don't say."

"They go with my Capone stripes. You know, the pants suit I got last week at Franklin Simon?"

"The one came with the hat?"

"It's a beret. Don't you know the difference?"

"Sure. Like the painters wear."

Olga wiggled one foot. "You likee?"

"Me no sabbee," said Vaughn, tapping ash off his cigarette. He'd be glad when this bullshit Bonnie-and-Clyde craze was done.

"Oh, Frank," said Olga with a roll of her eyes.

Olga tied an apron around her waist, went to the sink, and began to wash their dishes. Frank watched her with affection.

From upstairs, he heard the thump of bass coming from the stereo in Ricky's room. It was Vaughn's own fault if it was driving him nuts. He'd bought the system for Ricky himself, a birthday present and also a little something to kick off his college education. It was a Zenith component setup, eighty watts, had a feature called "Circle of Sound." The salesman at

George's, over there on Queen's Chapel Road, said it was a nice "unit," then said it was "only" one hundred and sixty-nine. When Vaughn heard the price he felt like grabbing his slacks and telling the guy, Turn around, I got a nice unit for you right here. But he just smiled politely and said he'd come back. Vaughn got his fence friend down off 14th to find a Zenith just like it, or one that was damn close. And it didn't cost him no buck sixty-nine. Course it was a little on the warm side. Only thing it didn't come with was a box and a warranty card. But for twenty-five dollars you could do without the cardboard and the serial number.

Vaughn had felt a little bad that the kid was living at home while some of his friends went off to school, so buying the system for him was like, what did you call that, a consolation prize. But now Vaughn had to pay the price.

When Ricky wasn't listening to music, he was gabbing about it with his friends. Talking about a group named Flavor at the Rabbit's Foot on Wisconsin and, all last summer, a guy named Hendrix who'd played the Ambassador and then "sat in" with another guy named Roy at a place called the Silver Dollar, and on and on. The kid could talk on the phone. He was like his mother that way.

"Does he ever study?" said Vaughn.

"He must," said Olga. "He got decent grades last fall."

"Three hundred dollars a semester and he's up there playin' that shit all day. He oughtta have his face buried in the books."

"Frank."

"That's not why I'm humpin' it out here," said Vaughn. "So he can live off my tit and listen to music."

"You bought that box for him," said Olga, "remember? You'll see, he's doing fine in college."

Anyway, thought Vaughn, it'll keep him out of the war.

Vaughn crushed out his smoke as Olga turned, drying her hands on a dishrag. She untied her apron, hung it back on its hook, and looked him over. He was wearing one of his Robert Hall suits. It was early for him to be dressed for work.

"Aren't you gonna take your nap?" said Olga.

Usually, he got some shut-eye after lunch while Olga watched what she called her "afternoon menu" on channel 7: *The Newlywed Game, The Baby Game, General Hospital, Dark Shadows,* and Mike Douglas. Around the time she was looking at that crazy vampire show, he'd dress, slip out the house, and get on his way to his four-to-midnight shift.

"Not today," said Vaughn. "I'm gonna get out early. Want to visit a few garages before they close."

"For what?"

"This young guy got hit-and-runned last night. I'm looking into it."

"He was killed?"

Vaughn nodded. "The car that was involved musta got smashed up good. It's gonna need repairs."

"You don't work accidental deaths."

"It's a homicide until I learn different. I think it was a race killing. Whoever did it, it was like they were joyriding. You know, having fun. The boy was colored."

"Frank."

"What?"

"What color was he?"

"Huh?"

"He was black, wasn't he?"

"Okay."

"Then call him black."

"Christ, Olga."

He had to stifle himself now. Olga and her girlfriends. He bet they had taught her to use that comeback on him when he called someone colored. *What color was he?* Clever. Them, who had no black friends. Them, whose only contact with black people was with their black maids and the black man at the

A&P who loaded their groceries into the back of their station wagons. And here they were, with their nails and their pool memberships and their mah-jongg tiles, thinking they were gonna teach him something, when he was out there in the actual world every day.

"What's wrong?" said Olga.

"Nothin', doll." Vaughn's eyes crinkled at the corners. "You just make me laugh sometimes."

"You're a real Neanderthal, Frank, you know it?"

"C'mere, baby," said Vaughn, patting his thigh. "Bring them gunboats with you."

"They're gun*boots*, you dummy," said Olga, already walking toward him.

Olga had a seat on his lap. Her face was caked with makeup and her helmet of black hair was frozen in place. But her eyes were soft, the same as the night he'd met her, at the Kavakos nightclub down on H Street, back in the early '40s. They looked at each other as the bass from upstairs buzzed the kitchen walls. Vaughn kissed her on the lips.

Olga moved her rump around as she settled into his shape. He felt himself growing hard beneath her.

"What's that?" said Olga with a lopsided grin.

"You said I was a caveman," said Vaughn. "That's my club."

Beneath his next kiss, he felt her smile.

STRANGE AND PETERS drove down Georgia in their cruiser. They were on the tail end of their eight-to-four. Their day had consisted of some field investigations, a report made at a home break-in scene, a petty larceny, one domestic disturbance, and the usual numerous traffic stops: exceeding the limit, red-light runners, incomplete stops, and the like. Nothing involving violence or, on their part, the use of force.

Peters was having one of his talkative spells, going on about LBJ, who would succeed him, King's scheduled return to Memphis, and what would happen down there next. Strange mostly nodded and shook his head.

He had been quiet since they'd made a stop at the station, where he'd overheard some comments made by a couple of white officers out in the lot. One of them called Peters "Golden Boy" as he and Strange were walking back to their Ford. The other called them "the Dynamic Duo" and added, "Better Peters than me." This was the same cop, Sullivan, who had called his nightstick a "nigger knocker" within earshot of Strange a few weeks ago, then smiled nervously and said, "Hey, no offense, rookie. I mean, we're all brothers in blue, right?" Strange had nodded but hadn't even tried to mask the hate in his eyes. He could take a lot, and he did, but there was something about Sullivan's face, those Mr. Ed teeth protruding out from thin lips, that just made Strange want to kick his ass real good.

"Derek, you got plans tonight?"

"Why?"

"Thought you might want to come over, have dinner with me and Patty."

"Thanks. But I was gonna hook up with Lydell. We were thinking of checkin' out this party he heard about, over near Howard."

"Some other time, right?"

Strange didn't think it was likely. But he said, "Sounds good."

They crossed the intersection at Piney Branch and approached the Esso station. Out by the pumps, a big pale guy, sleeves rolled up to show his arms, looked to be arguing with another guy, had full black hair and a solid build. Both wore uniform shirts. The bigger of the two was working his jaw close to the other guy's face. Peters recognized the smaller guy as the pump jockey they'd seen the day before, when they'd stopped to talk to Hound Dog Vaughn.

"Looks like something," said Peters.

"I don't think so," said Strange.

"Maybe we ought to stop."

"The guy with the black hair will walk away. He liked to fight when he was younger. But I don't think he does anymore."

"You know him?"

"Ran with him some when I was a kid. We did a little shoplifting together one day, a long time ago."

"You guys get away with it?"

"I got caught. He didn't."

"His lucky day," said Peters.

"No," said Strange. "It was mine."

SEVENTEEN

ALVIN JONES HAD been driving a green-on-green Buick Special for the last six months or so. It was a basic four-door, radio-and-heater, bench-seat, automatic-on-the-tree model, and it turned no heads. Despite the name, wasn't nothing special about it. Point of fact, it looked like something an old lady would be driving, her white gloves at the ten-and-two position, sitting up on a pillow so she could see over the wheel.

The Buick was a '63. Dealer made him pay for it in full with cash money before he got handed the keys. Four hundred dollars, not a whole lot, but still, he wasn't accustomed to laying out the ducats on the front end. Contrary to what he'd told Lula Bacon, there came a time when people really did stop giving you credit, and his credit was about as fucked as a man's credit could be.

Anyway, the price was right and it was his. Soon as his luck changed, and it was gonna change real soon, he'd be under the wheel of something right. Recently, he'd seen this white-over-red '67 El Dorado coupe with factory air, vinyl roof, electric windows and seats in the showroom of Capitol Cadillac-Olds, on 22nd, across town. That was gonna be his next ride. Once you got your mind set on a car, it was like seein' a woman in a club and knowing you were gonna be killin' it in your bed by the end of the night. He knew he was going to own that Caddy in the same way. Thing that hurt him, though, he'd owned a Cadillac nine years ago, at twenty-two, and here he was, grown man of thirty-one, driving a Buick. Seemed lately like he was walking backward through his life, passin' hisself on the way down.

But right now, Jones felt good. He was wearing a new button-down from National Shirt Shop, his Flagg Brothers, and his favorite hat, black with the gold band, picked up the gold off his eyes. A .38 was wedged tight between his legs, right up against his dick. "Funky Broadway" was on WOOK, and Wicked Wilson was singing it loud. Broadway. He was gonna get up to that motherfucker someday, show them how they did in D.C. Drive up there in his Cadillac, too. By then he'd have it tricked with spokes.

Jones cruised down H, along the retail center of Northeast, heading toward 8th, where his cousin Kenneth lived in that little place he'd been staying in for a while, over the liquor store. Whole lot of grown people and kids were on the sidewalks, some carrying bags, some playing, some just moving along. Outside the liquor store stood a wino, asking passersby for change. Jones saw Kenneth's Monterey, parked up a ways, and looked for a place to put his Special. They were gonna take the Mercury, on account of it was more reliable and had a little more horse. Jones wasn't nervous about the robbery or nothin' like that. Plus, he'd had a couple of drinks.

Jones saw a police car in his rearview and his hands, due to habit, tightened on the wheel. Then the car pulled over and stopped a little bit up from the liquor store. Jones looked ahead. Another police car was coming from the opposite direction. It went by him and he watched as it, too, slowed near the liquor store and came to stop, nose to ass with the first squad car. Alvin made a turn onto 9th, found a space, and cut the engine. He slid the pistol under the bench seat, got out of the Buick, locked it, and jogged on up to H.

When he got there, the squad cars had moved on. But he saw a couple of white men in street clothes, looked like police with their builds and the way they moved, kind of hurrying around the area of the liquor store. One of them ducked into the outside foyer area of a market and the other positioned himself with his back against the bricks beside the stairwell entrance to the second-floor apartments. The wino was gone.

Jones went to a pay-phone booth on the corner, dropped change into the slot, and dialed his cousin's number. The phone rang and kept on ringing. The ring became a scream in Alvin Jones's head. It told him that he was never going to see Broadway or ride down the street in that white El D.

"Come on, Kenneth," said Jones. "Pick up the got-damn phone."

KENNETH WILLIS HAD dressed in dark clothing and was rifling through his dresser drawer trying to find a pair of stockings this big redbone had left at his crib. He was gonna put one of the stockings over his face when the time came, the way his cousin Alvin had told him to do. "Funky Broadway" was playing from back in the living room, out this box he'd bought from the local Sears. He was charged up for what he was about to do, and Wilson going, "Shake shake shake," and growling, "Lord, have mercy," was charging him further still.

He found the stockings, a pair of fishnets. Well, Alvin had said stockings; he hadn't said what kind.

Willis took one and, couldn't help it, sniffed it before he stuffed it in his front pocket. He looked in the mirror. He was a big man with a chest and some big-ass arms on him, too. Wasn't no one in that market gonna hesitate to hand over whatever he was asking for, they had a look at him. Also, he had a gun.

Willis went out of his bedroom to the small living-room area of his place, stepping on some stroke magazines he had left on the floor. The apartment was all messed up, like it always was. Ashtray was overfilled with butts, beer bottles sat on the eating table, and in the kitchen sink were dishes from last week, still had food on them, with water bugs crawling across the food. Even Willis knew this shithole needed cleaning. Maybe he would pay a woman to do it, soon as he had some money.

He pulled his shirttail out to cover the gun, which he had slipped behind the waistband of his slacks. Cheap gun, but damn sure looked like a gun when it got pointed in your face. It was a pocket .32 with a six-shot magazine, and it was pressing into his back. He'd put it somewhere else once they got in the car. His cousin had told him they'd meet on the sidewalk, out in front of the liquor store. Willis hoped he wasn't late.

There was an Earl Scheib commercial on the radio now, and Willis turned it off. He went out the front door, locked the door, and headed down the stairs. He saw a white man with some shoulders coming into the foyer at the bottom of the stairs, where they had the mailbox slots on the wall, and then he heard the phone ringing back in his place, and he stopped where he was. The white man, a look on his face like he'd never seen a black man before, backed up and went outside. Must be one of them working for the landlord or something, come to collect. He was paid up, so it wasn't no concern of his. . . . *Damn*, that phone. Willis looked up the stairs to his place, wondering if he should go back in and catch it. Might be his cousin calling him about a change of plans. But he knew Alvin was already driving over here, because Alvin had told him the time to meet out front, and Alvin was never late. So it couldn't be him.

Still, whoever it was, they were trying to get him for something. They were just ringin' the *shit* out of that phone, too.

Willis went down the stairs. He didn't want to keep Alvin waiting.

The sunlight was bright as he exited the front door of the building. Nice day. Wasn't many people out, though, not even that wino who folks called Cricket, usually stood out front. Willis turned his head to the left and saw the white man he'd seen before rushing toward him. He had a revolver in his hand and his gun arm was out straight. Willis reached his hand up under the back of his shirt. He heard his back crack and felt a snap in his neck as arms wrapped around him and he was tackled from behind by someone strong. His chest and face hit the sidewalk at the same time, and he said "uh," and tasted blood in his mouth, and heard tires screeching to a stop in the street. White voices yelling at him not to move, and some people in the neighborhood cussing at the police who had taken him down, and the hard feel of cuffs locking on his wrists.

"What we got here?" said the white police who had tackled him, the man's knee now pressing into his back. Willis felt the .32 ripped out of his waistband, the automatic's grip scraping his skin.

"Motherfucker," said Willis, spitting blood on the concrete.

"Keep talkin', nigger," said a low voice in his ear.

Way he got yanked up off the sidewalk then, felt like his arms were gonna tear right off.

Across the street, down near 9th, Alvin Jones came out of the phone booth and watched as his cousin got took right outside his place. He watched them cuff him and bring him up to a standing position, rough, like they liked to do, and he watched them walk him to a squad car and push him inside. Somewhere in all that, he hoped he had caught Kenneth's eye. Remind him that his blood was still out here, waitin' on him, and everything was gonna be all right.

Kenneth was cool. Kenneth would not give him up. Jones wasn't worried about that.

But it *was* a damn shame. All that money for the taking, and now it was out of reach. They'd been cheated out of a big opportunity. Wasn't no guarantee something this good was gonna come around again.

He walked quickly back toward his car, his lips moving, his face contorted, fussing all the way.

Someone had fucked up their plans. Couldn't be no random shit that got the law on his cousin.

Jones came to his Buick. Looking at it, knowing he had to get inside it, hating that he had to get inside it, 'cause he deserved a more stylish ride than this.

Why someone would do this to him and Kenneth he didn't know. But that someone, whoever it was, was someone who needed to be got.

DEREK STRANGE HAD a one-bedroom place in an apartment house on the northeast corner of 13th and Clifton, just above Cardozo High School, a handful of blocks up from the very heart of Shaw. It was close to his parents, Howard University, U Street, and everything else a young black man could want or have need for in a city. The building sat atop the very edge of the Piedmont plateau. The landscape and the street dropped down sharply from there, with the downtown skyline, including the monuments, spread out below. The apartment was not plush in any way, and the neighborhood was what it was, but Strange had a million-dollar view.

That view was no secret, either. Consequently, the apartments in this building rarely turned over. When one had come up empty, Strange had gotten in over the other candidates when the landlord found out he was a cop. Strange had emphasized it on the application and told the man he would keep an eye out for any criminal activity around the building, though he had no plans to do so at all. Using his uniform to get the place he wanted, well, that was just another perk of having the job.

Except for the view from his window, Strange's place was unremarkable, a bachelor's crib that appeared to be furnished with one eye on economy and the other shut. His couch, eating table, and chairs were secondhand. He didn't have an interest in that kind of thing anyway, and if he knew a woman was coming up, he could make the place look reasonably neat in a matter of minutes. For art and decor, he had hung a couple of posters. On one wall, the Man with No Name, wearing a poncho, that little cigar hanging out his mouth. On another, Jim Brown, grenades in hand, readying himself to make that run across the courtyard of the chateau in *The Dirty Dozen,* which Strange had seen first run at the Town theater on 13th and New York two times. He had yellowed newspaper clippings of Brown in uniform as well, from his playing days with Cleveland, which he'd framed on the cheap and hung up around the place in a haphazard way. He had a TV set that he hardly used. He was happy here. Only thing wrong with this building, they didn't allow dogs. He'd seen this boxer at the pound, a tan female, who looked good and had a real nice disposition, too. That would have to wait.

The dominant feature of the living room was Strange's sound system, purchased at Star Radio on Connecticut and Jefferson, and his music. He had sprung for the components, powered by a Marantz tube amplifier, the previous year, and he would be paying on them through '68. The purchase was an extravagance, given his salary, but to Strange it made coming home every night worthwhile.

Around the stereo was his wax collection, stored in fruit crates, arranged alphabetically. From his father, Strange had gotten full-length albums by Ray Charles, Sam Cooke, Jackie Wilson, and others, along with some gospel recordings by groups whose members had gone on to careers in R&B. But Strange kept these records mainly because they were a gift from his father; these days he rarely pulled them from their sleeves. Strange was into the new soul thing. To be precise, he was a lover of southern soul. There were exceptions, like the Impressions, who were out of Chicago and making some beautiful, politically courageous music, and some of the artists recording for the Blue Rock and Loma labels, but generally he went for the southern sound.

Otis Redding, the greatest soul singer who ever lived, was his man and would be his man forever, wasn't any question of that. But there were others. He especially liked James Carr, the personification of deep soul, a gut-wrenching, from-the-bottom vocalist who seemed to be intimate with heartache and pain. Also, O. V. Wright, the self-proclaimed Ace of Spades who brought muscle and real emotion to every track he cut, and Solomon Burke, a survivor who always surprised and could work up a head of steam like no other, his songs often climaxing in thrilling ways.

To find his bounty, Strange visited small record stores in Shaw and Petworth, and spent too much money at the Soul Shack, on 12th and G, and Super Music City, down on 7th. He only bought albums that he felt were keepers, those that he suspected he would still be listening to in thirty years: *Otis Blue* and *The Great Otis Redding Sings Soul Ballads*, Aretha's *I Never Loved a Man the Way I Love You*, and the one full-length that every brother and sister he knew seemed to own, James Brown's legendary *Live at the Apollo*.

But mainly Strange was a collector of singles. He would buy damn near any 45, unheard, if it carried one of "his" labels, because he had come to recognize that these labels had a certain sound. He'd been told by the counter clerk at the Soul Shack that it was session men from Booker T. & the MG's who were doing most of the playing on the hottest songs, but he already knew, without having to be told, that Atlantic, Atco, Dial, Stax, and Volt shared musicians. You could hear the same rhythm and horn sections on cuts from Wilson Pickett, Otis, Rufus and Carla Thomas, Sam & Dave, Aretha, William Bell, Joe Tex, Johnnie Taylor, and others. You could hear this same kind of rough old sound on releases from smaller labels like Goldwax and Back Beat. Most of these recordings, he noticed, came out of Memphis or Muscle Shoals. James Brown was an exception. He recorded on King and Smash, and had a sound that was all his own, but JB, a man who seemed to have dropped down from another planet, was an exception to everything. But there was something about those southern singers and the cats who were backing them up that separated them from their counterparts coming out of Detroit. Some said that the Motown machine had purposely tried to take the sexuality and rawness out of their tracks so they could sell records to the masses in general and to white teenagers in particular. Some went even further and more to the point, saying that Motown got you thinking on kissing, while Stax/Volt made you want to fuck. But that wasn't exactly fair or right. True, the southerners' vocals were wet with sex, but in them you could also hear the joy and hurt that came along with love. This combination of blues, country, gospel, R&B, and hard history could only have risen up from the area south of the Mason-Dixon Line.

Whatever it was, it had gotten into Strange. He had even begun to catalogue the release numbers of each single he owned in a notebook he kept by the stereo. It was a sickness with him, almost an obsession, and he couldn't talk about it or explain it, but what he did know was that when he listened to this music, it just about moved him to tears.

And here he was, feeling that way now. Sitting on the couch, his eyes closed, listening to James Carr singing his new one, "A Man Needs a Woman," Goldwax number 332.

He heard a knock on his door and got up out of his seat. He looked through the rabbit hole and opened the door.

Dennis stood in the frame, wearing yesterday's clothes. There was that smell coming off him, the sweetness of smoke and the cut of cheap wine, that Derek Strange had come to know as his brother's since he'd been back from the service. He was always walking around with some book, and he had one in his hand now. Everything was like it always was, except his eyes, which looked different today, brighter somehow than they had in a while.

"Young D."

"Dennis."

"What, you gonna make a black man stand out in the hall?"

"Come on in," said Derek.

Derek closed the door behind Dennis. Both had a seat on the couch.

"You want a Coke, somethin'?" said Derek.

"Nah, I'm good."

Dennis commented on the stereo, how clean the sound was and how the speakers must have cost big money. Derek told him it was the tubes in the amplifier, not the speakers, that gave the sound its crispness, as it had been explained to him by the salesman, as he'd explained it to Dennis many times before.

"Gonna get me a box like that someday," said Dennis.

"You should."

"Gotta get my own place first, I guess."

"You should do that, too."

Dennis looked around the room and took it in. "You got it all, don't you?"

Derek had heard this kind of remark from his brother before, usually said in a different way. But there was no jealousy or rancor in Dennis's voice now.

"I don't have a penny," said Derek, downplaying the surroundings and also telling the truth. "Payin' rent money's like throwing your money out in the street. What I need to do is like Pop did. Invest in a house."

"Sounds like a plan to me."

A silence came between them. The music ended, and the silence was amplified. Derek didn't know why his brother had stopped by or what they were supposed to talk about now. Lately, they'd had less and less to discuss.

"Look here, Dennis . . ."

"What?"

"I'm going out soon. Lydell and me are going by this party, over near Howard."

"Can I come?"

"Wouldn't be a good idea," said Derek, too quickly. "I mean, it's not like you'd know anyone, right?"

"Relax. I'm just playin' with you, man. You and me don't exactly swing with the same crowd."

Derek was instantly ashamed for trying to talk his brother out of coming with him and Lydell. There was a time when he'd looked way up to Dennis. When, aside from his father, his big brother had been his main hero. Back then, he would have given anything for Dennis to ask him to come along to a party or anywhere else. In those days, it felt like a privilege just to walk by his side.

"You're welcome to stay here tonight," said Derek. "Put some space between you and Pop. I know it's been rough lately between you two."

"Yeah, it's been rough. On my side of things, it's hard to live up to his expectations. But I can dig it. I been a disappointment to him, I know."

Derek said nothing.

"Think I might have turned a corner, though," said Dennis.

"How's that?"

"Seein' things more clearly, is all I'm trying to say."

"Somethin' happen?"

"Wasn't like a lightning bolt came shootin' out of heaven. It came to me slow. The point is, it came. What I was thinking was, a man's got to have a plan."

"True."

"Doesn't have to be a big plan."

"I hear you."

"You were talking about trying to hook me up with a job. I think I'd like to look into that. I mean, it would be something, right?"

"Sure would be," said Derek. "It would be a start."

"Nothing too strenuous, 'cause of this back of mine."

"Right."

"Anyway," said Dennis. "I was on the bus, heading down to U. Saw Clifton Street and pulled the cord. Thought I'd stop by and see you. If you were wondering why I came by."

"You're welcome anytime."

Dennis picked his book up off the coffee table and rose from the couch. "Well, let me get on out of here, then."

"You're not gonna stay?"

"I don't think so. Gonna catch a movie, somethin', then head back to the house. Talk to Pop the way I talked to you."

Derek stood and shook Dennis's hand. "Thought you looked different when you walked in here."

"I'm still me."

"So we shouldn't be expecting you to buy any tickets to this year's policemen's ball, huh?"

"I'm angry, man. I'm always gonna be angry about the way things are. And I'm gonna keep speaking my mind."

"Nothin' wrong with that."

"I just hope I live to see a better world."

"I do, too."

"But I want you to know somethin', Derek. I been angry, but I ain't never been angry at *you*. Matter of fact, I always been proud of you, man. Always."

Derek took a step toward his brother. Dennis brought him in and held him tight. They patted each other on the back. They broke apart and Dennis stood straight.

"I felt that," said Dennis, wiping at his eye.

"What?"

"You tried to grab my rod."

"No, I didn't."

"You damn sure *did*."

"Go ahead, man."

"I'm gone," said Dennis. He smiled and went out the door.

Later, Derek Strange stood at his southern window, watching his brother limping down the hill of 13th Street. Thinking, I should've told him I was proud of him, too.

EIGHTEEN

A FTER WORK, DOMINIC Martini went down to the 6,000 block of Georgia, entered John's Lunch, and took a seat on a stool at the L-shaped counter. He ordered a Swiss steak dinner and had a smoke while old man Deoudes prepared the meal. There was no kitchen in the back, so Martini knew the place was okay. That was one of the few useful things his father had taught him: "Eat in a place has the kitchen out front. That way, you gonna know it's clean."

John Deoudes's wife, whose name was Evthokia but who the customers called Mama, was behind the counter. Their youngest son, Logan, back from the navy in '65, was working the grill. On the stools and in the booths were neighborhood old-timers and other locals who were just getting off work. Martini saw one of the butchers from Katz's, the kosher market across the street, take two steaks from inside his jacket and slip them to Mama. She put one in the refrigerator for her family and gave the other to Logan to cook for the butcher. Martini realized he knew everyone in here by name or sight. This place hadn't changed since he was a kid.

He had his food, a cup of coffee, and another smoke. Logan Deoudes, compact and muscular, came by and said hello.

"Whaddaya know, Dom?"

"Nothin' much. You still got that dog?"

"Greco? He's breathin'."

"Nice dog."

Deoudes looked him over. "You all right?"

Martini paid up, put some change on the counter, and left John's. He went south on Georgia Avenue. He loved his Nova but usually walked from his mother's house to the station and back again. He was never in a hurry to get home.

Across the street, a small crowd was gathered around the box office of the Sheridan. When they were teenagers, Martini and his brother, Angelo, used to climb up a fire ladder that led to the roof and sneak in a window that opened to a hall near the projection booth. If the manager, a guy named Renaldi, didn't nail them right away, they'd hide in the men's room until the show began, then take their seats in the dark. The theater was the hot spot of the neighborhood, an A house that was also a good place to try and pick up girls. Now they ran second-bill westerns, Universal Bs, and Greek movies on Wednesday nights.

Tonight was a George Peppard picture, *Rough Night in Jericho*, had Dean Martin in it, too. All Italian Americans knew that Martin's real name was Martini. Angie used to ask him, "Hey, Dom, you think we're related, like?" and Martini would smack him on the back of the head and say, "Yeah, and Nancy Sinatra's our sister, too."

Dominic Martini would have given his life, right now, to take back all the times he'd smacked his brother or called him stupid or a fag. He was only trying to toughen him up, but still. If he could see him again, just once more, he'd hold him tight.

He went down to Lou's, a pool hall next to the firehouse, and got a game. Someone put "The Ballad of the Green Berets" on the jukebox, and a couple of drunks started singing along. Martini called his pocket, sunk the eight, and handed his stick to a guy he didn't know. One of the drunks stepped out of his way as he walked across the poolroom. Martini was known around the neighborhood as the marine who'd seen action in Vietnam. He supposed he was feared. What the drunk didn't know, what none of them knew, was that his fighting days were done. He lit a cigarette as he left the place and headed west.

He walked onto the grounds of Fort Stevens, going along the cannons, hearing the pop of the flag and the lanyard clanging against the pole. His history was in this park. He'd had his first smoke here, got shitfaced on hard liquor here, hid beer and things he'd stolen in the ammo bunker built into the hill. As a kid, he'd run across this field from Officer Pappas, laughing and yelling "Jacques" over his shoulder as he hotfooted it in the direction of his house. He'd busted his cherry here one night, when he and a couple of his buddies pulled a train on a girl named Laurie, who they all called Whorie, after she'd dared them to. He thought it was all good fun and he never thought the things he was doing would have any bearing on what he would be as a man. But now it seemed that all of it had brought him to where he was today.

He'd read the newspaper on his break, back at the station. Buzz had said not to worry, that a hit-and-run on a colored guy wouldn't even make the news. He was wrong. It was only a few paragraphs in the City section, but it was there. Vernon Wilson was seventeen, nearing graduation at Roosevelt High School, working, at the time of his death, as a delivery boy for Posin's deli. He had been accepted to Grambling College and was planning to start there in the fall. He was survived by a mother and a brother. Police were said to be working on the case but had no concrete leads at this time.

Martini cursed himself as he left the park and walked down Piney Branch Road.

Buzz had been wrong about plenty. The newspaper people and the police did "give a shit." They were going to look for the killers, even though the boy was "just a coon."

Buzz had told him to stop crying about something he couldn't change. Buzz had *told* him to keep his mouth shut. He would do that, because he always did what Buzz said. But there was a part of Martini that hoped the truth would come to light. He felt it was important for people to understand that what happened to Vernon Wilson was unprovoked and in no way his fault. Wilson's mother deserved to know this. His brother did, too.

Martini entered his house on Longfellow. The smell of garlic and basil was heavy as he went through the door. The air inside was warm and still. His mother, Angela, sat in his father's old chair, wearing black, watching a *Hazel* rerun on their old RCA Victor. She turned her head and looked at him. Her face was waxy in the light.

"Ma."

"There's Sunday gravy and pasta in the kitchen."

"I already ate."

His mother turned back to the television. Martini went up to his room and lay down on the bed.

———

THEY HAD PUT Kenneth Willis in one of those rooms at the Ninth Precinct house, had a table and a chair and nothing else. The table was bolted to the floor, and beneath it ran an iron bar. They had cuffed one of his hands to the bar. His face was fucked from when he'd fallen to the sidewalk, and also from

the beat-down they'd given him in this room. He'd said something smart to one of the arresting officers, and that had set
them off. They must have known about his priors, too; the
statutory rape charges on his sheet always got their blood up.
Willis was used to getting hit by the police, he expected it,
even, so it wasn't any shock. He could have used a little whiskey, though, something, to rub on his gums. White boy had
knocked loose one of his teeth.

The one who'd hit him, Officer James Mahaffie, and another one, Officer William Durkin, both in plainclothes, were
in the room with him now. Standing over him and getting real
close, how they liked to do.

Willis knew how to play these two. Give them back the lip
they gave you. That's how you got respect from their kind.

"What were you gonna do with this, then?" said Durkin,
holding the single stocking they'd recovered from Willis's
slacks.

"This girl I been datin'," said Willis, "she left it over my
crib. I was gonna return it to her."

"What, this girl only has one leg?"

"She has one pussy. That's all I need to know."

"You're a real stud. I'm just curious: You ever had a
woman over the age of fourteen?"

"Your mother was," said Willis.

Mahaffie, big and blond, slapped him viciously across the
face. Willis put his tongue to the loose tooth, moved it, and
tasted blood. He felt dizzy and hot.

"A gun and a stocking," said Durkin. "You were on your
way to knock over something when we nailed you outside
your place. Isn't that right?"

"Huh?"

"Tell us about your accomplice. Where were you headed
when we picked you up?"

"I was just goin' out for a walk."

"Liar."

"What'd you say?"

"You're a lyin' piece of black shit."

"*Fuck* you, whitey."

Mahaffie threw a deep punch into Willis's jaw and knocked him off his chair. His arm twisted in the fall, and he felt an arrow of pain in the wrist still cuffed to the bar. Something had torn in his shoulder, too. Mahaffie righted the chair, and Willis struggled to his knees. He retched as he managed to get back in the seat. He spit blood and his tooth on the table. He looked them in the eye in turn.

"Hey, Jim," said Durkin, smiling jagged teeth. "You see this?" He let the stocking dangle from his hand.

"Yeah, I see it."

"Stupid sonofabitch was gonna pull a robbery with a fishnet stocking. Oh, shit."

Durkin and Mahaffie laughed.

"What's the charge?" said Willis.

"That thirty-two you were carryin'," said Durkin. "Big surprise, someone filed the serial number off it. Guy like you gets popped with a weapon altered like that, you're lookin' at a felony."

"So? How come I ain't been brought before no judge?"

"We're gonna let you think about it."

"I don't need to think on nothin'," said Willis. "I'll take the charge."

"You're lookin' at time," said Durkin.

"I wanna speak to an attorney."

"Yeah, okay."

Mahaffie put his finger in the mess on the table and flicked the tooth against Willis's chest. "Here you go. Put it under your pillow tonight. For the fairy."

"I get a phone call, don't I?" said Willis, over Mahaffie and Durkin's laughter. He watched them walk from the room.

Later, Willis stood out in the hall, a desk sergeant nearby, and made his call on a pay phone. He spoke softly so the sergeant couldn't hear.

"I'm in trouble, cuz."

"You need to stand tall," said Alvin Jones.

"You *know* I will."

"They gonna try and make you talk."

"They already did," said Willis, sick from the coppery taste in his mouth.

"You got a lawyer?"

"They gonna give me one, I expect."

"You can beat a little old gun rap."

"Yeah, but they ain't even charged me yet. They just gonna let me sit here for a while, I guess."

"That ain't legal."

"Black motherfucker like me, legal ain't got nothin' to do with it." Willis shifted his eyes to the sergeant, then back to the wall in front of him. "Thing of it is, they knew about our plan."

"Say what?"

"The market," said Willis. "They knew. Now, why you think that is?"

Alvin Jones let that lie in his brain.

"Kenneth."

"Yeah."

"You call here again, I might not be in, you understand?"

"You goin' back with Mary?"

"Nah, man. That baby's got the cryin' disease, and I cannot take it. I'll be at cousin Ronnie's crib, over there off 7th. But that's for you only. Don't you tell no one where I went."

"I won't say nothin'."

"I know it. You a soldier, Ken."

Jones told his cousin to be strong, then hung up the phone. His eyes went narrow and he began to mumble. Sitting there in the living-room chair of Lula Bacon's apartment, rattling ice cubes in a highball glass where bourbon had been.

They knew. His cousin's words burned through his head.

"What's wrong with you?" said Lula, standing over him, her hand on her hip.

"Nothin'," said Jones.

"You talkin' to yourself and your eyes are funny."

"Go on, bitch," said Jones, holding out his glass. "Get me another drink."

Jones watched her head into the kitchen. He lit a Kool and dragged on it deep.

Okay. They knew. But *how*'d they know? Who the *fuck* would have the nerve to talk to the police about their plans, and why? Lula? Nah, he never told her anything. Only one he could think of . . . that smart-mouthed boy Dennis, one had the police brother. Yeah, he was the one. Had to be. Tryin' to be all Dudley Do-Right and shit.

Jones remembered Dennis, right in this very spot, advising him on how to draw the number out the box score. Telling him that Frank Howard was seven 'cause he played left.

Jones grabbed the phone off the stand, dialed, and got his bookie on the line.

"Alvin," said the bookie. "How's it goin', brother?"

"What the number was?" said Jones.

The bookie told him he hadn't hit. The numbers that had come out weren't even close to the ones he'd played.

Jones hung up the phone. He pictured Dennis Strange in his head. Acting superior, talkin' all that clever shit, looking to play him. Defying him, sitting in the backseat of the Mercury the night before, holding one of his dumb-ass books, like he was better than him and Kenneth, his so-called friend. The friend that he'd betrayed. Boy gave out bad advice, too.

Alvin Jones watched his hand shake as he ashed his cigarette. He felt his blood go *tick tick tick*.

NINETEEN

DEREK STRANGE WAS listening to a Dial single, Joe Tex doing "A Sweet Woman Like You," when Lydell Blue buzzed him from the lobby. Strange turned off the music, checked himself in the full-length mirror he had hung by the front door, and went down to meet Lydell. Night had fallen on the streets.

Strange dropped into the bucket of Lydell's gold Riviera. Blue's big arms and chest stretched the fabric of his shirt as he put the car in gear.

"Where we headed, Ly?"

"Barry Place."

"Shoot, we coulda walked."

"I walked a beat all day. Besides, we meet some girls tonight, you think they're gonna want us to walk them home?"

"You got a point."

"I ain't makin' payments on this Riv for nothin'."

They went down the hill alongside Cardozo, then east on Florida. Blue punched the gas, and the car seemed to lift off.

"What you got in this thing, the Apollo rocket?"

"Four-oh-one Nailhead," said Blue, stroking his thick black mustache.

Strange had a look at the interior of the car. Blue kept it spotless, in and out; you could groom yourself looking into the mirror finish on the body. It was the '63, the first year Buick had offered the model. Auto turbine, power windows, power seats, even had an antenna went up and down when you pushed a button. He'd bought it used, off that little old lady from Pasadena that every car lover was looking for. Still, even though it was five years old, it hadn't come cheap. Blue still lived with his mother and father over there in Petworth because he couldn't afford both an apartment and the nut on this car.

"It is nice," said Strange.

"What is?"

"Your ride. But the question is, you do meet a girl tonight, where you gonna take her later on?"

"Your place," said Blue, like he was telling a stupid man his own name. He used Strange's apartment regularly for just that purpose.

"Fine with me, long as it ain't like it was with that last girl you had."

"What was wrong with it?"

"Y'all kept me up half the night."

"One of those churchgoing types," said Blue with a wink of his eye. "Girl sings gospel."

"Sounds like she screams it, too."

"Go on, Derek."

Strange smiled. As kids, he and Blue had stood up for each other in the schoolyard and on the streets. At Roosevelt High, both had played football, with Strange going both ways at tight end and safety, and Blue a star halfback. Strange was more a blocker than he was a receiver and had opened many holes for Lydell, who had set that year's Interhigh record for ground yardage gained in his senior season. It was in one of those final games that Strange had torn the ligaments in his knee, an injury that would keep him out of the draft. After graduation, Blue went into the army while Strange worked a succession of futureless jobs and recovered from the operation that fixed his knee. Then, when Blue returned from the service, both applied to the MPD and entered the academy. You made new friends all your life, but none were as special as the ones you'd made early on.

"Wanna hear somethin'?" said Blue.

"Pick it," said Strange.

Blue reached over and turned on the AM. DJ Bob Terry was introducing Marvin Gaye's brand-new one, "You," on WOL. Blue kept his hand on the dial and with a smirk on his face looked at Strange.

"That's good right there," said Strange.

"Thought you didn't like Motown."

"I make an exception for Marvin."

"It's got nothin' to do with him bein' local, does it?"

"A little."

"You are your father's son," said Blue.

In more ways than you know, thought Strange.

They parked on Barry Place. Ahead, halfway up the street toward Georgia, they saw young people outside a row house, on the concrete porch and in the small yard, talking, dancing a little, getting their heads up on things they were drinking out of bottles and paper cups. Soul music was coming softly down the block.

Strange and Blue walked toward the house side by side. Both were dressed clean; both moved with their shoulders squared and their heads held up. To be young, handsome, and employed, to walk into a party looking strong, standing with your main boy from childhood, trusting him to watch your back, there wasn't a feeling much better than that.

"Feels good," said Blue.

"What does?"

"To be out of uniform for a change. Not that I don't like my job, because I do. It's just, you know, nice to have brothers and sisters lookin' at me like I'm one of them."

"You are."

"I mean like I'm on their side."

"You don't have to explain it," said Strange. "I know exactly what you mean."

"It's just hard. On top of it, I got a genuine sonofabitch for a partner. Old brother is always schoolin' me. To him, if I open my mouth, I better be just breathin', 'cause if I speak, I'm wrong."

The comment made Strange think of Troy Peters. He tried too hard sometimes, but his heart was right. All in all, he was about as good a partner as a man could have.

"Come on, Ly," said Strange as they hit the steps going up to the house. "Let's have a little fun."

Strange and Blue waded into the outdoor crowd. They got a couple of Miller High Lifes out of a washtub filled with ice and popped the tops with an opener hung on a string from the tub. Blue introduced Strange to the host, a young Howard student named Cedric Love, who was renting the house with two other young men. Lots of Bison here on Barry Place and the surrounding streets, as Howard U wasn't but a long spit east. Strange looked around, moving his head to the Wilson Pickett, "Don't Fight It," coming from a couple of speakers set up on the porch. People in the yard were coupling up and dancing to the driving rhythm, the Stax/Volt horns and Wilson exhorting them on. Up on the porch, Strange saw the back of a young woman, had a short baby-blue dress on, going into the house. Strange knew those legs and that shape.

"Excuse me," said Strange to Cedric Love, "I'm gonna see what's going on inside." He was looking to catch Blue's attention, but Lydell was already asking some girl to dance.

Strange went up on the porch. A guy he knew from high school said, "What's goin' on, big man?" and Strange said,

"Everything's cool, George, how you been?" and gave the guy the soul shake and moved on. Then he was in the house.

It was warm inside and packed with folks. People against the walls and tight in groups, and men and women leaning into each other, Afros on the men and some of the women, the women wearing big hoop earrings and a few of the dudes wearing shades. Tobacco smoke, and the smoke and fragrant smell of marijuana, hung thick in the air. Conversation and laughter rumbled up under the music, louder in here than it had been outside.

Strange caught some eyes as he walked slowly through the crowd. He saw two fine young women, Rachel Phillips and Porscha Coleman, who had come out of Cardozo a few years back. He recognized many of the faces here. The people who recognized him knew he was police.

He went into a room that was more crowded than the one before it. An O. V. Wright song, "Eight Men, Four Women," came up on the system, with those lazy-voiced female backup singers he liked to use, and Strange thought, Back Beat number 580. And then he thought, Someone at this party knows his shit.

"Derek," said his friend Sam Simmons, tall and rangy, who came up on him suddenly out of the hall. "My brother."

Simmons was with a dude, had a black beret and a soul patch, who Strange didn't know. Probably a college boy, 'cause many of them had that ready-for-the-revolution look going on.

"Cootch," said Strange, using Simmons's nickname, giving him skin.

"Here you go," said Simmons. "Groove on this."

Simmons passed Strange a lit joint. Strange looked at it for a moment, then put it to his lips and hit it deep. Smoke was still streaming from his nose when he hit it again. It was smooth to his lungs, which meant it would be good to his head.

Strange passed the joint to the man in the beret, who

looked at Simmons first, then took it after Simmons made a small go-ahead motion with his chin. Simmons, who'd played end for Dunbar when Strange was playing safety for Roosevelt, smiled at his former adversary. There had always been respect between them, especially when a game had been on the line.

"My man's all right," said Simmons to his companion.

"I am now," said Strange.

"Heard you been keepin' the streets safe," said Simmons.

"Streets gonna have to do without me for a little while," said Strange. "I'm layin' back tonight."

They talked about football and who was coming out of what high school and what colleges they were going on to. The dude with the beret never did warm up to Strange, but that was all right with him. Strange was higher than a mother-fucker by the time he finished his beer and could muster no bad will toward anyone. He shook hands again with Simmons and went to the kitchen, where he found another High Life and opened it. He drank its neck off down to the shoulders and drifted into another room.

It was an all-couples room. Someone had cleared the furniture and changed the bulbs in the lamps so the room was bathed in blue. Solomon Burke was on the stereo now, singing "Tonight's the Night," Solomon telling his woman, "And when the lights are low, I'm gonna lock all the doors," and some couples were slow-dragging on the hardwood floor, others just holding each other, standing still, kissing each other deep. Strange smiled and leaned his back against the wall. He felt a tap on his shoulder and turned his head. What he saw made him smile even more.

"Carmen," said Strange. "How you doin'?"

"I'm good."

She had a little blue ribbon tied in her hair, the same color as the dress. She had big dark eyes, dimples in her cheeks, and smooth, deep-brown skin. She had a figure that caused his breath to come up short. Carmen Hill had it all. The memory of her naked in his bed made Strange's mouth go dry. He had a sip of his beer.

"What you doin' in the blue-light room all by yourself?" said Carmen.

"I was waitin' on you, girl."

"Go ahead, Derek." Carmen laughed, looking into his heavy-lidded eyes. "You're high, aren't you?"

"A little."

"I just had some nice smoke myself."

"You gonna be a doctor, you need to quit it. Can't be, like, *operatin'* on people with your mind messed up."

"I'm just an undergraduate. I got time to have fun. Anyway, what you gonna do, write me a ticket?"

"I'll let you off with a warning tonight."

Strange held his beer out to Carmen. She took it, drank, and gave the bottle back. Strange reached out and wiped his thumb across some foam that had gathered at the corner of her mouth. She leaned a little into his touch. She looked at him and looked away. Then she looked back into his eyes.

"I was thinking of you last December," said Carmen. "The day Otis died."

"Yeah, December tenth," said Strange. "I was in my squad car when the news came on the radio, said his plane had gone down in Wisconsin."

"He left some music, though, didn't he."

"Always gonna be there," said Strange. His eyes went to one of the speakers in the room, where King Solomon's voice was still coming out strong. "This is real pretty right here, too."

"Sure is."

"Wanna dance to it?"

"Okay."

He placed the beer bottle on the floor and as he stood tall she came into his arms. He trembled a little as she put her head against his shoulder. He smelled that shampoo of hers and her dime-store perfume. Her breasts were firm against his chest, her fingers warm through his. They moved slowly and easily, as if she'd never left him, as they'd danced all through high school and beyond, until the trouble had come between them and she'd told him to go.

Otis Redding came on the box, the song with that beautiful piano introduction that always gave Strange chills. "Nothing Can Change This Love." It had been one of theirs. Strange held Carmen close and breathed her in.

"I been missin' you," said Strange.

They kissed. Her lips were warm, and he felt the heat come off her face. Otis sang to them and there was no one else in the room.

LATER, AS THE crowd thinned and the music notched down, Strange and Carmen Hill sat outside the house on the front steps, sharing another beer. Lydell had gone back to Strange's place with a girl he'd been on and off with for some time. The alcohol had brought Strange down nice, taking the edge off his high. His thigh touched Carmen's as they talked.

"Tonight was good," said Strange. "Good to relax some, you know? Good to see you."

"Was for me, too."

"It's easy with you, Carmen. Always has been."

"You can pick up the phone, Derek. You want to talk, you can call me."

"I feel like I need to sometimes. Been rough, with my job and whatnot, these last few months."

"You knew it would be."

"I knew some of the white police would resent me. I was ready for that. What I didn't expect was my own people lookin' at me like I'm the enemy. I'm just trying to do my job and I'm duckin' fire from both sides."

"Then do your job," said Carmen. "That's what you always told me. Keep your head down and go to work. That's what grown folks do."

"I guess you're right."

"Anyway, you always did want to be like one of those dudes from those westerns you love. 'A man who protects the community but can never be a part of it his own self.' Isn't that how you described it to me once?"

"I might have," said Strange.

"You're luckier than most, then. You're the man you wanted to be."

She found his hand and laced her fingers through his. He looked her over with deep affection.

"Where you stayin' at now?" said Strange.

Carmen Hill nodded across the street. "I'm right there on the corner, up on the third floor. See that light up there? That's me. Finally got a place that's walking distance to my classes."

"I heard you moved."

"You did?" said Carmen in a slightly mocking way.

"Saw your sister one day, on the street."

"You sure it was like that? 'Cause she said you called her up and asked her where I'd gone to."

"I don't remember the particulars. Point is, your sister told me."

"Okay," said Carmen with a little laugh. She squeezed his hand.

"So, seein' as how you ain't but a few steps away . . ."

"What?"

"Aren't you gonna ask me over?"

"I don't think so."

"Why not?"

"I been talkin' to people, too. You still seeing that little hairdresser from Northeast, right?"

"That ain't nothin' serious."

"It never is with you."

"She's just a girl, is all I'm sayin'."

"But she's not the only girl, *is* she, Derek?"

"I ain't married to her, if that's what you mean."

"And now you're lookin' to get with me tonight, too."

"What's your point?"

"You got the same problem you always had. And that will not work with me, Derek; not again."

"If I could be with you, it *would* be only you."

Carmen leaned in, kissed him on the side of his mouth, and stood.

"I always knew, Carmen," said Strange. "Even when we were kids . . . you standing down by the corner market in that Easter dress of yours and those patent leather shoes. I knew."

"So did I. We try it again, though, this time it's gonna be on my terms. You need to think on that, Derek. You come to a decision, well, you know where to find me. Now that you know where I live."

"You remember where *I* live, don't you?"

"Yes. I still have your key."

Strange watched her go down the steps and across the street to her row house. He wondered if he would ever be capable of committing to one woman or if it was just that he was young and would change in time. He *wanted* to change. 'Cause there wasn't any question about it: Carmen was the one.

He got up and went down to Barry Place, then onto Florida Avenue. He walked east through a quiet city. He stopped to tell a boy of nine or ten, dribbling a basketball alone on the sidewalk, to get inside his house. The boy asked him why it was any business of his.

"I'm a police officer," said Strange.

He waited for the boy to do as he was told, and then he walked on.

TWENTY

ON TUESDAY, IN Memphis, Negro leaders announced plans for a massive march at the end of the week, with trade union members and civil rights spokesmen from across the country due to attend. A settlement of the garbage workers' strike would postpone the march, but no one expected that to happen. Dr. King had been scheduled to arrive in Tennessee that day to prepare for the demonstration, but he had been held up in Atlanta. His people promised that he would begin to head the operations in Memphis on Wednesday instead.

On Tuesday, in Milwaukee, Senator Eugene McCarthy celebrated his victory in the Wisconsin primary, having soundly beaten noncandidate Lyndon Johnson as well as write-in candidates Robert Kennedy and Hubert Humphrey the night before. In the Republican primary, Richard M. Nixon had won 80 percent of the vote to Ronald Reagan's 10 and seemed well on the way to his party's nomination.

On Tuesday, in D.C., the Cherry Blossom Festival of 1968

officially commenced. Over the Potomac River in Virginia, U.S. Park Police removed a Vietcong flag found flying over the Iwo Jima monument near Arlington Cemetery. Later that afternoon, two brothers were busted in the parking lot of a Northwest drive-in restaurant on Wisconsin Avenue, netting the largest seizure of hashish ever made in the Washington area.

At the same time, Buzz Stewart and Dominic Martini worked uneasily together at the Esso station on Georgia Avenue while Walter Hess, without remorse or anything else clouding his head, did his duties at the machine shop on Brookeville Road. Darius Strange flipped eggs and burgers on the grill of the Three-Star Diner on Kennedy Street while his wife, Alethea, cleaned a house in the Four Corners area of Silver Spring, Maryland. Their older son, Dennis, slept late, watched television, and read the want ads in the *Post*. Their younger, Derek, had a slow morning, reading and listening to records, then dressing to meet Troy Peters for their evening patrol.

Frank Vaughn heard the hash bust story on all-news WAVA as he drove his Polara south on a downtown Silver Spring street. It made him think of Ricky, and the small pipe he'd found in his son's car the week before.

"I was driving around with a bunch of guys the other night," explained Ricky. "One of them must have dropped it under the seat or somethin'. I swear, Dad, I don't even know what it's for."

Bull*shit*, thought Vaughn. But to his son he said, "Just get rid of it, okay?"

Vaughn turned onto Sligo Avenue, then made a quick right onto Selim. He parked in front of a beer garden called Fay and Andy's, where drinkers stared at Georgia Avenue and the B&O railroad tracks when they weren't staring into their glasses or the ashtrays in front of them. There were several garages, engine repair businesses and body shops alike, on this strip. Vaughn was out of his jurisdiction, but that meant jack to him, and anyway he was off the clock.

Vaughn had gotten his lab man, a guy named Phil Leibovitz, on the phone that morning. Leibovitz had studied the grillwork, glass, and logo left at the hit-and-run scene and discerned that the car involved was a '63 or '64 midsize Ford.

"It's not a Falcon or a pony car," said Leibovitz. "I'm sure of that. Different kind of gridwork. You need to be looking for a Fairlane or a Galaxie Five Hundred."

"What the hell, Phil?" said Vaughn. "Which one?"

"The Galaxie."

"How come?"

"I'm assuming the impact knocked the emblem off the front of the car. The Fairlane doesn't carry the Ford logo on the grille."

"You're a genius."

"Compliments don't pay my bills."

"The next beer's on me."

"Beers don't pay my bills, either, Frank."

"I'll get you when I see you," said Vaughn.

Vaughn spent the next hour doing walk-ins, questioning mechanics and metalworkers, trying to get a line on a damaged red Ford. He talked to grease monkeys, straights, near idiots, guys who looked like they'd done time, and guys who looked like candidates for time. He turned up squat.

Vaughn drove into D.C. He still had an hour before his shift. He was the primary on a fresh homicide in Petworth, and that would cut into the time he could devote to the hit and run. From the history they'd turned up, the young man, Vernon Wilson, was clean. He had a steady job and was going on to college. He came from a family he loved and who loved him back. He was murdered, Vaughn decided, because he was colored. Vaughn felt he was close to nailing Wilson's killer, and that got his blood up. All he had to do was find the car.

Vaughn went down to Arkansas Avenue between 14th and Piney Branch Parkway. A one-bay garage stood there near a glass shop and a commercial-refrigeration outlet. Vaughn knew the head mechanic, a huge colored guy named Leonard White, who he'd dropped on a B&E charge many years ago when Vaughn was working Robbery, his first position out of uniform.

Vaughn parked near a pay phone and tapped his finger on the wheel. He thought of a friend in Prince George's County who might be of some help. First he'd play the long shot and talk to White.

White's head was under the hood of a '63 Valiant when Vaughn walked through the open bay door. Music came loud from the shop radio. Another colored guy, slim in his coveralls, with a watch cap cocked on his head, was handing White a ratchet arm. He cool-eyed Vaughn and said, "Leonard, the Man here to see you." White looked up, squinting through the glare of a droplight hung over the Plymouth. The light gave the illusion of warmth, but the interior of the cinder-block box was cool as a tomb.

White stood to his full six-feet-something, wiped his hands off on a shop rag, and walked over to Vaughn. He wore black-rimmed eyeglass held together at the bridge with surgical tape. His head was the size of a calf's. He looked like Roosevelt Grier.

"Officer Vaughn."

"Leonard. See you're still working on those Valiants."

"Long as they keep puttin' push-button trannies in those Signets, I'm gonna stay in business."

"I talk to you a minute outside?"

White walked out without answering, and Vaughn followed. Vaughn shook an L&M from his deck. White took a pack of Viceroys from his breast pocket and put one between his lips. Vaughn produced his Zippo, lit White's smoke, lit his own, then snapped the lighter shut.

"There was a homicide the other night over on Fourteenth."

"That ain't no surprise."

"Not down in Shaw. A mile or two from here. Car ran down this colored kid, wasn't doin' anything but walking home."

"I heard about it."

"*What*'d you hear?"

"That it happened."

White dragged on his Viceroy and let the smoke out slow.

"I'm lookin' for a red Ford," said Vaughn. "Galaxie Five Hundred, sixty-three, sixty-four. Damage to the grille, headlights, front quarters, like that."

"Ain't had nothin' like it come through."

"Here you go." Vaughn handed White a card on which he'd scribbled his home number next to the printed station number. "Anything at all, you get up with me, hear?"

White nodded.

"Everything okay?" said Vaughn.

"God is good," said White.

Leonard White finished his smoke and watched Frank Vaughn cross the street, heading for a pay phone near the bus stop. Vaughn amused him. He was like one of those dinosaurs, didn't know the other dinosaurs had all laid down and died. Also, like many men who'd done time, White had a strange fondness for the one who'd sent him up. In a very direct way, Frank Vaughn had done what his mother, father, girlfriends, and minister had been unable to do: He'd turned his life around.

At the pay phone, Vaughn flicked away his cigarette. He pulled his wallet and ratfucked through its folds until he found a phone number jotted down on a piece of matchbook cover. He dropped a dime into the phone and dialed the number of a homicide cop over in PG County, a guy named Marin Scordato he'd befriended on the shooting range over in Upper Marlboro many years ago. Scordato kept a notebook detailing the current whereabouts of the men he'd arrested who'd done time and been sent back out into the world. He often squeezed these men for information. Almost all of them were parole violators in one way or another, and they readily responded to his threats. It was harassment, and very effective.

"Marin, it's Frank."

"Hound Dog, how's it hangin'?"

"My meat's okay," said Vaughn. "But I got a problem with a case."

MIKE GEORGELAKOS HAD torn the register tape off at three o'clock and was entering the day's take in his green book. He sat on a stool near the register, glasses low on his nose, penciling figures into the book. Any sales made after three would go into his pocket and remain unreported to the IRS, a common practice among small businessmen in D.C.

Down behind the counter of the Three-Star Diner, Darius Strange used a brick to clean the grill while Halftime, Mike's utility man, washed dishes on the other side of the plastic screen, humming the chorus of "I Was Made to Love Her" over and over as he worked. Ella Lockheart filled the Heinz bottles with A&P-brand ketchup as gospel music came from the house radio. They went about their tasks in an unhurried way. Lunch rush was over, and the end of the workday was near.

Derek Strange and Troy Peters sat at the counter eating cheeseburger platters and drinking Cokes, getting fueled up for the start of their four-to-midnight shift. They were in uniform, and their service revolvers hung holstered at their sides. Peters was thinking of his wife, Patty, and how she'd looked in sleep, her blond hair fanned out on the pillow, after they'd made it the night before. Strange had been dizzy with the thought of Carmen Hill all day, the curve of her backside in that dress, the cut of her thighs, the warmth of her privates against his as they danced. Those deep brown eyes. In addition, Strange and Peters were concentrating on the food that was before them, loving it the way they loved women, as young men tended to do.

"How's that burger, son?" said Darius Strange.

"It's good, Pop."

"You do somethin' long enough, I guess you get it right." He looked over his shoulder at his son, and as he shifted his weight he felt a sharp pain down by his tailbone.

Derek watched his father wince, then return to his task. He had that big old chef's hat, which he called a toque, on his head. Recently, Billy Georgelakos had taken a photograph of his own father, Mike, standing alongside Darius, with Darius wearing the hat and holding a spatula up in his hand. The photograph had been framed and hung by the front door.

Mike had upped Darius's pay through the years. Currently, he was making a hundred and ten dollars a week. Alethea was getting seventeen dollars now to clean houses and had cut her workweek down from six to five days. On their combined take, they managed to pay their bills. So they were doing all right. But Derek was worried about his father. Lately, his flesh looked loose on his face, his cheeks drawn. For a man in his fifties, he seemed to be aging fast.

The *Daily News* man came into the diner and dropped his stack atop the cigarette machine, removing the unsold copies from the previous day. Derek got off his stool, picked one from the top of the stack, and walked it back to the counter, where he spread it out to the left of his plate. The *News* was D.C.'s tabloid paper, convenient to read because of its size. The easy layout style and the dramatic edge put on the stories also made reading the *News* fun. Even had puzzles near the funny pages, Jumble and such, which Derek still liked to do. He opened the paper to the movie section and checked out the scheduled openings for the first-run houses downtown.

"Anything good coming up?" said Peters, wiping mustard from the side of his mouth.

"*The Scalphunters*," said Derek. "I been waitin' on that one."

"Burt's all man," said Peters.

"Don't forget about Ossie Davis. Got that bald-headed dude, too, played Maggott in *The Dirty Dozen*."

"Savales!" said Mike Georgelakos, suddenly animated, from the other end of the counter, and Derek heard his father chuckle under his breath.

"You gonna take your little hairdresser?" said Peters.

"I don't think so," said Derek, thinking, Darla doesn't even like westerns anyway.

Darius turned and stepped up to the counter, placing his palms on it and facing his son. "You finished?"

"Thanks, Pop," said Derek.

"You tryin' to do my job now?" said Ella Lockheart, stepping quick over the mats, reaching across Darius to clear Derek Strange's empty plate. "I'll just take that up."

In doing so, she brushed her hand across Darius's forearm. Her touch seemed natural and did not appear to discomfort him at all. Ella placed the plate on a bus tray beneath the counter and went back to her ketchup bottles. Darius looked at her for a moment, then back at his son.

"Dennis and I had a talk last night," said Darius.

"He told me he was gonna speak with you."

Darius's eyes went to Troy Peters, then back to Derek.

"It's okay, Pop," said Derek. "My partner and me, we already discussed it."

Peters nearly smiled. It was the first time he could recall Derek calling him partner.

"You think it's for real this time?" said Darius.

"*He* thinks it is," said Derek. "Whether Dennis follows through or not, I don't know. I guess we'll have to wait and see."

"Maybe the three of us could check out that movie you

were talking about. You, me, and Dennis, I mean. We could go downtown and see it this weekend. It's playin' at the Keith's, right? We haven't seen a picture together at one of those old palaces in a long time."

"I'd be into it," said Derek.

"I'll talk to your brother," said Darius. "See if he's into it, too."

Darius went back to his work. Derek looked down the counter at Ella, smiling to herself, singing along softly with the gospel tune coming from the radio.

Derek remembered a time when he was a kid, when he'd walked uptown after school one day while the magnolias were in bloom, hoping to surprise his old man. Derek was coming up the alley, headed for the rear door of the diner the way he and Billy liked to do, when he saw his father and Ella Lockheart talking real close on the back stoop. In his father's eyes and smile Derek saw something familiar. It was the way he looked and smiled at his wife, Derek's mother, on certain nights when they were happy and getting along. Later, on those same nights, Derek would hear them laughing and making noise in their bedroom. Seeing his father look at Ella that same way unsettled him. He backed himself out of the alley and walked home, never mentioning to his father that he had come to visit him that spring day.

He guessed he had known even then. But for a boy it was all too confusing to deal with directly, so he had put the incident, mostly, to the back of his mind. He loved his mother and father equally. He was sorry for her and disappointed in him. Disappointed, too, that the bond between his parents, which he had held to be simple and sacred, was as complex and fragile as everything else. But he couldn't bring himself to hate his father. Judge not lest you be judged, that's what their minister always said in church. It seemed to apply to both Darius and the adult Derek Strange.

You are your father's son. That's what Lydell had said to him the night before.

He reckoned that he was. He sure had gotten his work ethic from his old man. His interest in local sports heroes, in music, even in western movies, it had all come from Darius Strange. And his reluctance to commit to one woman, truly commit, even when someone as good as Carmen was looking at him square in the face, well, he supposed that had come from his father, too. Course, knowing where all his baggage came from didn't make the load any lighter. You just put one foot in front of the other every day and did the best you could.

"We gotta get moving," said Peters, looking at his watch.

"Right," said Derek.

They paid up, half the amount that was printed on the menu, and left change on the counter. They waved good-bye to Mike, whose lips were moving as he counted out a stack of ones.

"Have a blessed day, young man," said Ella Lockheart, now filling the salt and pepper shakers, her final task of the day, as Derek Strange and Troy Peters headed for the door.

"You, too, Miss Ella. See you, Pop."

"Son."

Outside the diner they moved toward their squad car. Across the street at the Kennedy, folks were gathering for the first showing of *Von Ryan's Express*. Girls were doing double Dutch in front of a church, and a woman pushed a baby carriage down the sidewalk, passing a man applying wax to his curbside Lincoln.

"Nice out," said Peters, looking up at the cloudless sky.

Strange smelled rain.

TWENTY-ONE

A LVIN JONES PARKED his Special on the corner of 2nd and
Thomas, and walked north into the heart of LeDroit Park.
As he moved along, he hard-eyed young men and let his gaze
travel soft over the women. He had left his gun in the apartment but hadn't come out naked. He carried a straight razor in
the pocket of his slacks.

Soon he came to the intersection across the street from the
market. It might have been that the owner of the shop or
someone who worked there had gotten suspicious, seen them
sitting in Kenneth's Monterey on Sunday night. Maybe it was
them who called the police on Kenneth after taking down the
number on his plates. Didn't seem like the MPD would arrest
someone on just a hunch, but still. Jones wanted to make sure.

The door was tied open with a string. He stared at the
market pointlessly, knowing he wasn't going to get any closer
or go inside. Then he saw a couple of boys a half-block down,
riding bicycles over a piece of plywood they had leaned up on

some bricks in the middle of the street. Jones went over to where the boys were playing and observed their game. They were getting some speed on the approach, riding their bikes up the shaky ramp, trying to get the bikes into the air. The kid who got up highest would win a bet of money that, Jones figured, neither of them had. But the bikes were old and heavy, and it wasn't working out the way they'd planned.

Least they had bikes. Jones had asked his father for a bicycle once, back in the early fifties, and his father had laughed. Jones asked him again, and his father slapped him so hard he saw stars, just like in the cartoons. Wasn't his real father anyway. Just some man his mother had ordered Jones to mind. When he wasn't laughing at him, the man used to beat him with a belt or closed hands. If Jones could see him now, he'd kill him. But the man had been dead for ten, twelve years. Got his heart stabbed in a fight over a woman, lived one floor down from where they all stayed.

Jones whistled to the boys. They rolled on over to him on their bikes, apprehension and curiosity on their faces. He introduced himself and told them what he wanted, holding two folded ones in his hand as he spoke. Telling them how he'd grown up around here, asking them, What was the name of that man owns the market down here, and the other man, works there, too? Claiming how he wanted to go in there and say hello but was ashamed because he wanted to call them by their names and couldn't recall. And, Oh yeah, had they seen this other cat hanging around the market or somethin' yesterday? Jones describing Dennis Strange and the kids not knowing any damn thing, but wide of eye and licking their lips over those dollar bills.

"Don't we get the money, mister?" said one of the boys, watching as Jones slipped the bills back into his pocket.

"Ask for the money up front next time," said Jones.

Y'all should have paid *me* for the lesson I just gave you, thought Jones, walking away. He always went to kids first for information, 'cause they were trusting and the first to give it up. But these kids here, they weren't worth a damn.

Jones went back down the street. He passed the market and at the next intersection cut right and walked into an alley that ran between two residential blocks. At the end of the alley, Jones could see the back door of the market, an overturned milk crate by its stoop. Cats of all kinds scattered as he moved along the cracked concrete. Up ahead, a boy in a striped shirt threw a tennis ball against a brick wall.

Jones came up on the boy and stood beside him. The boy didn't move away. He had an old face for his years, with eyes that had lost their innocence too soon. All of this, to Jones's mind, was good.

"What's goin' on, young man?"

The boy said nothing.

"You got an arm on you like Bob Gibson, boy."

The boy whipped the ball against the wall.

"All right," said Jones. "You just listen."

Jones fed the boy the same stories and questions he had given the kids on the bikes. The boy continued to throw the ball, catching it bare-handed off one hop, as Jones spoke. When Jones was done, he waited for the boy to say something. But the boy did not react at all.

Jones had lost half his patience. He put fire to a Kool and looked the boy up and down. "Somethin' wrong with your tongue?"

The boy shook his head. "My uncle told me not to talk to no police."

"He told you right."

The boy held the ball and stood straight. He looked Jones in the eye for the first time. "You got money?"

"I might."

"I might know somethin', then."

"*Tell* me what you know."

"Where the money at?"

224

Jones chuckled low. He reached into his pocket and handed the boy two one-dollar bills. "Say it."

"White man who owns the market, everyone calls him Mr. Ludvig. Man who works for him, we all call him John."

"John's a black man. . . ."

"Dark-skinned, got gray in his hair."

"What about the rest?"

"Rest of what?"

"What I asked. Did you see a young brother come and talk to those men yesterday? I'm sayin', someone who wasn't from the neighborhood. Like a stranger. Most likely, this cat would've talked to John."

The boy frowned as he thought. His frown broke as the image came to his mind. "There was this one man, came around early. Right back here."

"In the alley?"

"Man walked by me. Talked to John behind the store. Tall, young dude, had an Afro that was all messed up."

"He ain't say his name, did he?"

"Nah."

"Anything else about this man?"

"Nothin', I guess. Except —"

"What?"

"Man was carrying a book."

Jones smiled. "He say anything to you?"

"Nothin' important. Knowledge is power, somethin' like that."

"That's bullshit right there," said Jones.

"*I* know it," said the boy.

"Street's the only teacher you ever gonna need. And books are for faggots, too."

"I aint' no punk."

"I can see that," said Jones. "Listen, you and me didn't talk today, hear?"

"For two more dollars, we ain't never talked *any* day."

"Boy," said Jones, reaching for his wallet, "you about to drive me to the poorhouse and drop me off out front, all those brains you got."

THE TROUBLE STARTED after dark, at the Peoples Drug Store at 14th and U, where trouble was not uncommon. Fourteenth and U's four corners marked the busiest and most notorious of all intersections in black Washington, a major bus transfer spot in the middle of D.C.'s Harlem, a hub for heroin addicts, pimps, prostitutes, and all manner of hustlers, as well as law-abiding citizens and neighborhood residents just trying to move through their world.

The Peoples Drug sat beside the Washington, D.C., office of Dr. King's Southern Christian Leadership Conference, housed in a former bank. The SNCC and NAACP offices were nearby as well.

Hostility between juveniles and the store's black security guards had become a regular occurrence at this particular Peoples in the past few weeks. On this evening, the guard on duty, employed by an outside service, confronted a group of young men who were swinging a dead fish outside the store and bothering passersby with lewd gestures and remarks. The security guard told them to move on, but the boys did not comply. They called him "punk" and "motherfucker," and when he retreated, a couple of them followed him into the store. The manager phoned the police. A physical altercation ensued between one of the boys and the guard, and the boys were expelled. The manager locked the front door. By now a crowd had begun to form outside the Peoples. As was common in the inner city, word had spread quickly via the "ghetto telegraph," and the story had mutated to suggest another beat-down of a black boy at the hands of the authorities. Confusion and curiosity turned to anger as the crowd grew. The crowd pushed against the plate glass of the front show window. The glass imploded just as MPD patrol wagons and squad cars began to arrive.

Available units had been called to the scene by radio. Derek Strange and Troy Peters were among the first to arrive. Strange got out of the car with his hand on his nightstick. He and Peters joined the other uniforms who had gathered around the lieutenant in command. The men were instructed to use their presence, rather than physical force, to restore order and protect the commercial properties on the strip. The crowd, now numbering in the hundreds, continued to swell as the men received their instructions. "Do not draw your guns unless it is absolutely necessary," said the lieutenant. Strange felt a trickle of sweat run down his back. His hand involuntarily grazed the butt of his .38.

Strange and Troy joined the police line in front of the store and spread out several arm lengths but remained side by side. From what Strange could see, he was the sole black officer on the scene. He heard screams of "Tom" and "house nigger," and felt a pounding in his head. He brandished his stick and slapped it rhythmically into his palm. He did not look the crowd members in the eye.

Serve and protect. Do your job.

A missile broke the pane of the Peoples door. Rocks, cans, bottles, and debris flew around them. A Doberman pinscher was unleashed into the crowd by a local store owner, further inciting the mob. A sergeant screamed at the civilian to get his "goddamn dog" out of there, but it was too late. A full bottle of Nehi grape soda hit a cop car, cracking its windshield. Two police went into the mob and pulled out a man, cursing and kicking, and threw him into the back of a wagon. A second man was cuffed and put into the wagon. Kids poured lighter fluid against a tree and set it aflame. They laughed and cursed at a fireman who put it out. Pebbles hit a squad car with the force of shot and twelve-year-old girls screamed out horrible things at the uniforms and Strange's hands felt damp upon his stick.

He looked at Peters and saw Troy's wide eyes and the sweat bulleted across his forehead. For the next twenty minutes it was like a flash fire that they were powerless to stop. A young officer drew his gun in fear, and the noise grew louder and Strange knew then that they had lost control. Their lieutenant ordered them to pull back.

But suddenly, as if spent from its own rage, the crowd began to calm down. Stokely Carmichael, wearing a fatigue jacket, arrived from the SNCC office, was given a bullhorn, and instructed everyone to "go home." He told people to disperse and clean the street of what they'd thrown, as this was, after all, their neighborhood. They did not move to clean a thing, but as he spoke the crowd quieted further and moved slowly away from the scene.

Police stood in the emptied street, surrounded by shattered glass and other debris. Smoke roiled in the strobing light of the cherry tops idling in the intersection. A boy rode through on a bicycle, his kid brother sitting on the handlebars, both of them laughing. A young officer lit a cigarette with a shaking hand.

"Troy," said Strange.

Peters's face was drained of color. He stared ahead, his feet anchored to the street.

"Come on, buddy," said Strange, tapping him on the arm.

They walked together to their car.

———

LIKE THE MAN who lived in it, James Hayes's apartment was clean and unpretentious. Its furniture came from a downtown store and would still be stylish in twenty years. The kitchen had been outfitted in new harvest gold appliances. A color television sat in the living room along with a console stereo. The shirts hanging in the bedroom closet were dry-cleaned and custom tailored. All of these possessions were of some quality but deliberately understated. The man showed no flash.

James Hayes had lived here on Otis Place long enough to have seen boys like Dennis and Derek Strange run the alleys and streets of Park View and grow to be men. He didn't talk to the young ones until they came of age, and when they got involved with him it was always of their own volition. He was not a good man, nor was he bad.

Hayes sat in his living room with Dennis Strange, having a couple of Margeaux cognacs, listening to a record, enjoying the music and each other's company but saying little because both of them were high. They had shared a joint of gage, and now the cognac was working on them, too, giving them that warm liquor thing on top of the head thing that blurred the edges of the room. Dennis had swallowed a red an hour earlier and was just about where he wanted to be. He had left the apartment before his parents came home from work, because he hadn't wanted to look them in the eye.

"There it is, right there," said Hayes. "Hear him growlin'?"

"Man can do it."

"They say Sam was soft. If the only Cooke you own is *Live at the Copa*, you might think so. But you got to listen to these old records to know."

Dennis smiled and nodded his head. Like Dennis's father, Hayes went for that old sound, the R&B singers with the gospel roots. Dennis had spent many a night up here, listening to Sam Cooke's Keen sides, the Soul Stirrers with R. H. Harris, the Pilgrim Travelers with J. W. Alexander, Jackie Wilson, and others. He was not religious, but he often got the feeling he got in church, listening to these records.

Dennis felt comfortable here. When they weren't deep inside their heads or into the music, he and Hayes often had long discussions about politics and the black man's future in America. Hayes was smart and sensible and put his words together right. Dennis knew enough to realize that James Hayes was a father to him in ways that his own father could not bring himself to be. He listened, for one, and was not quick to judge. Dennis also knew that it was easy for a man to let you slide on things, and be your friend, when you were not his son.

"I've got a woman," said Hayes.

"Ray Charles," said Dennis, laughing at his little joke, laughing because he was high.

"What I'm sayin' is, I've got a lady friend comin' over tonight."

"I hear you."

"I don't mean to put you out."

"Ain't no thing," said Dennis. "We're cool."

Dennis didn't want to leave. He had no place to go. But he got up from the floor, where he had been sitting cross-legged, and stretched. He finished his cognac and put the empty snifter on the small table beside the chair where Hayes always sat. He shook Hayes's hand.

Near the front door of the apartment, in a bowl on a telephone stand where Hayes kept his keys and things, Dennis saw the check, written by Jones's lady friend, that he had brought over on Sunday night.

"You ain't cashed this yet?" said Dennis.

"Was feeling poorly the last couple days. Haven't had the chance to get to the bank."

"I was just wondering if it was any good."

"If it isn't, I'm gonna need you to *make* it good."

"You *know* I will."

Dennis said this with bravado, but he didn't know what he'd do if the check were to bounce. He didn't want to deal with Jones again, not after what he'd done to him and especially Kenneth. He wondered what had happened to Kenneth, if the police had took him in, and if they had, would he do time. He hadn't really thought the whole thing through, the consequences and such, when he'd talked to that old man down at the market. Just an impulse, really, nothing like a plan. He wasn't sorry he'd done it or anything, 'cause it was the right thing to do, but . . . whatever. He didn't want to think on it, not right now. His head was up too good.

"Take it easy, young man," said Hayes.

"You, too."

Dennis went out the door. He took the stairs down to the foyer of the row house where Hayes had his place and stepped out to the street.

The moon hung low and bright. Dennis could see no clouds. But to him it smelled like rain.

He walked up Otis toward the school, passing many parked cars. Mustangs and Novas for the cock-strong, Dodge Monacos and Olds 88s for the middle-aged and elderly, Caddys and Lincolns for those who liked to show. This was not his street, but he could match many of the vehicles to the houses where their owners stayed. He could match them all when he was straight. He passed a green Buick Special, then a VW Bug owned by this brother he knew who was always high, and a new Camaro, white with orange hood stripes, whose owner was a mechanic up near Fort Totten. Dennis had always been able to identify large things with small pieces of information. Like the dogs barking in the alleys. He could tell you the names of those dogs. Though maybe not right now. His head was all torn up.

He found himself on the grounds of Park View Elementary. He limped across the weedy field. He found the last quarter of the joint they'd smoked in his pocket and lit it with a match. He had a seat on a swing that he barely fit into and hit the jay. He snorted up the smoke that was coming off its tip and held the whole draw in his lungs.

His parents had finished dinner by now. His mother had washed the dishes, taken her bath, and gone to bed. His father would still be up, nursing his one beer, watching television. What was it, around eleven? He would be into *Wanted: Dead or Alive* on channel 20. A rerun, but his father didn't care. Long as it had horses and guns.

Dennis chuckled as he exhaled his smoke. He rubbed at the top of his head.

His father had listened to him the night before, when Dennis had told him about his plan. How he was gonna turn it all around, get a job, work hard like his brother, and get his own place like his brother had, because his eyes had opened up and he'd learned. His father had nodded patiently the whole time he was talking. Yeah, there was the usual flicker of doubt in his eyes, and his hands were opening and closing at his sides, the way they did when he was impatient. But he had *listened.*

That plan thing, it was all bullshit, anyway. Dennis had looked through the want ads in the morning but had made no calls. Basically, he'd done nothing all day. And here he was, sitting on a swing set late at night, no friends, no woman, no one to talk to and no one looking to talk to him. Just high. Sitting in the same swing he'd sat in over twenty years ago. Still a child, gone no further than a child.

His plan had felt electric last night. It felt like nothing now.

Derek'll find me something, though, thought Dennis. My little brother will hook me up.

He wet his fingers and extinguished the roach, putting it into his pocket because there was a hit or two to be had later on. He got up and limped across the field.

Otis Place was up ahead. He could hear the bark of the dogs in its backyards. He cut into a short stretch of alley that joined the long common alley that ran between Otis and Princeton. Behind the corner house, he passed a mongrel named Betty who was growling with her face up against her owner's fence.

Betty knew him by sight and smell. Dennis said a few calm words, but Betty did not cease, and Dennis shrugged and moved on.

He knew every stone in this alley. Didn't even have to look at his feet to mind the uneven parts. When he and his father had played catch back here in the late '40s, around sundown on summer nights, his pop would throw him grounders along with flies. Got so he knew when the ball would take a hop, depending on where it got thrown. He could picture his father, the white sleeves of his work shirt rolled up on his strong forearms, the easy motion of his throws. Coming out here and playing ball with his boy, even though he was bone tired from his job.

I didn't hug my father last night, thought Dennis. That's what I forgot to do. I am high tonight and I might be high tomorrow, but I will hug my father when I get inside his place and I will tell him how good it felt for him to listen. What it meant, and how good it felt to me.

Halfway down the alley, a German shepherd mix ran back and forth behind the fence, baring his teeth and gums, barking rapidly. The shepherd's name was Brave, and Dennis stopped to pet him every day. Dennis approached the fence and leaned forward, extending his hand so the dog could smell it through the links.

"Come here, boy. It's me."

Brave barked wildly, snatching at the air with his jaws. Saliva dripped from his mouth, and his eyes were feral and desperate. The dog snapped at Dennis's hand.

Dennis drew back and stood straight.

"Smart nigger," hissed a voice in his ear as the edge of a straight razor was pressed against his throat.

Pop, thought Dennis Strange.

TWENTY-TWO

O N WEDNESDAY, THE Reverend Dr. Martin Luther King Jr. arrived in Tennessee. The city of Memphis received a Federal Court Restraining Order against Friday's planned march, claiming that officials there would be unable to "control" the participants.

On Wednesday, in New Haven, Connecticut, Senator Eugene McCarthy, energized by his primary victory in Wisconsin, appeared at a rally six thousand strong. A band played "When the Saints Go Marching In" as he entered the aisle of the meeting hall, some supporters running their hands through his hair as he passed. Later, McCarthy traveled to a north Hartford ghetto and spoke through a bullhorn to four hundred blacks, promising a "new set of civil rights," detailing his proposals, but reminding them that the most important thing government should do is "find out what you think, what you want." The reaction to his comments went unreported.

On Wednesday, in Washington, D.C., in the evening, five to ten thousand people attended a rally at the corner of 14th Street and Park Road, where Robert F. Kennedy arrived via convertible motorcade and stepped up onto a makeshift platform set on the back of a flatbed truck. Banners and signs reading "RFK, Blue-Eyed Soul Brother" could be seen in the crowd. A street party atmosphere ensued as Kennedy spoke of "Washington's monuments to failure, to indifference, to neglect." People stood in the street and on rooftops, telephone booths, and trash cans, cheering wildly. One blond woman fainted in front of Kennedy's wife. Down the block, at a much smaller gathering, a couple of Black Nationalists spoke to their predominately black audience, urging them not to vote for "another whitey." According to the *Washington Post* reporter on the scene, their comments drew "little attention."

At the same time, in Memphis, Dr. King spoke to more than two thousand supporters. Friday's march had been moved to Monday, but the city was still seeking an injunction against it, in part because of threats made to the reverend's life.

"It really doesn't matter what happens now," said Dr. King. "I've been to the mountaintop."

Very early that day, just around dawn, the body of Dennis Strange was discovered in the alley shared by Princeton Place and Otis Place, near the row house where he had lived with his parents, by a neighbor who was headed off to work. As the neighbor walked toward his Oldsmobile sedan, his tired eyes not yet focused, he saw starlings alighting on something heaped on the stones up ahead. The birds took flight as the man approached. He knew it was a dead body he was nearing, having seen much death in the Second World War. He recognized the victim immediately, though he looked very different in the grotesque freeze of violent death than he had in life. His head had been nearly severed from his shoulders; it rested at an unnatural angle to his body, as if hinged. His teeth, stained with blood, protruded from lips drawn upward, a grimace of agony common in slaughtered animals. His eyes were open, fixed, and bulging. And there was all that blood. The blood, a pond of it beneath him, had soaked into his clothing and turned much of it black.

"Lord," said the man, his voice not much more than a whisper.

He went back to his house and phoned the police, then woke his wife and sat on the edge of their marriage bed.

"Poor Alethea," said the wife.

"I know it," said the man, shaking his head. Their words were minimal but mutually understood. He and his wife had grown children of their own.

"You think he was robbed?"

"Of what? Boy never had twin dimes." The man squeezed his wife's hand and got up off the bed. "I better get back out there. They'll be wanting to talk to me, I expect."

By the time the neighbor had returned to the scene, two squad cars had arrived, and soon thereafter came the meat wagon, photographer, and lab man. Last to arrive was a homicide detective named Bill Dolittle, who was working a double and had the bad luck to catch the case just an hour before break time. Dolittle was a slack-jawed alcoholic, prone to seersucker suits, whose stick never shifted past second gear. He had the lowest closure rate in his precinct. Other cops called him Do-nothing and laughed at the mention of his name. He didn't mind. He was working for his pension and his next drink.

Dolittle dispatched one of the uniforms to talk to the old man whose house was behind the fence where the murder had occurred. The man, a gnarled-faced gentleman who went by R. T., said he knew the victim and nothing else. He had let his dog, Brave, back in the house at a late hour but had seen "not a thing."

"Your dog stays out all night?" said the uniform.

"Usually he does. That's my security guard right there. But he was barking at nothin' last night. Leastways nothin' I could see. I was up there on my stoop with the kitchen lights shining behind me. All's my eyes could make out was the black of night."

"Why'd you let him in?"

"Dog was barkin' at a ghost, far as I could tell, and he wouldn't stop. I was afraid Brave was gonna wake someone up."

After getting a statement from the neighbor, Detective Dolittle went to notify the victim's parents. He found the mother, Alethea Strange, drinking a cup of coffee at an eating table, wearing a uniform-style dress, preparing, she said, to head up into Maryland to her "Wednesday house," where she worked as a domestic. The father, Darius Strange, had already left for his job as a grill man in a diner. The woman broke down briefly when Dolittle gave her the news, Dolittle standing before her, jingling the change in his pocket and staring impotently at the floor. She then composed herself, rose abruptly from the table, and phoned her husband. When she was done talking to him, she phoned her younger son.

FRANK VAUGHN HAD closed his fresh Petworth homicide the night before, the way most cases got closed: via a snitch. A parole violator brought in on a marijuana charge offered up the killer, with whom he regularly played cards, and cut a deal. Uniforms arrested the suspect at his grandmother's apartment without incident. Vaughn interrogated the suspect at the station, but it was a formality, as he had already signed a confession he had written out, in pathetic grammar, before Vaughn arrived.

"Why'd you do it, Renaldo?" said Vaughn.

"Does it matter?"

"That's up to your attorney to decide. But I just like to know. Off the record."

Renaldo shrugged. "Man was fuckin' my woman. I don't even *like* the bitch, understand? But there's some things you don't do. I heard about it at a card game; all these boys I run with . . . everyone knew but me. Didn't even bother me he was jammin' this girl. He just shouldn't have talked so free, is all it was. It shamed me. When a man don't have his pride . . ."

He ain't got nothin' at all, thought Vaughn, tuning out Renaldo's voice and finishing it off in his head. He'd only heard this story, in variation, about a hundred and fifty times. He had thought this might be the interesting exception here, something different to make his buddies down at the FOP bar laugh, but it was always the same. Now Renaldo, a triple offender, just like the solid citizen who'd ratted him out, was going to do twenty-to-life for defending the honor of a bitch he didn't even like.

"Take it easy, Renaldo," said Vaughn before leaving him in the box. At least you got your pride.

Now Vaughn was free to work the hit and run. He had pulled an eight-to-four and his plan was to pursue it all day.

At around nine, Vaughn was still in the station, drinking coffee and having a smoke, sitting at his desk, scanning the night sheets, when he read about the fresh victim down in Park View. Alethea's oldest was named Dennis. Had to be the same man.

He picked up the phone, talked to Olga, gave her the news, listened to Olga's theatrics, and got Alethea's phone number. He phoned the Strange residence, and a man came on the line. He recognized the voice.

"Strange residence."

"Frank Vaughn here."

"Detective."

"I just heard. It *is* your brother, right?"

"Yes."

"My sympathies to you and your family. Please tell your mother that I was . . . that she's in my thoughts."

"I will."

"Young man?"

"Yes."

"Who's the primary? Do you know?"

"A Bill Dolittle."

"Okay. You tell him I'm at his disposal, hear? And the same goes for you and your parents. Anything you need. Anything, understand?"

"Thank you, Detective," said Strange, and hung up the phone.

Billy Do-nothing. That was a bad break. Unless the perp walked right into the station with pen in hand, or there was a forthcoming wit, or there was a plea-out involved, the case would go cold.

Vaughn rubbed at his face. The young man, Derek, had seemed unemotional, considering. Well, he was police. Some of them just felt they had to put up a hard front all the time. Secretly, Vaughn was relieved that the son, and not the mother or father, had picked up the phone. But he hoped Derek would pass on the message that he had called.

Vaughn sat there smoking his cigarette. What he knew of Dennis Strange came from Alethea, and Alethea gave up little of her private life. He remembered vaguely that the older son had been in the service, but that was long ago. There was little else to recall. When Alethea spoke of her sons at all, it was usually about Derek, the cop. He wondered if Dennis, the murder victim, had shamed her in some way or if it was just that Derek gave her such pride.

Vaughn crushed his L&M out in the ashtray before him, found an unmarked out in the lot, and went to work.

He visited several garages on the D.C. border. He went

back down to 14th and recanvassed a few of the neighbors who lived close to the accident scene, and turned up jack.

Shortly thereafter, he sat at the lunch counter in the Peoples on Georgia and Bonifant, eating a burger-and-fries platter and washing it down with a chocolate shake, his basic early lunch. The steel cup used to make the shake sat next to his glass. The soda jerks here didn't pour the extra out and waste it like they did at other five-and-dimes, and that was why Vaughn always came back.

He pushed away his plate and lit a smoke. When he was done with it, he took his notebook and pen out of his inside jacket pocket, went to a wooden phone booth in the drugstore, dropped a dime in the slot, and got Scordato, his PG County cop friend, on the line.

"Marin, it's Vaughn."

"Hound Dog, how's it hangin'?"

"Straight down the middle," said Vaughn. "Gimme somethin', will you?"

"Get a pen."

Vaughn drove into PG County. He visited a garage off Riggs Road, in Chillum. He got shrugs and the usual passive hostility. His next stop was a place near Agar Road, in West Hyattsville, near the Queens Chapel Drive-in, an unmarked garage on a gravel road set behind a strip of speed and tire shops.

Vaughn parked behind a Dodge Dart, a plum-colored GT with mag wheels. A Hi Jackers decal and another reading "WOOK: K Comes Before L," were affixed to the rear window. He studied the car as he passed it and headed for the garage.

Vaughn walked through the open bay door. A white guy and a colored guy, both good sized, had their heads under the hood of an all-stock, pearl-finish Chevelle SS. "Windy" came from a radio set high on a shelf.

The white guy, light and freckled, wearing coveralls cut

off at the shoulders, a cigarette dangling from his lips, stood free as Vaughn cleared his throat. The colored guy's eyes came up, but only for a moment, returning his attention to the Chevy's water pump, illuminated by a droplight. He worked a flathead to a clamp, tightening it around a hose. Vaughn saw homemade tattoos, probably done with a heated wire, on both of his forearms.

"How's it goin' today?" said Vaughn.

"We help you?" said the white guy, real chipper voice, smiling, looking Vaughn over, making him as a cop.

"I hope so," said Vaughn, badging the white guy, replacing the badge case inside his jacket. "Frank Vaughn, MPD. I'm lookin' for a Patrick Millikin."

"You found him."

"Can I get a minute?"

Millikin pointed his chin in the direction of the Chevy. "Just about."

Vaughn stepped forward, closing the space between himself and Millikin, intending to crowd him. Millikin did not react.

"A homicide occurred a few nights ago involving a red Galaxie or Fairlane, sixty-three, sixty-four. Might be damage to the grille or the hood. Headlights, quarter panels..." Vaughn looked at the colored guy, whose eyes had flashed up again, then back at Millikin. "I was wondering if a car like that might have come through."

"No, sir."

Millikin picked a shop rag up off the cement floor and rubbed at his hands. The ember flared on his cigarette as he drew on it, Millikin squinting against the smoke coming off its tip. He dropped the rag, ashed the cigarette into his palm, and rubbed the ashes into the thigh of his coveralls.

"You *sure*, now," said Vaughn.

"Haven't seen a car fitting that description."

"You talk to the other garage owners around here, don't you?"

"Sometimes."

"Any of them mention a car like that?"

"No."

"Nothin', huh?"

"Not a thing."

"You got a brother in the joint on a manslaughter beef, right?"

"He don't know about no red Ford, either."

Millikin dragged on his smoke, double-dragged, pitched the butt out the open bay door. His pale freckled face had gone pink.

"You're a funny guy," said Vaughn.

"I was just sayin' he don't know."

"Well, I mention prison 'cause . . . hell, Mr. Millikin, I know all about the code. How people like your brother and some of the people you might, uh, *associate* with now and again don't like to talk with the police. But see, this isn't one of those honor-among-thieves things."

"That's nice. But I still ain't seen the car. Now look, I gotta get to work. I promised the man who owns this Chevy here that I'd have it for him this afternoon."

"Here's the deal," said Vaughn, taking another step forward. "The driver of the car I'm describing, he ran this colored boy down in the street for no reason at all. Broke his neck, severed his spinal cord . . . left his brain fluid all over the street. Boy had a steady job, was off to college in the fall, the whole nine. Looked to me like this driver, he was havin' fun doing it. Boy wasn't hurting no one."

Millikin's eyes had lost some of their light. "That's rough."

"Someone spray-painted 'Dead nigger' on the asphalt, too, with an arrow pointing to where the body dropped. Can you imagine?"

"Damn shame," said Millikin, looking away from Vaughn.

"Yeah," said Vaughn. "It's just wrong." He reached into his pocket, retrieved his badge case, and withdrew a card, doctored to include his home phone. "You hear anything about a red Ford, sixty-three, sixty-four, damage to the front, you give me a call."

"I surely will."

Vaughn looked to make eye contact with the colored guy before he left, but the man's face was buried in his work. He walked from the garage, the lousy music trailing him like a bad joke.

Outside, he stopped by the plum-colored Dart. He withdrew another business card from his badge case, reached into the open window, and dropped it onto the driver's bucket. He knew that the call-letter decal on the back window was for one of those local radio stations played soul, R&B, race music, whatever they were calling it this week. It was all jungle-jump to Vaughn. What the sticker meant was, this here had to be the vehicle of the colored mechanic, had the prison tattoos. Maybe the lie Vaughn had told, about the spray paint in the street, would get the guy going. Maybe not. Anyway, it was all scatter shot. Once in a while you got a hit.

Vaughn got into his car and headed back into D.C. He had promised Linda Allen he'd drop by.

Back in the garage, Pat Millikin and Lawrence Houston waited for the sound of the cop's engine to fade.

"Stupid sonofabitch," said Millikin, lighting another smoke. "He backed my brother on the inside, so it was on me to back him, too. But after this, I'm done."

"You finished with his car?"

"I got it over in Berwyn Heights, workin' on it nights. Gonna be a few days before I'm done."

"That big boy he was with, you say he wanted a rental, too?"

"Buzz Stewart. Well, he ain't gettin' one now. I'm gonna call him at that gas station he works at right now and give him the news. Make it simple: I got no cars to rent."

"You gonna tell him about our visitor?"

"Not my lookout. We didn't say nothin' to that cop, so Stewart's got no reason to know. I want as little contact with those two as possible." Millikin looked at Houston. "Listen, Lawrence . . . brother or no brother, if I had known what those guys did, I never would have took in that car."

Houston shrugged. "Ain't no thing to me."

He tugged at the pump hose, testing the strength of the clamp. He reached to close the Chevy's hood and saw the tremble in his hands.

You hit a monkey, huh?

His hands shook when his blood was up.

TWENTY-THREE

FIVE MINUTES INTO meeting Billy Dolittle, Strange marked him as lazy, incompetent, and "that way." The man wearing his seersucker suit, red-and-blue rep tie, and cheap brown shoes, writing things down in a notebook, one of those schoolkid tablets, black with white spots. Talking down to him, speaking slowly and repeating himself as if Strange were a child. Dolittle chewing on wintergreen Life Savers during the interview, Strange wondering if he had been drinking this early, 'cause he sure did look the type. Also wondering how much to tell him: what to give up and what to hold back.

It was Dolittle who suggested that Strange officially ID his brother, that, as a cop, he could "handle it" and in the process spare his parents the pain of seeing their son "like that." By then his father had arrived at the house and, as Strange knew he would, insisted on coming along. So together they went to the alley and stood over Dennis and saw him "like that," and neither of them got sick or turned his face away. Instead, Darius put his hand on his younger son's shoulder and said a low prayer, and Derek Strange closed his eyes, not thinking of God or his brother's spirit but instead thinking, I will kill the motherfucker who did this to my brother, and, That man is going to die.

Back in the kitchen of his father's house, both of his parents seated at the table in the living room, his father holding his mother's hand, Strange talked to Dolittle and told him some of what he knew about his brother's life. He told him about Dennis's stint in the navy, his disability, and how he had no current job, and he mentioned his running boys, Alvin Jones and Kenneth Willis, and suggested that Dolittle definitely speak to them, because both of them were wrong. He did not tell Dolittle that Dennis moved small amounts of marijuana for the neighborhood dealer, James Hayes, because he had no desire to taint his brother further or to get Hayes, a nonviolent man who had hurt no one, in trouble with the law. Also, he wanted to talk to Hayes himself.

"Where can I find Jones and Willis?"

"Jones stays with this woman name of Lula Bacon, down in LeDroit Park. Far as I know, he has no job. Willis is a janitor in some elementary school up off Kansas; I don't know which one. He's got an apartment over on H, in Northeast, above a liquor store. Eighth, Ninth, around there. My mother might have Kenneth's number."

Dolittle scribbled in his notebook, his lips moving as he worked. "Anything else you can think of?"

Strange shook his head. "Not now."

Dolittle handed him a card. "You can get ahold of me here."

Strange saw that there was only the precinct house number on the card. When Dolittle was off the clock, he was off.

"I'm gonna call you this afternoon," said Strange, "see if there's been any progress."

"We haven't even finished canvassing the neighbors yet. These investigations take time."

"They take too much time, they get cold."

"I can understand you being anxious," said Dolittle, scratching at a thick nose spiderwebbed with red veins. "But you need to let me do my job. I been at this a long time."

Too long, thought Strange.

"Don't worry," said Dolittle, touching Strange's arm gingerly. "We'll get this guy."

You'll get him if you get lucky, thought Strange.

"That it?" said Strange.

"I'll see myself out."

Strange listened to Dolittle talking to his parents out in the living room. He heard the phone ring and he heard his father tell his mother not to pick it up. As word had spread in the neighborhood, the calls had begun to increase. Soon folks would be dropping by with food and drink, and the apartment would be crowded with visitors. He hoped his mother could handle it. She was doing all right so far.

Strange went to the window over the sink, where his mother's square of cardboard had come free in two corners and was arcing back. Strange reaffixed the corners to the glass.

He heard the front door open and shut. He heard his mother sobbing. He heard his father say, "Come here, Alethea," and the rustle of their clothing as they embraced.

Strange wanted to be with them and hold on to them, too. But this was their moment, and he was no longer a boy. He sat down on the kitchen floor beside the sink, where he'd sat at his mother's feet many times as a child, leaned his head back against the cabinet, and, very quietly, allowed himself to let go.

BUZZ STEWART FLICKED ash off his Marlboro. "There it is, right there."

"It doesn't look like much," said Dominic Martini.

"That's right. It ain't no big deal."

They were parked in Stewart's Belvedere, the nose of the Plymouth pointed south, on the west side of Georgia Avenue, not too far over the District line in Shepherd Park. "Once Upon a Time" came from the radio, Buzz Stewart nodding his head to the busy Motown arrangement as he kept his eyes fixed on the strip of businesses clustered on the east side of the street.

Nearby was Morris Miller's liquor store, a landmark whose rear parking lot was a meeting spot for D.C. and Montgomery County teenagers, a starting place to buy beer and make plans on Friday and Saturday nights. Years earlier, owner Morris Miller could not live in the neighborhood where he owned his business, as Shepherd Park had covenants restricting the sale of its houses to Jewish buyers. Since then, the neighborhood had become progressive. In '58, white and black homeowners, angered by the practices of blockbuster real estate agents, had formed Neighbors Inc. to support integrated streets. Now the area was heavy with Jewish residents, as well as blacks, with pioneering interracial couples in the mix. Its high school, Coolidge, was still called "Jewlidge" by Stewart and Hess, but its student body was now primarily black.

Across the street, an A&P grocery was the largest store of the bunch. Also on the strip sat a drugstore, a dry cleaner, and a speed shop, and, on the corner, a bank. Stewart and Martini were looking at the bank.

"What they call a savings and loan," said Stewart.

"You been inside?"

"Once. Shorty's been in there, too. We seen everything we needed to see. A single armed guard, guy's older than dirt. We ain't gonna fuck with no safe. Gotta be thousands behind that counter alone. It's a cakewalk, Dom. I shit you not."

Martini stared at the bank, openmouthed. "What now?"

"We're meetin' Shorty for lunch up at the Shepherd. We'll talk about it then."

Stewart put the Belvedere in gear, pulled off the curb, and swung a U in the middle of Georgia. He turned up the Mary and Marvin; he'd seen Wells and Gaye sing this one together onstage at the Howard, back in '64, and the song made him smile, remembering how happy he'd felt that night. He goosed the gas. It wasn't but a short hop to the Shepherd Park Restaurant, but Stewart liked to hear his Plymouth run. They parked in the side lot, next to Hess's mother's car, a three-on-the-tree pea green '64 Rambler Ambassador, which Walter Hess had been driving the past two days.

The familiarity of the Shepherd hit Martini as they came through the front doors. He'd come here with his family in the '50s, when Angelo was his shadow and his old man was still occasionally sober. Back then, the place was owned and run by brothers George and John Glekas. Its signature was its burgers and steaks, and a waitress with a shrieking laugh. Prominent Maryland politicians shared the dining room with families and local eccentrics. Mrs. Glekas, George's wife, could often be seen at one of the tables, typing menus with one finger while she gave emotional orders to her daughter Angie. The restaurant had since been sold to three other Greeks, but the pleasant smell of grilled beef and the sound of that waitress, laughing at something back in the kitchen, told Martini that little here had changed.

The tables and wall booths were half full. A bar separated by a load-bearing post ran along the back wall, its stools occupied by workingmen. It was a no-tablecloth, no-linen eat house, with basic service and good food, common in Greek ownership. Soon it would become one of the most notorious, raucous strip bars in the area. But for now it was frozen in time.

Hess was seated at one of the dining-room tables, wearing his blue uniform shirt with "Shorty" stitched to a patch.

"That your hot rod out front?" said Stewart, pulling a wooden chair out from under the table and resting his huge frame upon it.

"Knock it off," said Hess.

"Rambler makes a real quality vehicle. Fast, too. That the Am-*bass*-a-dor or the A-*mer*-ican? I never can tell them race cars apart."

"I said knock it off. I'm gonna be drivin' my Ford any day now."

"I wouldn't count on it," said Stewart. "And we got another problem, too."

Stewart told them about his phone call from Pat Millikin, which he had taken at the Esso station just before he and Martini had gone on break. The Galaxie was going to be in the shop a few more days. Also, Millikin claimed that he had not been able to find them a rental. Stewart had pressed him on it, but Millikin had assured him there was nothing to be had.

"What's goin' on with him?" said Hess.

"I don't know. He says the market's dried up."

"Dried up, huh? He needs to remember that back in the joint, I shanked some coon who was white-eyein' his brother. Man owes me big. You tell him that?"

"I did. And I got the same answer he gave me the first time." Stewart looked at Martini. "We're gonna have to use your car."

"*What?*"

"Well, we can't use mine. Way it looks, bright red, with the wedge and all, everyone around this part of town recognizes that car. Hell, you hardly even drive that Nova anymore."

"What about my plates?"

"Shorty's gonna provide us with some new ones."

"A car'll come up soon," said Martini. "Why can't we wait a few days?"

"'Cause we can't," said Stewart. "That little accident we had the other night kinda changed everything. Me and Shorty been talkin'. We ain't stickin' around to find out if that comes back on us, see? We're leaving town, soon as we score that money. Myrtle Beach. Daytona, maybe. Someplace down South."

"I'm out," said Martini with a small wave of his hands, as if he were trying to push them away.

"Pretty Boy don't get it, Buzz. Boy is thick."

"Shut up, Shorty."

"Nah, see, he just don't get it." Hess pushed his face close to Martini's. "You're in, *Dominic*. You were with us the other night when we pegged that coon, and you are in now. You better pray we do this job right and make enough jack to get out of this situation clean. You gonna help us do that. We ain't askin' you, dad."

"Look at me, Dom," said Stewart. "*Look* at me."

Martini met Stewart's eyes.

"All's we need is a driver. Me and Shorty'll do the rest. We get gone, you go on about your life. Hear?"

"When?" said Martini.

"I'm off tomorrow. You can just call in sick. We'll go before they close the bank, late in the afternoon."

A waitress, flame-red hair and wide of hip, arrived at their four-top, a small pad and pencil in her hand. The men, who had been grouped tightly around the table, leaned back in their seats.

"Three cheeseburger platters, all the way around," said Stewart. "Three Cokes."

"How you want those burgers cooked?"

"Medium," said Stewart.

"The same way," said Martini.

"I like mine warm and pink inside," said Hess, smiling at the waitress, winking one of his crossed eyes.

"That would be medium rare," said the waitress, writing on her pad, not looking once at Hess. She walked back to the kitchen, fatigue in her step.

"She thinks I'm the most," said Hess.

"The most repulsive," said Stewart.

Stewart and Hess laughed.

When the waitress brought the Cokes, Stewart tapped his glass against Martini's.

"All for one," said Stewart.

Martini looked away.

ALVIN JONES HAD thrown the gloves he'd worn down a sewer hole in Shaw, then driven to another street a few blocks away and lost the straight razor the same way. He'd boosted the gloves from the D. J. Kaufman's near 10th and Penn, so there wasn't any loss there, and you could always get your hands on a knife. Anyway, it wasn't like he was naked; he still had his gun.

After getting rid of the evidence, Jones had driven over to Lula Bacon's place, woke her and her baby up, got his favorite hat and the few other things he owned out the closet, put them in a duffel bag, and left. Bitch asked him where he was going as he headed out the door, but he felt no need to answer. Wasn't none of her business, anyway. He'd slept on the couch at his cousin's place, over off 7th. Had to wake him up, too, to get inside.

Now Jones was sitting in the cramped living room of Ronnie's apartment, watching television, wanting a drink. But Ronnie wasn't into liquid heat. Boy didn't even keep beer or wine in his crib, and he didn't like to burn the gage, either. Jones couldn't relate to a man wasn't looking to get his head up in some way.

Every man had something, though, made him get out of bed in the morning. For Ronnie it was ass. Sure, it drove every-goddamn-one, but Ronnie was sick behind it. Even took those instant photographs of all the girls he had, kept the pictures in a book, had a label glued on the front of it with childlike handwriting scribbled across it, read, "My Pussy Portraits." Matter of fact, Ronnie had recently bought a new Big Swinger, thirty dollars at the Peoples Drug, 'cause he'd worn out the Polaroid he had.

Ronnie had gone off to his job after lunch. He worked as a stock man down at George and Co., the big-and-tall-men's shop on 7th. Ronnie went six four or five and claimed he took the position there for the discount. He couldn't find clothes anywhere else that fit him right.

Soon as he was gone, Jones went and got the photo album. All kinds of girls in that book: dark-skinned girls, white girls, redbones, skinny bitches, and some fat-ass heifers, too. All cupping their titties, pushing them together and out, smiling and lying across Ronnie's bed, some kind of stuffed bunny rabbit placed beside 'em, the same pose every time. Some of these girls were so ugly, God couldn't love 'em. At least no one could accuse Ronnie of discrimination. All kinds of females, and Ronnie didn't have any problem getting them over to his place or getting them to pose. Jones had seen him plenty of times, walking around the apartment in his altogether. Man should have been wearing a saddle on his back, with that pipe of his.

After Jones had looked at the pictures and jacked his rod, he had sat down to watch TV. Nothing on but the *Match Game*, Mike Douglas, and *Pat Boone in Hollywood*, had Flip Wilson as a guest. Flip was wearing a dress and looking like he was digging it, giving white people their idea of black, talkin' about "Sock it to me," that same old tired shit. Jones changed over to channel 20, the UHF station, where sometimes they showed the bullfights from Mexico. He often wondered what that would feel like, to push a sword down into the head of one of those motherfuckers, straight into its brain. You got to wear those tight pants, too, and hear those cheers from the stands. In that way it was different than killing a man. But only in that way. You got down to it, anything alive just suffered in the end.

The bullfighting show wasn't on. Just something called *Wing Ding,* had to be for kids. He switched over to *Movie 4.* They were running some picture called *Francis of Assisi.* He wasn't gonna watch no sissy movie, that was for damn sure.

Jones decided to go out, get a cheap bottle of something, and bring it back. If he was going to have to be bored, he might as well be bored with his head on fire. He was out of Kools, too.

STRANGE WENT UP to 9th and Upshur and made the funeral arrangements at a home his father had used for his own mother. He had always liked this short stretch of 9th, which was quiet, faced Georgia Avenue from the east, and held a few small businesses: a barbershop and a butcher and such. Inside the home, he met with an overly polite, fastidious man in a pinstriped suit. Strange arranged it so that the viewing would be closed-casket, with the schedule dependent upon the completion of the autopsy and lab work by the police.

When he came out of the funeral home, Lydell Blue was waiting for him, standing on the sidewalk, in his uniform. They hugged roughly and patted each other's backs.

"Your father told me you'd be here," said Blue.

"Glad you got up with me, man."

"Us," said Blue, rapping his fist to his chest.

"Us," said Strange.

His parents' house was crowded with sympathizers upon his return. As it tended to do in the city, word had spread of Dennis's death. Relatives, neighbors, friends of Derek and his parents, and some of Dennis's friends from Park View Elementary, Bertie Backus Junior High, and Roosevelt High had gathered in the apartment. Dennis had lost touch with many of them since going off to the navy, but they had not forgotten him. Alvin Jones and Kenneth Willis had not dropped by or phoned.

Someone, maybe his father, had put an old Soul Stirrers record on the box, Sam Cooke singing pretty and rough, and it was playing low under the conversation in the room. People were having cigarettes and cigars, and the smoke lay thick in the air. A little bit of beer and wine drinking had commenced. Mike and Billy Georgelakos were standing in a corner together, still wearing their work clothes from the diner. Derek went to them, shook Mike's hand, hugged Billy, and thanked them for coming, knowing they were uncomfortable being here, knowing it was an effort, appreciating the effort, making a point of telling them that they were family. Derek had a conversation with Troy Peters, who had arrived in his uniform, his hat literally in his hand. He told Troy how much it meant to him that he had stopped by. He spoke to James Hayes and said he would get up with him later. He spoke to the German, now an old man, now contrite, who had once thrown hot water at him and Dennis when they were kids. He spoke to Mr. Meyer from the corner market. He took a condolence call from Darla Harris, who asked him to stop by that night. He told her that he might, and ended the call. And he went to Carmen Hill as soon as he saw her come through the door. As he brought her into his arms, it seemed they were alone in the room.

"I love you, Derek," she said, her mouth close to his ear.

"I love *you*."

When she had gone, he looked around the apartment and noticed that his parents were not among the crowd.

He asked the woman who lived downstairs if he could use her phone. In her apartment, he phoned Detective Dolittle at the station. Five minutes later, his call was returned. There was little to report on the case. No usable fingerprints had been turned up at the scene. No witnesses had come forward. Kenneth Willis had been picked up on a gun charge the Monday afternoon before the murder. Dolittle said he would interview Willis in his holding cell soon as he "got over that way," and when Strange suggested he do it now, Dolittle said, "Don't worry, Willis isn't going anywhere." Lula Bacon had been located, but Alvin Jones was not at her apartment. He had left her place, she said, in the middle of the night, and had not revealed his destination.

"You talked to Bacon?" said Strange.

"On the phone."

"Why don't you go over and see if he's there instead of taking that woman at her word?"

"That's an idea," said Dolittle, his voice slow and heavy with sarcasm. Strange wondered what bar Dolittle had come from last.

He asked for the location of the Bacon apartment, and Dolittle gave him the address. He asked for the make of Jones's car, and Dolittle told him that a green Buick Special was registered in his name.

"Find him," said Strange. "Focus on *him*."

"I'm workin' on it," said Dolittle.

Strange hung up the phone, his eyes fixed on nothing across the room.

He returned to the impromptu wake, made his way through the crowd, and found his parents back in Dennis's room. He closed the door behind him, muffling the rumble of conversation coming from the main area of the apartment. His father stood with his back against the wall, a beer in his hand, his sleeves rolled up. His mother sat on Dennis's bed, her hands folded neatly in her lap.

Alethea looked up. "Who would do this, Derek?"

"I don't know. But I'm going to find out."

Alethea glanced at her husband, then stared at Derek in a way that made him feel ten years old. "You've got to let the Lord settle this in his own way. Do you understand me, son?"

"Yes, ma'am," said Derek.

CHARLIE BYRD HAD that sound. You could close your eyes and listen to his guitar and know that it couldn't be anyone playing it but him. Frank Vaughn found himself smiling, hearing it now.

He sat at the bar of the Villa Rosa, on Ellsworth Drive in Silver Spring. The place was done in dark wood and paneling, and it was a pleasant place to drink. Married couples, adulterous couples, and singles sat around him, talking low, as Charlie and his quartet played that jazzy samba sound from back in the Byrd's Nest, the show area of the restaurant and club.

"How's it goin', Frank?" said a smooth voice as a man in a turtleneck and a bright sharkskin sport jacket passed behind him.

"I can't complain," said Vaughn to Pete Lambros, the owner of the club. Lambros had owned the Showboat, down on 18th and Columbia, for years and had recently opened the Villa Rosa out in the suburbs. Crime and a lack of Adams Morgan parking had driven him north, over the D.C. line.

"Another?" said the bartender, long sideburns, longish hair, had that Johnny Reb–Civil War look going on. He had just come on shift. Vaughn didn't need another. He was on his fourth.

"Beam," said Vaughn.

"Rocks, right?"

"Make it neat."

The tender free-poured bourbon into a heavy glass and set it on a cocktail napkin. Vaughn drew an L&M from the deck and used his Zippo to give it fire. With the fetishism common in bar lovers, he placed his lighter squarely atop his pack of smokes and pulled a tray to within ashing distance of his hand, leaning his forearm just so on the lip of the stick. Cigarettes, whiskey, and walking-around money. What more, thought Vaughn, did a man need?

Well, there was work. And women. He had two of those. One for companionship and memories, and one for sex. He'd been with Linda that afternoon, and it had been good. He'd fucked her strong, and she had given that strength back in equal measure. Her thighs were in spasm when they were done. Their lovemaking had been so physical that when it was over, the bed was halfway across the room from where it had started.

"You know those little round rubber things," said Vaughn, "you put 'em under the rollers of the bed frame? You need to get a set of those."

"That would spoil the ride."

Vaughn chuckled low. Linda kissed him hard on the mouth, her long brown hair damp with sweat.

He wasn't in love with her, and he wasn't with her just for sex. He could get that free and clear from any one of the many prostitutes he knew downtown. Vaughn needed to know that there was a woman out there who still wanted him, waited for him to drop by or call, thought about him *that way* when he wasn't there. Not out of marital duty or mercy but because it made her dizzy to imagine him. It meant he was still in the game and still very much alive. And that's what it came down to with him. That's why he fucked a woman he didn't love instead of staying faithful to one he did. When he was deep inside that silk, he was laughing at death.

Vaughn drank off half his shot. He dragged on his cigarette and tapped ash off its tip.

At least he was pure at work. Not honest, but pure. His job was to close homicide investigations, and, regardless of his methods, there was no one better at it than he. But he had been a genuine sonofabitch to his family. He'd been a real failure with Ricky, who he hardly knew. The best he could say was that he'd kept Ricky out of harm's way.

Not that anything could guarantee your kid's safety. You could still lose them, even if you did them right. Look at Alethea and her husband, what was his name, Darrin, somethin' like that. No, he was thinking of Derek, the young man, the cop. That good young black cop. There, I said *black* instead of *colored*. You happy, Olga? God, I am drunk.

Alethea had lost her oldest to the streets. Wasn't surprising, where they lived. Down there, coloreds were the perpetrators and the victims. But it never should have happened to a nice family like that. What they needed now was the satisfaction and peace of knowing who killed their son. That false pat on the shoulder, telling them the murder had been "solved." Of course, no murder ever got solved, not unless you could bring back the dead. And there'd always be another grieving mother, right behind the last. Like the mother of that boy who got run down on 14th, and now Alethea Strange. There just wasn't any way to protect the ones you loved. Even when you did them right . . .

"You all right here?" said the bartender.

"Gimme my check," said Vaughn.

He raised his glass, looked at his heavy-lidded eyes in the bar mirror, and killed his drink.

LATE IN THE evening, Strange left his parents' apartment, drove over to his place, showered, and changed his clothes. He put on a black leather car coat, dropped his badge into one of its pockets, and slipped his service revolver, a .38 Special, into the holster he had clipped onto his belt. He went back out to his Impala, parked on 13th, and drove down the big hill alongside Cardozo High.

He had no destination in mind. He rolled down the windows and let the cool, damp air of April hit his face. He got the all-news station on the radio, listened to a report on a massive rally for RFK on Park Road in Columbia Heights, and switched the radio off. He drove into the heart of Shaw.

Heading west, he passed the Republic Theater, the London Custom clothing store, National Liquors, and the Jumbo Nut Shop, and came to the intersection of 14th and U, which had been cleared of debris from the disturbance on the previous night. On the northeast corner, cardboard had been in-

serted in the broken glass door of the Peoples Drug. Hustlers,
pimps, whores, men dressed as women, pushers and addicts,
workers who had gotten off buses and had not yet gone home,
and kids who were out too late for their own good cruised the
sidewalks.

Strange turned around at 16th Street and doubled back to
7th, checking out the action near the Howard Theater and the
active life on the street. He was killing time. He had told Darla
Harris he might get up with her, but he had no intention of
meeting her tonight. Seeing Carmen the other night, seeing
her come into his parents' apartment today, knowing she had
missed her classes to do so, still feeling her hot breath in his
ear, had erased Darla Harris completely from his mind.

Down below Howard University, he drove into the low-
numbered streets of LeDroit Park. He went by the row house
where Lula Bacon had her apartment and slowed his Chevy.
The lights inside her place had been extinguished. He circled
the block, saw no green Buick Special parked in the vicinity,
and drove on. Dennis had spoken of another woman with
whom Jones had fathered a baby. Dennis, Willis, and Jones
had been at her place, getting their heads up, on Sunday
evening. But Strange did not know her name or where she
lived. He'd come back and speak to Lula Bacon. Also, he'd
speak to James Hayes. If that woman had been involved in
some kind of dope thing with Dennis and them, Hayes would
know. But for now, all Strange could do was drive.

He ended his night, as he knew he would, parked on
Barry Place, in front of the row house where Carmen stayed.
He went up the concrete walk to the house, then took the
wooden steps to the third floor and knocked on her door. Carmen did not answer. A middle-aged woman with a hard face
came out of her apartment and asked Strange what his business was in the house. Strange said he was calling on his
friend Carmen Hill.

"She went out with some of her college friends," said the woman, looking him over. "You want to leave a message, somethin'?"

"No," said Strange.

He went back to his parents' apartment because he couldn't stand to go back to his place alone. His father was seated in his chair, in the dark, watching *Wanted: Dead or Alive* with the sound down low. Derek stood behind him and placed one hand on his father's shoulder, noticing his father's fingers tight on the arms of the chair.

"Derek," he said, staring at the screen, his shoulder relaxing under his son's touch.

"You don't mind," said Derek, "I'm gonna stay the night."

"I was hoping you would."

"Pop?"

"What?"

"I don't want you to worry. I'm gonna take care of this, hear?"

"Your mother told you something tonight. I want you to mind it."

"I will."

"You been given a responsibility, son. You're not just protecting your community out here. You're representing us, too. You do something to betray that, you don't deserve to be wearin' that uniform."

"Yes, sir."

"Go on, boy," said Darius. "And be quiet goin' along back there. I don't want you to wake your mother."

Derek fell asleep in Dennis's bed, the smell of his brother in the room.

TWENTY-FOUR

O N THURSDAY, APRIL 4, in Memphis, Dr. King met with his staff in a room of the Lorraine Hotel and made plans for Monday's march.

At midmorning in D.C., Alethea Strange answered a knock on her door. In the open frame stood a dark-skinned man, near her husband's age, with gray in his close-cropped hair. A bag of groceries was cradled in his arm.

"My name is John Thomas. Is this the Strange residence?"

"Yes."

"Are you the mother of Dennis?"

"I am."

"My sympathies on the death of your son."

Alethea cocked her head. "Were you a friend to Dennis?"

"Not exactly. We spoke briefly this past Monday. I read about his death in the *Post* this morning. I was up here, picking up a few things from Mr. Meyer, down on the corner. He and the man I work for, Ludvig, they both own markets. They're friends, from synagogue. . . ."

"Yes?"

"When one runs out of something, the other helps him out. I volunteered to come pick this stuff up, after reading the papers. . . . Your son told me you lived up on Princeton, so I asked Mr. Meyer where your place was."

"I don't understand." Alethea had backed up a step and was holding on to the door for support. "Why have you come here?"

Thomas knew he was talking too fast, confusing the woman, who was obviously weak with grief. But he was nervous, too, and didn't quite know how to get to the point.

"I knew your husband," said Thomas.

"I don't recall him ever speaking of you."

"We weren't tight. . . . What I mean is, I knew him by sight, from the American Legion. Post Five? I used to see him at those meetings at Republic Gardens, long time ago. We talked a few times, you know." Thomas cleared his throat. "I was wondering, could I speak with him for a minute, if he's not too busy? I've got some information about your son."

"My husband is at work," said Alethea.

Darius had gone in early, despite the fact that Mike Georgelakos had insisted he take the day off. Darius felt that the place would fall apart without him, and anyway, it was worse for him to be sitting around the apartment with nothing to occupy his mind. Alethea understood. She was not physically ready to return to work, but she would be soon. In fact, she planned to go to her regular Friday house, the Vaughns', the next day.

"Maybe I ought to stop by later," said Thomas. "I don't mean to trouble you."

"Please come in," said Alethea, pulling back the door, stepping aside. "My younger son, Derek, is here."

"I should stop by later," said Thomas, not wanting to say what he had to say to some kid.

"If you have some information," said Alethea with a sudden firmness, "you should speak to my son. Please come in."

Thomas did as he was told and stepped into the apartment. As he entered, Derek Strange emerged from a hall leading to the bedrooms.

"What's goin' on?" said Derek.

"This man is here to see you," said Alethea.

"About what?" said Derek, in no mood for pleasantries.

"You can speak freely," said Alethea, looking at the man with the gray hair and the kind eyes. "My son's police."

———

VAUGHN SAT AT the kitchen table in his boxers and a T-shirt, nursing a hangover that two Anacin, coffee, eggs and bacon, and a couple of L&Ms had not yet cured. He read the sports page, mechanically saying "yep" and "uh-huh" and "yes, Olga" every so often, as his wife described a pair of double-strap sling-back patents she'd seen at the Franklin Simon in the new Montgomery Mall. She leaned against the sink, her yellow apron standing out in contrast to her helmet of raven black hair.

"They're only sixteen dollars," said Olga. "It's not like it's gonna break us."

"It's only money," said Vaughn, his lids at half-mast, his eyes squarely on the paper spread before him. "Easy come, easy go."

Vaughn read that the Baltimore Bullets, who had finished in last place the previous season, were looking to draft Wes Unseld, the big All-American kid out of Louisville.

"I can put them on our Central Charge," said Olga.

"That's an idea," said Vaughn. Not a good idea, but an idea.

The Kentucky Colonels, from that new league, were trying to get Unseld as well. Coach Shue would pull it off. Shue was all right. Vaughn had seen him in a bar one time, with a nice-looking redhead, lighting her cigarette. A man's man.

"Frank, are you listening to me?"

"Yes, Olga."

The phone, canary yellow like Olga's apron, rang in the kitchen. Olga crossed the linoleum and snatched the receiver off the wall.

"Vaughn residence . . . Just a moment." She held the receiver out for Vaughn. "It's you. Business."

Vaughn's arm shot out with a rush of energy he had not felt all morning. "Frank Vaughn here."

He listened to the man on the other end of the line. He told the man that he needed an hour, to "shit, shower, and shave."

"See you there," said Vaughn before hanging up the phone.

"What're you smiling about?" said Olga as Vaughn got out of his chair.

"I got a hit," said Vaughn.

Going up the stairs to the split-level's second floor, he passed Ricky, coming down with books under his arm on his way to classes. Vaughn said nothing to his son, thinking only about the phone call and what it meant. He had that feeling he got, light on his feet, when he was close.

———

"THIS WAS WHEN, exactly?" said Strange.

"Sunday evening," said Thomas. "They had parked that Monterey under a streetlight. It was lit up there enough for me to see 'em and write down the tag numbers, too."

"You're certain of the car?"

"Monterey's the only car I know got that squared-off rear window."

"Right," said Strange. "And Dennis tipped you to the robbery on Monday?"

"Uh-huh. Early in the day. Said those other two were planning to take the place off."

They were in Dennis's bedroom, Strange standing, his back leaned against the wall, John Thomas seated in a chair. Strange had closed the door so that his mother could not hear their conversation.

"What'd you do next?"

"I called an MPD lieutenant I grew up with. Man named William Davis." Thomas saw recognition creep into Strange's face at the mention of Davis's name. "You know Bill?"

"Not personally. Used to notice him when I was a kid. At the time, he was a beat cop up in the Sixth."

"Wasn't many black patrolmen then."

"Why I noticed him, I guess," said Strange. "Keep going."

"I told Bill what I knew, leaving out your brother's name to protect him. Bill told me later that they'd picked up the driver of the Monterey on a gun charge. The other man in the passenger seat, I don't know what happened to him. What I do know is that we didn't get robbed. So what your brother did was right."

"Describe the other man," said Strange, without emotion.

"Light-skinned, looked to be on the small side, maybe because he was sitting beside the one under the wheel. *That* boy had some size on him. The little dude wore a hat. That's all I could make out."

That's plenty, thought Strange. That is more than enough.

"Did you call Lieutenant Davis when you saw my brother's obituary?"

"No, I didn't." Thomas stared at Strange thoughtfully. "Do you want me to?"

"No," said Strange. He uncrossed his arms and softened his tone. "I'd appreciate it if you didn't say anything to him, not unless I . . . not unless my family asks you to. I don't mean to cause you any trouble with your friend. It's just that, you know, we'd like to go about this in our own way and time. Anyway, you've done plenty for us already."

"I don't know about that," said Thomas. "It's been hard for me to deal with this today. Truth is, I feel like I set something in motion that got your brother killed."

"You're wrong to feel that way," said Strange. "I'd say you gave him hope. He was happy the last time I saw him, like he'd confessed. You did him right. You'd be doin' him right again if you keep this between us."

"I will," said Thomas, getting up from his chair. He went to Dennis's nightstand, picked up a book off the top of a stack, and examined its cover. "We had a nice discussion about this one the day he visited me."

"He could talk," said Strange, smiling a little for the first time in the past two days. "Argue, too."

"There was truth in what he was sayin'. He had a right to be angry. We all do."

"Yes."

"Young black men out here, killin' each other. Someday we gonna focus our anger in the right direction."

"Sounds like somethin' Dennis would say to my father to get him fired up."

"My son does the same way with me. If I remember correctly, the few times I talked to your father at those meetings, he was just as angry at the injustices out here as your brother was. If he disagreed with your brother, I suspect it was because he was trying to calm him down, protect him from harm. The same way I do with my son."

"My father couldn't protect him."

"Young men from good homes find trouble, too. Anyone could see that your brother had come on rough times. But there's something you should tell your parents: When he came by to see me, he told me how proud he was of his family. I think it's important that they know."

"Yes, sir," said Strange, a crack in his voice.

"All right, then. Let me get out of here."

"Thank you." Strange looked away, ashamed at the tears that had come to his eyes. "You don't mind, I'm just gonna stay here a minute, get my thoughts together."

John Thomas nodded and left the room.

FRANK VAUGHN AND Lawrence Houston sat in the front seat of Vaughn's Polara, in the parking lot of the Tick Tock liquor store at University Boulevard and Riggs Road, drinking Schlitz from cans wrapped in brown paper bags. Houston's plum-colored Dart GT was parked nearby. The first beer had erased the last of Vaughn's headache but had gone down bitter. This one, his second, was going down good.

Houston still wore his coveralls from the garage. He had told his boss, Pat Millikin, that he had to run his sister to the doctor's and needed an hour, an hour and a half of break time. He had suggested the Tick Tock location to Vaughn because it wasn't far from the garage. Also, he wanted a cold can of beer.

"Tell it," said Vaughn. "Time's gettin' short."

"We need to get straight on somethin' first."

"Okay."

"I ain't used to talkin' to police."

"You're here, aren't you?"

"*I* know it."

"You called *me*. You told me you had something on that Ford."

Houston shifted in his seat. "Pat's been good to me, man. Gave me my job straight out of the joint. I mean he *always* did me right. And you know, when I came out, people weren't interested in hiring no violent offender. Pat took a chance on me, treated me with respect."

"So Pat's a swell guy."

"What I'm sayin' is, I don't want to wrong him."

"Listen, Lawrence, I'm not looking to jack Millikin up, if that's what you're worried about. The Prince George's police already know all about the phony inspection certificates coming out of that garage, and they haven't made a move on him yet. They're waitin', see? At some point, they're gonna squeeze him for something big. He's more valuable as a source of information than he is in jail."

"I don't want Pat to get in no trouble over this, is all."

"I can't promise you that. If he's involved with that vehicle in any way, we're gonna need his testimony to support the charges. Yours, too, most likely."

Houston had a long swig of beer, then turned the brown bag in his lap.

Vaughn looked him over. "What were you in for?"

"Manslaughter."

"Musta had a temper on you."

"I still do." Houston side-glanced Vaughn, veins standing out on his temples, veins shifting on his wrists and the backs of his hands. "Why I'm here, I guess."

"Come on, Lawrence. Talk to me."

Houston reached inside the chest area of his coveralls and withdrew a cigarette. Vaughn shook an L&M from his deck. He flipped open the lid of his Zippo, lit Houston's smoke, lit his own, and snapped the lighter shut. Vaughn let the cigarette dangle from his mouth as he opened a small spiral notebook and thumbed down the top of a ballpoint pen.

"I got a kid brother, took the straight road," said Houston. "Went to one of those good Negro colleges down South, got a government job, owns a house, has a wife and kids . . . I mean, he did it all right. That could have been my brother got run down in that street. Cut down for nothin' but his color, you understand?"

"What about the car?" said Vaughn.

"Couple of men brought it in on Monday. Red Galaxie Five Hundred, all messed up in the front."

"Sixty-three or sixty-four?"

"Sixty-three and a half," said Houston with a hint of pride.

"And these guys said what?"

"Driver of the Galaxie, little sawed-off, cross-eyed white boy name of Walter Hess. Goes by Shorty? Said he hit a monkey in the street. Was smilin' about it, too. He was talking about that young brother you described, I expect. "

"Walter Hess," said Vaughn, writing it down.

"White boy he came in with? Big dude, wears his sleeves rolled high to show his muscles. Last name Stewart. I don't know what his Christian name is, but he goes by Buzz."

"They came in two cars."

"Yeah. This Buzz Stewart was drivin' a red Belvedere, white hardtop, tricked out with a Max Wedge hood."

As Vaughn wrote, he felt his face flush with blood. He knew that car. "Tag numbers?"

"I got 'em off the Ford," said Houston. He pulled a crumpled piece of paper from his pocket and read the numbers off to Vaughn.

"Anything else?"

"The Belvedere had a name, kind of scripted on its side, you know how them gearheads do."

"What was the name?"

"Bernadette," said Houston.

Vaughn closed his eyes and tried to picture the car. He saw it parked beside the garage of the Esso station at Georgia and Piney Branch. He saw the big mechanic, the unfriendly greaser with the sleeves of his uniform shirt rolled up high, gunning the lugs off an Oldsmobile that was up on the lift in the bay.

"Bernadette," said Vaughn, nodding his head. "I guess this Buzz has a girlfriend, huh?"

"I'd say he's a Levi Stubbs fan."

"What's that?"

"The Four Tops," said Houston with a small smile. "You listened to the radio the last ten years, you'd know."

Vaughn shrugged.

"By the way, you overplayed it with that story, too," said Houston. "You know, about them spray-paintin' *nigger* in the street."

"You didn't buy it, huh?"

"It was the arrow-pointin'-to-the-body thing that did it. Too complicated for those two."

"I guess I took it too far."

"Thing was, you had me goin' without it."

"Thanks, Lawrence." Vaughn reached across the bench and shook Houston's hand. "You did right."

Houston drove off in his Dart GT. Vaughn killed his Schlitz, flicked his smoke out the open window, and walked to a phone booth in the corner of the lot.

TWENTY-FIVE

STRANGE STOOD ON the landing of the second floor of Lula Bacon's row house, knocking on her apartment door. He wore his black leather car coat over gray slacks and a charcoal shirt, his service revolver in a holster clipped onto the belt line of the slacks. His badge was in the pocket of his coat.

"Yeah?" she said from behind the door.

"Lula Bacon?"

"Who's askin'?"

"I'm a police officer."

"You got some identification?"

Strange badged the peephole, which had darkened in the door.

"What's this about?"

"Open the door, Miss Bacon."

"You don't look like no police."

"You need to open this door right now."

"Or what?"

"Or I come back with the welfare man," said Strange. "He's gonna be real interested in your lifestyle, I expect."

Strange knew nothing about her lifestyle, but his limited experience told him that this was an effective way to gain entry. He heard a chain sliding off a catch and the turn of a dead bolt.

Strange had been to James Hayes's place on Otis first, but Hayes was not in. Morning had become noon. He was due in at work for his four-to-midnight. He had decided to stop calling Dolittle and work this himself. What he was doing wasn't procedure. It was beyond his duty limit and probably illegal. But he felt he was running out of time.

The door opened. A petite woman wearing a short navy blue shift stood in the frame. She had shapely legs and hips. She had big eyes accentuated by dark makeup, large hoop earrings, and store-done hair. A glass of amber-colored liquor over ice was loose in her hand. She smelled of whiskey and cigarettes. Bacon looked like a sloppy Diana Ross.

Strange did not move to go inside. "I'm lookin' for Alvin Jones."

"He ain't in. I don't expect him back, neither."

"Any idea where he went to?"

"No idea," she said lazily, leaning her figure into the door. A baby cried from far back in the apartment.

"He's got another girlfriend, right?" said Strange, unconcerned with diplomacy or her feelings.

"That ain't news."

"Maybe he moved back in with her."

"So?"

"You know her name or where she stay at?"

Bacon shrugged and drank off some of her liquor.

"Well?"

"I don't know nothin'."

"You lyin', I'm gonna come back."

"Big man," said Bacon, looking him over, "you can come back anytime, even if I'm tellin' the truth."

"I'm spoken for," said Strange.

"Then send your brother over, you got one. That is, if he looks like you."

"Your baby's crying," said Strange in an even way. "You best get yourself together and see to that child."

"You run into Alvin, you tell him he done lost this good thing forever."

She was talking to his back. Strange had already begun to take the stairs down to the street.

VAUGHN COMMANDEERED THE phone booth in the lot of the Tick Tock. He phoned the Esso station and got the correct name of the employee, Carlton "Buzz" Stewart. He was told by the manager, who sounded harried, that this was Stewart's day off. Vaughn then called the Sixth Precinct station and told the guy manning the Homicide desk what he needed. It required more than a little work, and he knew it would take time. While he waited, Vaughn stood in the lot, smoking and guarding the phone, and drinking Schlitz from a can wrapped in a brown paper bag. A county cop approached him about the open beer; Vaughn badged him and showed him his uppers, and the cop shoved off. By the time Vaughn got the return call, it was after noon. He put all the information into his notebook and went to his car.

He had instructed his man to put out a bulletin, with descriptions, over the radio: two men, Walter Hess, aka Shorty Hess, and Carlton Stewart, aka Buzz Stewart, were wanted for questioning in the hit-and-run death of Vernon Wilson. It was the very soft version of an all-points bulletin. If they were to be stopped for, say, a traffic violation, and the uniform radioed in the information, the bulletin would send up a flag. Both men had sheets, and Hess was an ex-con. But Vaughn suspected that their crime was the result of a drunken night, and though he thought they were stupid and probably cruel, he did not believe them to be dangerous. Plus, he wanted the collar for himself.

He drove to the 700 block of Silver Spring Avenue off Georgia, a quarter mile northeast of the District line. The street consisted primarily of bungalows set close to the curb, with deep, sloping backyards lightly forested in oak, walnut, and pine. The residents were second-wave, postwar, blue- and gray-collar workers, many of German descent, who had purchased these houses, built in the 1920s, on the GI Bill. Their kids were going or gone. Bikers and young tradesmen had begun to rent the houses as the homeowners neared retirement age and drifted off. Vaughn knew that some of these renters used and possibly dealt marijuana and speed. He had sat beside them at the bars up on Georgia on a couple of occasions, had struck up conversations with them and seen the drugs in their jacked-up eyes.

According to his information, Walter Hess lived with his parents in a baby blue bungalow with white trim and a broad front porch, located at the crest of a hill. Vaughn found Hess's mother at home. He told her that he and Shorty had worked together at the machine shop on Brookeville Road before he'd moved on, and that he was just dropping in on his old bud on the long shot that he might be in.

"He's at work," said the woman, who was not old but had whiskers sprouting from her chin. She hung back in the doorway and did not step out into the natural light or ask him in. The house smelled of cabbage and dog. There was dog hair swirled upon her embroidered apron. Her eyes were close set. She breathed through her mouth and looked slightly retarded. She was no taller than a child.

"I shoulda known," said Vaughn. "That Galaxie of his ain't around."

"It's in the shop. He's drivin' our Rambler."

"Oh, yeah, he mentioned once that you all had one. That old blue one, right?"

"Green. You want me to tell him you stopped by?"

"I think I'll surprise him at the shop," said Vaughn. "Thank you, ma'am."

Vaughn drove over to Mississippi Avenue, looking for Buzz Stewart's house, looking for his Belvedere. But it was not parked along the curb or in the open freestanding garage, which he could see from the street. He didn't want to talk to Stewart's people even if they were in. He had already risked too much with Hess's mother.

Vaughn went out to Brookeville Road, a few miles away, to an industrial area near Montgomery Hills, not far from his own house. He found the machine shop, did not see a green Rambler in the vicinity, and parked nearby. Shortly thereafter a man in a blue work shirt with his name stitched on the breast patch walked out of the shop and lit a cigarette. Vaughn rolled down the window of his Polara and shouted to the man.

"Hey, fella, you seen my buddy Shorty? We supposed to meet here on his break." Vaughn doing his idea of redneck, which was not much of a stretch.

"His whole life's a break," said the man, dragging hungrily on his cigarette.

"Where's he at, then?" said Vaughn.

"Called in sick," said the man, flicking ash at his work boots. "Must have that Irish flu."

Vaughn rolled his window up, turned the key in his Dodge, and took off up the road. So neither Hess nor Stewart was at work. Maybe they got so shitfaced the night before they couldn't work. But Hess had told his mother he was going to work. Maybe what it was, Hess and Stewart had anticipated the heat and left town. Vaughn didn't think the little grease monkey would leave D.C. without his Galaxie. But he couldn't be sure.

He drove to a phone booth outside a body shop. He phoned the station to see if there had been any flags on the bulletin. The desk sergeant told him there was nothing to report. He had received only one message, from a cop named Derek Strange. Strange had asked that Vaughn give him a call.

"Gimme the number where he's at," said Vaughn. He pulled his notebook and pen from his jacket, and wrote the number down.

STRANGE SAT IN the living room of an Otis Place apartment, talking with James Hayes. Hayes had gone out for his morning walk, on which he regularly picked up a *Post* and a pack of smokes. The newspaper sat in a heap at the foot of his chair, and a cigarette burned in an ashtray beside him. Hayes wore a velvet jacket. He had changed out of his street shoes and now wore soft leather slippers. He held a cloth handkerchief, which he used to wipe at his runny nose.

"He left out of here when?" said Strange.

"I'm not sure," said Hayes. "Maybe 'round eleven o'clock. I had a woman friend coming over here. She works late on Sunday nights."

"Eleven would fit," said Strange.

"I *had* to put him out," said Hayes. "We were having a good time, just sitting here, listening to some old records and discussin' things. But he had to go."

"Ya'll were gettin' high?"

"Sure."

"Was he lucid?"

"He was a little down on reds. And we had drunk some Margeaux and burned a little smoke. I can't speak for his head.

Far as his feet went, though, he wasn't gone. I wouldn't have let him out the door had he been stumblin'."

"What about his mental state?"

"Good," said Hayes. "He seemed good to me."

"He didn't indicate that he was in danger, anything like that?"

"No."

"The two of you made a transaction, didn't you, on Sunday night?"

Hayes dragged on his cigarette, released two streams of smoke through his nose. He squinted at Strange through the smoke. "That's right. He had delivered a little somethin' to a couple of friends of his."

The phone rang on the stand by the front door. Hayes got up and answered it, then said, "He's right here." He held the phone out to Strange, who crossed the room and grabbed the receiver.

"Derek Strange."

"This is Vaughn."

"Thanks for returning my call."

"What can I do for you?"

"You said you'd help."

"Talk to me."

"I'm out here, seein' what I can piece together."

"About your brother's murder."

"I decided to go around Dolittle," said Strange.

"I don't blame you."

"There's two men I need to talk to. Alvin Jones and Kenneth Willis. They —"

"Slow up. I'm writing this down."

"Alvin Jones . . . Kenneth Willis."

"Okay."

"Willis and Jones were planning to rob a corner market down in LeDroit Park. My brother tipped off the man at the market about the robbery. This man called the police. The police picked up Willis on a gun charge before they had a chance to pull it off."

"What police?" said Vaughn.

"Ninth Precinct," said Strange.

"Who knows what your brother did?"

"The man he told," said Strange, fish-eyeing Hayes. "Other than him, you and me."

"Willis is in custody now?"

"Last I heard."

"I know some people in the Ninth. What about the other one?"

"Jones is in the wind. I'm having a little trouble locating him."

"You gonna be there a minute?"

"Yeah."

"I'll call you back."

Strange hung up the phone. He stayed where he was and looked at James Hayes.

"You hear all that?"

"Maybe I did and maybe I didn't," said Hayes. "You tell me."

"Those names sound familiar to you?"

"No."

"You said that Dennis had sold a little somethin' for you on Sunday night. Did he sell it to Jones and Willis?"

"He could have," said Hayes. "But neither of those names is on the check."

"Say what?"

"Look in that basket right there in front of you," said Hayes. "Should be a check lyin' in there. I been too sick to cash it. Takes enough out of me just to walk to Meyer's for my newspaper and cigarettes."

Strange read the name off the top of the check and scanned the address. "Dennis gave you this?"

Hayes nodded. "That's how he paid for the gage."

The phone rang. Strange picked it up.

"Strange here."

"I spoke to Jim Mahaffie down in the Ninth. Bad news on Willis."

"What is it?"

"He got bounced. They arraigned him on the gun charge, but they couldn't hold him; Willis had soft priors. The attorney they assigned him got him off on a bond."

"When?"

"This morning."

"Damn."

"Look at it like this: You can talk to him alone now, you want to, in your own way."

"Right."

"You know where he stays?"

"Somewhere on H."

"I got his permanent right here," said Vaughn. He gave Strange the address.

"Thanks, Detective."

"Anything," said Vaughn. "You gonna be in today?"

"Four o'clock."

"I'll see you then."

"You're workin' a double?"

"I'm on somethin'," said Vaughn.

Strange cradled the receiver, folded the check, and placed it in his breast pocket. "I'm gonna need this."

"Take it," said Hayes. "Listen, young man . . ."

"You don't have to say it. We're all feeling the same way. There ain't but one man responsible for Dennis's death."

"Good luck," said Hayes.

Strange checked his wristwatch and went out the door.

———

AFTER VAUGHN HUNG up with Strange, he phoned the Stewart residence and got a woman on the line. She sounded tired and old. Vaughn didn't identify himself or use any kind of ruse. He simply asked her if Buzz was in, and when she said no, he asked if she knew where he was.

"He met some friends."

"What friends? Shorty?"

Vaughn heard the woman draw on a cigarette and exhale. "I suppose."

"Was he leaving town?"

"What?"

"Did you see him putting a suitcase or anything like it into his car? Did he act like he wasn't going to be seeing you for a while?"

"Who am I speaking to?"

Vaughn killed the line. He stepped out of the phone booth and went to his car.

TWENTY-SIX

THE WOMAN LIVED on Fairmont Street, west of 13th, just two blocks from Strange's apartment building. Strange stared at the check in his hand, reading the address at the top of it, and then he looked up at the tall row house at the end of a concrete walk. It was one of those old houses capped with a turret, a common architectural touch unique to D.C. The house had probably been fine once, maybe even grand, but it was in disrepair and in need of paint now.

Strange went up the walk and into the ground-floor foyer. He matched the woman's name to the name on one of the mailbox slots and took the stairs up to the second floor. He knocked on her door.

She opened the door without asking who was there. She was young, on the tall side, not yet twenty, her face a mess of large, wide features, her eyes almond shaped, her skin light. Her figure had been lush, most likely, in her early teens, but it had gone to fat. She held a baby wrapped in a blanket, and the baby was fussing, its eyes closed tight, its tiny fingers reaching out. It was trying to get to one of her breasts, which it had been suckling moments before. The woman's shirt, unbuttoned halfway down, was wet with her own milk. She wore bright orange plastic earrings showing a silhouette of an Afroed woman with the words "Black Is Beautiful" written below the silhouette. A crucifix hung between her large breasts.

"Afternoon," said Strange. She had trusting eyes and had opened her door to a stranger without caution. He decided to use that naïveté against her and not tell her that he was police.

"Derek Strange."

"Mary," she said.

"I'm lookin' to get up with Alvin Jones."

"He's not here," said the woman, her voice soft and high.

"Alvin ran with my brother, Dennis. Dennis was killed a couple of nights back."

She nodded slowly and kept her eyes on his. "I'm sorry for your loss."

"I just want to speak with Alvin, see if he can give me some information regarding my brother's last hours."

"I'd like to speak to him, too," she said with a long, tired exhale. "You wanna come in? I need to finish feedin' my little boy."

Strange went through the open door.

THE HOUSES ON the north side of Longfellow Street, between 13th and Colorado Avenue, were detached, with small back-yards ending in garages built along the alley. In the kitchen of the Martini house, Angela Martini prepared her weekly batch of Sunday gravy. Angela had begun by browning pork neck bones, veal shoulder chops, and sausages in hot oil. She was working on the base now. The sauce itself would take three hours to cook. Its garlic and basil smell would linger in the house for days.

In the garage, Dominic Martini, Buzz Stewart, and Walter Hess stood grouped around Martini's Nova. The space was tight, packed with garden implements, a manual push mower, automotive tools, a gas can, and a small bale of chicken wire. Angelo Martini's old bicycle, which still had baseball cards clothespinned to the spokes, leaned against a wall. Two nylon-stocking masks and two plain unbelted raincoats, purchased by Stewart at Montgomery Ward's, hung on pegs.

The door to the garage was closed. Stewart's Belvedere was parked in the alley, tight to the yard. Behind it sat the green Rambler owned by Mrs. Hess.

Walter Hess threw his head back and killed the Schlitz he'd been drinking, then crushed the can in his hand and tossed the empty into a box. He dipped his hand into a brown paper bag and pulled another can free. He pulled the ring, dropped the ring into the hole in the top, and took a swig of beer.

"You better slow down," said Stewart.

"I'm thirsty."

"It's that speed you ate."

"Who don't know *that?*"

"Slow down."

"I could drink a case."

Stewart didn't doubt that he could. Up on Beauties, Hess could take alcohol forever. When he was using amphetamines, beer didn't slur his speech or lame him. It just took the edge off Shorty's hot nerves.

"Dom," said Stewart, "you check the gauges?"

"Pressure's fine," said Martini, staring at his car with dead eyes. "Fluids are tight."

The Nova would not attract attention. It was a two-door Chevy II SS, black over black, and stock in appearance. It had a four-speed Hurst between the buckets and a 350 engine with a four-barrel Holly carb under the hood. It was light, tight, and fast. The Cragar mags were the sole adornment indicating that the car could run.

Hess put himself down on the concrete floor in push-up position and looked under the car.

"No leaks," he said as he rose to his full five foot four inches.

"Said I checked it."

"Just backin' you up, Pretty Boy."

"You get them plates?" said Stewart to Hess.

"They're out in the Rambler. Took 'em off a Mustang out at PG Plaza."

"Told you to get 'em someplace far away."

"I just boosted 'em an hour ago. By the time it gets reported and into the system, them plates'll be down some sewer hole, and you and me will be rich and gone."

"All right." Stewart pointed his chin over the shoulders of Martini and Hess toward the workbench. "Let's see what we got."

An open duffel bag sat on the workbench, and in the bag were guns: the Italian double-trigger twelve-gauge with the cut-down barrel and stock; two S&W .38s with nickel finish, walnut grips, and four-inch barrels; and a Colt Combat .45. The guns had been passed along through the criminal underworld for years. All had been thoroughly cleaned and oiled. All serial numbers had been filed off. Also in the bag were three sets of thin leather gloves, a harness for the cut-down, two shoulder holsters, bricks of bullets in both calibers, a full magazine for the Colt, and shotgun shells with copper-covered loads.

In addition, Stewart had his .38 caliber single-shot derringer slipped into his right boot. Hess was armed with a commando knife with a five-inch stainless blade, sheathed in a scabbard.

They grouped themselves around the bag. Stewart withdrew the shotgun, harness, and shells, and placed them on the bench as Hess dressed himself in the shoulder holsters. Stewart handed him the .38s.

Hess holstered both, cross-drew them, and dry-fired at the wall. He had practiced this in the mirror of his bedroom many times. He stared at the guns for a moment and smiled. He turned, pointed one of them at Martini's face, and pulled its trigger. The hammer fell on an empty chamber, its dull sound echoing in the garage.

Hess cackled like a witch. "Shit, boy, you oughtta see the look on your face."

"That ain't funny, Shorty," said Stewart.

"Aw," said Hess, "old Dom can handle it. Him and his rough-and-tough soldier-boy friends, I bet they seen all sorts of things scarier than that over in 'Nam. Ain't that right, *Dominique?*"

Martini said nothing.

"Here," said Stewart, pulling the Colt from the bag, handing it to Martini. He then handed him its magazine.

Martini palmed the magazine into the grip of the automatic. He thumbed off the safety and racked the receiver. He flashed the gun up and touched the muzzle to Hess's cheek. Hess moved back a step, and Martini went with him. Hess could go no farther than the workbench, and Martini pushed the gun into his cheek and dented it. Hess could do nothing but turn his head. Martini moved the muzzle and pressed it into the side of Hess's porcine right eye. Martini pulled back the lanyard-style hammer and locked it in place.

"Easy," said Stewart, who had not moved at all.

"Those men I served with?" said Martini. "Don't ever mention them again."

"All right," said Hess, his rasp not much more than a whisper. "All right."

Martini stepped back and hefted the heavy steel-framed

Colt. He hadn't held one since his discharge. It felt like part of his hand.

"I need to talk to my mother," said Martini.

"You go on," said Stewart.

Martini placed the automatic on the workbench and walked quietly and ramrod straight from the garage.

"I was only playin' with him," said Hess, rubbing at his cheek.

"All for one," said Stewart with a crooked smile. "That boy's ready now."

VAUGHN DROVE UNDER the B&O railroad tracks at Sligo Avenue, going south toward D.C. He dragged out the last of his L&M. If Hess and Stewart were leaving town, what would be their last stop? Visits to girlfriends. Road beer and cigarettes from Morris Miller's, for sure. The very last stop would be the Esso station, where Stewart could fill up with gas on credit or for free.

Vaughn pitched his smoke out the window. He passed over the District line, then by the Shepherd Park Restaurant, Morris Miller's, the A&P, the drugstore, the dry cleaner, and the small bank at the end of the shopping center, the Capitol Savings and Loan. He goosed the gas and headed for the Esso station at Georgia and Piney Branch Road.

THE APARTMENT SMELLED of soiled diapers and cigarettes. The baby boy, who Mary said was two months old, had been fed and now slept in an old bassinet beside the sofa. Strange sat on the sofa, sipping coffee from a chipped cup set on a dirty saucer, Mary beside him.

"I don't know where he be stayin' at now," said Mary.

"He was here the other night, wasn't he? With Kenneth and my brother?"

"Alvin and them came over to give me a little smoke and take some of my money. He comes by from time to time, when he needs somethin'. But not too much anymore. Basically, he left out of here soon after my baby got born."

"It's hard for some men to handle it."

"It sure was hard for *him*."

"Isn't the boy his?"

"Yes. But that didn't make no difference to Alvin. He said he couldn't stand to hear him cry. I said, 'Alvin, that's what babies do. They just askin' for somethin' when they cryin', the only way they know.' But he didn't want to hear about all that. I woke up one morning and he was just gone."

"No idea where he went to, huh?"

"I got an *idea* it was to another woman, 'cause that's how he did. He never had a job long as I knew him. He charmed women and he lived off them until he found a new one. I know because he came to me the same way, full of promises and smiles. But I don't know the new girl's name."

Strange lifted his saucer and saw antennae moving behind the cup. A roach emerged and crawled around the saucer. Strange placed the cup and saucer back down on the table in front of the couch.

"Where would he be staying if he wasn't staying with a woman?" said Strange. "He mention any relatives that you can recall?"

Mary stared at the television set, running without sound. Strange recognized the program, *Eye Guess,* had that crippled game show host, wore the thick glasses. Dennis had liked to look at those shows sometimes in the afternoons, shout the answers out before the contestants had a chance to. Drove their father crazy to see Dennis in his underwear, watching that show. "Man's playing games," he'd say, "while other men go to work."

"Any relatives?" said Strange.

Mary cleared her throat. "Kenneth."

"Anyone else?"

"Alvin did have a stepbrother, but he's in Leavenworth forever. His mother's dead. The only time he mentioned his father was in hate. He had this other cousin he talked about, lived down off Seventh, worked in a big-man's store down that way. Ronald, Ronnie, somethin' like that. Maybe he can tell you where Alvin's at."

Strange made a mental note of the information.

"If you do run into Alvin," said Mary, "tell him he needs to come see his son."

"I will."

"Alvin ain't right. But I believe that a child can change a man. A boy needs a father in his life to make him whole."

"I agree," said Strange.

"You say Alvin and your brother were friends?"

"Yes," said Strange, the simple lie coming with difficulty from his mouth.

"I hope your brother's at peace with the Lord."

"I better get goin'," said Strange, rising quietly so as not to wake the baby. "Thank you for the coffee."

"Was it all right? You ain't hardly drink any."

"It was fine."

He looked at the clock on her wall. He had time for one more stop before his shift.

"MAMA," SAID DOMINIC Martini to his mother's back. She stood facing the stove in her black dress, socks, and thick black shoes, stirring the contents of a pot set over a gas flame.

"What, Dominic?"

"I'm goin' out."

"Who you goin' with, eh?"

"Buzz and Shorty."

"Those guys are bums," said Angela. "You gonna get in trouble with those two."

"Ma."

"Come here and taste the gravy before you go."

Martini crossed the linoleum kitchen floor. On the way, he hung the key to the garage padlock on a nail driven into the molding. He reached his mother and stood beside her as she dipped a wooden spoon into the mix of chopped tomatoes, tomato paste, pork neck bones, veal shoulders, sausages, garlic, basil, and pepper. She blew on the spoon to cool the sauce and held it up to her son's mouth.

Martini leaned into it, the garlic coming strong from the steaming spoon, bringing a pleasant burn to his nostrils. He tasted the sauce. "It's good. But it needs a little salt."

"I'm gonna add it later!" said Angela with great emotion.

Martini looked down at her with affection. "Awright, Ma."

Her eyes, magnified behind their lenses, blinked one time. "You gonna be home for dinner?"

"Yeah," said Martini. "I'm gonna come home."

He kissed her cool cheek.

TWENTY-SEVEN

VAUGHN GOT OUT of his car and stood beside it as the Esso man, a fat guy breathing loudly, pumped eight gallons of high-test into the Polara. There was a car behind Vaughn waiting for gas and another, its driver staring at the fat man with impatience, on the far side of the pumps. The fat man removed the gas gun, closed the tank door, and reholstered the nozzle in the cradle of the pump. Vaughn handed him bills and waited for the man to make change from a coin bank he wore on the front of his belt.

"No help today?" said Vaughn, reading the "Manager" patch on the man's chest, seeing the sweat on his brow and temples.

"My mechanic's off and my pump boy called in sick."

"The young guy who's always here?" Vaughn was picturing him, dark-haired, good-looking kid with the haunted eyes, in his head.

"Yeah, Dominic," said the manager, handing Vaughn his change. "If I find out he *ain't* sick, his ass is gone."

"What's his last name?"

"Christ, can't you see I'm busy?"

Vaughn produced his badge case and flipped it open. "His last name."

The manager used a dirty shop rag to wipe at his face. "Last name's Martini. Like Dean Martin's before he changed it."

"Martini was in the military, right?"

"He served."

"He friends with Stewart?"

"Yeah. They're asshole buddies."

Vaughn chewed on his lip as he tossed over the new information: Stewart, Hess, and Martini had all made themselves absent from work on the same day.

"What's Martini drive?" said Vaughn.

"A black Nova," said the manager, moving to the car on the other side of the pump, adding over his shoulder, "but he better not be drivin' it today. If he's doin' anything other than lyin' in a sickbed . . ."

His ass is gone, thought Vaughn, finishing the manager's sentence in his mind as he got back under the wheel of his Polara.

Vaughn drove to the Sixth Precinct station, a half mile down the road, to dig up Martini's address.

DEREK STRANGE WENT through the residential entrance beside the liquor store on H, took the steps two at a time, and reached the second-floor landing. He found the door of Willis's apartment and began to pound on it with his fist. He stopped pounding when he heard heavy footsteps approaching from behind the door.

"Who *is* it?" said Willis, his voice muffled, angry, and filled with attitude.

Strange did not identify himself. He waited for the peephole to darken. When he was certain that Willis was there, his face up against the wood, Strange stepped back and kicked savagely at the area of the doorknob. The door splintered and gave in.

Strange stepped into the apartment and shut the door behind him. Willis was on his back, one hand holding his jaw. He rolled over, moaned, and got to his knees.

Willis spit on the floor.

"Get your ass up," said Strange.

Willis got to his feet slowly and turned around.

"Fuck *you* want?" he said.

Strange stepped in quickly and grabbed ahold of Willis's shirt with his left hand. He threw a short right into Willis's mouth, turning his hip and body into the punch. Willis's head snapped back. Strange felt a burn in his knuckles and, as Willis's head sprang forward, punched him again. Willis's eyes went funny and he lost his legs. Strange took his shirt in both hands and pushed him. Willis tripped backward and landed in a heap on the couch.

Strange drew his .38 from his clip-on. He went to Willis and put the muzzle of the gun to his temple and then moved it to his eye. He pulled back the hammer and locked it in place.

"Who murdered my brother?" said Strange.

Willis's eyes were glassy and afraid. Close up, Strange could see the bruises and swelling alongside his jaw, and, with his mouth stretched back the way it was, a space and black blood where a tooth had been. New blood flowed from his upper lip, which Strange had split with the second right.

"Dennis?" said Willis, his voice quavering and high. "*I* don't know. Dennis was my boy. . . ."

Strange believed him. But he pressed the revolver harder to the corner of Willis's eye.

"Where's Jones?" said Strange.

Under the pressure of the gun, Willis tried to shake his head. Some of his blood dripped onto Strange's hand.

"*Where?*" said Strange, his teeth bared, his hand slick with sweat and tight on the grip of the .38. "I will *kill* you, motherfucker, I swear to God."

"He stayin' with our cousin Ronnie. Ronnie Moses."

"Say where that is."

Willis described the approximate location of Moses's apartment. He claimed he didn't know the exact address.

"You got his number?"

Willis pointed weakly to a phone on a stand. Beside the phone was a small book with a marbleized cover.

"You got something to write with?"

"Under them magazines," said Willis, pointing with his chin.

Strange stepped back and holstered the .38. He looked for paper and a pen, found both under some stroke magazines topped with an ashtray. Strange swept the magazines and ashtray to the floor. He went to the address book, got the number on Moses, and wrote it on the paper. He went to the front door, then turned to speak to Willis. Willis was hunched over on the couch, looking at his shoes, too ashamed to look at Strange. Bright red blood colored the front of his white shirt.

"I wasn't here," said Strange.

Willis nodded. Strange went out the door.

———

AT THE PRECINCT house on Nicholson, Vaughn scored the information he needed: Dominic Martini lived on Longfellow, two blocks away. He got the tag numbers of the Nova, a black-on-black '66, registered in Martini's name, and wrote them in his spiral notebook. Martini's sheet was relatively clean: a couple of minor FIs from his youth and no adult priors.

Vaughn traded his Polara for an unmarked Ford and

asked a couple of uniforms smoking cigarettes back by the Harley garage to come along in a squad car. He told them to keep in radio contact.

Vaughn drove slowly past the house on Longfellow, saw curtains drawn in all the windows. Halfway down the block, going west toward Colorado, he turned the Ford into the alley break. The squad car was idling near a garage at the edge of the Martini yard. Parked beyond the cruiser, tight along the property line, sat a green Rambler shitbox and, behind it, a red Max Wedge Belvedere.

"Bernadette," said Vaughn, his mouth spread in a canine grin.

He threw the tree up into park and got out of the Ford. He walked to the driver's side of the squad car.

"What's goin' on, Detective?" said the fresh-faced blond kid behind the wheel. His name was Mark White.

"Stay here, White," said Vaughn, studying the drop-down door on the garage, padlocked at the latch. "Anyone comes for that Rambler or the Plymouth, hold him."

Vaughn walked through the backyard and around the side of the house to the porch, where he knocked on the front door. An old Italian woman in thick eyeglasses and a black dress answered his knock.

"Yes?"

"Frank Vaughn, ma'am," he said, smiling, showing her his badge.

"Is my son all right?" said the woman, often a mother's first question when a cop came calling at her door.

"Dominic?" said Vaughn. "Far as I know. Is he in?"

"No," she said, looking away quickly.

"I'm looking to talk to his friends."

"Buzz and Shorty," she said, with a tinge of contempt. "I told him, stay away from those two."

"They're all together, right?"

Angela Martini nodded. "They went out."

"You wouldn't know *where* they went, would you?"

"No," she said, blinking her eyes heavily. "Dominic said he'd be home for dinner."

"I'm gonna need to get into your garage."

That's where I'll find something, thought Vaughn. That's where greasers like them make their plans.

"What for?"

"There might be something in that garage that will help me with a case I'm working on. It has to do with his friends." Vaughn gave her the most sincere look a guy like him could manage. "Your son's not in trouble yet. But Stewart and Hess might find him some."

She looked back into the house, then back at Vaughn. She rubbed her hands. He knew she had no understanding of search warrants. He knew she didn't care for his "friends." She'd help him if it meant helping her son.

"I'm gonna get the key for you now," she said.

In the garage, Vaughn found a duffel bag holding boxes of shotgun shells and bricks of ammunition for a .45 and a .38. A half dozen shells and many of the bullets were missing from the boxes. A set of D.C. license plates that matched the plates registered to the Nova was lying on the workbench as well. Vaughn now surmised that the three men were out on the street, armed, in a car bearing phony plates, and about to commit a robbery.

He came out of the garage, removed his gloves, and thanked Angela Martini, who was standing in the driveway. He told her not to worry, that everything would be all right, her son would be fine. He said he would only be a moment longer here, and that she should go back into her house.

When she did, Vaughn radioed in an all-points bulletin on Dominic Martini's Nova, plate number unknown, along with an armed-and-dangerous description of Martini, Stewart, and Hess. He cradled the mic in his unmarked and walked back to the squad car.

"You guys sit tight and keep an eye on these vehicles," said Vaughn to Officer Mark White.

"You leavin'?" said White.

"Gonna cruise around some," said Vaughn. "See if I run into the owners of these cars."

DEREK STRANGE AND Troy Peters came out of the precinct house on Nicholson in uniform and picked car number 63 for their shift. They pulled out of the station's horseshoe-shaped drive-way, going by Vaughn's Polara, parked in a patch of dirt.

Peters went up 13th, passing Fort Stevens, and at the Piney Branch–Georgia intersection turned right, circling the Esso and American stations there. They were working the APB. Strange had recognized Martini's name and told Peters to drive by the station.

"Nothin'," said Peters. "You know one of those guys, right?"

"Same one I was telling you about the other day," said Strange. "We saw him arguing with that big man, right there by the pumps."

"Report said they're wanted on a hit-and-run homicide. Think he's right for that?"

"I don't know. I don't know anything about him any-more. I didn't really know him then."

"I'm gonna cruise up to the District line," said Peters. "We'll turn around up there and do the north-south run."

Peters kicked it coming out of the turn at Tuckerman. They went along past the Polar Bears ice cream and the Hub-bard House. Strange could almost taste the sugar in the lay-ered chocolate pie, see his father carrying that white box across the street, late on Saturdays, when they'd bring it home together to share with his mother and Dennis.

"You okay?" said Peters.

"Just thinking on something is all."

"I mean your hand."

Strange looked at his right hand, resting on his thigh. His knuckles, pink against his dark brown skin, were still showing a little blood. He'd cleaned the scrape but not covered it, not wanting to bring attention to the injury, not wanting anyone to tell him he couldn't work. He needed to go to work.

"I punched a wall," said Strange.

Peters looked him over. "It's gonna be rough for a while."

"Feels like it's *always* gonna be."

"Anything on the investigation?"

"No."

Up past Aspen Street, they went by the Walter Reed Army Medical Center, and then a mix of low-rise commercial and residential structures. Peters accelerated as the squad car hit a long grade.

"I talked to your mother yesterday," said Peters, side-glancing Strange. "Nice woman."

"None better."

"I mentioned her job in the dentist's office."

"That right."

"She didn't know what I was talking about. Told me she'd been working as a domestic most of her adult life."

"You got me, Troy," said Strange unemotionally. "You caught me in a lie."

"Question is, why'd you feel like you had to tell me that story?"

"I wasn't ashamed of my mother, if that's what you think. I'm proud of her, understand?"

"What, then?"

"It was all about me. Me, with nothin' in my background but a high school degree, riding with a Peace Corps and Princeton man. By elevating her, I was trying to elevate myself. Once I told it that way, it was too late to tell it true."

"I ever try and make you feel small?"

"You never did."

"Where you think I come from, Derek?"

"Money, I expect."

"You mean you assumed."

"That's right."

"I come from dirt. That's all I'm gonna say, because you don't want to hear it. But to have a family like yours . . . Look, I was envious of you. Didn't matter to me what your parents did for a living. Point is, they were there for you. Not like mine."

"I didn't know."

"You never asked me," said Peters. "You weren't interested."

Strange didn't offer any kind of rebuttal, because Troy was right. When he looked at Peters, he saw a white man first and a man second. As far as getting underneath the surface of his partner and looking at his heart, Strange had not been interested. Knowing all the while it was the same way many white men looked at him.

"I apologize," said Strange.

"Forget it," said Peters.

Strange and Peters relaxed their shoulders and said nothing further. The silence was not uncomfortable.

A quarter mile ahead, on the left, stood the Morris Miller's liquor store. On the right sat a shopping center, book-ended by an A&P supermarket on one end and, on the other, the Capitol Savings and Loan.

TWENTY-EIGHT

Wait for a spot out front," said Stewart.

"There," said Hess from the backseat. "Money says the old lady's gonna get in that Buick."

"That ain't no surprise," said Stewart. "She pulls away, back this race car in, Dom."

"Right," said Martini, his lifeless eyes tracking the elderly woman emerging from the bank and walking to her Skylark, parked in a space out front.

They were in the idling Nova, fitted in a slot at the far corner of the A&P portion of the lot. The center was only half filled with cars, as this was the time of day during which mothers were typically home awaiting the arrival of their children from school. A woman got out of her station wagon with her toddler, found a shopping cart that had been abandoned, and pushed it with one hand toward the supermarket, her left hand pulling on her child's sweater. A man with a flattop haircut carried paper bags from the market to his Olds, a lit cigarette dangling from his lips.

Buzz Stewart and Walter Hess wore their raincoats over blue jeans, Dickie work shirts, and black bomber-style boots. Their stocking masks and gloves sat in their laps. Both had loaded and holstered their weapons. Additonal loose shotgun shells and revolver rounds sat in the side pockets of their raincoats. Martini's .45 rested on the bucket between his legs, steel grip out, the barrel pressing against his genitals.

Hess found a Black Beauty among the bullets in his pocket and pulled it free. Hunched in the backseat, he drew one of his .38s and ground its butt into the pill, which he held in the palm of his callused hand. The pill broke into bits and dust. Hess reholstered his gun, leaned forward, put his face into his palm, and snorted the amphetamine.

"*Fuck*, yeah," said Hess, throwing back his head, feeling the burn in his nasal passages and a bright burst behind his eyes.

"Go on, Dom," said Stewart. "Take the space."

As the Buick Skylark pulled out of the lot, Martini put the Hurst in gear and motored slowly past the space, getting reverse and backing in cleanly between a Satellite and a Bel Air. Looking over his shoulder to navigate, Martini saw Hess, amped on speed, his jittery, piggish eyes pinballing in their sockets. Behind the Nova was the sidewalk, and then the plate-glass window of the bank atop a three-foot marble base.

"You ready, Shorty?" said Stewart, his face colored by a head rush of blood.

"Born ready, dad. We gon' get it *all*."

"Look at me, Dom," said Stewart. "*Look* at me."

Martini turned his head and stared into Stewart's eyes.

"You're gonna wait for us," said Stewart. "You keep it runnin' and wait. We won't be but five. When we come back, you make it scream. Head south and work the side streets back to your alley. This ain't nothin' but a cakewalk, I shit you not."

"I'll be here," said Martini.

I've been headed here all my life.

Stewart and Hess fitted the stocking masks on their heads and pulled them down over their faces. They put on their gloves. Stewart, his features mutilated by the mask, his lips fishlike against it, made eye contact with Hess and nodded one time. He got out of the car first, then waited for Hess to push the front seat forward and climb out. Stewart shut the door. Martini looked in the sideview and watched them cross the asphalt and white concrete. Stewart opened the door to the bank and let Hess pass. Stewart drew the cut-down from the harness beneath his raincoat as he followed Hess inside. The door closed quietly behind them. Then there was only the sputtering of the Nova's 350 rumbling beneath the hood.

Martini's eyes stayed on the mirror, not looking ahead, not seeing MPD squad car number 63 as it slowly passed on Georgia Avenue.

———

VAUGHN FLIPPED OPEN his Zippo, lit a cigarette, and snapped the lid shut. He rested his elbow on the lip of the driver's window as he smoked, one meaty hand atop the wheel. He went down Georgia to the business district around Sheridan, checking out the sidewalk in front of Victor Liquors, Vince's Agnes Flower Shop, John's Lunch, the Chinese laundry, and, on the corner, the 6200 tavern. He kept going and cruised slowly by Lou's, where men who looked liked Martini, Stewart, and Hess drank, smoked, and shot pool. He saw no trace of a black Nova curbed along the Avenue or on the immediate side streets. He continued down Georgia, knowing in his gut as he saw the dark faces of the residents here that he was getting cold. These were men who had run down a man who had done them no wrong, and that made them cowards. They would never try to pull a job in the colored part of town.

He was turning the unmarked in the middle of the street when the 211 came over the radio, describing a robbery in progress at the Capitol Savings and Loan, up near the District line.

Vaughn grabbed the portable magnetic beacon light sitting on the passenger floorboard beside him. He put the cherry out the window and onto the roof, its power wire lying across his lap. He hit the siren and light switches on the console before him. He pegged the gas. The Ford lifted from the power surge. It fishtailed on the lane change as Vaughn swerved to avoid hitting a D.C. Transit bus.

———

STRANGE, ON THE shotgun side of the squad car, was the first to spot the black Nova in a space out front of the Capitol Savings and Loan. Exhaust drifted up over its trunk line.

"Slow down a little, Troy," said Strange.

"What's up?"

"Just slow it down."

Strange had learned from the bulletin that the plates were stolen and their numbers unknown. But he could make out the full head of wavy black hair on the man behind the Nova's wheel.

"Pull over," said Strange. "We got a hit on that all-points."

They were on Georgia, well past the bank now, directly in front of the A&P.

Troy took the Ford over to the curb as Strange radioed in the sighting. He was instructed by the voice on the other end to wait for backup. He ten-foured the desk man and cradled the mic.

Peters looked over his shoulder at the Nova and the bank. He looked at Strange.

"What now?" said Strange.

"You heard the man," said Peters. "Won't be but a minute or two before backup comes."

Peters pulled his service revolver from the swivel holster of his gun belt, freed the cylinder, checked the load, and snapped the cylinder back in place. Strange did the same. He opened his dump pouch and checked it for backup rounds as well. Both had done this before leaving the station. Their nerves told them to do it again.

They heard the siren of a car approaching from the south.

They heard the unmistakable pops of a handgun and the roar of a shotgun blast come from the far end of the shopping center. Before they could gather their thoughts, the shotgun sounded again. Light flashed through the plate glass of the bank.

Peters pulled down on the transmission arm and gave the Ford gas as Strange flip-switched the sirens and the cherries, keyed the mic, and reiterated the certainty of the 211. Peters swung into the lot of the A&P, braked, skidded to a stop, and slammed the trans into park.

"Take it," said Peters.

"Take *what*, goddamnit?"

"Stay with the vehicle. Get out and take cover on your side of the car."

Peters drew his sidearm as he opened the door of the squad car and moved across the lot in a crouch. He made it to the doors of the A&P, opened one, stood in the frame, and shouted something to a worker inside. The young man came forward and positioned himself near the entrance, his hands out in a "stop" position, warning customers who were attempting to leave to stay back. Peters put his back against the exterior wall of the supermarket and cautiously edged his way in the direction of the bank.

Strange got out on the passenger side of the squad car,

drew his .38, rested his gun arm on the roof of the car, straightened it, and aimed the gun at the bank. He moved his aim to the windshield of the Nova. He shouted at the man behind the wheel, who he recognized as Dominic Martini, to get out of the vehicle and lie down on the pavement. Martini looked at him blankly and did not move.

Strange heard the cry of tires and the whoop of a siren. Behind him, Frank Vaughn's unmarked entered the lot.

———

BUZZ STEWART'S PLAN was for him and Shorty to show the guns immediately, state their intent to use them, and make a lot of noise, scaring the tellers and security guard into instant submission. Because it was a simple plan, he knew it was one Hess could follow.

Hess entered first and cross-drew his .38s. Stewart pulled the shotgun from its harness before the door closed behind him, locking both hammers back.

"Eyes on me!" shouted Hess.

"This is a robbery!" shouted Stewart. "Hands up!"

Stewart put one hand around the shortened barrel, the other inside the guard, his forefinger grazing the dual triggers. He pointed the shotgun in the general direction of the tellers, their heads, shoulders, and torsos visible through the bars of their cages, their mouths open, their faces gone pale, and the two customers, a middle-aged man and a young woman, standing before them.

"Don't nobody move or touch no buttons!" shouted Hess, pointing one .38 at the white-haired security guard and the other at the bank manager, a thin, balding man behind a desk.

All did as instructed. All put their hands up, and none moved or spoke.

"*Keep* 'em up, grandpa," said Hess, stepping to the old man in the dark blue uniform, as he holstered one of the .38s and pointed the other at the man's face. The old man's spotted hands, raised in the air, shook, and his mouth worked at words without sound. Hess unsnapped the old man's holster strap and pulled his .45. Hess slipped it, butt leaned to the right, into the waistband of his jeans. He redrew the second .38. "Now lie on your belly and put your face to the floor."

The old security guard did as he was told. He grunted as he went to his knees and then his stomach.

The bank was small, with a marble floor and three teller cages behind a marble counter and brass bars. Behind the tellers was the vault, the door of which was closed. To one side of the lobby was the business and reception area, carpeted in green, where the balding manager now sat, his hands up, behind a cherrywood desk. In the center of the lobby was a marble island holding black pens on chains and topped with a slotted wooden rack housing deposit slips, withdrawal slips, and envelopes.

A customer stood at the island with his hands up. His name was Alex Koutris. Koutris was an American citizen born on Naxos, an island off the coast of Greece. He was a medium-height, medium-build forty-six-year-old man with a dark mustache who co-owned a small diner in a rough neighborhood downtown. He came on at five o'clock for the night shift and worked until closing, leaving his place with the day's cash at three a.m., when he walked through an unlit alley to his car. He carried a gun for protection. He had survived Guadalcanal and other fierce campaigns in the Second World War and was comfortable with the weapon. He was here to make his daily deposit before going into work. An envelope holding three hundred dollars was on the island before him. He had stood ten hours behind a counter to earn it, which made the money real. His gun, a snub-nosed .38, lay free in the side pocket of his yellow Peters jacket.

"Cash in the bags!" shouted Stewart, stepping around the

wall, kicking open a swinging gate hinged in the middle of a fence. He stood behind the tellers, moving the shotgun from one to another, one woman and two men, all young.

They worked quickly, pulling the folding money from their cash drawers and placing it in white cloth bags they drew from under the counter.

"Thirty seconds!" shouted Stewart. "I will *use* this shotgun."

The female teller stopped working, stood straight, and staggered. She lost her feet and fell to the marble floor. Her head made a hollow sound as it hit the floor. A circle of urine darkened her spring green skirt, fanned around her legs where she lay.

"What's goin' on?" said Hess, moving his guns catlike from the guard to the manager to the calm-looking man at the island, who was staring at him with no fear or expression at all on his face.

"Girl fainted, is all," said Stewart. He pointed the shotgun at one of the two remaining tellers and swept the barrel to the fallen woman. "Finish what she was doin'," he said. "Move!"

The young man went to her station and hand-shoveled cash into her bag.

Hess noticed the fat envelope on the island in front of the man with the mustache and calm eyes. He walked toward him, keeping his guns moving from the customers to the manager to the security guard lying on the floor. The female customer began to sob.

"What you got there?" said Hess, ugly beneath the mask, his mouth dry and frozen in something that was more grimace than smile. "What's in that envelope?"

Koutris didn't answer.

"I asked you a question."

"It's mine."

"Step away from that table," said Hess, and when the

man didn't move, he clicked back the hammer on one of his guns and put it to the man's face. Koutris moved back two full steps, his eyes unwavering, and Hess snatched the envelope off the island top and slipped it into the pocket of his raincoat.

"I got the gun," said Hess. "That makes it mine."

"*Koritsi mou*," said Koutris. It meant "my little girl."

"What'd you call me?"

Koutris looked him over with contempt.

"What'd you *call* me?" said Hess, moving forward.

Koutris said nothing. Hess laughed and flipped one of the guns so that its barrel was in his hand. He swung the butt violently into the man's nose. His nose shifted and caved, and his hands dropped to cover his face. Blood seeped through his fingers.

"Hey, Buzz," said Hess with a witch's cackle, looking for his friend through the bars. "I just fucked this greaseball *up*."

Hess turned his head to look back at the man. The man held a snub-nosed revolver in his hand and there was blood on his smile. The man squeezed the trigger, and as Hess heard the shot he felt his throat tear open and saw blood dot his stocking mask. He fell backward and felt the sting and shock of the second shot as it entered his groin and he said "Buzz" and was on his back watching the pressed-tin ceiling of the bank spin and double.

Alex Koutris began to turn toward the tellers' cages, seeing movement from the side of his eye, and was lifted off his feet by the blast of a shotgun. The copper load tore flesh off his face and peppered his neck. He tumbled and came to rest on his side, his cheek and shoulders slick with blood. His ears rang against the scream of a woman, and he thought, I survived the Japanese to die like this for a lousy three hundred bucks. He spit something pink and thick to the floor.

Koutris looked up and saw the big white man pointing the shotgun down at his face and saw the man's finger press one of the two triggers inside the guard and closed his eyes and saw fire and his mother and nothing at all.

Stewart stepped away from the body, broke open the shotgun, held it vertical, and let the hulls of both shells drop to the floor. He leaned the barrels on his forearm, found two shells in his pocket, thumbed them into both chambers, and snapped the barrels shut. Stewart didn't bother looking at the customers or tellers or the old security guard, now praying aloud, and he didn't try to quiet the female customer, alternately screaming and crying, completely out of control. None of them would try anything now.

Stewart walked through smoke to a wheezing Hess, who was leaving a slug's trail of blood as he back-crabbed convulsively on the marble tiles, still gripping both .38s. He stopped moving and his crossed eyes pinwheeled beneath the mask as he struggled to fix them on his friend. He voided his bowels. He arched his back and fought for breath.

"Shorty," said Stewart, looking down at Hess. "We gonna get you out of here, son. You gonna be all right."

Hess died as the words came from Stewart's mouth.

Stewart looked through the plate-glass window at the Nova, still idling out front. He had heard sirens. He could not see the squad car out in front of the supermarket or the unmarked that had joined it. He could not see the uniformed patrolman, Troy Peters, edging his way along the storefronts toward the bank.

Stewart harnessed the shotgun inside his raincoat. He bent down, drew the security guard's .45 from Hess's waistband, released the magazine, palmed it back in the grip, and thumbed off the safety.

"Bring me them bags," said Stewart dully, talking to the tellers who were still standing.

Stewart jacked a round into the chamber of the Colt. He blinked against the smell of gunsmoke, excrement, and blood.

One of the young men came from behind the tellers' cages and handed Stewart three cloth bags heavy with cash. Stewart bunched them in his left hand, his right gripping the Colt. He walked slowly to the front door.

VAUGHN AND STRANGE watched Peters move along the drugstore and then the dry cleaners, signaling the occupants of those stores to step back and stay where they were as he kept one eye on the bank, his gun at his side.

Another squad car had come into the lot and blocked the exit. Vaughn had drawn his weapon. He stood with his gun arm on the roof of the Ford, aiming at the bank. Strange's arm was fixed the same way, his gun sighted on the Nova. They were waiting for a white shirt with a bullhorn from the Sixth, along with more backup and an ambulance. The siren of the ambulance could be heard as it approached.

"What'd you hear?" said Vaughn.

"Gunshots and a shotgun," said Strange.

"What *exactly*?"

"Two gunshots, evenly spaced. A shotgun blast right after that, and then another, ten, fifteen seconds later."

"Sounds like we got some dead."

"Shouldn't we rush the place?"

"Hell, no," said Vaughn. "The thing to do is save the ones still alive. You don't want them killin' hostages. Wait for Stewart and Hess to come out. Don't let 'em get in that car."

"What about Martini?" said Strange, one eye shut, sighting him down the barrel of the .38.

"We don't have to take him now," said Vaughn.

"Okay," said Strange.

"Can you hit his tires from here?"

"I can try."

"Because you gotta disable that car. I'm gonna be busy with Stewart and Hess."

"I'll try."

"Look at your partner," said Vaughn, admiration in his voice. "That's a smart young man right there."

"Troy Peters," said Strange.

"You both did good."

Strange blinked sweat from his eye. He steadied his hand.

MARTINI, HIS EYES on the sideview mirror, had witnessed the violence inside the bank. He'd seen Buzz standing over the body of Shorty. He'd seen Buzz take the gun off Shorty's body and take the cloth bags in his hand. And now Buzz was coming for the door. Buzz had heard the sirens, most likely, and knew that the police had arrived. He didn't know that the big homicide cop, the one who got his gas at the station, had his gun trained on the front of the bank. He didn't know that Strange, the black cop Martini had known as a kid, had his gun on the Nova. He didn't know that the blond policeman was edging his way along the fronts of stores toward the bank.

Martini had not touched the gun resting between his legs. He wasn't going to touch it. He'd never told Buzz that he would. Buzz had ordered him to wait, and that's what he was doing. That's all he would do. He wasn't going to shoot at these men in uniform, who served like he'd served, like his friends had served, in the war.

Dominic Martini depressed the clutch and put the Hurst in gear. He thought of the men in uniform and found another gear. He revved the gas against the clutch. The needle swerved toward the red line on the tach.

Buzz Stewart pushed on the front door, opened it, and walked quickly out onto the sidewalk, directly behind the Nova. He heard a cop shouting from his right and, without turning, blind-fired his gun.

STRANGE HEARD TROY Peters's command and saw his hesitation as the big man shot blind. He saw Peters take a bullet, drop his weapon to the side, and fall.

Vaughn fired at the big man and hit him high. Strange, as he had been ordered to do, shot at the tires of the Nova, hitting the grille and fender instead. The big man fired back at them, sending him and Vaughn down for cover as the rounds took a beacon light out and some paint off the roof of the squad car.

"We gonna go up together, young man," said Vaughn to Strange with calm and assurance. "Now."

Strange stood with Vaughn, ready to fire. They cleared the roof with their gun arms. They saw the Nova's tires screaming on the asphalt, and the big man standing behind the car.

STEWART CHARGED OUT of the bank and saw two cops leaning over the roof of a squad car, pointing their guns at him. From his right he heard a man shout, "Police, drop your weapon!" and Stewart fired the automatic in that direction without turning his head. In his side vision he saw the cop go down. Stewart heard shouts from the lot and turned his gun that way and saw smoke and felt a slug hit him like a sharp punch. He stumbled back, firing wildly at the squad car, seeing a cherry light pulverized and rounds spark off the roof and the cops dropping behind its far side. He stood behind the Nova, hearing the clutch pop off the gas, seeing smoke pouring out from under the rear tires as they sought purchase, thinking, Those wheels are turning the wrong way.

The Nova caught asphalt and roared toward him. It jumped the sidewalk and lifted him up off his feet, taking him back through the window of the bank. Glass exploded sonically around him.

I been hit by Dominic's car. I have been shot.

His legs were pinned between the rear bumper of the

Nova and the edge of the marble wall that fronted the bank. A .38 slug had shattered his clavicle, tumbled, and lodged in his deltoid. He felt little pain.

That boy Dominic was born to fuck up. God, I am cold.

Stewart's torso hung backward over the lip of the wall. He had dropped the bags of money. He had dropped the .45. The shotgun was harnessed, and he did not have the strength to pull it free. He heard men shouting and their footsteps as they ran toward him.

I've murdered a man and maybe a cop and they are going to kill me for what I've done. Well, I will take one of them with me. They'll talk about me in bars forever if I do that last thing. I still have my derringer. It's here in my boot.

He reached for his right boot and felt slime and cloth. He looked down. There was no boot or anything else below his right knee. A portion of his left leg hung there, smashed flat, connected only by nerves and muscle and the shredded fabric of his jeans. Most of it was gone. What wasn't gone was red and wet.

Stewart screamed.

TWENTY-NINE

T ROY PETERS HAD been shot in the right thigh. The bullet had exited cleanly, missing his femoral artery. The paramedics were able to stanch the flow of blood before loading him onto a gurney and into the van. The ambulance took Peters to the Washington Sanitarium, the Seventh-Day Adventist Hospital in Takoma Park, Maryland, not far from the Capitol Savings and Loan. Strange decided to ride with him and told Vaughn that he'd see him at the Sixth Precinct station, where he would give his official statement on the events.

A doctor who had been shopping at the A&P attempted to stabilize Buzz Stewart, who had gone into convulsions, as a second ambulance arrived. Stewart's blood ran from the sidewalk down to the street.

Dominic Martini sat in the cage of a squad car, his hands cuffed behind him, a bruise darkening his swelling jaw. He had been tackled to the pavement as he got out of the Nova,

314

his arms raised in surrender, by one of the young policemen who had been blocking the exit of the lot, who then punched him repeatedly in the face. The young policeman's partner, a thirty-year-old army veteran, went into the bank and tried to calm the survivors, keeping them away from the corpses of the shotgun victim and Walter Hess.

Strange sat on a bench beside Peters's gurney as the ambulance sped down Eastern Avenue, heading into Takoma Park. Against the orders of the paramedic, Peters removed the oxygen mask that had been covering his nose and mouth.

"Call Patty," said Peters.

"Vaughn's gonna do it," said Strange.

"I want *you* to tell her what's goin' on. Tell her it's not serious."

Strange motioned to the oxygen mask, lying loosely around Peters's neck. "You better put that back on."

"I don't need it," said Peters. "I'm fine."

"You don't look so fine to me. You got no color in your face."

"That again."

Strange chuckled and looked down at his friend. "Badass."

"Go on, man."

"Had to be the hero."

"But I wasn't."

"You did okay."

Peters shook his head. "I should have shot that sonofabitch where he stood. Instead, I hesitated. I didn't have the guts."

"Doesn't take any courage to kill a man. What you're talkin' about, that ain't nothin' to be ashamed of."

"I'm not ashamed," said Peters. "But if that guy had shot you because I didn't shoot him first . . ."

"Forget about it."

"I'm in the wrong profession."

"Let me tell you somethin', Troy: For a minute back there, I thought Vaughn was gonna order me to take out Martini. When he told me to hold my fire, I was about as relieved as I've ever felt."

"So?"

"So, you're not alone."

The ambulance hit a bump and the gurney rocked. Peters winced, closed his eyes, then opened them and looked up soulfully at Strange.

"Derek?"

"What."

"Hold my hand."

"You ain't even all that hurt."

"Hold it anyway," said Peters. "At least until we get to the hospital."

"Aw, *fuck* you, man."

Strange left Troy Peters, sedated and sleepy, in the ER of the hospital at around 5:30 in the evening. When he went out to the lot he found his squad car waiting for him, along with the two cops who had been blocking the exit of the parking lot.

"Hound Dog said you'd be needing your car," said the older of the two.

Strange thanked him, got under the wheel of the Ford, and drove back into D.C.

STRANGE WAS CONGRATULATED by several uniformed officers and the desk sergeant as he arrived at the station, for what he did not know. He took the handshakes and the pats on his shoulder without comment but wondered why they were directed toward him. It was his partner who had gone beyond the call. He did not feel that he had acted with any particular heroism; rather, he had merely survived a dangerous situation by acquitting himself in a passable, cautious, and workman-like way.

In the squad room, he found an open desk and phoned Peters's wife at her job, assuring her that Troy was going to be okay. She was on her way out the door to join him at the hospital and thanked Strange for the call.

"Troy thinks so much of you," said Patty, a touch of the South in her voice. "You need to get over here for dinner, Derek. We been talkin' about it too long."

"I will," said Strange.

He vowed to make the effort. There were already too many things to regret.

Strange hung up the phone and began the process of filling out the necessary forms related to the event, in triplicate, which the prosecutors needed before they could begin to make their charges. He smelled cigarette smoke and looked up. Vaughn was standing in front of the desk, a butt burning between his thick fingers.

"Detective," said Strange. "How'd we do?"

"We got a full statement from Martini. He cleaned up a hit-and-run I been workin' on, too. He was a passenger in the car that ran down this young colored guy the other night on Fourteenth."

"Who was the driver?"

"Walter Hess. Buzz Stewart was riding shotgun. Martini gave it up on one condition. I told him it wouldn't be a problem."

"What was the condition?"

"He wanted to speak with you."

"Now?"

Vaughn nodded. "See me when you're done."

Strange went to the block of cells located on the right side of the station. A uniform standing guard let him into the cell that held Dominic Martini. Martini sat on a spring cot covered by a thin mattress, his upswept black hair disheveled, his eyes hollow. One side of his face was purple and misshapen from the punches he'd taken to the jaw.

Strange leaned his back against the bars and folded his arms.

"I finally made it," said Martini, softly, bitterly. "Just like my old man."

Strange said nothing.

"I used to watch the cops go in and out this station," said Martini. "I acted like I was against them, but really I admired 'em. I wanted to wear a uniform like them, but I never thought I could. Anyway, when I came back from the service, I got asshole tight with Buzz and Shorty again, so . . ."

Martini stared at the cell wall.

"I can tell you what's out there," said Martini, his eyes fixed on the cinder blocks. "I don't need no window, 'cause I got it memorized in my head, see? The driveway, the goldfish pond. The fence. Past the fence, that big old oak tree we used to hide behind. Throw rocks at the police and run if we were in the mood to get chased. Officer Pappas, with his little mustache. We used to call him Jacques, you remember?"

Strange shook his head.

"You were with me once. You and that heavyset Greek kid. One day you stopped me from throwing a rock at that black cop, Officer Davis."

Strange couldn't recall much about Martini except for that shoplifting episode they'd had together over at Ida's. He remembered that Martini liked to fight. He remembered that he had a younger brother who was gentler than him. That was all.

"How about my kid brother, Angelo?" said Martini. "You remember him?"

"A little," said Strange.

"I used to try and toughen him up, y'know? I made him fight other guys even though he didn't want to. I tried to make him fight you once, over at Fort Stevens. But you wouldn't do it."

Strange shifted his weight against the bars.

"That's right," said Martini, looking at Strange, seeing the incomprehension on his face. "You wouldn't fight him, even though you knew you could take him. You did somethin' good for my brother that day. You weren't much more than a kid, but you acted like a man. I didn't forget that, see?"

Strange said nothing.

"I never told him that it was all right not to fight. I called him fairy and faggot and every other goddamn thing you can think of his whole life. I should've known he'd follow me into the service. Try to prove to his big brother that he was tough enough. But he wasn't tough. Just good." A tear broke free from Martini's eye. "I wonder why they'd ever send a kid like him to war. Angie didn't want to hurt no one."

Strange dropped his arms to his sides and looked down at his shoes.

"Anyway," said Martini. "He died. Angelo stepped on a mine. They had him out on point, on his very first recon patrol. For what I don't know. He wouldn't have killed no one." Martini's eyes had lost their focus. "He stepped on a mine."

"I'm sorry," said Strange.

"I knew you prob'ly wouldn't remember none of it," said Martini. "I just wanted to thank you, is all."

Martini lay back on the cot and covered his eyes with his forearm. Strange called for the guard, who came and unlocked the cell door. As Strange walked down the hall of the block, he checked his wristwatch. It was 7:15.

Vaughn was waiting for him outside the cell block door.

"What was that all about?"

"He just wanted to get straight with me on somethin'," said Strange. "Somethin' going back to when we were kids."

"You knew him?"

"Not really," said Strange. "I wouldn't say I knew him at all. What do you reckon's gonna happen to him?"

"Murder One. Doesn't matter that Martini didn't pull the trigger in that bank. He's lucky he was a hundred yards inside the District line, if you wanna call it luck. Anywhere else he'd fry. He's gonna get life."

"What about Stewart?"

"They put amputees in prison, too. If he lives."

"Cripples don't last long inside."

"They buy the full ticket, just the same."

Vaughn shook an L&M halfway out of his pack and offered it to Strange. Strange waved it away. Vaughn drew the cigarette the rest of the way out with his mouth and lit it with his Zippo.

"You ought to call your mother," said Vaughn. "She might hear about a cop gettin' shot in your precinct over the radio. She'll be worried sick, especially living with your brother's death right now."

"I'll call her."

"She okay?"

"She's strong."

"Good woman."

"Yes."

"Been a rough couple of days for you, too," said Vaughn, looking him over.

"Guess I'll feel better when my brother's killer is arrested."

"You think so? You think you're gonna feel better then?"

"What're you gettin' at?"

"Is that all you *want?* To see him put in jail?"

Strange stared into Vaughn's eyes. "No."

"Like I said, I want to help."

"I appreciate it."

"Anything new?"

Strange told him, in detail, about his afternoon. He described his last stop, at the apartment of Kenneth Willis, and how he'd shook Willis down. He told him about his lead on Jones, and the cousin he was staying with over off 7th.

"Where's this Ronnie Moses live, exactly?" said Vaughn.

"I don't know. I did get a phone number, though. I was planning on getting an address through the number."

"You got the number on you?"

"It's in my locker."

"We'll Criss-Cross it now," said Vaughn. "You're certain about Jones, right?"

"I don't have any hard evidence. But I'm certain as I can be."

"You carry an unregistered piece?" said Vaughn.

"No."

"I do," said Vaughn. "You're gonna need to get one, too."

Strange considered stopping Vaughn right then. But he held his tongue.

They walked together into the squad room. Some officers were grouped around a desk radio, listening to a news broadcast. One of the uniforms, a black rookie named Morris, broke away from the group. His partner, a white cop named Timmons, tried to grab Morris by the arm, but Morris pulled free and stalked out of the room. As he passed, Strange saw anguish on his face. Strange and Vaughn went to the radio and listened to the announcer repeat the bulletin.

At 6:05 p.m., central standard time, the Reverend Dr. Martin Luther King Jr. had been shot in the neck by a sniper while standing on the balcony of the Lorraine Hotel in Memphis, Tennessee.

For the next hour, the police officers stayed in the squad room, taking calls and calling loved ones, talking quietly among themselves. Vaughn went outside to the station steps to have a smoke in the night air. Strange phoned his mother, as

Vaughn had told him to do. They spoke about the robbery and the awful thing that had happened in Memphis, and she told him she loved him and he told her the same thing. As he hung the phone up the announcer returned to the air.

Dr. King had been pronounced dead at St. Joseph's Hospital at 8:05 p.m., eastern standard time. Officer Morris, who had returned to hear the news, punched his fist into the squad room wall. Strange went to the bathroom, where he could be alone.

On 14th Street, in Shaw, the news came first to a boy who was walking down the sidewalk, carrying a cheap transistor radio on a strap.

"They killed Dr. King!" he shouted to no one in particular. "They killed Dr. King!"

People stopped to look at him as he ran down the street.

THIRTY

A S THE NEWS spread by mouth and phone call, people began to turn on their transistor and tabletop radios, and their television sets, to get the details of the King assassination. Many inner-city residents tuned their dials to 1450, the home of soul station WOL. DJ Bob Terry, a familiar, comforting voice to his black audience, urged listeners to reflect on the news in a spiritual way.

"This is no time to hate," said Terry. "And let me tell you something, white man . . . you better stop hating, too."

After speaking on the phone with leaders in Memphis, black activist Stokely Carmichael went to the SNCC offices on 14th Street, a couple of blocks north of U, and conferred with some of the leaders of its Washington bureau. He proposed a strike that would force closure of area businesses in honor of Dr. King. He reasoned that stores should shut down out of respect, as they had upon the assassination of JFK. While the officers of the SNCC favored some sort of protest, they did not approve of such a drastic move. Carmichael, wearing shades and his trademark fatigue jacket, disregarded their wishes and left the office to begin rounding up supporters who could help him facilitate his strike.

Soon after, Carmichael and a group of followers entered the Peoples Drug at 14th and U, the site of Tuesday night's disturbance, and asked the manager to close the store in honor of Dr. King. The manager complied, darkening the lights in the store. Carmichael then led a crowd, now grown to thirty or forty individuals, from shop to shop, going from dry cleaner to liquor store to barbershop, speaking to the owners or managers on shift, telling them all to close up shop. All complied.

The crowd then headed east on U. A light drizzle had begun, not uncommon on an April night.

The owner of the Jumbo Nut Shop, a woman, was asked to lock her doors. Ushers and box office attendants at the Republic Theater were told to terminate their first evening showing. A couple of Carmichael's followers walked into the auditorium of the Lincoln Theater and shouted to the audience, watching *Guess Who's Coming to Dinner,* telling them that their evening at the movies was done. The houselights came up, and patrons abandoned their seats.

At 9:30, someone shattered the plate-glass window of the Peoples Drug.

The Reverend Walter Fauntroy, chairman of the Washington City Council and a close confidant to Dr. King, watched the trouble begin from the second-floor offices of the Southern Christian Leadership Conference, next to the Peoples Drug. He went down to the street to talk to Carmichael and his followers, whose numbers had now swelled even more. Carmichael shook his arm from the diminutive Fauntroy's grasp and walked north on 14th, with hundreds in tow. Fauntroy would spend the balance of the evening going from TV station to radio station, urging "black brothers and sisters" to react to their grief "in the spirit of nonviolence." His words came too late and went unheeded.

The impromptu parade of protesters closed restaurants and businesses on 14th as they had done on U. Behind them, a trash can finished the Peoples window. Next, a bottle crashed through the window of National Liquor. Chants of "Black power," "Kill whitey," and "We gonna off some motherfuckers now" were heard in the night. Carmichael talked to the crowd and told them not to initiate any violence, that it would be harmful to them, as they were outnumbered and would be outgunned. He did this as he continued to lead them up the hill of 14th, where scores of mom-and-pop businesses, chain stores, and apartment houses lined the strip from U to Park Road.

As of 10:00, there appeared to be little police presence on the street. Officials were aware of the growing problem and had begun to send units down to the scene. Public Safety Director Patrick Murphy instructed officers to try to maintain order but retreat from any "imminent confrontation."

Five blocks north of U, at the top of the hill, a woman pushed her backside through the plate-glass window of Belmont TV. A few people tried to get into the display area to take some televisions but were blocked by Carmichael and a couple of SNCC workers. Carmichael produced a pistol from his jacket, waved it, and told his agitated followers that this was not "the way."

Meanwhile, crowds had regathered at 14th and U. As he walked south and neared the intersection, Carmichael could clearly discern that he was no longer in control of the situation. The crowd had grown considerably and its movements were erratic and unbridled. The voices of the participants had risen in anger and something like glee. Carmichael got into a waiting car and sped away. He would not be seen for the remainder of the night.

At around 10:30, the crowd broke the windows of Sam's

Pawnbrokers and Rhodes Five and Ten, both south of U, and began to steal jewelry, television sets, transistor radios, appliances, useless trinkets, and anything else that was not locked up or nailed down. SNCC volunteers tried to stop them. They were laughed at and brushed aside.

Imploding glass sounded as the display windows of many stores around 14th and U were shattered. The London Custom Shop was looted, as were the surrounding shops. North of U, people began spilling out of tenement-style apartments, some in curiosity, some in anger, some with the purposeless mentality of a mob, and began to damage and rob stores.

An informal command post was set up at the Thirteenth Precinct station near 16th and V. There, Mayor Walter Washington, Police Chief John B. Layton, and Patrick Murphy developed a rough consensual plan. The Special Operations Division (SOD) of the Civil Disturbance Unit (CDU), which had extensive training in counterriot activity, was called to duty. In addition, the four-to-midnight shift of active Thirteenth Precinct street officers was ordered to perform a double and work the midnight–to–eight a.m. as well. All available units were to report to the disturbance area of Shaw.

Officer Lydell Blue of the Thirteenth was among many to arrive in this wave.

Officers from other precincts who were not otherwise engaged were encouraged to join the Thirteenth's effort in quelling the riot.

At the Sixth Precinct station house, Officer Strange, along with Officer Morris and two other uniformed cops, volunteered for duty. They got into a squad car and headed south.

Detective Frank Vaughn drove to the house of Vernon Wilson and told his mother that her son's murderers had been found, and that those who were not killed in the attempted robbery would spend the rest of their lives in prison. He then went to the Villa Rosa, in downtown Silver Spring, and had a couple of drinks.

━━━━━━

STRANGE AND THE others, grouped down near U, got their orders from a sergeant out of the Thirteenth.

"Maintain order through intimidation and threat. Use your nightsticks and tear gas only if you have to. Do not draw your guns."

"Gas?" said one of the young police officers. "We don't even have masks."

"We're short on masks," said the sergeant.

"So we can't draw our weapons," said the young policeman, looking around at his fellow officers for support. "They're lootin' this whole block. We supposed to, what, stand back and let 'em?"

"Orders from above," said the sergeant, repeating the command. "Intimidation and threat."

Strange looked to the south. CDU officers wearing white riot helmets, gas masks, long white billy clubs on their belts, and armed with tear gas canisters, were not far behind them. They had formed at 14th and Swann and were marching north in a streetwide wedge, using their clubs to move looters toward MPD officers accompanying them in squad cars and paddy wagons. As they marched, they passed Nick's Grill, owned by Nick Stefanos. As of yet, its plate-glass window and the window in its door had not been touched.

Strange started up the hill on foot with two other police. He passed a used-car lot at Belmont Street, where a Chevy had been set on fire. Orange light colored his uniform and danced at his feet.

The drizzle had turned to hard rain. Strange adjusted his hat, pulling it down tightly on his forehead so that its bill would deflect the water away from his face. He could see other police on side streets, inside and outside their cars, talking nervously among themselves, trying to light damp cigarettes. He walked on.

At the top of the hill at Clifton, youths hurled rocks and bottles at buses and the last of the cars that were still using 14th. A bottle went through the window of a squad car parked sideways in the street. Strange chased one rock thrower down but lost him as he cut into an alley. The boy looked to be in his early teens. A young woman cursed at Strange from an open apartment window as he walked back to 14th. He didn't even turn his head.

Strange walked north. He saw some police regrouping at Fairmont Street. He saw the broad back of an officer who was gesturing with his hands as he spoke to the others. He knew from the broad gestures and the way the man stood that it was Lydell Blue. Strange came upon the group and shook hands with his friend. He and Blue stepped back from the others.

"What's goin' on with you, brother?" said Blue. "Heard from my man Morris up in the Sixth that you thwarted a robbery today."

"I didn't thwart shit," said Strange. "My partner got shot while I was duckin' behind a car."

"I expect it took the juice out you, man."

"I'm good."

"You're on your second shift, right? You all right to be here?"

"I *got* to be here, Lydell."

Their attention went north as the voices of the crowd there neared a frenzied pitch. Between the next street, Girard, and beyond to Park Road, hundreds of young people began smashing the windows of clothing, liquor, and hardware stores, and looting their contents. Uniformed police waded into the crowd, waving their clubs.

"We better get to it," said Strange, pulling his nightstick

as other officers gathered around them. Blue pulled his night-stick, too.

The officers went into the crowd with their sticks high. They apprehended some looters and chased others into alleys. These same people, mostly youths and young men, emerged from the alleys minutes later and resumed their looting. Strange took a rock to his back, felt the sting, and turned and saw the man who'd thrown it, who was smiling at him from the crowd. He chased the man with an explosion of energy fueled by adrenaline, and as he reached him swung his nightstick, clipping him on the shoulder. The man, who was Strange's age, tripped and went down. Strange held him there until a paddy wagon, slowly collecting looters, arrived.

"Tom-ass nigger," said the man.

Strange led him without comment to the paddy wagon and pushed him roughly into the back.

Strange's next capture was a running boy who had bumped into him, looking over his shoulder as he tried to carry a stereo system down the street. The boy dropped the stereo to the asphalt as Strange got him in a hug. He looked into the boy's eyes, saw himself at twelve, and let him go.

About five hundred MPD officers and CDU police had now arrived on the 14th Street corridor due to the call-ups and overlapping shifts. Fire trucks had arrived as well. Still, the police and firemen were badly outnumbered by rioters, un-prepared for the frenzy that had ensued, and rendered impo-tent by the restraint orders they had been given.

At half past midnight, fires were set at the Central Market and the Pleasant Hill Market on opposite corners of the inter-section at 14th and Fairmont. The Pleasant Hill fire spread to Steelman's liquor store beside it and to the apartments above. Firemen tried to extinguish the blaze as they were surrounded by taunting crowds and pelted by rocks and bottles from the street and from the rooftops of the adjacent buildings. Police threw tear gas canisters into the crowd. They tossed them from on foot and out the windows of roving squad cars and paddy wagons. CDU officers used grenade launchers to shoot tear gas onto the roofs from which offenders were attacking them with projectiles.

The rain had stopped. Burglar alarms rang steadily in the night. Smoke drifted in the street through the light strobing off the cherry tops of the squad car roofs.

Strange sat on the running board of a fire truck, a wet rag in his burning, tearing eyes, his throat raw, his breathing short. A fireman had handed him the rag. The tear gas had driven back the crowd, but it had also incapacitated many of the uniformed officers, who had no masks. Strange watched two women coming down the street, laughing and holding up dresses against one another to check their fit, tears running down their faces. They were of his generation. They were his color.

He looked around the street and saw no police he knew. He could not see Lydell.

A white police officer walked by him, dirt on his face, rubbing at his eyes, unaware that Strange was sitting on the truck. The police officer said, "Fuckin' niggers" to no one, then repeated it, shaking his head as he walked on. Strange watched him pass.

He thought of Carmen: where she was and what she was doing tonight. She was with her friends, probably, from Howard U. Talking about this, getting behind it, most likely, while he was out here fighting it. He thought of his brother and what he would say if he were still alive. His father and his mom. The conversations they'd all be having, the spirited debate, if they were together again on Princeton. What would his father tell him to do if he were here right now?

Strange dropped the rag to the street, got up, and walked to an area of disturbance to the south.

At the Empire Market at 14th and Euclid, a group of youths had attempted to set fire to the looted store. Police had driven them away with tear gas, but they had returned. One of the young men threw a canister back at the officers who had thrown it at him. Strange joined the officers in their attempts to repel the assault. The boys disappeared into a nearby alley, returned fifteen minutes later, and tried again. Police were successful in chasing them off but were called back north to quell more rioting. When Strange returned with other police, the store had been set ablaze.

Strange stood in the street as firemen trained their hoses with futility on the store.

A woman his mother's age, wearing a housecoat, came out from a nearby apartment building and handed him a teacup full of water. Strange thanked her and drank it down, lapping at it like a dog. Strange and the woman watched the market burn, their faces illuminated by the flames and embers that rose into the night.

STRANGE FOUND BLUE down around U Street near dawn. Police now lined the strip, and most of the citizens had gone indoors. Tear gas and the smoke of fires still roiled in the air, and burglar alarms continued to sound. But it seemed as if the trouble was done.

Two hundred adults and juveniles had been arrested. Two hundred stores had had their windows broken, and most of those stores had been looted. Many buildings had been destroyed by fire.

Some windows of the F Street Hecht's had been broken, as had the windows of D.J. Kaufman's at 10th and E, near Pennsylvania Avenue. Scattered window breaking had been reported on Mount Pleasant Street, 7th and Florida, and in Park View, where kids had hurled rocks from moving cars. But the rioting seemed to have been contained to the 14th Street corridor.

"Go home," said Blue, his face streaked with dried tears of dirt.

"I'm on till eight."

"I talked to my CO," said Blue. "He said you can go. Take those boys you came with, too."

Strange nodded. Blue tapped his fist to his chest. Strange did the same.

Strange and his fellow officers from the Sixth took their squad car up to the precinct house. Those that did not go to sleep immediately in the car did not speak. At the station, Strange picked up his Impala and drove down to his parents' row house. As he turned off Georgia onto Princeton, he noticed that the window in the door of Meyer's market had been broken. Mr. Meyer was there, taping a square of cardboard over the glass.

Derek Strange's parents were seated at the eating table of the living room as he entered the apartment. He hugged his mother, who stood to greet him, and shook his father's hand. Derek had a seat at the table and rubbed one hand over his cheeks while his mother went into the kitchen to get him a cup of black coffee.

Darius Strange looked at his son's dirt-streaked face and the areas of his uniform darkened by ash and perspiration.

"You had quite a day," said Darius.

Derek nodded. By his tone Derek knew that his father was telling him he had done well.

"I want you to take care of yourself, you hear me, boy?"

"Yes," said Derek.

"Your mother can't take another loss."

"I'll be fine."

"Look at me, son." Darius leaned forward and lowered his voice. "I'm sick, Derek."

"What you mean, *sick?*"

"I mean I don't know how much longer I have on this earth."

"Pop . . ."

"Ain't no need for you to stress on it. I'm tellin' you now so you think about it the next time you step out that door."

"How do you know?"

"I *know*. Now, listen, you're gonna need to stay healthy for your mother. She's strong, but there is only so much a person can take."

"Have you told her?"

Darius shook his head. He kept his gaze on his son, telling him with his eyes not to speak about what had been said, as Alethea returned to the table and placed a cup of coffee before Derek.

"Thank you, Mama," he said.

"We should say some words," said Alethea.

Darius led them in a prayer. They prayed for Dr. King and for what he stood for, and for peace to come to the streets. They prayed for justice. They prayed for Dr. King's soul and for the soul of their son and brother, Dennis Strange.

"Amen," said Alethea and Derek when Darius was done.

Darius cleared his throat. "This trouble is gonna change the funeral plans."

"I'll call the home today," said Derek. "See what they say."

"You need to get some rest first," said Alethea.

"I will." Derek noticed his mother's uniform dress and his father's starched white shirt for the first time. "Y'all are going in today?"

"Everybody is," said Darius. "Business as usual, that's what they're sayin' on the radio and TV."

"They need to close everything down," said Derek. "Show some respect for the reverend. That's what most folks are lookin' for."

"I agree," said Darius. "But the decision's been made. Even the government's open. "

"You don't work for the government."

"True. But I'm not gonna leave Mike shorthanded. And your mother's got her obligations, too." Darius looked at his wristwatch. "I better get goin'. I need to fire up that grill."

Darius got up from his seat, went to Alethea, and kissed her on the edge of her mouth. He took his jacket off a limb of the coat tree and put it on. Derek followed him to the door.

"You remember what I told you," said Darius. "You mind yourself out there."

"I'll do my best."

Darius eyed Derek up and down. "You got tested, didn't you?"

"You *know* I did. I got called every name in the book by my own kind. I got looked at with hate by folks who been looked down on their whole lives, just like me. I'm tellin' you, there were times when I felt like joining those people last night."

"You want the truth?" said Darius. "I felt like joining them, too."

"Why didn't you, then?"

"'Cause that's not me. Doesn't mean I can't recognize that what happened last night was necessary. People gonna listen now. They *have* to."

"So what do *I* do?"

"You made a commitment," said Darius. "Folks always gonna respect you for that, even if they say different."

"What are you tellin' me?"

"Do your job."

Darius hugged Derek and patted his back. He nodded to Alethea before heading out the door.

Derek took his seat at the table again and sipped his coffee. "Anyone call me?"

"You mean Carmen?"

"Anyone."

"Carmen didn't call." Alethea reached across the table and touched Derek's hand. "Go get a shower while I make you some breakfast."

Derek took off his uniform in his brother's bedroom and folded it neatly, placing it on a chair. He showered and changed into pants and a shirt that were Dennis's and smelled like Dennis. As he dressed, his mother used some grease from an old Wilkin's coffee can to fry bacon and eggs in a skillet. She served them along with toast, hot sauce, and another cup of coffee as Derek came back to the table. She sat and watched him eat.

"You need a ride?" said Derek, sopping up the yolk of the eggs with a triangle of toast.

"I'm gonna catch the uptown bus," she said. "You finish your breakfast and get yourself into bed. I want you to sleep."

Derek did as he was told. He fell asleep quickly in his brother's bed and did not hear his mother leave the house.

THIRTY-ONE

O N FRIDAY MORNING, Strange slept soundly.
As he slept, commuters from the suburbs drove cars and
rode buses to their downtown jobs. One hundred fifty thousand students and teachers reported to D.C. public schools,
which had been decreed open by Mayor Washington after he
had conferred with school superintendent William R. Manning.
It was decided that activities related to the annual Cherry Blossom Festival would also go on as planned. Despite the rioting
of the night before, public officials and police administrators
expected it to be a quiet day.

From the start, there were indications that this would not
be so.

All night and into the morning, tales had spread throughout the city of the exploits of the Shaw rioters and looters.
They spread via phone and ghetto telegraph: street talk at bus
stops, in living rooms, at corner markets, and at predawn
pickup points for day laborers. The stories became romanti-

cized with each telling; they fired up the anger, imagination, spirit of adventure, and ambition of the young.

Many black working-class men and women, along with black government workers, managers, and bureaucrats, stayed home from their jobs. Black teachers, and some white teachers, called in sick in protest or asked outright to be excused from work so they could attend memorial services for Dr. King.

Shortly after the opening bell, school officials began to report massive student absences, as well as a general unruliness and insubordination among the students who had reported to class. An SNCC official tried to persuade Superintendent Manning to close the schools, but he did not. As the morning went on, increasingly frustrated principals, some with panic in their voices, reported that the situation was deteriorating and claimed that the students could no longer be controlled.

Based on history, officials believed that riots occurred, for the most part, at night, after extended lulls in activity during the daylight hours. Accordingly, D.C. National Guardsmen had been ordered to be prepared for possible action on Friday night and were in the early stages of assemblage at the downtown armory. The CDU riot police were not due to report back until five p.m. Also, because of the relative quiet at dawn, many cops working double shifts had been dismissed early. Consequently, on Friday morning, police presence on the street was not noticeably heavier than it was on any other day.

Youths began congregating and drifting in roving bands on 14th and 7th Street, along H Street Northeast, and in east-of-the-river Anacostia. They stood in the doorways of retail establishments and taunted white store owners and clerks who had reported in for work. They shook the cars of white drivers stopped at red lights. A young white man was dragged from his automobile on 14th Street and brutally beaten. His life was saved by a Catholic priest.

Just below the apartment house of Derek Strange, at 13th and Clifton, the students at Cardozo High School began to walk out of classes. By midday, half of them had left the grounds. Along with students of other nearby high schools, many joined their friends on 14th and 7th Streets. Some walked to the grounds of Howard University, where Stokely Carmichael was scheduled to speak.

At a news conference that morning, Carmichael had said, "When white America killed Dr. King last night, she declared war on us. There will be no crying and there will be no funeral." And: "There no longer needs to be intellectual discussion. Black people know that they have to get guns. White America will live to cry that she killed Dr. King last night."

At Howard U, there had been an early service for faculty and students in Crampton Auditorium. Following a speech by university president James Nabrit, a choir led the attendees in Brahms's *Requiem*, along with "Precious Lord," which Dr. King had asked to be sung at Thursday night's gathering moments before he was shot. The final song, "We Shall Overcome," was reportedly less well received. Many young people in the Crampton audience refused to sing along.

Afterward, outside the steps of Frederick Douglass Hall, a more aggressive rally had begun, as speakers stepped up to denounce white racism to an audience of several hundred listeners. The crowd was heavy with serious faces, black turtlenecks, fatigue jackets, goatees and Vandykes, naturals, and shades. The American flag, flying at half-mast, was lowered, and the flag of Ujamma, a campus Black Nationalist organization that advocated a separate black nation, was raised. A female speaker came out against nonviolent response. "I might die violently," she said. "But I am going to take a honky with me." Stokely Carmichael, in sunglasses and fatigues, stepped up to the microphone next.

In the crowd stood Carmen Hill. She had been up half the night with her friends discussing the events and watching them unfold on TV. Most of her friends were in favor of the violence that had erupted Thursday night. None of them had participated. She had called Derek twice during the night at his apartment to make sure he was all right. There had been no response.

Carmen knew intellectually that what had happened, what was going to happen, had been coming for some time. She was a black woman, and in her heart she stood with her people. Like many young black people, she felt invigorated and emboldened by the response to the King assassination. She was also afraid.

Carmen listened to Carmichael's speech. She watched him produce a gun from his jacket and wave it above his head, as he had on 14th Street the night before.

"Stay off the streets if you don't have a gun," said Carmichael, "because there is going to be shooting."

Carmen thought of Derek and prayed to God to keep him safe.

A LITTLE AFTER noon, on 14th Street, just south of U, a fire broke out at the local Safeway. Four minutes later, eleven blocks north of the grocery store, a mob of young men set fire to a clothing store on the corner of Harvard Street.

Firemen and available police were called back down to 14th.

Almost immediately, teenagers and young men, who had been gathering all morning on the strip, began to initiate further activity. Fires were set in Belmont TV, the London Custom Shop, and Judd's Pharmacy, which had already been damaged and looted the night before. As firemen tried to hook up their hoses to hydrants, they were bricked, assaulted, and verbally abused, protected only by small groups of baton-wielding police who had arrived on the scene. The fires spread to the apartments above and the tenement buildings behind the stores. The Worthmore Clothing store on Park Road began to burn.

The mob moved from one spot to the next, undaunted by tear gas canisters and gas grenades. They began to break into stores between Columbia and Park Road, a retail strip of chain and white-owned businesses. They used small missiles and trash cans, and kicked in windows with their feet. They uprooted street signs and used them as battering rams. Rioters swarmed into the Lerner's and Grayson's dress stores, Irving's Men's Shop, Carousel, Kay Jewelers, Beyda's, Cannon Shoes, Howard Clothes, Mary Jane Shoes, Woolworth's, and the G.C. Murphy's five-and-dime.

Many black business owners had spray-painted or soap-written the words "Soul Brother" on their store windows or doors in the early morning hours. Many of these businesses were spared.

Middle-aged men and women began to loot. Families stole together. Parents and their children carted entire dining-room, bedroom, and living-room sets out of the Hamilton and Jordan Fine Furniture store at Euclid.

"Animals," said one policeman, standing impotently on a street corner as a father and his sons carried clothing, still on hangers, on their backs, laughing as they walked without fear of reprisal down 14th. The cop could only watch. Few arrests were being made. The police were outnumbered and completely unprepared.

Molotov cocktails were concocted in alleys and thrown from sidewalks. Hahn's shoe store burned after being picked clean. Beyda's burned. Hoses lay serpentine in the street as firemen scrambled to find water sources amid the jeers and general confusion.

The G.C. Murphy's was engulfed in a tremendous, raging blaze. Two teenage boys were trapped in the fire. Both died. One was burned beyond recognition and never identified.

Three hours after the first arson at noon, a large portion of 14th Street above U was on fire. By now, other parts of the city had begun to experience the same kind of devastation as Shaw.

Police officials called all available officers to duty and ordered scheduled late-shifters to report immediately as well. Lydell Blue arrived on 14th in a squad car packed with five men. He stepped out of the car, wide-eyed, and drew his stick.

DEREK STRANGE HEARD a phone ringing in his parents' living room. He fell back to sleep. The phone began to ring again and continued to ring until he got off the bed, his head unclear, and answered the call.

The rioting, looting, and burning had spread to 7th Street and the H Street corridor in Northeast. Ed Burns, his duty officer, was on the line, telling him that he was needed. He'd been trying to reach Strange at his apartment and was now using the alternate number Strange had left on file.

"You don't have to do this," said Burns. "I know what you been through these past few days. I hated to even call you up, but I'm callin' everyone, understand?"

"I'm fine," said Strange, thinking of Alvin Jones, thinking of where Kenneth Willis had said he'd be. "I'm right off Georgia Avenue, just a couple of miles north of Seventh. I'll head down there now."

"Good luck."

Strange went to the stove in the kitchen and used a straight match to light the gas of one of the burners, where his mother had left half a pot of coffee. He returned to the living room and turned on the television news.

Fourteenth Street was burning. Hundreds of youths were reported to be moving south on 7th Street, looting and starting fires. The Charles Macklin Furniture Store, at O, had been looted and was now aflame. Crowds were forming on H Street, where a liquor store was on fire. Sporadic burning and looting had begun east of the Anacostia River. In the downtown shopping district, the Hecht's and Woodward and Lothrop's flagship stores had shut down and carpenters had boarded their windows after youths ran through the aisles, stealing small items and yelling obscenities and threats at customers and clerks.

Strange got a cup of hot black coffee, came back out to the phone, and looked up the number of the Washington Sanitarium in the book. The receptionist put him through to Troy Peters's room. He told Troy about his night and relayed the current situation.

"I'm watching it on TV," said Peters. "The reporter said that LBJ's gonna call in the army and the guard."

"You're gonna miss all the action."

"Looks like I caught a lucky bullet."

"I guess you did. You, who wanted to be on that welcome wagon come revolution time."

"It shouldn't have happened like this."

"Wasn't but one way *for* it to happen. Everybody saw the fuse burnin', but they turned their heads away."

"Listen . . ."

"Lotta people sorry now," said Strange. "I gotta get to work."

"Take care of yourself, Derek."

"You, too."

Strange built a sandwich, not knowing when he'd get his next meal, and washed it down with two glasses of water. He drank another cup of coffee while he got back into his uniform in his brother's room. The uniform stank of last night's dirt and sweat. He fastened his utility belt around his waist, patted his handcuffs at the small of his back, and felt for the backup ammo in his dump pouch. He pushed his nightstick down through its loop. He checked the load of his .38 and slipped it into his swivel holster. He looked at his brother's unmade bed before walking back out to the living room and picking up the phone.

Strange called his father at the diner. He told him that he was going in and suggested that his father get back home.

"I'm leaving now," said Darius. "Mike's about to close."

"What about Mama?"

"I called her at the Vaughns'. She says that Frank Vaughn's heading into town. He's gonna drive her in."

"Vaughn's okay," said Strange. "He'll make sure she gets in safe."

"Right."

"I might be out here for a while, Pop. I don't want y'all to worry about me."

"I'll see you at supper on Sunday," said Darius, trying to steady the catch in his voice.

"I'll be there," said Strange.

He left the apartment, went down Princeton, and turned left on Georgia Avenue. He walked south, hearing the sirens of police cars and fire trucks coming from all directions. A young man yelled something angrily at him from a passing car, and Strange did not react. He stopped for a moment at the crest of the long hill that descended along Howard University and looked down to the Florida Avenue intersection, where Georgia became 7th Street. People swarmed in the canyon there under a smoke-dark sky.

THIRTY-TWO

OUTSIDE THE THREE-STAR Diner, on Kennedy Street, young men stood on the sidewalk, occasionally looking through the plate-glass window, alternately laughing and hard-eyeing Mike Georgelakos and his son, Billy, both behind the counter. Mike knew all of them by sight and many by name; he knew their parents and had served a few of their grandparents as well.

Darius Strange had used a brick to clean the grill, left his toque lying on the sandwich board, and was in the process of putting on his jacket. Ella Lockheart had finished filling the ketchup bottles and the salt and pepper shakers, and now sat on one of the red stools, applying lipstick that she had taken from her purse. Halftime, the dishwasher and utility man, had phoned in sick.

"*Mavri*," said Mike with disgust, looking at the kids.

"Dad," said Billy.

"What the hell," said Mike.

Darius had heard all the bad Greek words come from

Mike's mouth over the years. He knew that *mavri*, in all its variations, meant black people, and usually when Mike added something before or after, or did that curling thing with his lip, its meaning was negative and foul.

Darius's and Ella's eyes met for a moment. She dropped her lipstick into her purse.

"I'm gonna be gettin' on," said Ella.

"You need a ride?" said Darius.

"No, thank you," said Ella. "I'll walk."

"I'm gonna call you both," said Mike, "let you know about tomorrow. I'm hopin' this here is gonna blow over and we're gonna open up."

Ella went out the door without a word. Darius watched her walk down the sidewalk through the group of kids, which parted to let her pass.

"You better get goin'," said Mike.

"You, too," said Darius.

"Ah," said Mike with a wave of his hand. "I don't worry 'bout nothin'."

"Where's Derek?" said Billy.

"Seventh Street, right about now," said Darius, turning up the collar of his jacket. "Working."

"God bless the MPD," said Billy. "Tell him I was thinking about him, okay?"

"I will," said Darius.

"Hey," said Mike, his voice stopping Darius as he reached for the door. Mike's forehead was streaked with sweat, and his barrel chest rose and fell with each labored breath. A cigarette burned between his fingers.

"What is it?"

"Thanks for comin' in today, Darius," said Mike.

Darius nodded, looking without emotion into Mike's eyes. Neither could know that they would both be dead within the year.

Darius walked from the diner to his car on the street.

"Let's go," said Billy to his father. *"Pa-meh."*

"I ain't goin' nowhere, goddamnit," said Mike. "Those boys gonna break my window, somethin'."

"We can fix a window," said Billy, putting his hand on Mike's shoulder. "C'mon, *Ba-ba.* It's time to go."

Mike left the register's cash drawer open, as he did every night at closing, so that anyone could see from the street that it was empty. He took the store keys from his pocket and locked the front door.

DESPITE THE WARNING from Derek Strange, Kenneth Willis had phoned Alvin Jones at Ronnie Moses's apartment on Thursday afternoon and told him that Strange was looking to hunt him down. Strange had put a scare into Willis, and a hurting on him, too, but it didn't stop Willis from making the call. He couldn't do Alvin like that. Alvin was kin.

On the phone, Jones denied any knowledge of the murder of Dennis Strange. He had decided not to admit it, on account of Dennis was Kenneth's boy from way back and he didn't want Kenneth to get upset. Also, he didn't care to give Kenneth anything the police could use against him if Kenneth got picked up on something later on. Kenneth was strong, but even a strong man could get flipped.

"All right, Ken," said Jones. "Thanks for the tip."

"What you gonna do?" said Willis.

"What you think?" said Jones, as if he were speaking to a child. "Keep my head low. Understand, I ain't have shit to do with your boy's demise, but I can't be fuckin' with no police nohow."

"You got a plan?"

"Man like me always got a plan," said Jones before hanging up the phone.

The riots of Thursday night had given him his plan. Jones had gone out, near midnight, and stepped onto an eastbound

D.C. Transit bus on Rhode Island Avenue with a stocking over his face and his gun in his hand, robbing the driver of eighty dollars in cash. It was the easiest robbery he'd ever pulled. Seemed like all of the police were over in Shaw. He knew they weren't gonna give a good fuck about some little old stickup job when 14th Street was going up in flames.

And here he was today, in Ronnie's apartment near 7th Street. Standing in front of the mirror, admiring his new shit, which he and Ronnie had looted from the Cavalier Men's Shop between L and K just a little while back. Looking at his new Zanzibar slacks, his Damon knit shirt, and his side-weave kicks. The shirt, especially, was right on, a real nice color gold. Picked up the gold band on his favorite black hat. He cocked the hat a little so it sat right on his head.

Ronnie had left the crib to get more vines. Said he was heading down to his place of employment, the big-men's shop, to get what he could, 'cause those clothes there were the only ones in town that could fit a horse like him. Said he knew where his sizes were and exactly the items he wanted, 'cause he'd had his eye on them for some time. Jones telling him he wasn't thinking straight, to be shittin' in his own feeding trough like that, but Ronnie had waved him away.

"I know what I'm doin'," Ronnie Moses had said, heading for the door. "You with me, blood?"

"Go on," said Jones. "I'm gonna take a little rest."

"Lock the apartment, man, you go out."

"Yeah, all right."

Jones thinking, Now I am really gonna roll. Take someone off for some real cash. 'Cause the police, they are busy. Too busy tryin' to contain those thousands of black motherfuckers out on the street to worry over *one* black motherfucker like me. Make a nice score, real money, none of this eighty-dollar shit, and leave town. Go down to South Carolina, where his mother's people still stayed, and visit for a while. See what he could score down there.

Thank you, Dr. King. Thank you for this opportunity.

Jones went to his bag, had all his clothes and shit inside it, which he kept beside the sofa where he slept. He withdrew his old .38, had the bluing rubbed off the barrel. Jones had wrapped black electrical tape around the grip; his hands tended to sweat when he was working, and he needed to have a tight hold on his gun. He released the cylinder, checked the five-shot load, and snapped it shut. He dropped the pistol into the right pocket of his Zanzibar slacks. He found a crumpled-up stocking in a bedroom drawer, belonged to Ronnie's bottom girl, and shoved it into the left pocket of his slacks. He checked himself in the mirror one more time, readjusted his hat, and left the apartment, locking the door behind him as he had said he would.

He went down to 7th Street and walked south.

There were hundreds of young people out on the street, looting stores, hollering and laughing, having fun. Boys and girls, and some older people, too. Cops trying to contain the rioters, having little success. Firemen hosing down burning buildings, ducking the occasional rock and bottle thrown their way.

Leventhal's Furniture Store, at Q, it wasn't much more than a shell now. The store had been stripped of goods and was burning inside. The apartment houses nearby were burning with it.

Leventhal's, thought Jones, stepping around a flaming mattress. Jew name, wasn't it? Like most of the stores down here, owned by Jews. Long after they'd moved out the neighborhood their own selves, they were still doing business on 7th, selling jewelry and furniture and stereos and appliances to blacks. Selling credit, really, and high-interest credit at that. Jones could see the glee on the faces of the looters as they broke into another store. Wasn't much about Dr. King anymore, *was* it? It was about getting things for free, and getting back at every motherfucker, Jew and white man alike, who'd been bleeding them and stepping on their necks their whole goddamn lives. Leastways, that's the way Jones saw it. His people, getting a little bit back.

His people. Truth was, Jones didn't give a fuck about them. When this was done, they'd go back to their sad-ass lives. While he, Jones, would be driving south with cash in the pockets of his new outfit, maybe under the wheel of that white El D he'd seen across town. Had electric windows and everything.

He passed a brother in the street, wearing shades and fatigues, imploring some other young brothers to drop the stolen shit they were carrying and go home.

"Dr. King wouldn't want this!" shouted the man.

Jones laughed. Now he'd seen it all.

A black man stood outside his deli, holding a pistol at his side, watching the neighborhood burn. His store was untouched. Jones passed other stores and heard dogs barking and growling viciously behind their doors. These stores, too, had gone untouched.

People ran around him and bumped and said not one thing. He coughed and rubbed at his eyes. The police had started using gas. He was sweating some, too. The fires in the buildings were throwing off serious heat.

Down by the big-men's shop, he saw Ronnie lying face-down in the street, a sweaty white cop over him, knee down, cuffing Ronnie's hands behind his back, other cops doing the same to some other young brothers, a paddy wagon parked nearby.

You fucked up, cuz, thought Jones. You have lost your job now, too. But I can't help you, can I? You'll be out in a few days, if you're lucky, and you can put your life together then. In the meantime, I got work to do.

Down below L, past the Cavalier Men's Shop, which had been picked clean, Jones could see a row of police and squad cars blocking off Mount Vernon Square. This was the line dividing black residents from the commercial center of downtown, white D.C. Isn't no surprise, thought Jones. They're protecting the master's castle, like they always do.

Jones cut right and then right again, going north of Massachusetts Avenue. He had parked his car over here the night before. He had heard talk on the street that 7th was going to burn the next day. Funny how most everyone down here knew, when the police, they hadn't known a thing.

———

THE HOUSE IN Wheaton had gone quieter through the morning and into the afternoon. Olga sitting at the kitchen table, smoking her Larks, watching the news broadcasts on the little black-and-white Philco set on a rolling metal stand. Olga telling Alethea how sorry she was for her "people," not meeting Alethea's eyes as she spoke. Frank lumbering around in his robe, reading the sports page, drinking coffee, smoking cigarettes, like it was any other day. Only their son, Ricky, had talked to her not as a Negro woman but as a woman. Asked her, also, if there was anything he could do to help her get back home.

"Your father's going to drive me," she said. "Thank you."

He hugged her outside the kitchen, unselfconsciously, as he had when he was a child. She had always been fond of him. Maybe there was hope in the young. Maybe she and the Vaughns and everyone like them needed to die out before this sickness was erased. It was a shame it had to be that way. But she had the feeling it was so.

Alethea stood in the foyer by the front door, waiting for Frank Vaughn to come downstairs and drive her back home. She could hear his muffled voice coming from his and Olga's bedroom, and the music behind the closed door of Ricky's room.

Up in the bedroom, Vaughn slipped his .38 Special into his shoulder holster and went to the small nightstand on his side of the bed. He opened its drawer and used a key on a green lockbox. Inside the box was another gun: a cheap .32 automatic holstered in a clip-on. He removed it from its holster, checked the magazine, and palmed the six-shot load back into the laminated-wood grip. He clipped the reholstered .32, which he had taken off a pimp in Shaw six months earlier, onto the belt line behind his back. He folded a cloth handkerchief into a small square and dropped it into the pocket of his pants. He shook himself into his Robert Hall suit jacket, gray with light blue stripes, and looked himself over in the mirror.

"Why do you have to go in?" said Olga, looking at him from across the room, leaning against the frame of their master bathroom door.

"I'm workin' a case."

"Today?"

"Homicide never sleeps."

"Haven't you been watching the news?"

Vaughn formed his mouth into an O, gave Olga a theatrical look of surprise. "Why, is somethin' goin' on?"

"Don't be an ape."

"I'm not goin' near the trouble spots, Olga. Don't worry."

"Promise me, Frank."

"Okay, I promise."

It was a lie.

"Come here," said Vaughn.

She crossed the room and put her arms around his waist. He lowered his face and kissed her on the lips. He pushed himself against her to let her know he was alive. He thought of Linda Allen and her warm box.

"I might be late tonight, doll."

"Call me. So I know you're all right."

Vaughn left the room and stepped onto the second-floor landing, glancing at Ricky's closed door before going down the stairs. Alethea Strange was waiting for him in the foyer, buttoning her coat over her uniform dress.

"Let's go," said Vaughn.

"Aren't you gonna say good-bye to your son?"

"What, you kiddin'?"

"Tell him you love him. *Hug* him, Mr. Vaughn." Alethea made a motion with her chin, pointing it toward the second floor. "Go ahead. I can wait."

Something in her liquid brown eyes told him not to protest. He went back up the stairs and knocked on Ricky's door.

DOWNTOWN GOVERNMENT WORKERS and private-sector employees, hearing the ongoing reports of escalating rioting on the radio, getting panic calls from spouses, and seeing the smoke drifting toward them from the eastern portion of the city, began to leave their jobs in numbers. Retail employees on F Street and in the rest of the downtown district did the same. Massive uptown and crosstown traffic jams ensued. Some citizens stepped into four-ways and tried to direct cars through gridlocked intersections. Others abandoned their automobiles and walked, trying to relieve the anxiety they felt at being trapped inside their vehicles.

On Georgia Avenue, the northbound lanes were at a virtual standstill. Vaughn drove his Polara south with relative ease, Alethea Strange beside him on the big bench seat. They had passed through Shepherd Park and Sheridan, where there had been scattered window-breaking and looting at places like Ida's department store, but nothing of the magnitude of 7th Street below. The sky had darkened and the smell of smoke grew stronger as they drove deeper into the city.

Vaughn lit a cigarette and kept it in his left hand, hanging it out the window so as not to bother Alethea. He turned on the radio and tuned it to a middle-of-the-road station just as the DJ began to introduce a song: "And here's one you're gonna like,

Frank and Nancy Sinatra doing 'Somethin' Stupid.' I'm Fred Fiske, and you're listening to twelve six-oh, WWDC."

Vaughn sang the Frank parts under his breath and let Nancy do her thing without his accompaniment. Alethea had to marvel at Vaughn's nonchalant attitude in the face of the ongoing events. But then, that was Frank Vaughn all over. Single-minded, unchanging, stuck in a time that never was and that existed, perhaps, only in his mind.

"Did you talk to Ricky?" said Alethea as the song came to an end.

"A little," said Vaughn, keeping his eyes on the road.

"He's a good boy."

"Yeah, he's all right."

"It's important to tell them that you love them," she said. "Every time they leave the house, or you leave . . . You just don't know if you'll ever have the chance again. Only the Lord has that kind of knowledge."

"Amen," said Vaughn clumsily.

He was sweating a little under his collar. He knew she was reflecting on the death of her firstborn son and her own regrets. He had never been comfortable with these kinds of conversations.

When he'd gone into Ricky's room, their brief exchange had been awkward and forced. Ricky hadn't even turned down the music, some guy singing about his "white room," something to do with drugs, most likely. Vaughn had given his son a hug before he left, as Alethea had suggested, the first one he'd given him in years. It felt as okay as an embrace could feel between two men. What he hadn't done was tell Ricky that he loved him. He didn't understand why you had to say you loved your kid or, for that matter, put your arms around him to show it. Hell, he'd been feeding him, clothing him, and buying him things his whole life. For Chrissakes, wasn't that enough?

"Thank you," said Alethea.

"For what?"

"Looking after Derek yesterday during that robbery. He told me the whole story."

"He . . ." Vaughn searched for the word. "He acquitted himself well. He's a fine young man. Gonna be good police."

They drove into Park View and neared her street.

"I'm worried about him," said Alethea. "Out there in all this."

Vaughn could feel her eyes on him directly.

"I'll look after him," said Vaughn as casually as he could. "I'm goin' down there now."

Down there, thought Vaughn, to find the one who murdered your son. I have fucked up everything good in my life, but there is one thing that I still do right.

"Thank you, Frank," she said.

He felt himself blush as he heard her say his name. He turned left onto Princeton and went slowly up the street. He stopped at her row house, where her husband, Darin or whatever his name was, stood out front. He turned to look at her. She nodded at him once and smiled with her eyes. Vaughn thinking, She's no Julie London. But, damn, that is a woman right there.

Vaughn watched husband and wife embrace on the front stoop of their row house before he turned the Dodge around. He felt an unfamiliar stab of jealousy as he drove down to Georgia Avenue and hung a left. He put this feeling from his mind and punched the gas. At Irving, a group of kids stood on the sidewalk yelling things at southbound cars. A kid screamed "white motherfucker" at Vaughn as he passed.

Vaughn flicked his cigarette out the open window and laughed.

THIRTY-THREE

T HE TROUBLE ON H Street in Northeast started later than the trouble on 7th and 14th, but it came intensely and all at once. Sometime after one p.m., more than a thousand people rushed onto the strip, burning and looting twelve city blocks of commercial businesses, the longest continuous shopping corridor in black D.C. When the riot erupted, only two dozen police were on the scene.

Police decided to protect the major stores as all available men from the Ninth Precinct sped to H. Shotgun-wielding cops patrolled the front of the neighborhood Safeway. Patrol cars blocked the front of the area Sears. But they couldn't stop the damage occurring in the form of fire between 3rd and 15th, where H Street met Florida Avenue and Bladensburg Road.

In alleys, looters collected their goods and made further plans of assault. Molotov cocktails were filled and ragged, tossed by men who were no longer interested in stealing liquor or merchandise. These arsonists went methodically from one store to the next, throwing their bombs. In this way, the Morton's clothing store at 7th and H, one of the largest employers of blacks in the area, was destroyed. A teenage boy was later found inside the ruins, charred beyond recognition and never to be identified. At the I-C Furniture Company at 5th, a thirty-year-old man was crushed to death when a burning wall collapsed on him. Police arriving on H did not hesitate to fire gas grenades from launchers into the crowd. It deterred the rioters briefly. But by then, the entire corridor appeared to be on fire.

Kenneth Willis walked down H with purpose. He had left his apartment and gone down to the strip, urging on the young men who were carrying the last of the beer and wine from the liquor store beneath his place, slapping others five who had gathered on the sidewalk. But Willis wasn't interested in liquor or anything that small. He had seen a nice watch, looked like it had diamonds around its face, in the window of this jewelry store up a couple of blocks from where he stayed. Could have been fake diamonds pasted on that watch; he wasn't sure. But a woman in a dark bar wouldn't know the difference. A woman would want to get with a man who wore a watch like that on his wrist.

Willis walked on, hoping these people out here hadn't got to that jewelry store before he could.

EAST OF THE Anacostia River, looting had become widespread. Police from the Eleventh and Fourteenth Precincts, showing less restraint than their fellow officers in other areas of the city, and fearful for their lives, began firing their guns over the heads of looters to scare them off. By the end of the day, in Anacostia, police had shot and killed two young men.

Police officials and Mayor Washington conferred with

LBJ. Schools were officially closed, as were government offices. Sixty-four District fire-engine companies were deployed or put on alert. A like number of engine companies from Maryland, Virginia, and Pennsylvania headed for D.C. Troops from the Sixth Armored Cavalry were called in from Fort Meade, Maryland, as were the Third Infantry troops of Company D from Fort Meyer, Virginia. The Third would guard the Federal City and police 7th Street; the Sixth would stage at the Old Soldiers' Home on North Capitol and proceed to H and 14th. The 91st Combat Engineer Battalion from Fort Belvoir, Virginia, was ordered into Far Southeast, Anacostia. The D.C. National Guard, now ready at the Armory, headed for Far Northeast.

ALVIN JONES PARKED his Special on 15th Street, along Meridian Hill, and cut through the park to 16th. He headed for a strip of stone-and-brick row houses, apartments, and a few small hotels. Real nice over here on the Avenue of the Presidents. A broad, clean street, lots of trees . . . usually lots of white people, too. But not today. They were all stuck in their vehicles, looking out the windows. Paler than usual, eyes full of fear.

It had taken Jones a couple of hours to get across town. He realized he would have to leave his car where he had parked it and walk back to Ronnie's crib. He hoped what he was about to do would be worth all this sweat and time.

Jones went up a sidewalk leading to the hotel. Looked like just another house, but it was not. He had cased it a couple of weeks back, walked right up to the registration desk and asked about their rates. Young white boy behind the desk, had doll lips, looked like he took it in his hind parts, had said, "Which type of room are you looking for?" not even thinking to call him "sir." Well, he was gonna show some respect now.

Jones put the stocking over his face right before he stepped through the door. He had the gun out of his pocket two steps in. A woman sitting in a chair in the lobby got a look at him and said, "Oh!" in a loud voice.

"Shut up, bitch," said Jones. She made no further sound.

Wasn't anyone else in the lobby. Jones walked right up to the desk where that boy with the doll lips stood. He had put his hands up in the air. They were already shaking before Jones spoke. Boy wore one of those shirts with the flaps and brass buttons on the shoulders, like he was an admiral in the navy, sumshit like that. Figured that this one would be wearing a sailor suit.

"You know what this is, motherfucker," said Jones, pointing the .38 at the white boy's chest. "Give it up."

Jones looked through the lobby window to the street as the desk boy extracted some bills from the cash drawer and placed them on the counter. Wasn't anyone out there except those who were jammed up in their cars. The guests who were staying in the hotel were probably all upstairs, holed up in their rooms.

"You got a safe in this piece?" said Jones.

"Yes, but —"

"Open it, slim."

"It will take a few minutes."

"It'll take a few minutes, *sir*."

"Sir," said the young man, his lips trembling.

Jones smiled through the mask. "I got time."

Fifteen minutes later he was walking east, his gun in one pocket, eight hundred dollars in the other, smiling occasionally at nothing at all, thinking on what a good day it had been, dreaming of a white El Dorado with red interior and electric windows and seats.

Here I go, thought Jones. No more police on my ass or women with babies trying to bust on my groove. I will be out of this motherfucker tonight. And: I am rich.

FRANK VAUGHN PARKED his Polara in a Howard University lot and walked with his shoulders squared into the fray on 7th. He had removed his badge from his case and pinned it on his lapel.

Everything around him was burning. Ladder trucks, now topped with plywood and wrapped with chicken-wire cages to protect the firemen, attempted to move through the crowds. White-helmeted riot police hung on the sides. Vaughn had not seen anything like this on the soil of his own country. It reminded him of the last days of the war.

He cut left down past P. Rats, fleeing the flames, smoke, and heat, scurried across the street. A couple of blocks in, he passed a corner market that had been looted and tossed, all its windows shattered. He had Criss-Crossed the phone number to the apartment and found the building, a common row house, where Alvin Jones's cousin Ronnie Moses had his place. Vaughn went into a small foyer and up a flight of stairs.

He knocked on the door several times. He knocked again. He said, "Police," just to have said it, and then he drew his service revolver and kicked in the door at the knob. He walked into Moses's apartment and closed the door behind him.

Vaughn went from room to room. He found nudie magazines and women's clothing in the bedroom. He found a Polaroid camera next to a photo album and an open duffel bag holding clothing and shaving equipment dropped beside the shredded couch in the living room. These items told him that Ronnie Moses was a gash-hound and that he was currently hosting a male guest.

Vaughn went back down to the street.

ON H STREET, the Sixth Armored Cavalry arrived in jeeps and trucks and blocked both ends of the shopping district. The soldiers wore yellow kerchiefs around their necks and black gas masks over their faces. They marched in combat formation down the center of the street, carrying M14s with sheathed bayonets, thrusting them at looters, throwing tear gas grenades liberally. Paddy wagons and police officers followed them, making arrests.

Kenneth Willis pushed a drunk down to the sidewalk as he made his way home, going by the big Western Auto store at 9th, completely in flames. There were plenty of drunks on the street, stumbling and laughing, feeling the effects of the liquor they had stolen.

Willis had gotten lucky. He had found that watch in the jewelry store, though it was not in the window where he had expected it to be; there was no window anymore, or anything behind it on display. The watch had been knocked to the floor and kicked by someone toward the back of the shop. The face was scratched some, but Willis knew that a little toothpaste would remove the marks. Willis wore the watch now on his wrist.

He neared his building. Firemen were spraying water into the liquor store and the units above. The fire had engulfed the apartments. The building was completely aflame.

Willis stood there frozen, watching. He had lost his job, for sure. He was up on a felony gun charge. In the last few days he had taken multiple beat-downs from various police. Now everything he owned was carbon and smoke.

He looked at the watch on his wrist. He saw that one of the diamonds circling the face had come loose. He picked it out and squeezed it between his thumb and forefinger. It turned to dust.

Rhinestones, thought Willis. He found this funny, and he laughed.

———

STRANGE HAD USED his nightstick and muscle to make some arrests. He had chased several kids off the corridor, into alleys and onto side streets, hoping they would stay off the main drag. He was doing what he could.

He walked down 7th at Q. An apartment house over a clothing store was burning. A man was screaming at firemen, telling them that his mother, too slow to get down the stairs, was trapped in the blaze. Newspapers would later report that the woman, who died of smoke inhalation, had weighed over four hundred pounds. Her son had begged arsonists not to set the building afire, but they had ignored his pleas.

Strange passed a small furniture store with a plate-glass display window that had not been looted or burned. A white man sat in a rocking chair in the window with a double-barreled shotgun cradled in his arms, a cigar wedged between his lips. The man winked at Strange.

Strange walked by a black man wearing fatigues and shades, pleading with a group of young men to get off the streets, invoking the teachings of Dr. King. Strange knew this was an undercover officer, a man trained in counterrioting techniques. He was not having much success today.

Strange wiped tears from his face. His throat was raw and his eyes stung mercilessly from the gas. His exposed skin felt seared from the heat. Seventh Street was burning down all around him.

Third Infantry soldiers had arrived on 7th and begun to teargas and pursue looters. They protected firemen whose hoses had been cut as they were shelled by bricks and beer bottles from all directions. The soldiers had also begun to make massive arrests. The worst appeared to be over. But there was little left of the street.

"Young man," said a voice behind Strange.

He turned. It was Vaughn. His face was smudged, and his hair had darkened from the soot drifting in the air.

"Detective," said Strange.

"I went to Ronnie Moses's place," said Vaughn, "looking for Alvin Jones."

"And?"

"Jones is staying there, I think," said Vaughn. "He's not in . . . yet."

"So?"

"You *want* him, don't you?"

Strange nodded tightly.

"I just spoke to a lieutenant down here," said Vaughn. "The powers that be are about to announce a curfew. They're gonna have this under control eventually. All these folks out here, they're gonna have to get back to where they live."

"What are you sayin'?" said Strange, raising his voice above the burglar alarms and shouts around him.

"Let's get outta here for a minute," said Vaughn. "All this bullshit, I can't hear myself think."

Vaughn and Strange cut down P, stepping around a steel girder that was glowing red in the street.

MAYOR WASHINGTON, in consultation with Police Chief John Layton, Director of Public Safety Patrick Murphy, and President Johnson, imposed a strict curfew on the District of Columbia to be in effect from 5:30 p.m. Friday evening to 6:30 a.m. the following morning. Police, firemen, doctors, nurses, and sanitation workers were excepted. Beer, wine, and liquor sales were forbidden. Gas would only be sold to motorists who were dispensing it directly into their cars.

Sixth Cavalry troops had arrived late in the afternoon on 14th Street. They assembled down at S and moved north in columns, chanting "March, march, march," in cadence. They threw tear gas canisters liberally and, with police, made sweeping arrests. They secured the top and lower ends of the corridor with two 700-man battalions.

As on 7th and H Streets, there was little left to protect.

Lydell Blue sat on the bed of a four-ton army truck, eating

a peanut-butter-and-jelly sandwich and drinking water from a canteen. A woman from the neighborhood had come with sandwiches to feed police and soldiers on a needed break.

Blue's uniform had taken on the color of charcoal. His back ached, and he could have slept where he sat. He had coughed up blood into his hands moments earlier.

With all of that, he felt good.

In the middle of it, at its worst, as he was protecting his city and his people, he had come to the realization of who he was and what he would always be. He was a black man, through and through. And he was police. The one didn't cancel out the other. He could be both, and be both with pride.

A BROTHER ON the street warned Jones about the curfew. Now Jones knew that he would have to travel with extra care across the city. His plan was to stay below Massachusetts Avenue, keeping close to the downtown buildings, in the shadows, out of sight of the soldiers and police. Then head east to 6th and up to his cousin's crib. Grab his duffel bag, which held his few possessions, and reverse his path. He could do it, the darker it got. All he had to do was reach his Buick, over there on 15th, and he'd be southern bound and stone free.

It took a while, but he reached 6th without incident and went north and east until he came to the block of Ronnie's apartment. He went by the gutted market on the corner, keeping his head low, and crossed the street. He entered the row house where his cousin had his place on the second floor.

Back in the depths of the market, looking through the space where the front window had been, Frank Vaughn stroked the wheel of his Zippo, got flame, and lit a cigarette. He snapped the lid shut.

Little black man with light, almost yellow-colored skin. Just as Strange had said, he was wearing a black hat with a gold band. Now all Vaughn had to do was look up at the window of Ronnie Moses's apartment. Watch for Strange's sign and wait.

Vaughn hit his L&M. Its ember flared, faintly illuminating the ruined market. The only light in there now was the dying light of dusk. There was little inventory remaining on the shelves. Paperback novels, boxes of cake mix and flour strewn about the tiles. Water dripped loudly from a busted pipe. A heap of half-burned newspapers sat piled in the middle of the shop. Someone had set the papers on fire, but the fire had not spread. The smell of carbon was strong in the shell of the store.

Vaughn stepped forward, close to the doorway. From here he could see Ronnie Moses's apartment on the second floor.

"Make him talk and let him go," Vaughn had told Strange. "Flash a light in the window if he confesses. I'll do the rest."

"Do what?" Strange had said.

Vaughn hadn't needed to spell it out for the rookie. He would let the young man make the decision himself.

Vaughn dragged deeply on his cigarette.

SOON AS HE had got to the landing, Jones could tell someone had busted through his cousin's apartment door. It opened, too, with just a little push. Someone had broke into his cousin's crib, that was plain, 'cause he remembered clearly that he'd locked the door. But Jones reasoned that the break-in was just part of the general mayhem of the day. Kids being kids.

He drew his gun from his slacks just the same. He stepped inside.

Strange came from behind the open door and put his service revolver to the back of Jones's head.

"Don't say nothin'," said Strange. "Let go of that gun and drop it to the floor."

"Gun could *discharge* like that," said Jones, not moving, not turning his head.

"Do it," said Strange.

Jones dropped the old revolver. It hit the hardwood with a hollow thud.

"Now move over there to the center of the room," said Strange, "and turn around."

Jones obeyed the command. Strange kept the gun trained on Jones and closed the door with his foot.

Jones smiled a little as he turned around and took in Strange.

"Lawman," said Jones. "Heard you were lookin' for me."

Strange said nothing.

"This about your brother, right?"

Strange did not reply.

"I heard he got hisself dead. My cousin Kenneth told me, man. Damn shame."

"Yes," Strange heard himself say, looking into the odd golden eyes of Alvin Jones.

"I don't know nothin' about it," said Jones. "I mean, if that's why you been huntin' me down, I'm just sayin' . . . I was with a woman the night he was killed." Jones chuckled. "The *whole* night. Bitch would not *let* me out the bed, you hear what I'm sayin'? I could give you her phone number, you want it. She'll tell you."

"I don't want any phone numbers," said Strange.

"*What*, then? You standing there holdin' a gun on me. Tell me what you want. I told you I don't know nothin', man. I don't know what else to do."

Strange stared at Jones.

"If you think I cut him," said Jones, "you are wrong. It wasn't me."

I didn't say anybody cut him. I didn't tell Willis he died that way. The newspapers, they didn't print it . . . so how could you know?

Strange lowered his gun.

"There you go," said Jones, smiling. "Now you seein'

365

things clear. No hard feelings, blood. I can understand you bein' upset."

"Get out of here," said Strange, very softly.

Jones went to the side of the couch, bent down, zipped his duffel bag shut, and snatched it off the floor.

"I'm gone," said Jones.

He walked toward the front door, eyeing the gun on the floor. Strange shook his head. Jones laughed a little, like a kid, and kept on going, straight out of the apartment. Strange listened to his footsteps on the stairs.

He turned off the main overhead light in the living room. He walked to the window that fronted the street. A naked-bulb lamp sat on a small table near the window. Strange put his finger to the switch on the lamp. He hesitated for a moment; Jones had not confessed, exactly. But he had known that Dennis had been "cut." Only a few friends, family members, and police had knowledge of that. And the killer. The killer knew.

Strange switched on the lamp, then quickly switched it off.

From the darkness of the apartment, he watched Jones cross the street. He watched Vaughn emerge from the corner market, a small automatic in his hand. He watched him say a few words to Jones in a threatening way, then point him toward the market with the muzzle of the gun. Vaughn stepped aside to let Jones pass inside the market before he followed him in.

Strange heard a popping sound from below, then two more pops right behind it. Light flashed from the market's depths and briefly illuminated the street.

Strange left the apartment in darkness and walked down the stairs. He exited the row house and headed across the street to an alley entrance beside the market. Vaughn came outside, looked around, and smoothed out his suit jacket. He joined

Strange, standing in a patch of black at the edge of the alley. He pulled a wad of cash from his pocket and handed it to Strange.

"Take it," said Vaughn. "I emptied his pockets and his wallet."

"I don't want it," said Strange.

"Take it. Throw it away or give it away, it makes no difference to me. It's gotta look like a robbery, so there it is."

Strange put the money in his pocket.

"It gets easier," said Vaughn, looking into Strange's hollow eyes. "Let's go."

They walked toward 7th Street. The sirens and burglar alarms grew louder, as did the upraised voices of the soldiers, citizens, and police. As they neared the commotion, they came upon a sewer that was taking in a river of water from the curb. Vaughn drew the cheap .32 from his belt line, wiped it off with his cloth handkerchief, and dropped the gun into the sewer along with the wallet he'd taken off Alvin Jones. Vaughn barely broke his stride.

At the intersection of 7th and P, amid the confusion, the strobing lights, the flames, and the noise, he shook Strange's hand and broke away.

Vaughn disappeared into the smoke. Strange walked north.

THIRTY-FOUR

T HE CURFEW, AND the presence of more than six thousand armed soldiers, National Guardsmen, and police, brought the city under control. Prisoners in overflowing precinct jails were transferred to facilities downtown. Rioters and looters who had escaped arrest began to return to their apartments, houses, and public housing units to examine their bounty, treat their wounds, and tell tales. A few law-abiding residents came out of their homes, in violation of the curfew, to give food and drink to exhausted firemen and police. For many, it was the first shocking glimpse of the streets and businesses they had frequented every day for most of their lives. The destruction of their neighborhoods had been devastating and complete.

By midnight, the capital of the United States was under occupation by federal troops. Sporadic rioting and civil disobedience would continue through the weekend at a greatly reduced degree, leading to a Sunday of relative peace.

By the end of the weekend, there would be almost 8,000 arrests, 1,200 reported injuries, and nearly 30 million dollars' worth of damage. Twelve citizen deaths were attributed to the riots. A thirteenth death was listed as a homicide. The body of a man was found in a gutted market near 7th Street, his death the result of close-range gunshot wounds to the head, throat, and chest.

The man was never identified. His killer was never found.

LATE FRIDAY NIGHT, a squad car went up Georgia, along Howard University. It occupants, two veteran white cops out of the Thirteenth Precinct, pulled to the curb, where a big white man in a cheap suit stood talking on the phone in a public booth, the door open to accommodate his bulk. The cop riding shotgun had recognized the man.

"Detective," said the cop, tilting his head out the window of the Ford. "Everything all right?"

Vaughn put his hand over the receiver. "Just out here solving homicides."

"You're behind enemy lines, case you haven't noticed."

"I'm undercover," said Vaughn, and the uniforms laughed.

"You been around forever," said the cop, winking at his partner. "Any advice for this situation we got here?"

"Don't shoot till you see the whites of their eyes."

"That ain't no trick."

"You be safe, hear?"

The patrol cops drove off. Vaughn removed his hand from the receiver.

"Couple of cops," said Vaughn into the phone. "Worried about the Hound Dog."

"I've been worried about you, too," said the woman on the other end of the line.

"Told you I'd call, didn't I?"

"Sure, only . . ."

"What?"

"I wanna *see* you, Frank."

Vaughn screwed a cigarette between his lips. "I could use a drink."

"I'll be waiting," said Linda Allen, and she cut the line.

Vaughn stepped out of the booth and lit his smoke. He'd go home to Olga and the kid. But not yet.

THE SQUAD CAR continued north. The veterans drove by a young black cop, slowly walking up the long hill.

Derek Strange saw the squad car pass. He didn't wave or acknowledge it. He crossed Georgia Avenue and walked west on Barry Place. He stopped at Carmen Hill's row house and looked up at her apartment and saw that it was dark. He stared at the blackness behind her window and then he walked on.

Despite the curfew, people were out, sitting on their stoops, the younger ones gathered in alleys, some at street corners, leaning against lampposts or perched atop garbage cans. Some cold-eyed Strange. A few nodded in a friendly way. None spoke to him at all.

In his mind, Strange pictured his brother. Standing in the living room, trying to school his family on the revolution that had to come.

"You missed, D," said Strange.

He wiped tears from his cheeks as a boy ran from an alley, carrying a dress over his shoulder. His eyes were wide as Strange reached out and grabbed his arm.

"What're you doin'?" said Strange.

"I'm just funnin'," said the boy. "This dress is for my moms."

"Where's your mother and father at? Didn't they tell you there was a curfew?"

"I ain't got no father, mister. My mother is out with a man."

"Go home," said Strange, releasing the boy's arm. "Go home!"

The boy dropped the dress and fled. Strange walked on.

He turned right on 13th Street and went up the hill alongside Cardozo High, not looking at the smoldering ruins of Shaw behind him. At the top of the hill he came to his building and glanced up at his apartment. His windows were wide open. He tried to remember if he had left them that way when he had gone out last.

Strange started up to the door of his building, went for his key, and felt the roll of cash folded in the pants pocket of his uniform. He stood there for a moment at the door, thinking of the boy he'd just rousted. Thinking of all the boys he saw out here every day. Thinking of the baby boy whose father he'd just killed.

Strange returned to the sidewalk of 13th. He walked north, past Euclid, to Fairmont. West on Fairmont, he came to the row house with the turret and the peeling paint. He went inside and up to the second-floor landing. He knocked on a door there and waited.

The door opened to reveal the tall, heavy woman with the wide features and the almond-shaped eyes. She wore an old shirt and the "Black Is Beautiful" earrings he'd seen before. She held her baby boy in the crook of her arm.

"Mary," said Strange. "Sorry to bother you so late."

"You look rough."

"Been workin' damn near two days straight. Can I come in? I won't stay but a minute."

She stepped aside to let him pass through, then closed the door behind him. They stood there awkwardly in her small foyer. The apartment smelled of baby and cigarettes.

"You want a coffee, somethin'?"

"No, thank you," said Strange, thinking of the cup she'd served coffee in before and the roach crawling on its saucer.

"Is this about Alvin again?" said Mary. "What, did you find him?"

"Looks like he's gone," said Strange. "I don't think he's coming back."

"I'm not surprised."

"Anyway," said Strange, reaching into his pocket and retrieving the roll of cash. "I just came to give you this. It's for your baby boy."

Mary eyed the bills in Strange's hand. "I don't understand."

"I took it off a suspect tonight," said Strange. "Down in the trouble, on Seventh. Had to be stolen out the register of some store. I couldn't keep it. And I couldn't see turning it in. Now, I don't mean to insult you, but . . . look, I *know* you can use it. You can use it to buy some things for your son."

Her brow wrinkled in suspicion. "How much is it?"

"Count it," he said, holding it out.

She hesitated for a moment.

"Hold my baby," she said.

Strange exchanged the money for the child. Mary's lips moved as she counted the bills. Strange looked down at the light-skinned baby boy staring up at him with odd golden eyes.

"There's eight hundred dollars here."

"It's yours," said Strange, still looking at the boy. "What do you call him?"

"Granville," said Mary. "Granville Oliver. I gave him my last name."

"He's gonna be handsome," said Strange.

"I hope he'll be a fine young man," said Mary Oliver, smiling at Strange for the first time. "Thank you for this."

It ain't nothin' but blood money, thought Strange. Something to ease my conscience, is all it is.

"I better be gettin' on," said Strange.

GOING DOWN FAIRMONT, Strange took in the fragrance of a lilac bush growing against a fence. He turned right on 13th and walked the two blocks south to his building without looking over the crest of the big hill.

He went through the double glass doors and into the lobby, where groups of young people sat, talking and smoking cigarettes. They fell silent at the sight of him. He wondered if they knew that this was his last night as police.

"You've been given a responsibility, son. You do something to betray that, you don't deserve to be wearing that uniform."

Up on his floor, he stepped down the carpeted hallway, hearing music coming from behind the door of his apartment. As he arrived at his place, he put his ear against the door and listened to a familiar voice. Strange smiled.

It was Otis, with those ace session men behind him. "That's How Strong My Love Is." Volt single number 124.

Strange used his key to enter his apartment.

She was there by the open windows, wearing that light blue dress, the blue ribbon in her hair. Strange crossed the room and moved into her embrace, taking in the smell of her dime-store perfume. He kissed her mouth full, then said her name.

Below, in Shaw, lights glimmered faintly through the curtain of black smoke that hovered there and darkened the night sky. A breeze came in through the windows. Magnolias, dogwoods, and cherry trees had bloomed around the city. The scent of their flowers, and the smell of things burned and cleansed, was in the air.

ACKNOWLEDGMENTS

Thanks to my friends Logan Deoudes and Jerome Gross, who gave me extensive, invaluable assistance during the research stages of *Hard Revolution*. Thanks go out as well to Dan Fein, Leonard Tempchin, Pete Glekas, Tim Thomas, Bob Fegley, Gary Phillips, Ruby Pelecanos, Bob Boukas, Paulina Garner, Billy Caludis, Frazier O'Leary, Mary Rados, Jim and Ted Pedas, Michael Pietsch, Reagan Arthur, Claire McKinney, Betsy Uhrig, and Alicia Gordon. In addition, I spoke to many active participants in the riots of April 1968 who will remain anonymous. Their candor and honesty was greatly appreciated.

As it has for me in the past, the Washingtoniana room of the MLK Library provided the tools and atmosphere I needed to write this novel. *Ten Blocks from the White House*, by Ben Gilbert and the staff of the *Washington Post*, provided the time line and factual backbone of the riot section of the book. Peter Guralnick's *Sweet Soul Music* and Mark Opsasnick's *Capitol*

Rock gave me the music details I needed. The recordings of Otis Redding, O. V. Wright, the Impressions, James Carr, Wilson Pickett, Johnnie Taylor, and others gave me inspiration.

This one goes out to all the good people — workers, parents, children, volunteers, teachers, clergy, and police — of Washington, D.C., and to my family: Emily, Nick, Pete, and Rosa. Much love and respect to you all.